BOOKISH

MATTHEW SWEET
BOOKISH

*Adapted from the TV series
created by Mark Gatiss*

QUERCUS

First published in Great Britain in 2025 by Quercus

QUERCUS

Quercus Editions Limited
Carmelite House
50 Victoria Embankment
London EC4Y 0DZ

An Hachette UK company

The authorised representative in the EEA is Hachette Ireland,
8 Castlecourt Centre, Dublin 15, D15 XTP3, Ireland (email: info@hbgi.ie)

Copyright © 2025 Eagle Eye Drama Limited

The moral right of Matthew Sweet to be
identified as the author of this work has been
asserted in accordance with the Copyright,
Designs and Patents Act, 1988.

All rights reserved. No part of this publication
may be reproduced or transmitted in any form
or by any means, electronic or mechanical,
including photocopy, recording, or any
information storage and retrieval system,
without permission in writing from the publisher.

A CIP catalogue record for this book is available
from the British Library

HB ISBN 978 1 52944 444 5
TPB ISBN 978 1 52944 445 2
US HB ISBN 978 1 52944 729 3
EBOOK ISBN 978 1 52944 446 9

1

This book is a work of fiction. Names, characters,
businesses, organizations, places and events are
either the product of the author's imagination
or used fictitiously. Any resemblance to
actual persons, living or dead, events or
locales is entirely coincidental.

Typeset by CC Book Production
Printed and bound in Great Britain by Clays Ltd, Elcograf S.p.A

Papers used by Quercus are from well-managed forests and other responsible sources.

For Freddie

23rd November 1962

Sir,

I received your package this morning. You were quite right to suppose that this volume would interest me, and it was generous of you to send it on approval before listing it in your catalogue. The price you mention is quite acceptable.

Your deductions about the identity of the author are correct. Under her pseudonym, she is now of course an accomplished writer with admirers all over the world. It touched me deeply, however, to be reminded of her early years behind the counter of the shop on Archangel Lane. They seem so very long ago, those months after VE Day and before the Big Freeze, when we were all so full of hope and optimism. The recent cold weather brought them to mind again – though thankfully none of us are now obliged to eat snoek or cadge chocolate from visiting Americans.

She has used my name, fragments of my biography and some details of the police cases in which I played a very minor role, but I feel I must make it clear that this is a work of fiction and not an account drawn from life. The possibility of confusion may be why she chose not to publish these three stories – although those who admire her present output will find clear echoes in her novels Prescription for

<u>Murder</u> (1953), '<u>And Cut . . .</u>' (1955) and <u>Blood Sisters</u> (1960). She now resides in California, where I believe she is adapting the latter for the motion pictures.

The binding is excellent and of a standard rarely lavished on unpublished typescript material (I confess I recognise the work of the firm). For the record, however, I should point out that I did not suffer from scarlet fever as a child, that the kingdom of Scutari would appear to be some lightly fictionalised version of Albania under King Zog, and the character of Jack Blunt is entirely the author's invention. I think also that she has misremembered some of the details of the chocolate ration: unlike me, she never had a sweet tooth.

I include a cheque made out for the quoted amount. Will I see you at Chelsea for the ABA meeting? I hear Walker acquired the library at Hessingdon. I fear he paid too much: I visited in the thirties and the place was damp even then.

Yours sincerely,

Book

10th December 1962

Dear Nora,

I hope that you did not greet the arrival of this package with dismay. One can't be sure, after all these years. I picture you by a swimming pool, with a portable typewriter and rattan furniture, thinking, perhaps, of this letter as an intrusion from our small and smoky world into your wide and sunny one. I know you will have recognised the handwriting. You were always complaining about it.

We have followed your career, of course. How clever of you to take the bones of those early cases and rebuild them as entirely different animals. Transplanting them to America was the cleverest part, I think. I always thought your gas station attendant in <u>Prescription for Murder</u> was modelled on poor Mr George Harkup. And the concierge in <u>Blood Sisters</u> — transparently poor old Edmund Kind.

Now, though, through a quirk of circumstance, I have had the opportunity to inspect your earliest drafts. I'm not sure how they came into the possession of the dealer who sent them to me — another mystery we might solve? — but he was very good and discreet about the matter.

They're juvenilia, I know, and perhaps it was wrong of me to read them at all, but I'm afraid my curiosity got the better of me. As you will recall, it often did. I can see that you wrote them on the shop typewriter. I still use it. This 'e' is unmistakable.

If I was a younger man I would quote Oscar and say that there's only one thing worse than being written about, but I am an old man, and I haven't the words to express how it felt to have those days recalled to me, in all their giddy speed and interest; all their pain, too.

I confess I considered destroying them. Consigning them to the flames. My instincts, however, prevented me from doing so. The smell of burning paper is the worst smell in the world. So I write, dear Nora, to return these stories to you. They are your property, not mine. But my secrets are here. And even after all these years, I keep them close.

My fate is in your hands.

Yours ever,

Book

SLIGHTLY FOXED

CHAPTER ONE

Jack feared that the light would dazzle him. The view from his cell window had offered as much sunshine as the port-hole of a submarine: victory in Europe had brought no more. Removing years of grime – the residue of the Blitz, the tidemark of London pea-soupers – had not, to his disappointment, proved a priority of the first six months of the Labour government. His final night in HMP Whitechapel brought little sleep and the prickling realisation that the world beyond its walls was as unknown to him as a Sanskrit manuscript.

Prison suits some people. It did not suit Jack. He did not relish the company of the habitual housebreakers and smash-and-grab men who traded stories like old actors in the green room. Nor did he care for the conchies, who, assuming he was one of their number, tried to engage him in discussions about the unintended consequences of Versailles. Of the racketeers and coupon-fiddlers, he preferred the ones who declared there was nothing wrong with eating horse meat to those who had some elaborate story about how they'd been sold something in waxed paper under false pretences. He was grateful that the trunk murderer of Surrey Green did not take a shine to him, as he had done to other unfingermarked young men on their landing. He did not curry favour with the warders.

His separateness hardly made his confinement pass more quickly, but it saved him from a beating. Prisoners without loyalties earned no rewards and received few punishments.

'I hope you enjoyed your stay with us, sir,' said the warder.

'I'd recommend it to my friends,' said Jack. 'But I don't have any.'

'You've got one,' said the warder. He tapped the suitcase containing the meagre belongings with which Jack had come through the door. A ticket bearing Jack's name was tied to the handle. Beside it, fixed with glue like a luggage label, was an envelope. Jack tore it open. Inside was a picture postcard of Shakespeare, yellow and faded, as if it had spent the inter-war years unbought on a rack outside a newsagent in Stratford-upon-Avon. Jack flipped it around.

158 Archangel Lane, WC2.

Keys rattled in old locks. The iron hinges of the prison door yawned open and discharged Jack into freedom. He had no need to blink or shade his eyes. Someone had stolen the sun from England.

London bus routes, Jack was relieved to discover, had changed little since the bolts had been thrown behind him. The number 15 still ran east to west, from Stepney Methodist Church past St Paul's Cathedral and the Aldwych to Charing Cross. The streets through which it moved, however, had been made strange by war. On the Whitechapel Road, rubble gathered in drifts. The teeth had been knocked out of the City. Once-elegant buildings leaned on wooden crutches. The ghosts of air-raid sticky tape haunted the windows of Fleet Street. The Royal Courts of Justice, he noticed, had survived without a scratch. As the bus rattled past, he averted his gaze from its entrance and read the newspaper vendors' boards clustered on the other side of the street. The Foreign Secretary had given a speech. Famine was imminent. Where, Jack wondered? In Germany? In England? Across the whole world?

Jack had not expected peacetime London to dazzle him with Technicolor, but he had hoped for more visible signs that the Allies had actually won the war. One of the warders had told him that in Berlin they were stripping wallpaper to make broth from the paste. Londoners, he noticed, also had a lean and hungry look. As he stepped off the bus, he caught a glimpse of himself reflected in a barber's shop mirror. Perhaps he had it too.

The sign for Archangel Lane was thick with soot and placed slightly too high on the wall. At first Jack walked straight past it. Retracing his steps, he found himself in one of those unironed creases of the capital; a byway that seemed to have escaped demolition because Edwardian developers had failed to notice its existence. Not that it was quiet: its narrow space was lined with small businesses, some thriving, some dying, some persisting in that state of commercial purgatory indicated by a faded window display scattered lightly with dead bluebottles.

The inhabitants, Jack discovered, were friendly. This put him on the back foot. In prison, common pleasantries were not so common, a smile was usually the portent of bad news, and only the screws wore hats. When Mr Eric Wellbeloved, the butcher of Archangel Lane, caught his eye and tapped the brim of his straw boater, Jack found the gesture hard to read. Mr Wellbeloved was a beast of a man, with flanks that would have borne subdivision into rump, beef and brisket. His eyes, heavily lashed, blinked in Jack's direction, then refocused on the window. The morning's offers – liver, kidneys, lights – written up in strokes of white paint, vanished under the impact of Mr Wellbeloved's wet cloth. Beside him, his assistant, Enid Clegg, was manoeuvring a great slab of pig onto a hook. She was a slight woman, but the carcass seemed to hold no difficulty or mystery for her; she moved it as easily as a demonstration dancer taking the floor for the *paso doble*. She did not look up as Jack passed.

'Afternoon,' said a man in a leather apron.

'Afternoon,' said Jack.

Mr Toovey, the cobbler, with a row of tools in his top pocket and a smear of Meltonian shoe cream on his right ear, was holding out his hand. It took Jack a moment to understand that he was asking to see the postcard of Shakespeare. Mr Toovey took it, read it and pointed down the street. Jack followed his gaze along the row of shops. The tailor's had an offer on made-to-measure morning suits: its proprietor stood in the window like one of his own dummies. The chemist was shuttered. It might have been closed for lunch; it might have been abandoned by its owners before the war. Beyond it was a wallpaper shop alive with floral patterns – the colour plate in the black and white magazine of Archangel Lane.

At the end of the street, Jack saw a woman who seemed

to be waiting for a pantechnicon to take her to a new home. She was sitting on the kerb surrounded by a collection of mismatched domestic objects – a painted coal scuttle, a Victorian washstand, a set of bentwood chairs. Was this the person he was supposed to meet?

'Bit lost, love?' she asked, as Jack realised that these objects were the stock of her junk shop, and that Mrs Acres was hoping for custom, not removal. She did not ask to see Jack's postcard. She seemed to know that a visitor arriving on Archangel Lane with a suitcase and an uncertain air was unlikely to be looking for Mr Quillian the tailor, or Mr Harkup the chemist, and still less a Victorian washstand, however reasonably priced.

'158, is it?' she asked.

Jack followed her nod to a shop that, like the entrance to Archangel Lane, he had entirely managed to miss.

It was a bookshop. The bottle-green paintwork had seen better days, but the glass in the windows had survived the war unpatched. A stuffed fox and a bust of Edgar Allan Poe peered out, as if to put off browsers who might have been attracted by the discounted volumes piled on a pair of wooden trolleys parked on the pavement. These books were protected by an awning, but the air was damp, and Jack felt he could almost see them swelling. The sign above them also drew his eye. The name of the shop seemed to contain a grammatical error of the kind that, while common among bakers and fruiterers, seemed an offence against a business that dealt in the printed word.

Book's.

Jack stood in front of the glass and shrugged his shoulders.

The jacket was two sizes bigger than the trousers, and both had the sour smell of clothes that have been stored for a long time in the unheated backroom of a charitable institution. He sniffed the cuffs, then his own hands. He worried that his skin carried the odour of prison – cabbage, carbolic, cold sweat – and that this would be obvious once he left the air of the street. He straightened his sleeves and pushed open the door. The bell clattered unmusically.

A man who has spent many months staring at whitewash and brown glazed bricks may feel overwhelmed by the plainest domestic interior. One old lag, a walnut-faced recidivist who forgot to put the stocking on his head before walking into the Charing Cross Bank and demanding a stack of used oncers, had told Jack that on his release he had been given a headache by the striped paper on the wall of his mother's parlour.

Jack felt some of this pain as he entered 158 Archangel Lane. It is hard to describe the sensation to someone who has not experienced the shift from prison plainness to the plenitude of ordinary life, but had you asked him, as his eyes moved from shelf to shelf, clocking green Penguins and Victorian yellowbacks and atlases in obscure scripts, Jack would have told you to think of eating rich cuts of unfamiliar meat – jellied, curried, spiced – after a long diet of oats and water.

The room was stuffed with books of every description. They lined the walls, crammed the groaning shelves, stood in tottering leathery stacks in every corner, their bindings plum, scarlet, buff. Jack squinted at the titles. His fingers gripped the handle of his suitcase. He could smell dust, ancient paper, the faint aroma of baking. Was the ticking of the clock really so loud?

It was at this moment that he noticed he was being observed. From a basket beside an unlit fire, a Labrador of a certain age regarded him with large lugubrious eyes, utterly unmoved. Jack nodded to the animal and might have made some greeting, had his attention not been distracted by the violent movement of the baize curtain that divided the floor of the shop from a domestic space at the rear.

An angular blur of three-piece porridge tweed moved across his field of vision. The man did not turn to face his visitor but had clearly noticed his presence because, as he sped from the kitchen to a set of wheeled library steps on the far side of the shop, he slapped a book into Jack's hands. Jack took it as he might have caught a football hurled in his direction.

'Hold that, would you?' said the man. It was a command, not a request. 'What can you tell me about it?'

Jack realised that he was not simply required to hold the book, as you might hold the umbrella of someone looking for a bus ticket, but was being asked to examine it. To appraise it. He flicked through its pages and regretted the action immediately. The paper was parched and friable and a small fragment of the frontispiece fluttered to the floor.

'Looks old,' he said, hoping that more would occur to him.

'It is,' said the man. He was now at the summit of the library steps and dancing his finger along a run of obscure-looking periodicals. 'Fairly indifferent Jacobean poetry.

Calfskin binding. Worth a couple of bob. Three if we were just that little bit closer to the Museum.'

'What are these brown spots on the pages?' asked Jack.

The man descended the steps so quickly that Jack feared he had offended him with an accidental insult – but at least he was no longer talking to the back of his head.

The man's reddish hair flopped forwards over a pair of round, amber-coloured spectacles. A beard, almost equally red, gave force to the jaw without betraying any history in the services. It was not a naval style, nor one of those unruly bohemian tangles grown by demob-happy Army and RAF men. Through it flashed a smile of such shocking width and intensity that Jack felt the sudden shadow of prison on his mind. He had no idea whether this man wanted to embrace him or kick him back onto the cobbles.

'You get straight to the heart of the matter, Mr . . . ?'

'Jack,' said Jack, a little too slowly. 'Just Jack.'

The man took back the volume of fairly indifferent Jacobean poetry and spread his fingers over the page, indicating the tea-coloured speckles as an astronomer might indicate the distribution of stars in a galaxy.

'That's called "foxing", Jack just Jack,' he murmured. 'It's what time does to books. To all of us, really. In the profession we say it's "slightly foxed". Interested?'

'There's a mistake,' said Jack.

This was not the expected answer.

'A mistake?' repeated the man.

'On the door,' said Jack. 'The sign.'

The man narrowed his eyes. 'What about it?' he asked.

'Well, it's wrong, isn't it?' said Jack. 'There's no apostrophe in "books".'

'There is,' said the man.

'There isn't,' said Jack.

'There is,' insisted the man.

'There isn't!' protested Jack, wondering if this would come to blows.

'There is!'

'There isn't!'

'There is,' said the man, looking strangely satisfied by this exchange, 'if your name is Book and you happen to own the shop. Which it is and I do.'

Book held out his hand. Jack took it. It was his first handshake in over two years, and its warmth left him speechless.

'My name's Book,' said Book. 'Book's books. Confusing, I know. Or is it handy? I can never decide. Anyway. I'm Book and I run a bookshop. This one, obviously. You must be here about the job. Tea?'

The handshake led to a chair in the back kitchen, the moan of a kettle on a dirty gas ring, and the sight of Mr Book risking his eyebrows by peering into the hot interior of the stove.

'Not quite there yet,' he said. Close enough, though, for him to keep the scorched floral oven glove on his hand.

The business of tea-making, Jack discovered, was also a test. Book indicated a battered caddy and a brown earthenware pot of the sort into which a Mad Hatter might have stuffed a dormouse.

'How much?' asked Jack, digging the spoon into the loose leaves.

It was as if Jack had asked for a prompt for the first line of the Lord's Prayer.

'Where were you dragged up?' Book roared. 'One for each person and one for the pot!'

The appearance of the Labrador through the baize curtain seemed to erase the offence from his mind. The animal padded into the kitchen and stood sentry by his master, expressing loyalty both to the man and the smell of hot dough that spilled from the oven.

'Well, Jack just Jack,' he said. 'This is Dog.'

'Dog?' queried Jack, feeling that he might be about to step into another grammatical minefield.

'Just Dog,' said Book, beaming downwards. He gave the animal an affectionate pat with his uninsulated hand, then turned his attention back to the stove. A moment later he had extracted a baking sheet loaded with dark brown biscuits and was peering at them as if they were the result of a complex scientific experiment.

'Ginger snaps,' he said. He tipped them onto a cooling rack and set it down on the kitchen table. 'I can never be bothered to wait, can you?'

Book pinched a biscuit between thumb and forefinger and was about to dunk it in his tea when he noticed that his cup was empty. Jack took the hint and poured. Steam rose agreeably. Book added milk from a bottle on the table and took an immense gulp.

'Oh God,' he breathed, 'that's better. I must have my tea. Without tea I am merely unreconstituted dust.'

Jack raised his own cup to his lips. Either he had grown

accustomed to the tepidities of prison catering, or Mr Book's mouth was made partly of asbestos.

'Now,' said Book, 'I have a little hobby on the side and I find it's taking me away from the shop more and more. And Nora – you'll meet her soon, I'm sure – can't be here all the time. So I require assistance.' He took another gulp of tea. 'Board and lodging come with the position and the remuneration is reasonable but not extravagant. Have a ginger snap, why don't you?'

Jack picked up a biscuit. Doing so, however, clarified his sense of unease. There were processes, mechanisms, whirling and moving around him, carrying him along, and he had no understanding of the nature of the machinery or the character of its operators. Did the consumption of a ginger snap constitute a contractual agreement?

'Look,' he said, shifting in his chair, 'this isn't really my sort of gaff. I thought they'd maybe send me to a factory or something.'

'They?' said Book.

The clock ticked. Dog received a biscuit from his master like a communion wafer. Jack again sensed that an odour might be clinging to the fabric of his suit.

'You do know where I've come from, don't you?' he said.

Book closed his eyes and raised a hand in protest.

'No need to mention it again!' he said. 'What are you hoping for now you've got the job, Jack just Jack?'

Jack contemplated his shoes. 'I want to keep my head down,' he said. But as soon as he uttered these words, he looked sharply upwards. 'I've got the job?'

'If you want it,' said Book, removing crumbs from his beard. He seemed to consider the matter settled. Perhaps, thought Jack, he should do the same. He had adjusted to the forced routines of an East End institution enclosed by railings and barbed wire. Archangel Lane was similarly separate from the world, but the regime appeared liberal and the food smelled sweet. He bit into his biscuit. The ginger tasted of liberty.

Before he had swallowed, the door jangled violently open, and a woman burst into the shop. With her came some of the colour Jack had hoped to see on the other side of the wall, conveyed in a bold floral-print frock and matching pillbox hat, both of which, though well made and perfectly fitted, gave the impression of having been put on, or put back on, in a hurry. Their wearer, a handsome woman in the foothills of her fifties, was pink with excitement.

'Darling!' she exclaimed. 'You must come at once!'

The woman noticed Jack, getting to his feet, putting down his teacup, negotiating a mouthful of biscuit.

'Oh,' she said. 'Hello.' She was friendly. But it was obvious, Jack thought, that this woman knew he was not a customer.

'Trottie, this is Jack just Jack,' said Book. 'Jack, this is Trottie. My wife.'

Jack returned the greeting, then felt himself falling down the agenda of the conversation. Trottie had information. Book was keen as a knife to know it.

'The bombsite,' said Trottie. 'The men clearing the bombsite – you know, where Inkerman Street used to be. They've found something. In suspicious circumstances.'

Book's eyes were illuminated. 'My favourite kind of circumstances!'

Jack did not need to be told to follow him from the shop. He had a job. Running after Mr Book was part of it.

The Blitz and its younger brother, the Baby Blitz, had carved great wounds into the body of London. The planes came first, in the autumn of 1940, scattering bombs like wheat. In the East End, spirits and oil bled from dockside warehouses and formed a burning lake that might have pleased Milton; clouds of hot pepper scratched the eyes of the men from the Auxiliary Fire Service. In the West End, the Café de Paris took one in the belly and the patrons of the Walsingham Hotel slept in the basement and hoped the management was telling the truth about the strength of the ceiling above their heads. Later, in the spring of 1944, the rocket bombs arrived in their hundreds, with a low whistle followed by a silence that told the hearer to prepare for death. One broke the back of Selfridges; one made a tomb for 168 in the New Cross Woolworth's; one turned Inkerman Street into the surface of the moon.

Newspaper reports ascribed its destruction to an exploding gas main. By 1944, however, readers knew what lay between those lines – the impact of a cigar-shaped black and white missile launched from somewhere in the Netherlands. Inkerman Street was reduced to a carcass, its standing walls and chimney stacks sticking upwards like the ribs of a rotting whale. Two years on, a barricade had been erected to discourage the curious, but little had been cleared or repaired. Rosebay willowherb had colonised empty windows and doorways. Pools of filthy standing water reflected the grey sky back at itself. On the corner of a surviving rooftop, the rusting form of an anti-aircraft searchlight gazed down sightlessly. There was little to illuminate. The street had lost its population, except for the odd shrapnel-hungry child, and the dossers who occupied the empty body of the old Crown and Anchor, who lit a fire each night in the roofless saloon and toasted each other with meths.

Today, however, the place was crowded. The inhabitants of the surrounding courts and alleys had arrived to inspect an unexpected new feature. A patch of Inkerman Street had sunk like a sponge cake in a draughty oven, revealing a large hollow space below. The depths of the pit were obscured by shadow and fresh falls of earth, but the visible part offered a lecture on the tissues of the city. Cobbles gave way to layers of clinker and broken brick, shiny red London clay and exposed innards of cellarage.

A trio of uniformed police constables had formed a human cordon around the crater to protect the reckless and the incurably nosy. Their sergeant, a long-limbed man with oiled black hair and a long face like a carnivorous horse, surveyed the scene impatiently. Had these rubberneckers nothing better to do than stare into a hole in the ground? Perhaps, thought Sergeant Morris, some of them had got wind of what had been discovered inside.

His fears were confirmed when Book and Trottie appeared from behind a pile of rubble and walked confidently — *shamelessly* — to the edge of the crater. Behind them was a young man whom the sergeant did not recognise. He was hanging slightly behind, his eyes downcast. He was holding a suitcase. Morris knew instinctively that this was a person who wished to avoid conversations with policemen.

'Morning, Sergeant,' said Book, pleasantly.

'I was wondering if you'd turn up,' said Sergeant Morris.

'I'm like a bad penny.' Book smiled.

'Well, you know my feelings,' said Morris.

'And you have made them exquisitely plain,' replied Book, fumbling in his jacket pocket and producing a creased paper from a little leather wallet.

'I have a special letter . . .' Book began.

'From Mr Churchill,' said Morris. 'Yes, sir. I suppose you've got Stalin and Roosevelt tucked away in there too.'

Now that Book had reached the edge of the pit, he could see it contained one of his closest friends. Six feet beneath the surface of the street — a height below which, in mysterious defiance of Metropolitan Police regulations, he fell considerably short — was Detective Inspector Bliss, a man with mild clear eyes and an expression as crumpled as his raincoat. For a man occupying a sinkhole in the middle of a bombsite, he looked remarkably cheerful.

'Oh, hello, Book!' he trilled. 'Thought this might be up your street.'

'Almost literally,' said Trottie.

Bliss was not alone in the hole. Beside him stood a familiar and mountainous figure wearing a battered metal helmet painted with a bold black letter 'W'. Mr Baseheart had been the district Air Raid Warden since the first week of the war, when he had gone door to door delivering leaflets explaining how to distinguish the smell of mustard gas from phosgene. The local ARP had been disbanded at the beginning of the year, but Mr Baseheart had found it hard to relinquish the role, and continued his rounds on the pretext that he had yet to receive his final payments and gratuities.

'I covered it with a tarp,' said Baseheart, indicating a dark shape at his feet. He had one of those rough tubercular voices, like someone rolling ball bearings in a tin bucket.

'Start at the beginning, Inspector,' said Book, 'and leave nothing out, especially if it's salacious, gory or vaguely scandalous.'

'Bit of a puzzle,' said Bliss. 'The borough has been promising to clear this rubble for months. But Mr Baseheart got a bit impatient.'

'Civil defence,' said Baseheart, 'doesn't stop just because the fire is out.'

'Inkerman Street caught it in '44, didn't it?' asked Book.

'Oh yes,' said Baseheart. 'Terrible pounding. You remember that raid, sir?'

'How could I forget?' said Book. 'Trottie and I ended up cheek by jowl in the Anderson shelter with a man from the Pru.'

'He had lovely fingernails,' sighed Trottie.

'And terrible halitosis,' said Book. 'Those shelters weren't meant for sharing. Still, we don't have to worry about that anymore. Though you're still looking out for us, Mr Baseheart. Will they want that uniform back, do you think?'

'There's still work to do,' said Baseheart. 'And I like to drop in on old Brenda.' For a moment Book imagined some elderly diehard refusing to evacuate from a half-demolished home; then he realised that this was a nickname for the anti-aircraft searchlight. Brenda was his pride and joy.

'Once it's been shook up, the ground doesn't rest easy,' said Baseheart. 'Chimney of the Crown and Anchor lasted until Christmas gone. Then it came tumbling down. And when that happens, I mark it on my little map. Send the gen off to the War Office.'

'What do they do with it?' asked Trottie.

'Add it to their big map,' said Baseheart.

'So here he was,' said Bliss, 'marking his map. When – *lo!* – what did he find?'

'Lo! What?' asked Book.

Bliss grabbed the edge of the tarpaulin and threw it back like a stage magician whipping away a tablecloth.

Book's first thought was of the ruins of Pompeii. Not just the images familiar from newspapers and scholarly publications, depicting the victims calcified in their houses, but quieter reports, given by old friends and associates, of Allied bombs raining below Vesuvius in the mistaken belief that a dead Roman city had become a German ammunition dump.

The pit contained bones. Skulls, ribs, vertebrae. Not laid out for the afterlife. Not laid out with any kind of order or decorum.

'Tossed together like a skeletal salad!' exclaimed Book, and with powder-monkey speed, he clambered down to join Bliss and Baseheart in the pit.

'How many, do you think?' he said, dividing crania by tibia.

'Dozen?' guessed Bliss. 'Baker's dozen?'

The inspector looked sternly towards the ARP warden. 'Quite why Mr Baseheart didn't tell the authorities about his discovery forthwith is another matter. Some kiddies who were playing here let us know.'

Mr Baseheart's interest in defence clearly extended to his own actions. 'I told you,' he said, unapologetically. 'I've got a theory.'

This was too much for Sergeant Morris. 'Obviously they caught it in the raid, didn't they?'

Book peered up with the air of a lecturer taking a comment from the auditorium. He ignored Morris, however: Jack had shifted forwards to the edge of the crater and was now standing just as close.

'What do *you* think, Jack?' asked Book.

The attention gave Jack a mild lurch of horror. Everyone was now looking at him. Book had undone his right to remain silent.

'Well,' he said. 'Yeah. That's what must have happened. The air raid killed them. Died two years ago and now they're all rotted away.'

'A logical assumption,' said Book, patting his pockets.

Bliss looked keenly at the lean young man. 'Who's this?' he asked.

Trottie had spotted Book's cogs turning. The question was ignored.

'So you *don't* think they died in the raid?' she asked.

'Inkerman Street was already empty before the raid, wasn't it, Mr Baseheart?' asked Book.

'Scheduled for demolition,' Baseheart confirmed, a little smugly.

'So there was nobody living here,' said Book. 'In which

case, who are these people?' He sank to his haunches and began poking at a ribcage with an HB pencil.

'They could be anybody,' said Morris. 'Cockneys. Empty house wouldn't be a bad place to shelter.'

'For a dozen people?' snorted Book. 'And what about clothes?'

'Clothes?' repeated Morris.

'All flesh is grass!' Book's eyes were fixed on the bones, but he had the sergeant's blood in his nostrils. Jack realised that he had been spared what Morris was now about to endure. 'No, no, no, Sergeant. The raid was only two years ago. Even if the flesh was gone, their clothes would still be intact.' He was back on his feet. In his eye was a jeweller's loupe. In his hand was a small round object. 'I think Mr Baseheart and I are thinking along similar lines,' he said. 'And this would appear to be the clincher.'

He tossed the object to Bliss. It was a coin. An old coin.

Bliss turned it between his fingers. 'I knew a Carol once,' he said. 'Lovely girl.' Book squinted at him. Bliss looked again. 'Why,' he said, 'it's the unmistakable bonce of King Charles the Second.'

'Is there a year?' asked Trottie.

'Year of our Lord 1665,' said Bliss.

'I didn't know there was a graveyard here,' said Trottie.

'Plague pit,' said Book.

Mr Baseheart's moment had arrived. 'It started with the rats,' he said, 'and then Samuel Pepys worrying that his wig was infected, and then all the burial grounds were overwhelmed. So they dug great big pits to dump the corpses in.' He gave a little twitch of pride. 'I'm a bit of an archaeologist,' he said. 'On the side. Strictly amateur, you understand.'

'So why didn't you tell us straight away when you found them?' asked Morris.

'Because I knew I wouldn't get a chance like this again! Just wanted a bit of time to excavate them.' This time Baseheart appeared contrite. 'I'm really very sorry, Inspector.'

'Yes, well,' muttered Bliss, 'I suppose there's no harm done.'

'I'm not sure about that,' said Book. 'These bones might still be . . . *lively*.'

Bliss looked at the coin in his hand and returned it hurriedly to its finder. 'You mean it's still catching?' He wiped his fingers on the lapels of his raincoat.

'The jury is out,' said Book, airily. 'But I think it's very unlikely.'

Bliss seemed unwilling to wait for the verdict. He scrambled out of the pit. Sensing that others might have noticed his anxiety, he then made a show of helping Book up out of the hole. Baseheart, despite his bulk and years, ignored the inspector's outstretched hand. The bombsite was his natural habitat. He mounted the shifting rubble with the agility of an oystercatcher in the moving tide.

Book passed the coin to Jack. 'Might be worth a bit,' he said. 'You can look it up when we get back home.'

Odd word, that, thought Jack. *Home*. He thought of remarking on it, but Book had already walked past him to join Trottie, who was talking to one of the bystanders – a wiry teenager with dark, observant eyes and hair pulled tight to her scalp.

'Hello, Nora,' said Book, as indulgently as a department store Father Christmas. 'Why am I not surprised to see you here?'

'Did you know,' she said, 'that in the Middle Ages, they used great catapults to toss plaguey corpses into besieged cities? To deliberately infect people?'

Nora's Uncle Yusuf owned the Istanbul restaurant on Archangel Lane: he announced the specials with similar gusto.

'That's horrible, Nora.'

'I know!' enthused Nora.

'And it's a split infinitive,' said Book. 'Will the horrors never end?'

They stood and watched the sad, slow business of exhumation. The closed ambulance, when it arrived, could only get as far as the junction with Archangel Lane; the toppled chimney stack of the Crown and Anchor allowed no further access. The crew was grateful to Morris and his constables, who helped them gather the bones from the pit in handfuls and stack them on a stretcher. It took seven journeys before the remains were cleared, during which time a light drizzle began to fall. Water droplets made the bones look deliquescent, as if something was escaping from them. On the final journey from pit to ambulance, one of the crew members stumbled over a broken paving slab. A skull jumped from the canvas, bounced in the mud and rolled back towards the crater. Jack's instincts were sufficiently quick for him to scoop it from the ground. He looked like Hamlet, standing on some rain-lashed escarpment of Elsinore, with Book, Trottie, Bliss and Nora as his audience.

The shriek of a police whistle cut through the drizzle.

A whey-faced officer was running towards them over the rubble. He was breathless and young, and he brought news of death. Not the kind that has been sitting patiently beneath the earth for hundreds of years, but the kind that is new and fresh and bleeds in the daylight.

CHAPTER TWO

Death has a process. The last breath, the last sight, that mysterious moment of extinguishment none of us can report. The end of ordinary business inside our tissues and organs, which fall idle like machines in a factory, before decay brings new kinds of industry. And beyond all this, the medical, juridical and bureaucratic work to which the flesh cannot but choose to submit.

In the case of Mr George Harkup, late of Archangel Lane, this work began quickly. For this he was indebted to the skeleton population of Inkerman Street, who had ensured that their little patch of London was thick with uniformed constables. Anyone sitting in Mr Harkup's little flat above his chemist's shop would have been able to monitor its progress. The sound of the whey-faced constable's whistle, the thunder of boots on the stairs, the hubbub of a crowd of onlookers blessed to have been provided with two sources of sensational interest in one day, gave way to the business of more cool and expert interest. Inspector Bliss and Sergeant Morris entered the premises, checked the gas in the kitchenette, the knives in the drawers, the cabinet in the tiny bathroom. They found no signs of forced entry. No latches or bolts were broken; the folded newspaper used to block a draughty window remained undisturbed. No third party betrayed their presence. One half-drunk cup of tea had been abandoned on the draining board. Last night's washing-up lay unattended in the sink, a smear of sardine sauce dry above the waterline.

Under the inspector's direction, the police photographer aimed his viewfinder at details worth documenting. A flash bulb fizzed over the twisted arrangement of Mr Harkup's cold limbs; the telltale bottle lying on the hearthrug. The camera came in close for a shot that would have dazzled Mr Harkup, had he still possessed the faculty of sight. His eyes were wide and black; his face contorted as if its muscles were trying to escape to some better place.

Book did not enter. Not for want of asking. He had to be content standing among the crowd.

'Suicide, I heard,' he said, as Bliss and his sergeant emerged from the shuttered shop.

'Heard from who?' asked Morris.

'Your colleague on the doorstep,' said Book, immediately regretting the admission. As Morris fumed, Book reflected on the specific violence of that common English expression about guts and garters. He wondered if the annals of English crime contained any example of the outrage.

'All right, Sergeant, all right,' said Bliss. 'Mr Book is always welcome to give us the benefit of his wisdom.' He pressed some recent examples upon Morris – the case of a bogus university man who had betrayed himself with a duff quote from Cicero; a thief who had made off with the wrong Benin bronze – but the sergeant was too preoccupied with the loose tongue of his immediate subordinate and was already crossing the street to tighten it.

'It's a bad business, Book,' muttered Bliss. 'Very bad. Poor sod. But Morris has a point. It's a common or garden suicide. I can be flexible, as you know. When something a bit more . . .' He groped for a word that could encompass nine-bob Latinists, Igbo artefacts and piles of diseased bones.

'Recherché?' suggested Book. 'Outré? Anything with an acute accent?'

'Unusual, Book,' said Bliss. 'Anything unusual. But this is a meat and potatoes job. Nothing that the sergeant and I can't polish off in an afternoon.'

Book was not dissuaded. 'Who found him?' he asked.

'Charwoman,' said Bliss. 'Ada Dredge.'

'Dredge,' mused Book. 'That rings a little bell.'

Bliss nodded towards a woman sitting disconsolate on a bentwood chair outside Mrs Acres' junk shop. Her raw eyes were staring into space.

'Been doing for Mr Harkup for donkey's,' said Bliss.

'Ding dong,' chimed Book, putting a face to a name and an occupation. Now, he realised, he had seen her many times, shuffling over the cobbles in a floral overall.

'Was there a note?' he asked.

'No note,' reported Bliss.

'How did he do it?' asked Book.

'Prussic acid.' Bliss said it quietly, with his eye on Morris.

'Nasty,' said Book. 'And old-fashioned. They put it in a Madeira cake and gave it to Rasputin. For some reason it didn't have much effect. Perhaps he ate a lot of apple pips and developed an immunity.'

'Where do you get this stuff from?' said Bliss.

'Nora, of course.'

'And where does she get it from?'

'My shop,' said Book. 'It's all on the shelves if you know where to look.'

Jack had not wanted Trottie to carry his suitcase up to his room. She was not his landlady and not his mother. There were, he imagined, rules to such situations, and he did not know them.

'It's just up here,' she said, as they reached the second landing. 'I hope he's cleared it out a bit. Paper things tend to migrate around here.'

The room, he saw, was smaller than his cell in Whitechapel. There was, however, a neat bed with a sprung mattress and an eiderdown covered with a crocheted blanket. The window, which was unbarred, gave a good clear view of the roof-tops towards the white art deco citadel of the Walsingham Hotel. He gazed up to the sky. The clouds, he saw, were beginning to disperse. He looked down into the lane. The police were not.

'Don't worry,' said Trottie. 'I'm not that fond of some of them myself.'

'Who?' said Jack. Was he really so transparent?

'I'd watch out for Sergeant Morris,' she said. 'He's a bit of a pill.'

'Me and coppers don't always get on,' said Jack. 'I've been away, you see . . .'

Trottie waved away the explanation. 'No need to worry about that,' she said. 'You're here now. You must stay with us, mustn't you, now you've got the job.' She began listing the local amenities. She told him about the little restaurant run by Nora's uncle, who made cheap meat pleasant by wrapping it in a queer sort of unleavened bread; the Covent Garden café where they did a suet pudding called a baby's head, which was excellent if you ignored the name. She told him which cinemas would take payment in lemonade bottles and named the pub where they put the least amount of water in a pint of wallop.

'You live over the shop, then?' asked Jack.

'I have the premises next door,' she said. 'Book has his books, I have my wallpaper. This darling little room is between the two. Now, did you need a toothbrush?'

'Why are you being so helpful?' asked Jack.

'Why not?' said Trottie breezily. She looked at him for a moment. 'I'll let you settle in.'

'That feller opposite,' said Jack. 'Those bones. Is it always like this?'

'Well,' said Trottie. 'Stay and you'll find out.' She gave him her warmest smile, then disappeared to the landing below. Jack realised that she must have passed through a door connecting the bookshop and the wallpaper shop. He sank down on the bed and felt the springs move beneath him. An unfamiliar sensation after two years on a hard block of horsehair. He pushed a finger through the hole in the middle of a crochet square.

Below, the doorbell clattered.

Book shouted up the stairs. 'Jack! Pile of newspapers on the first landing. Third stack from the right from the bathroom door. *Charing Cross Dispatch*. Under two volumes on

Eleanor of Castile and a wilting aspidistra. Fetch it for me, would you?'

'Okay,' said Jack. 'What happened over there?'

'Suicide!' called Book. 'Would you put the kettle on? We're going to have company.'

Company was Mrs Ada Dredge, a once-fastidious woman who now seemed to be losing a war of attrition with life. She took the armchair in the back kitchen with pitiable gratitude. Her eyes were red from crying. This, and the recent loss of her reading glasses somewhere on the District Line, obliged her to hold Book's special letter as far away from her face as she could reach.

'Oh well,' she said, passing it back to Book. 'Seeing as it's from *him*. He came to me in a dream once.'

Mrs Dredge, it emerged, was *sensitive*. 'I've pierced the veil a few times,' she said. 'And I know what the leaves mean.'

Jack settled a cup of tea beside her. 'I'll put this here,' he said.

'You can read it later,' said Book. Mrs Dredge responded by digging into her shopping bag and producing a metal tin commemorating the coronation of George V. 'I brought a coffee and walnut for Mr Harkup,' she said. 'You may as well have it.' She handed the tin to Book. 'Used my last drop of Camp for that.'

Book took the tin graciously. The job of cutting the cake was delegated to Jack.

'This was your usual char day, was it?' asked Book.

'Oh yes,' said Mrs Dredge. 'Every week, regular as clockwork. But I saw him yesterday, too. Popped round to get some bandages. My boy was injured in the war, you see.

He needs constant attention. His dressing.' She produced no further details.

'What time was this?' asked Book. 'The popping round?'

'Six,' said Mrs Dredge, uncertainly. 'Six-ish.' She was thinking of her moment of dread discovery: Harkup on the hearthrug, dead as a turbot in a fishmonger's window. She felt the tide of tears rolling in. 'Doesn't seem possible,' she whispered. 'He was so full of life.'

The wave crashed. Mrs Dredge issued a great wet gulping sob.

'You're doing very well,' said Book. 'And was he?'

'Was he what?' said Mrs Dredge, dabbing her eyes with a handkerchief.

'Full of life?' said Book. 'When you saw him? In good spirits, I mean.'

'Not really,' said Mrs Dredge. 'I'd say there was something on his mind. But why he'd want to go and do a horrible thing like that to himself . . .'

The waters burst again. Book waded in.

'Did Mr Harkup have any vices?' he asked.

The question was confusing. Disturbing. 'Vices, sir?'

'Alas, dear lady,' said Book. 'We must investigate all angles.'

Mrs Dredge frowned. 'Man of very regular habits, he was,' she said. 'Church every Sunday. Always took the wine and the wafer. Kept all his accounts in very neat order. Lovely straight columns. I think that was the soldier in him. He did play dominoes, though. Every Monday and Thursday night in the Bull. With Mr Baseheart and some others. Does that count as a vice?'

'I hardly think so,' said Book.

Jack presented him with a doorstop slice of cake on a willow-pattern plate. Book looked at it as if it were the north face of Mont Blanc.

'Did Mr Harkup have any family?' asked Jack. Book raised an eyebrow.

Mrs Dredge stiffened. Her sensitivity, it seemed, was not limited to the supernatural realm. 'My mother always said, if you can't say anything nice about someone, don't open your trap.'

'There was bad blood?' asked Jack.

Mrs Dredge did not reply. Book pushed on down the path that Jack had opened. 'There's a daughter, isn't there? Were they estranged in some way?'

'I wouldn't like to say,' she replied. 'It doesn't seem right, what with Mr H not cold in his grave.' Harkup's corpse now reappeared to her: a grimacing thing on the floor in front of the gas fire. A great wail escaped her lungs. Book's eye-roll was even less voluntary. He plunged his fork into Mrs Dredge's coffee and walnut like an ice-pick.

'Heavens, this cake!' he exclaimed, smacking his lips at a volume to match its maker's howls. 'It's absolutely first class. But then, I'd expect nothing less from Miss Lyons Corner House 1921.'

Mrs Dredge flinched. The allusion astonished her tears away. 'Fancy you knowing that!' she exclaimed. 'It was 1922, though.'

Book apologised for the error. He put down his plate on a copy of the *Charing Cross Dispatch* to conceal a photograph of the young Mrs Dredge in a starched white cap and black ribbon, beaming beside a potted palm.

'I bet you made a fabulous Nippy,' he said.

'A fabulous *Gladys*,' corrected Mrs Dredge. 'We weren't Nippies until '26.'

'I'll take the note,' said Book.

'Never felt so glamorous!' enthused Mrs Dredge. 'I had my hair bobbed. And the Lord Mayor winked at me.'

'Fancy,' said Book.

'Worked there for years, I did,' said Mrs Dredge, now luxuriating in a warm bath of nostalgia. 'So I got very good with the baking. All done on the premises. Mr H used to love my pineapple upside-down.'

Her lip began to tremble. Book observed it, and cut in. 'It really would be most helpful to know why he and his daughter Sarah no longer saw eye to eye,' he said.

'Merula,' corrected Mrs Dredge.

'Merula, that's right,' said Book, taking his prize.

'Well,' said Mrs Dredge, 'seeing as you've been so kind, sir.' She seemed about to divulge some delicate secret. 'She was a cow! A horrible, money-grubbing little cow!'

'I see,' said Book.

'Apple of his eye, she was. After the wife passed on. But she knew how to twist him round her little finger. Nothing was too much for his little princess! And then she has the gall to run off with *him*!'

'Him?'

'Mickey,' hooted Mrs Dredge. 'Mickey Hall. Right ne'er-do-well. Up to all sorts in the war. Spiv stuff, you know. Black market. He's a motor mechanic. They have a garage. Out Mile End way.'

'Mile End,' said Book. 'Charming.'

'And now Merula will inherit the lot,' rumbled Mrs Dredge. 'Don't seem right, do it?'

'No,' agreed Book. 'It *don't*.'

Book became aware that something long and sudden was happening on the step of the shop. It was Sergeant Morris, peering at this conversation through the glass, and already foaming with disapproval. He burst through the door.

'What the hell do you think you're doing?' he asked.

'Your witness, I think, Sergeant,' said Book.

The February sun died quietly that afternoon. On Archangel Lane, the police moved gravely from door to door. One by one, the shopkeepers turned their signs and submitted to questions about the last movements of Mr Harkup. Mr Wellbeloved and Mr Quillian both expressed regret for not having felt more suspicious about the closed shutters of the chemist. Mr Toovey wept. Mrs Acres said that Mrs Dredge had had a lot to put up with: Mr Harkup was not the sort of employer who ran his fingers over the wainscot and tutted, but he always kept his eye on the clock. Mr Baseheart, though not a witness of any sort, insisted on making a statement, and amplified the opinion of Mrs Acres. Mr Harkup, he said, was a little Hitler, who sometimes abused his powers of discretion.

Book, keeping an eye on these activities through the window of his shop, noted the departure of Morris and his gaggle of constables. One remained behind to guard the door of the chemist. The removal of the body, however, had yet to occur. Bliss, he calculated, was now alone with the corpse. Much to his relief, the constable on the door proved biddable, and his calculation correct.

'I'm just thinking,' said Bliss, as Book entered. 'I'm not sitting shiva. Dr Calder will get him soon enough.' The light had faded from the room. Harkup's body was a pale bundle lying in the gloom. Bliss was sitting in an armchair by the cold fire. He stood up to flick on the electric bulb. Book, he saw, was wearing his smartest three-piece suit.

'Off to the pictures?' asked Bliss. 'They're running a Sandra Dare at the Rialto.'

'The opera,' said Book. 'Your tiny hand is frozen, that sort of thing. Speaking of which, may I?'

Book pulled back the sheet covering the corpse. The passage of the day had not made it more beautiful: the electric light now added a yellowish tinge. Book traced his hand over the cold bowl of Harkup's skull and found there was blood on his fingers. He pulled out his handkerchief and wiped his hand clean.

'There's a daughter,' he said. 'But they didn't get on.'

Bliss was looking out of the window. 'We're endeavouring to trace her.'

'She has a garage in Mile End,' said Book.

'Oh,' said Bliss. 'Right. Thanks.' He sounded tired.

Conscious that his visit might soon be cut short, Book turned his attention from the body to the room. A sideboard, too big for the space, drew his eye. It was ranged with dozens of little ornaments, most of them blue-green in colour. A little elephant held up a clear glass marble representing the world. A wise mandarin bowed to a turtle. A cicada preened on top of a smooth pomegranate.

'Mrs Bliss goes in for something similar,' said Bliss, noticing where Book's attention lay. 'Little knick-knacks. She sends off from the *Daily Express*.'

'These are jade,' said Book, peering closely. 'Rather fine. Mr Harkup was a connoisseur.'

He picked up a small carved equine figurine and turned it over in his hand. As he put it back, he noticed that the dustless area beneath the ornament was wider than its base.

Bliss put out the light. It was time to leave. They descended the staircase and walked through the pharmacy. The shutters were drawn. Book could see all the medicines rowed in bottles and ampoules but could not read the labels in the gloom.

'Do you think it was suicide?' he asked.

'You have doubts?' replied Bliss, locking the door of the shop.

'I do,' said Book.

'What's your theory?'

Book did not divulge it. Baseheart and Wellbeloved were walking in the lane. The butcher appeared to have joined the ARP warden on one of his ceremonial laps of honour. They were looking up at the rooftops, pointing out gaps in the guttering, cracks in the brickwork. Baseheart offered a polite 'Good evening'.

'Oh, Eric,' said Book. '*Black Lamb and Grey Falcon*.'

'Eh?' said Wellbeloved, thinking fuzzily of meat and game.

'That book for Sheila,' said Book. 'It's arrived.'

The butcher's face broke into a wide, childlike grin. 'Oh,' he said. 'Smashing. She'll come over tomorrow for it.' He and the warden moved on, taking their conversation to the end of the lane.

'So?' asked Bliss, softly. 'What is your theory?'

Book watched Baseheart and Wellbeloved disappear from view. 'Patience, Inspector! Patience!' he whispered. 'The two most powerful warriors are patience and time.'

'Who said that?' asked Bliss.

'Tolstoy,' said Book.

'Oh.' Bliss sniffed. 'Couldn't get into him. Tried that one where she chucks herself in front of a train.'

The light snapped on in the wallpaper shop. For graduates of the blackout, the sudden appearance of a radiant yellow square in the gloom of the street still brought a faint churn of anxiety. *Put that light out.*

The window of Trottie's premises was stacked with paint tins and samples, but it did not obscure the view of the shop completely. He could see Jack standing in the doorway that led to the stockroom. Trottie was at the counter, wearing a new frock that he had seen on her sewing machine the previous morning. They were talking. There was a bottle of gin between them.

'See you in the morning, then,' said Bliss.

Trottie's dress was not made from a pattern: she had seen it wrapped tightly around Carole Landis in a copy of *Picture Post* and deduced its structure like a palaeontologist producing an iguanodon from an incomplete fossil. The fabric was unfussy wool-weight rayon, pleated, but not so extravagantly as to draw the jealous eye of those who knew the rules on controlled commodities. The pattern, however, gave two fingers to austerity. Its colour and form owed something to the prints displayed in Trottie's shop, but Jack had never seen roses of such eye-popping pinkness beyond the cinema screen. He did not, however, think of the headache experienced by the man who had robbed the Charing Cross Bank: the sensation it caused was entirely different. He tried to avert his eyes and focus his attention on a display of new wallpaper samples. These were also sizzlingly bright.

'Too much?' asked Trottie.

'No,' breathed Jack. 'Not at all. You look *amazing*.'

'I meant the paper,' said Trottie, not remotely displeased. 'Book says it's an affront to good taste. But I don't know. I think it has a certain something, don't you?'

Jack attempted to construct an opinion about wallpaper, a task nobody had ever asked him to perform.

'Since you mention it,' said Trottie, 'I did make the dress, too. I'm good at knocking things together,' she said. 'Always have been. Wireless sets. Wardrobes. Heads. I was in the Land Army. And the International Brigades. Gin?'

Jack's reply was unnecessary: she had broken out the bottle and two tumblers from a glass-fronted cabinet containing pots of paint, and was already pouring.

'You're going out?' he asked.

'We're *always* going out. Do me up, would you?' She whirled round and presented her back to Jack. He saw a small metal fastener loose at the nape of her neck. For a moment he stared at it, dumbly, as if he were being asked to conjugate a Latin verb. His fingers, however, seemed to possess the necessary knowledge.

'One has to live, doesn't one?' said Trottie, draining her

glass. 'Especially after the time we've all had. There're some chops in the larder. I think. Do you like chops?'

'I do like chops,' said Jack. The answer was correct and ordinary but felt like the most foolish words that had ever left his lips.

Trottie, however, did not register his embarrassment. Her husband, she saw, was waiting in the lane. Book, lit by the glow from the window, gave a polite bow.

'No need to wait up for him,' she said, and switched off the light, leaving Jack standing in the gloom holding a medicine glass full of gin.

Trottie stepped out into the evening. Jack drained his glass and felt the unfamiliar heat of alcohol. He did not much care for gin: he had spent his childhood around those who cared for it too much. But he did like the warmth, and the way it held his throat in the dark.

Out in the lane, the fog was gathering itself for the night. Trottie and Book stood within its folds and kissed. As their lips met, Trottie detected a certain nervous energy in her husband. A quickness of the eyes. A twitch around the mouth, as if he were eager to give a speech.

'I know that look,' she said. 'You're on to something.'

'Nonsense,' said Book. 'Just the happy look of a contented man. I have my lovely wife. My lovely bookshop. My lovely dog. What more could a man want?'

She was being teased. This behaviour merited a playful punch.

'Fraud,' she said. 'Charlatan.'

'All right,' said Book. 'I'm on to three things.' They

linked arms and walked together over the cobbles. 'George Harkup collected Chinese jade figures of exceptional quality. But dust is eloquent. Dust doesn't lie. One figure has been replaced with some piece of cheap trash. A chess piece made of green Bakelite. But the larger outline of the original figure remains clear. Mrs Dredge hasn't cleaned for a while, despite what she said. Secondly, Mr Harkup has a small lump on the back of his head. Not caused by falling, though, I would say. More like a blow with a blunt instrument. A blunt instrument that didn't break the skin. And yet there was blood on Harkup's scalp. And thirdly . . .'

Book came to a sudden halt. His eyes snapped shut. He inhaled deeply, as if trying to swallow the fog.

'Are you all right?' asked Trottie.

'*Darkling I listen;*' he whispered, '*and, for many a time I have been half in love with easeful Death, Call'd him soft names in many a mused rhyme, To take into the air my quiet breath.*'

'Pardon?' said Trottie.

He opened his eyes. 'Why,' he said, 'would a chemist, with every known gentle poison in the shop below, choose to kill himself with something as horrible as Prussic acid?'

Trottie attempted to think of a plausible answer. She could not.

'There we are then,' breathed Book. 'It's murder!' He sounded like a man who had been presented with an exceptionally fine jar of marmalade.

Book reattached his arm to Trottie's, and together they walked towards the lights of the Strand. A bus huffed past in the direction of Charing Cross, its windows glowing yellow.

When they reached the end of the lane, they stopped and faced each other.

'Book,' said Mrs Book.

'Mrs Book,' said Book.

It was a moment of courtly solicitude, which, having been concluded, sent them both off into the fog, in entirely separate directions.

CHAPTER THREE

Jack did not hear Book return. Nor did he hear the jangling of keys, the night-screech of iron hinges, the moans of men spending their first night behind bars. Finding that the small bed in the small room in the attic of 158 Archangel Lane was inconceivably soft, he sank back, allowed it to swallow him, and did not awake until his dreams were invaded by a vision of the whey-faced policeman, blowing sharply at his whistle.

The sound persisted after he had opened his eyes. Someone, he thought, should remove the kettle from the hob. That person seemed to be him. Going downstairs, he found the kitchen empty: the absence of the lead hanging by the baize curtain told him that Dog was being taken for a walk. The moaning kettle seemed to indicate that his master required a cup of tea on his return. Book came through the door with a satisfied smile on his face. Jack had passed another test.

'Never worked in a shop before,' said Jack. 'Unless you count selling fish round pubs.'

'I don't,' said Book. 'But I'm sure it'll go swimmingly.'

Book's Books was not the most popular business on Archangel Lane. Eric Wellbeloved had the stuff that brought the queues; some of the trade at 158 came from people who wanted something to read while they waited in line for pork loins and best ends of neck. On Jack's first morning he watched Book sell *The Hand of Ethelberta* to a Thomas Hardy completist, disappoint an elderly gentleman in search of unusual postcards, and fail to persuade a poetic young nurse to dip her toe into Vorticism.

Book had a ginger snap in his mouth when a middle-aged woman and her sour-faced husband crossed the threshold.

'I'm after a book,' said the woman.

'You are very much in the right place,' said Book. He looked the customer up and down, as if he were estimating how far he could throw her, then turned his gaze on Jack, whose period as an observer had clearly come to a sudden end.

'What do you think, young man?' he said. 'What would suit the lady? Dickens? Wilkie Collins? Henry James?'

Jack knew the names, but little more.

'Do you have the new Georgette Heyer?' said the woman.

'Ah,' said Book.

'I've read all her others,' said the customer.

'Me too. And what a smasher she is. But that'd be a *new* book, Miss . . . ?'

'*Mrs* Goodwin,' said Mrs Goodwin, more pleased by the error than her husband.

'Mrs Goodwin.'

'Jean,' she added.

'Well, Jean,' said Book. 'We don't really go in for new books.'

'We should try Foyles,' said Mr Goodwin.

Book winced. So did Mrs Goodwin. 'It's a bit of a schlep, Gerald,' she said.

Book glanced downwards. There was, he noticed, something angular about the line of Mrs Goodwin's toes that her shoes and thick woollen tights could not disguise.

'I have the perfect alternative,' he declared. 'An author who was spinning romantic yarns before Miss Heyer was out of the cradle. Probably.'

Book clapped a hand to his head and appeared to have forgotten his own recommendation. He waved his other hand in the air, as if batting dandelion seeds away from his face. When Mrs Goodwin asked for the name, Book shushed her.

'Beg your pardon, I'm sure,' said Mrs Goodwin.

'Sorry,' said Book. 'Thinking.'

Some eureka moment occurred inside his skull. He leapt towards an overstuffed case and began rooting through its volumes like a terrier after a rat. Sinking down on his hands and knees did not reduce the effect.

Jack gave Jean Goodwin an apologetic smile.

'Orczy!' declared Book, back on his feet.

'Never heard of him,' said Mrs Goodwin.

'*Her*,' said Book.

'Not smutty, is it?' asked Mrs Goodwin, suspiciously.

'Oh no,' said Book. 'Orczy's a Baroness. Hungarian. Lives in Henley-on-Thames.'

'*The Scarlet Pimpernel*,' said Gerald Goodwin, complacently.

'Oh, I've heard of that,' said Jean. 'French Revolution.'

Book gave her a conspiratorial smile. 'You won't regret it,' he said. 'When you've finished, bring it back and I'll find you the sequel. It's around here somewhere.' His eyes were back on the shelves.

'Well, that's very good of you,' said Jean. 'What do I owe you?'

'Let's call it a bob,' grinned Book. Mr Goodwin put his hand in his pocket and would have handed over the money instantly, but Book was already scaling the library steps to extract another volume from a high shelf, a thick blue block with the title embossed in gold: *Podiatric Ailments and Their Remedies*.

'That's free,' said Book. Mrs Goodwin spluttered some polite objections. Book dismissed them. 'It's nothing,' he said, his eyes on Mr Goodwin. 'But sending you on the bus contemplating the end of your discomfort – well, that has a price above rubies, wouldn't you say, Jean?'

Bunions. Jean did not care to draw attention to her affliction. However, she was so touched by the sentiment that she left the shop with the blue volume pressed against her bosom like a billet-doux. Gerald Goodwin opened the door for her. As he left, he cast a resentful look in Book's direction.

'I'll never make any money like that, will I?' Book sighed, flipping the silver shilling in his hand. 'But then, neither will Miss Christina Foyle.' He pronounced the name like Sherlock Holmes speaking of Professor Moriarty. 'Still got that coin from Inkerman Street?'

'Of course,' said Jack.

'Good,' said Book. Something, thought Jack, had been ticked off a list. But Jack had a list of his own. He had been observing his employer all morning and done more than study the quality of his salesmanship. 'I don't mean to pry, Mr Book,' he said, 'but what exactly do you *do*?'

Book waved at the multicoloured wall of spines before them. 'I would have thought that was obvious.'

'But that's not all, is it?' pushed Jack. His eyes were bright and hungry. 'Out there. Yesterday. The bombsite. And your chat with the charlady. Is that your hobby?'

'Hobby?' repeated Book.

'The way you talk to the coppers,' said Jack. 'And the way they let you roam around that pit. Are you, like, an advisor to them or something? I mean, why should they listen to you?'

Book snorted. 'They frequently don't. More fool them. I did the inspector a favour once, during the war. He hasn't forgotten. Also, I have a special letter—'

'A letter from Churchill, yeah,' interrupted Jack. 'Saying what?'

Book ignored the question. 'It's a chaotic world, Jack. I have a system. Sometimes the police need people like me to give an opinion. Impose a little order on that chaos. That's all. You can read all sorts of things, as well as books.'

His eyes were back on the shelves. Jack followed his gaze, taking in a jumbled field of penny novelettes, cookery manuals, poetry anthologies and academic Festschrifts.

'This is your system?' he asked.

'What's wrong with it?' asked Book, stung and bothered.

'Well, they're not in any kind of order!' said Jack. He pulled a volume from the shelf. *Cataracts of the Nile* (Hurst and Blackett, 1910, third impression, struck with a silver Eye of Horus).

'Not bad,' said Book. 'A little browning to a few pages. Otherwise a clean copy.'

Jack pulled out the next title. *Diseases of the Eye and Their Treatment* (HK Lewis and Co., 1907, ninth edition). He handed it to Book.

'Cataracts!' exclaimed Book. 'Eye disease! Logical! Absolutely logical!'

Jack slipped out the next three volumes. *The Guillotine: A Practical Guide* (contemporary half calf, drab blue boards); *The Life and Death of Alfred Muttings, Gent* (bound chapbook, ex libris Hon Mrs Radlett); *Coins of the Realm* (first edition, buckram in purpose-made slipcase).

'There's no system,' said Jack. 'No system at all!'

He loaded these volumes into Book's arms. Book seemed flustered, like a conjurer to whom someone has given a pack of cards and then demanded to see a trick. The trick was forthcoming. 'Alfred Muttings was a career criminal,' he said, laying the chapbook on the counter. 'Very successful forger in his day. Which was Queen Victoria's day. Extraordinary chap in his field. He was a coiner. A forger of coins.' Down went *Coins of the Realm*, then *The Guillotine*. 'But his luck ran out in Paris and they chopped off his head. So that's why those books are all clumped together. You see?'

'That's silly,' said Jack.

'Nevertheless,' said Book, drily. 'Put those back, would you?' He began dragging on his coat and heading for the door. Dog looked up in expectation.

'Well, I'll leave you to hold the fort,' he said. He left, quickly, fretfully and doglessly.

Maybe, thought Jack, that was that. Perhaps his relationship with a sprung mattress and soft eiderdown was doomed to be brief. Dog regarded him balefully, as if blaming him for not being out in the February air, inhaling near lampposts and restaurant bins.

Jack sank into a chair with the pile of books in his lap. He stared at the cover of *Coins of the Realm* and noted a scattering of little brown flecks on its pages. Slightly foxed. He gazed at an engraving of a Queen Anne gold guinea; a silver half-groat bearing a blank-eyed full-face portrait of Henry VII. He reached into his pocket to retrieve the coin pulled from the pit. There it was, or something similar, rendered in the book. King Charles II, with a nose as Roman as the laurels on his head, and on the reverse, the four crowned shields of England, Scotland, France and Ireland arranged in the form of a cross (British monarchs, the text reported, claimed a right of kingship over France until 1801). He held the coin up to the light. Between the harp of Ireland and the three lions of England was an imperfection on the metal.

A search of Book's desk drawers produced a magnifying glass that revealed this to be a hardened patch of transparent powder. Jack had the pleasant sensation that he had passed another test.

The shop bell broke the moment. A young woman in a tank top and oatmeal plus fours was moving towards him with the speed and certainty of a torpedo scudding towards a U-boat.

'I'm Nora,' she said. 'We've got lots to talk about.'

Bow Street police station had a bouquet. The tang of carbolic, formaldehyde and varnished oak, intermixed with cigarette ash, stewed tea and the sour-sweetness of the tank into which the meths drinkers of Covent Garden were poured during the small hours. It was Book's third-favourite smell, after lapsang souchong and incunabula.

The terms of his access to the building were complex and depended on the patronage of Inspector Bliss. If the inspector was present and prominent, Book was often waved straight through to the warren of back corridors. If Bliss was absent, or ensconced in some obscure corner, Book was made to wait under the eye of the desk sergeant, like some stage-door johnny seeking an audience with a Cochrane girl. If Morris was visible in the entrance hall, Book sometimes took a turn around the fruit market until the sergeant had moved elsewhere.

Today, the whey-faced constable was at the desk, and sufficiently friendly to reveal that Morris had been called to a punch-up on Lisle Street. Book nodded gratefully, then passed through the enamel-brick corridors towards the lab. Here he found the pathologist, Dr Calder, hunkered over the human puzzle pieces recovered from the pit on Inkerman Street. Book always delighted in watching Dr Calder at work: the dexterity of her scalpel, the clarity of her eye, the gentle creak of the leather skin of her prosthetic arm. The jumble of bones had given her no great trouble. It had only taken her the night to resolve them into people. Dr Calder was keen for Book to cast his eye over a particular set. On a long, pale femur, she had detected a series of marks.

'Where better to hide a tree,' said Book.

'. . . than in a forest,' said Dr Calder.

They admired the skeletons as if they were on display in a vitrine at the British Museum.

'The blood test will help,' said Book. 'Don't forget it!'

'Are you my boss now?' asked Dr Calder.

They both looked up. Bliss was peering around the door with undisguised surprise. In the corridor behind him was a young woman in a raincoat with the belt hanging loose. She was tense as a piano wire and lighting herself a cigarette.

'What do you think?' asked Bliss, acknowledging Book with a watery smile. 'Any risk of infection from these old bones?'

'Quite safe on that count, Inspector,' she said. 'However—'

'Ah!' Book interrupted. 'Loose lips drop slips, as they say in the knicker trade. Let's not spoil the surprise, eh?'

Bliss rolled his eyes, but the presence of the woman in the corridor prevented him from prosecuting the matter further. He motioned for Book to join him.

'This is Miss Merula Harkup,' said Bliss. 'She's just performed the sad duty of identifying her father's body.'

Merula Harkup took a long, grim drag on her cigarette.

'I'm so terribly sorry,' said Book, softening his voice to meet the tone of the moment. 'We were all very shocked by his death.'

Miss Harkup gave a desultory nod and expelled a tight line of smoke. Book had seen commuters express more emotion in response to an apology for a late-running tube.

Bliss led them both to the interview room beside his office. It had once had a series of frosted windows, but most of these had been patched with board. A constable furnished Miss Harkup with a mug of tea, which she ignored.

'Suppose you think I'm hard,' she said. 'Not blubbing all over the shop. Well, it's just not the way I'm made. So there.' She stubbed out her cigarette, which she had smoked right to the tip. 'I'm sorry he's dead. 'Course I am. He was my dad, in spite of everything. He didn't make it easy to love him, though.'

'Can you think of any reason why he would want to take his own life?' asked Bliss.

'None,' said Merula. 'He was nicely set up with his shop. And Mum left him a few bob when she died.'

Bliss wondered if estrangement from his family might have been a motive for his actions, but Merula Harkup cut him off with a snort. 'No,' she said. 'Nothing to do with that. He wasn't the sentimental type. Maybe that's where I get it from. He made it very clear that he didn't approve of me and Mickey. But he'd hardly have gone and killed himself in a fit of the glums about it. Weren't the type, as I say.'

'Tell us about Mickey,' said Bliss. Book was also curious.

'What's to say?' replied Merula. 'He's my feller.'

'Well,' said Book, 'I know how much your father appreciated the armed forces. Always wore his medals with great pride. On Armistice Day he positively rattled.'

'Yes, well. Mickey wasn't so lucky. His eyes. They're not good. Maybe that's why he ended up with me.' The self-deprecation suggested the possibility of something tender beneath Merula Harkup's armour. 'Mickey wouldn't have been much good against Jerry with eyes like his. Dad didn't like that. Thought he was a shirker. That was the start of it.'

'What was the finish?'

'Dad was convinced Mickey was thieving from him.'

'Cash?' asked Bliss.

'Morphine,' replied Merula. It was a sad little story. Mickey, she said, had bent a few regulations during the war. Nothing serious. Nothing that had resulted in a charge. 'Stockings and cigarettes,' she explained. 'Packet of razors here and there. But a drinking pal of his got into proper bother with the police. Something to do with horse-doping at Newmarket. Never really got to the bottom of it.'

'And your dad noticed morphine missing from his shop?' asked Bliss.

'He stopped speaking to us,' said Merula.

'What a terrible pity,' said Book, quietly, 'that you couldn't tell him your good news.'

Merula frowned, then realised that she had her hand planted on her belly. It was the third time during their short conversation that she had made this gesture.

'Thought a little one might be the thing that brung us back together,' she said mournfully. 'But that's that, I suppose.'

She got to her feet and pulled the raincoat around her. Inspector Bliss accepted that the interview was at an end. As he escorted her from the station, he offered more words of condolence. Merula Harkup did not reply. She was thinking of her husband, and had already decided that when she got home, she would kiss him deeply and place his hands upon her body, no matter how thick they were with oil and grease.

It had been a slow afternoon at 158 Archangel Lane. A clerk with necrotic breath came seeking something on pest control: Jack swallowed the temptation to tell him to exhale on his problem. A twitchy schoolboy, clearly troubled by something he had seen in the night, sought a book on the interpretation of dreams (Freud came to the rescue).

The most interesting visitor did not even cross the threshold. He was a middle-aged man in a tailored suit who stood opposite the shop, occupying himself with a cigarette. A businessman of some kind, perhaps; a more respectable figure than most of those who loiter on the pavements in the middle of the day. A leather patch covered one of his eyes. A war wound, Jack assumed. When the man registered that Jack had noticed him, he moved on. But not before finishing his cigarette.

Nora, though she was also an employee of Book's Books, did not assist Jack with these customers. Instead, she jammed herself into an armchair and observed him as if he were a rare kind of amphibian that had turned up in her garden pond. The most she would do was offer another example of Book's system, through which she had once located a copy of Samuel Johnson's *The Journal of a Tour to the Hebrides* by looking next to Hensel's biography of the Mendelssohn family. 'I took a punt on *Fingal's Cave*,' she said, bafflingly.

'You know them well, then?' asked Jack. 'Mr and Mrs Book?'

Nora knew Jack was fishing, so threw him a few morsels. The Books were a dream. They were sweethearts. Mrs Book had shot a Fascist in Spain in the 1930s. Mr Book's first name was Gabriel.

'Like the angel?' asked Jack.

'Archangel,' corrected Nora.

'And you know about his little hobby?' asked Jack.

'Bloody hell, yes!' enthused Nora. The floodgates opened. 'It's *all* I think about! Mr Book saw Crippen once. Outside the Old Bailey. Being led in by handcuffs. Crippen! Imagine that!'

'Don't have to imagine,' muttered Jack.

'Sorry?' said Nora.

'Nothing,' said Jack.

'You know Crippen's big mistake?' asked Nora, eager to fill a sorry gap in Jack's education. 'Saying she'd died in America. Mrs Crippen, I mean. Maybe if he'd just said she'd left him. But a death obviously rouses suspicions. And then it's a short step to finding bits of her in the coal cellar.'

'Isn't all that,' mumbled Jack, 'I mean . . . isn't it a bit—'

'Unhealthy? I should think so!' Her eyes shone with delight, like a schoolgirl contemplating the end of the sweet ration. 'It's going to be my career.'

'Murder?' asked Jack. Nora was so full of italic energy that it was not impossible to imagine her standing proudly in the dock, as a lawyer quizzed her about where the bodies were buried.

'*Writing* about murder,' Nora clarified.

'What do your mum and dad think?' asked Jack.

'Don't have any,' said Nora. 'The war, you know.'

The shop bell clattered. Enid, the butcher's assistant whom Jack had seen handling a pig carcass with such ease, was standing at the counter.

'I've come to collect a book,' she said.

'What was the name?' asked Jack.

'Sheila Wellbeloved,' said Enid.

The shelf housing customer orders was a tiny enclave in which the alphabet was given the respect it deserved. Jack found *Black Lamb and Grey Falcon* quickly.

'Looks interesting,' he said, looking at the coloured map in the endpapers.

'Does it?' said Enid.

'The Balkans,' said Jack.

'I'm sure,' said Enid. Her lack of interest followed her through the shop door like the odour of her scent. Nora ignored the exchange. She was back in the armchair with her head buried in the newest edition of *Tribune* magazine. After five minutes, she put it down with a frown. 'Up to a point, Lord Copper,' she exclaimed. The remark meant so little to Jack that she might as well have addressed it to Dog, which, on consideration, he realised she had.

'I've got so many ideas,' said Nora. This, it seemed, *was* intended for human ears.

'For what?' asked Jack.

'Detective stories,' she said. 'That's what I want to write. It's such an exciting new world out there. So inspiring.'

'Inspiring?' said Jack. 'Everything's been smashed up. And no one knows what to do anymore.'

'Well,' countered Nora, '*I* do.' She looked at Jack with a forensic sharpness that again made him feel like a visiting frog. 'The war turned everything upside down,' she enthused. 'Shook it up. But that's great. There's no going back to how things used to be.'

'Including murders?' asked Jack.

'Including murders,' she confirmed. She was on home territory. 'Half the soldiers in Britain have come home with pistols they stole from dead Nazis. The country's awash with them. We only seem civilised in this country because we're not *armed*. Think of all that throbbing suburban passion. Husbands having affairs with secretaries. Ladies having affairs with their chauffeurs. All those contested wills and domestic rows. People used to kill each other by boiling down arsenic from their wallpaper. Now they just have to reach for a Luger!'

She pointed two fingers at Jack. '*Pow! Pow! Pow!*' In some part of Nora's imagination, he was now lying on the bonnet of a Baby Austin, his body riddled with smoking lead.

'What happened to your parents?' he asked.

'*I'm* the writer,' she said. 'You tell me *your* story. Maybe I'll make something of it.'

'I'm an orphan too,' said Jack. 'Never knew my mum. Got a photo of my dad. That's the lot.'

Nora was disarmed. Her invisible Luger returned to its invisible holster. She might have apologised to him had the shop door not rattled open to admit a breathless middle-aged man in a tight tweed waistcoat.

'I'm looking for something on the cataracts of the Nile,' the man panted.

Jack made an instant sale. *Diseases of the Eye and their Treatment* would now require attachment to some other chain of association.

'It was an incendiary,' said Nora, as the man went happily away.

'What?' said Jack.

'Set the roof on fire,' she said, her eyes cast down. 'In the Blitz. Mum got me out and went back for Dad. Then the roof fell in. I just sat there in the garden looking at the house. Just felt sort of numb. The ARP warden found me. Then my uncle took me in. So now I have to help him out with the restaurant.' She raised her eyes from the floor to meet Jack's.

'Much more exciting over here, innit?' She smiled.

Was any of this true? Jack decided to behave as if it was. Prison had taught him not to pick unnecessary fights.

'I suppose it is,' he said.

Nora slapped the copy of *Tribune* into Jack's hands. 'Have a read of that, mate. "Decline of the English Murder". Feller says they've gone off. That the Yanks and the movies have spoiled us. We used to have respectable killers. Now our girls go out like they go out jitterbugging and do people in for kicks. What do you think?'

Jack liked dancing, but he had never jitterbugged. He loved the movies, but he had not seen a film since 1943. 'I've no idea,' he said.

'Well,' said Nora. 'I think Mr Orwell is wrong. I think we're at the start of a golden age.'

That night Book went to bed with George Orwell; also with his wife and most loyal companion, that is to say, with Mrs Trottie Book and with Dog, who never saw an eiderdown upon which he did not wish to curl. Trottie was at her dressing table, applying cold cream. Dog snored lightly. Book, *Tribune* balanced on his chest, was wrestling with the essay to which Nora had taken exception. The subject was the Cleft Chin Murder of 1944, in which two GIs had gone on a killing spree with a teenage waitress from Neath who dreamed of a career in striptease. The genteel canonical slaughter of the Victorian and Edwardian past, the writer contended, was deeper and richer than this 'meaningless story, with its atmosphere of dance halls, movie palaces, cheap perfume, false names and stolen cars'. The crimes of Elizabeth Jones and her conspirators were a dubious foreign import, like the grey squirrel or Spam.

Book folded the magazine with a sceptical smile and thought of Mr George Harkup, dead on his parlour carpet with a fatal mouthful of acid.

Somewhere above the bedroom, a floorboard creaked.

'I put him in the attic room,' said Trottie, trying to climb beneath the covers without disturbing Dog.

'Like Mrs Rochester,' replied Book. 'But slightly more butch.'

Trottie moved closer to her husband. It was a cold night and he was always warm. His flannel pyjamas were pleasingly soft.

'Has it ever occurred to you,' she asked, her eyes already closing, 'that you are such a bibliophile because of your name?'

'Nominative determinism?' mused Book.

'If you'd been called "Butcher", you might be slicing up choice cuts of meat,' said Trottie.

'*Flensing*,' said Book, pushing his spectacles back on his nose. 'That's the word. For removing fat from a carcass. Wonderfully descriptive. *Flensing*. I shall endeavour to bring it back.'

'I wish you joy with that,' said Trottie, sleepily. 'You could be slipping me black-market chops under the counter like Mr Wellbeloved. Much more useful than books these days.'

'I could have been an Archer,' Book reflected, following her line of thought. 'Or a Baker. Or a Chandler. Which reminds me . . .'

He reached towards a tower of volumes on the bedside table. Reluctantly, Trottie opened her eyes and moved aside to allow his search.

'*Farewell, My Lovely*,' he muttered.

'Oh, are you going out again?' asked Trottie.

'You're so sharp you'll cut yourself,' said Book, extracting a lipstick-pink hardback novel from the pile.

Another creak came from upstairs.

'How sharp is he?' asked Trottie.

'Oh, Jack shows definite promise,' said Book, steadying the tower. 'And he didn't try to flog that coin.'

'So jail hasn't made him a wrong'un for life?'

'Touch wood,' said Book, settling his head back on the pillow and opening up the novel.

'And the other matter?' asked Trottie, a note of delicacy in her voice.

'It's too soon to tell him,' said Book. It was the certainty of wisdom, or the certainty of fear.

Trottie rolled in closer. Book put an arm around her and pinched the book between his fingers to hold it steady. American accents were not Book's forte, and rather than alarm her with his rendering of the patrons of a second-floor dine-and-dice emporium on Central Avenue, he read silently and waited for his wife to fall asleep.

Little disturbed the night: Book could hear the door of

Yusuf's restaurant opening and closing as the last of the diners went home; the faint rumble of the traffic at the end of the lane. Philip Marlowe was in the thick of the action, but Book found himself noticing Chandler's descriptions of clothes – a yellow tie, a pink garter, a grey coat stitched with a golf-ball pattern – and then noticing nothing.

Book was thinking of another bed and another book on one of the dank spring mornings of his childhood, when the old queen was dead and the new king seemed just as old. He was not at home. He had not been at home for some time. He was in a low wooden pavilion where twenty identical iron-framed beds were rowed beneath windows that gave a view of flat land a long way from anywhere but the grey English coast.

The book in his hands was illustrated. The cover depicted a golden afternoon of cricket: a clean-limbed boy was running in to bowl across a public-school lawn. Quite suddenly, however, the image vanished from view. The book was now in the fist of a granite-faced nurse who was moving through the room with a haul of confiscated objects.

Other children clamoured around her. Protest, however, was futile. After the ward door clicked shut there was nothing to do but imagine a metal drum stacked with blazing coal and the heads of wax dolls suppurating, and knitted items from home blackening, and a fine copy of *Tim* by Howard Sturgis (blue cloth binding, second impression, 1894) going to scorched oblivion.

One more possibility presented itself. Sobbing and staring at the grey afternoon, which might have been enough for

Book, had not the new girl appeared by his bedside; twelve years old in a scruffy pinafore dress and baggy cardigan, her face bearing a sympathetic smile and livid scarlatina rash.

He found it hard to recall the precise point in the day when this happened, but the words exchanged stood as brightly as the text of an illuminated manuscript beneath an electric lamp.

'Why did they take your book?' she asked.

'Germs,' he said.

'Do you lick your fingers when you turn the pages?' she asked.

'Yes,' he said.

'Why don't they speak to you here?'

The girl was rude. Friendly but rude.

'Why don't you ask them?' he replied.

'They don't speak to me, either,' she said, settling on the edge of the bed. 'What was so special about your book?'

'Nothing, really. It's just about some chaps. At school. Playing cricket.' He found himself unwilling to elaborate.

'And what do you think of Carol Darley?'

The question stunned him.

'You've read it?' he asked.

'Started it,' she said.

'When?'

'This afternoon. After I saved it from the incinerator.'

From the folds of her cardigan, she produced the fat blue volume. He was astounded. The treasure had been returned. The flames and the authorities had been defeated. It was time to introduce himself.

'Book,' he said.

The girl turned the object over in her hand. 'Pages. Lots of words. I think you may be right.'

'No,' he said. 'That's me. I'm Book. What's your name?'

'Budge over,' said the girl, pushing him from the centre of the bed.

'Queer name,' said Book.

Once he had made room, she passed him the book. He held it up to the light, inspected it carefully for damage, smoothed down the corner of a crumpled page.

'You lied about licking your finger,' she said.

'They don't like me reading this sort of story,' he replied. 'The doctor said—'

'Bugger the doctor,' snapped the girl. The word shocked Book. He had never dared to say it aloud.

'Thank you,' he breathed.

'Trottie,' said the girl. 'Short for Strotford. Strotford Perry.'

'That's even queerer,' said Book.

'It's a long story,' said Trottie. 'I shan't ever tell you it.'

'I shan't ever ask,' he said.

'That's settled, then,' said Trottie.

They gazed at each other. 'You're splendid,' said Book.

'You owe me,' said Trottie, blowing a corkscrew curl from her face. 'When I get into trouble here, will you help me out?'

Book nodded. 'Let us make a solemn pact.' They did not exchange thunderous oaths, nor mingle their blood. They were not storybook pirates or brigands. They were serious people. They shook hands.

'I was up to page 316,' said Trottie.

Book realised that he was expected to read aloud. He found the place with nervous fingers and cleared his throat. He kept his voice low, and not just because he did not want to disturb the other children on the ward.

'*Put your strong arms around me, Carol,*' he read, '*and raise me a little; I can talk better so.*'

An uncertain pause followed. Nobody on the ward was paying them the smallest bit of attention. Book continued.

'*He laid his head on his friend's breast and closed his eyes; the effort of talking so much had tired him. "Do you remember, Carol? I lay on this sofa when you first came to see me after the accident. I had been dreaming of you without knowing it; I thought you were an angel. And then I turned and saw you standing there in the doorway. You kissed me that day, Carol. Will you kiss me now?"*'

Trottie let her head fall on Book's shoulder. A little gesture of trust that would be repeated down the decades.

'*Carol bowed his head without a word and kissed him,*' read Book. '*And thus their friendship was sealed.*'

Trottie woke as Book slipped out from beneath the eiderdown.

'Goodnight, Mr Book,' she whispered.

'Goodnight, Mrs Book,' he replied.

She kissed his cheek, put out the bedside light and stretched out under the eiderdown.

Dog followed his master through the door that connected the two halves of the building. As Book crossed the uncarpeted landing, he murmured a little rhyme.

The daughter, the spiv, the char, the warden
Who gave Harkup the ruddy poison?

On the other side of the landing was a sparse little room with a plain single bed and a baize-topped wooden table piled with documents and books. He picked one up. *Chemical Compounds and Their Effects* (ES Livingstone, 1920, fair copy). He read the entry on Prussic acid with a frown.

'Robs the blood of oxygen,' he said. 'Like a dry drowning.'

He moved to the window and looked down upon Archangel Lane. The streetlamps were lit and the night was settling around them. Book pictured himself climbing a lamppost, reaching up to catch the banks of the fog, and finding that they were sufficiently solid to support his weight. He imagined kicking his legs like a swimmer and moving upwards into the air to peer through the upper-storey windows of the houses; that under his gaze, roofs could be obliged to turn to glass and reveal the movements of their inhabitants; that minds, too, could be made transparent, to expose the thoughts darting within, like the fishes in an aquarium; that all London was beneath him, its bright desires unmasked by blackout blinds, burning up the evening.

Had he possessed this power, he might have seen a little group playing dominoes in the Bull, and Mr Baseheart's grim, cold face as his friends toasted to the memory of George Harkup. He might have seen Mr Harkup's picture in an expensive frame on the mantelpiece of Mrs Ada Dredge, and her gazing sweetly upon it. He might have detected, in a room above Mrs Dredge's parlour, a shape turning beneath damp sheets, and loosing a long, low moan of pain.

Book, though, was no airborne angel; no demon Asmodeus, spying on human folly from the air. He was an earthbound mortal who noticed things and did his homework; a man who studied the text and the footnotes. He sat down, spread his books around him on the baize-topped table, adjusted the angle of the lamp, and began to read.

CHAPTER FOUR

It was raining on the night that Strotford Perry shot a Fascist. A memorable occasion: on the banks of the Ebro in the summer of 1938, rain was rarer than untinned milk. As many British volunteers in the International Brigades discovered, it would have been an event even on the plain: Spain was so dry that they were forced to clean the kitchen utensils and mop the operating theatres with sea water. And there were many mouths to feed, and there was much blood to be washed away.

It was not the first time Trottie had seen a Francoist soldier, separated from his unit and on the wrong side of the line. This one was a good-looking boy in his twenties, brown-eyed, unusually tall, with the firm and pitiless eye of a seducer. All these qualities might have held some appeal in peacetime, but in war, they carried no such charm. Her target had come staggering into the field hospital – a convent with the misfortune to be close to the fighting – intending, she was sure, to finish off the broken men she was helping to put back together. He walked through the ward, his pistol levelled, smoothly and deliberately, at nuns, volunteer nurses and the wounded of the Garibaldi

Brigade. Trottie had been sent to the hospital because it was enduring an outbreak of scarlatina. Given that she had endured it in childhood, she was unlikely to get it twice. But she also had other skills. She pulled the Mauser from the belt of an Italian sergeant with a missing leg and fired without blinking.

The man in the entrance of her shop was not armed, but he had a loping, qualmless, dangerous look. He had pushed open the door, clocked Trottie behind the counter and turned instantly to whip off his wire-framed spectacles and smooth his hair. He was vain. He was confident. He smouldered and looked used to starting fires. He seemed to think himself a fox with the good fortune to have found a goose that might take him at his word. He had no such luck.

'Can I help you?' asked Trottie.

'Oh *yes*,' said the man, as if he were already upstairs with his belt unbuckled.

'With wallpaper,' said Trottie. 'It's a little early for *that*.'

'I'm looking for a Mrs Book,' said the man.

'You found her,' replied Trottie.

'Oh,' he said, pressing his palms on the glass top of the counter. 'Crying shame.'

'What is?' asked Trottie.

'You being married.' His studied insolence might have impressed a woman who had not heard the line a thousand times before. Mercifully, Dog appeared from the bookshop and padded towards Trottie.

'Stay,' said Trottie. Dog obeyed.

Dog, unlike this person, was a gentleman.

'I got a message,' said the man, 'from your husband. Said

you was having trouble with your alternator. In your car. That's what I do, see. Cars.'

Trottie did not do cars. If she had, she would have driven ambulances in Spain, and not run a field hospital.

'So you're a mechanic, are you, Mr . . . ?'

'Hall,' said the mechanic. 'Mickey Hall.' He rubbed a thumbnail over his two-day stubble in a gesture that made Trottie wonder how it would feel it against her skin.

'I see,' she said. 'And Mr Book sent for you?'

Mickey Hall nodded. 'No idea why he couldn't have got someone more local. But you go to where the work is, don't you?'

Dog was not the sort of animal to question an order. He seemed, however, to be experiencing a conflict of interests. His paws were in the air, as if requesting permission to speak. Trottie understood the gesture immediately. Her silver cigarette case was beside the cash register. She slipped a cork-tipped Kensitas between her lips and asked her visitor for a light. As Mickey patted his pockets, she ducked down to stroke Dog's head and saw, as she expected, a piece of paper rolled inside the small metal cylinder attached to his collar. She pulled it out. The note was in Book's italic handwriting.

Your visitor is here to fix a car. Mrs Wellbeloved's should do the trick. Could you bear to take him for a ride? GB x.

The price of the time to read this message was the sensation of Mickey Hall's eyes raking her as he moved in close to light her cigarette. She hoped that he would not register her confusion: sometimes, thought Trottie, it would be nice to be married to someone less cryptic.

'Permit me,' said Mickey Hall. He had heard it in a film.

Trottie accepted the light, inhaled, and, holding his gaze, sent a stream of smoke sideways from her mouth. As she did so, she crushed the little note in her hand.

'Would you excuse me just a moment?' she said.

Mickey smiled and sank easily into an armchair as if he thought Trottie might return in a fur-trimmed negligee. Instead, she disappeared through the front door and dashed into the butcher's, where she found Mr Wellbeloved alone, dressing a yard of tripe.

'The very man!' she declared.

Mr Wellbeloved beamed. Every visitor to his shop received this smile. He had decided long ago that cheerfulness was best for business. The rosy-cheeked butchers in books of nursery rhymes might have used him as a model.

'Awful about Mr Harkup,' said Trottie.

'Terrible,' agreed Mr Wellbeloved. 'Poor soul.' Customers in search of credit, he noted, often used such opening gambits. If they manoeuvred you into personal territory, it was much easier to ask for a meat-related favour.

'I wonder if you'd be an absolute darling for me, Eric?' said Trottie.

'Anything for a lady.' He grinned. Trottie, he noticed, had no handbag and was not holding her ration book. Perhaps the wallpaper business was not as lucrative as it looked.

'Sheila's little Daimler,' said Trottie. 'I was wondering. Could I just pop up and ask to borrow it?'

Nothing to do with meat, then. 'No need for that,' he said, producing his broadest grin. 'She wouldn't mind. The keys are in it. Help yourself.'

★

Merula Harkup hated being alone in the garage. It was not her lack of technical knowledge that made her anxious – the thought of being mystified by a question about a fan belt, for example – she simply preferred to have her husband where she could see him, and when he was lying beneath a car, at work on its greasy innards, she could be quite sure that his marriage vows were not in danger. She had seen the way he talked to lady customers when he imagined the attention of his wife was elsewhere.

Sitting in the office beside the workshop, listening to the trains thunder over the railway arch above, catching the quick streak of a rat along the brickwork, she remembered that this was not the future her father had intended for her. Nor had she intended it. Before Mickey had grabbed her by the waist at the Hammersmith Palais de Danse, cutting in to relieve a stumbling Army gunner of his duties, Merula had dreamed of a career that matched the aspirational sound of her name. She did not know what this would be, but she imagined a marble-topped reception desk bearing a bowl of lilies, and her finger on the button of an intercom.

The girl she could see standing in the yard outside did not make her feel any better. She wore a college scarf and the basket of her Raleigh cycle was stuffed with books. She was good-looking in a faintly foreign sort of way, which, as she called through the open door of the workshop, made her voice all the more surprising.

'I say,' she said. 'Would you mind awfully taking a look at this?' She pushed the bicycle forwards – the wheeled equivalent of getting a foot in the door. 'Puncture, I think,' she said. 'As bald as Daddy. I told him, these won't get me to Cambridge. This is the Cambridge Road, isn't it?'

Merula nodded. 'Bicycles aren't really my department,' she said. 'I'm just minding the shop.'

'Don't you have a repair kit anywhere?' asked the girl. 'I'd be most awfully grateful.' The flat tyre scrunched on the concrete floor.

Merula was puzzled by her visitor. She talked like those girls in public-school stories who considered each other absolute bricks and thought men were quite too, too beastly. Her plumminess, however, did not seem quite natural. Perhaps, thought Merula, her father had also sent her to an elocution class in Wimbledon that he hoped would be her ticket out of trade. George Harkup would not have been fooled. Not because he had a good ear for received pronunciation, but because he would have recognised her instantly as the niece of the owner of the Istanbul restaurant on Archangel Lane.

'All right,' said Merula, relenting. 'Bring it through. I'll have a look.'

Merula began rooting in a likely cardboard box. The activity prevented her from noticing Nora deliver an unsubtle wink to a bespectacled man peering around the workshop door.

Gabriel Book moved quickly. He darted into the little office and ducked down under the desk. Merula and Nora had the bicycle on its back and were removing the punctured tyre. Nora was chatting noisily about her life among the dreaming spires. Book hoped that Merula was not a reader of Dorothy L. Sayers, lest she guess the origins of Nora's monologue about the Gaudy at Shrewsbury College.

Crouched on the floor of the office, he eased open the cupboard below the desk. It proved a little treasure trove of cigarette cartons and packets of nylons fresh inside cellophane wrappers. Mickey Hall kept a hand in the black market. The drawer above the cupboard was locked. He found the key stowed in an old coffee tin sitting on the desk. The drawer was sticky. He synchronised the unavoidable creaks with the honks of Nora's bicycle pump, and found his diligence rewarded. Inside was a portable chess set. Green Bakelite pieces offered a feeble imitation of jade. One of the white knights was missing: its comrade was an exact match for the piece secreted in George Harkup's collection. The back of the drawer produced a better prize: a pale celadon jade carving of two boys riding on the back of an elephant. Property of the late Mr Harkup.

Merula Harkup banged the tyre with her fist. Hard as a rock. Her husband, she reflected, would be proud of her. Her customer could not contain her enthusiasm: she drawled her thanks with every superlative that Enid Blyton might have mustered. It was at this point Merula noticed the tall man with horn-rimmed spectacles standing in the garage office. He had been making a telephone call. His eyes met hers at the precise moment he replaced the telephone receiver in its cradle.

Bow Street station absorbed Mickey Hall like the sea on a cold morning. It was not where he wished to be. He had enjoyed his drive around the backstreets of Covent Garden. The job was easy to the point of non-existence. The alternator was working perfectly. Each rev of the engine produced a reassuringly loud roar. The accelerator worked smoothly beneath the force of his foot. Trottie's perfume smelled good and she seemed impressed by his command of the Daimler. Certainly, her eyes flashed every time he made the speedometer needle jerk strongly to the right. It was hard to be completely sure without his spectacles, but experience had taught him that ladies preferred him without a glass barrier. Such are the everyday problems of a man who is both myopic and priapic.

There were only two moments of difficulty. The first came when Trottie asked about the ownership of the garage, and he almost mentioned Merula. The second came when, delivering her outside the wallpaper shop with a screech of brakes, he had reached his arm over her head and asked her if she was busy on Sunday.

'I find I'm washing my hair that evening,' she said. 'And I think perhaps your dance card may soon be a little full. Other parties are demanding your attention.'

One was tapping on the driver's window; smartly dressed in blue serge, buttons polished, asking him to get out of the car. Sergeant Morris was not Mickey Hall's usual type, but he found himself quite unable to resist. Handcuffs proved unnecessary. Mickey allowed himself to be walked over the road to Bow Street, where the desk sergeant filled out his forms so swiftly that other men waiting to help the police with their enquiries grumbled as if he had jumped the queue at the barber's.

The boarded windows of the interview room suggested the possibility of rough treatment. Mickey had known such things, in the quieter corners of police stations. His hosts at Bow Street gave quite the opposite impression. The plain-clothes detective with the crinkly grey hair and crinkly grey suit sat and smiled indulgently. His taller friend laid out a series of objects on the table – a fountain pen, a notebook, a packet of Murray Mints and, finally, a brass bell of the sort often seen on the reception desk of a hotel.

Book pushed back his spectacles and settled in the chair beside Bliss.

'We thought, Mr Hall,' said the inspector, 'that it was high time we had a little chat.'

Mickey leaned forward. 'Listen,' he said. 'I know my rights—'

Book slapped his hand down on the bell.

Ding!

The bright little chime surprised Mickey into silence.

'Straight out of the blocks!' said Bliss, shaking his head sorrowfully.

'Disappointing,' tutted Book. 'Dear me, Mr Hall. One point deducted already.'

'Point?' frowned Mickey. 'What are you talking about? Listen, you can't stick anything on me.'

Book hit the bell again.

Ding!

'Textbook!' he hooted. 'Banal! Quotidian!'

Mickey felt a twinge of panic. If these men were trying to confuse him, they were succeeding.

'The inspector and I have been through this routine a hundred times,' explained Book, as though he expected Mickey to feel their pain. 'And you wouldn't believe how tedious it is having to listen to the same old stock responses from gnarly old lags. Like something from the music hall.'

'*Hold your hand out, you naughty boy,*' sang Bliss, in a little treble voice, and might have reached the verse had this not produced a sharp look from Book.

'So,' said Book, the humour fading from his voice. 'Here's the question you would ask were it not for your fear of me dinging you: "Why would I want to kill poor Mr Harkup?"'

Mickey thought this fair. 'Absolutely. Why would I? I wouldn't hurt a fly!'

Ding!

'I never did it!'

Ding!

'But you admit you went to the flat?' demanded Book. This was now a proper interrogation, and, absurdly, each sweet chime of the bell seemed to Mickey as bad as a cuff round the head.

'I just wanted to talk things over,' said Mickey. 'Reason with him. Now me and Merula have the little one on the way.'

'Or,' suggested Bliss, 'did you go with the express intention of filching the jade elephant and replacing it?'

Mickey banged his fist on the table. 'That's a dirty lie!'

Ding!

'Bravo!' exclaimed Bliss. His pleasure seemed to be genuine.

'Haven't heard that one in a while,' cooed Book, nodding like a Wagnerian during a big aria at Bayreuth.

'Should have put "copper" at the end, though,' added Bliss. '"That's a dirty lie, copper." Much more effective.'

'But you ain't a copper, is you?' said Mickey, staring at Book. The seriousness of the question cut through. The parlour game appeared to be over.

'Ah,' conceded Book. 'Fair point. No, I ain't. Isn't. *Am not*. But I do have a special letter from Churchill.' He tapped his top pocket.

Mickey shrugged. 'So what? Anyway, you can't prove I did that.'

'No,' said Book, 'but the elephant was in your drawers, and the elephant was not yours. So it's all very probable, I think you'll agree. What happened, then?'

'I hung around outside the shop,' said Mickey. 'I knew he'd be in. He never really went anywhere. Except on Mondays and Thursdays to play dominoes at the Bull. I waited till well after seven but there was no sign of him.'

'And so you went to the flat?' said Book.

'No sign of him. But first the char come out.'

'The char?' asked Book. 'Mrs Dredge, you mean?'

'She come out of the chemist's looking pretty shifty,' said Mickey. 'Had summat in her coat. Trying her best to keep it hidden.'

Bliss and Book exchanged looks. This was new.

'When was this?' asked Bliss.

'About six o'clock,' said Mickey. 'Then someone else come. I couldn't see him clearly. My eyes ain't so good.'

'But it was a him?' asked Book.

'I think I know the difference, mister.'

'Your reputation precedes you,' said Book.

'He was all bundled up,' said Mickey. 'Hat, scarf, overcoat. After he was gone, I went inside. The door was shut but I know my way around a lock. So in I went. And that's when I found him. Merula's dad, that is. Stone dead. Foam round his mouth and everything.'

'So, naturally you thought you should call the police,' said Bliss, drily.

'That wouldn't be very wise, would it?' snapped Mickey. 'I was going to leg it but then I remembered the ornaments. The jade figures. He'd told me about them months ago. How they was precious.' His bravado was draining away. 'Business ain't been too good lately. And I got a few personal expenses that it's best the missus don't know about. So I thought, well, no one's gonna notice one of them missing. So I swapped one. I had me little chess set with me, you see. Then I took off. Straight home. That's all.'

Mickey let his eyes fall to the table. When he looked up, he saw that both his interrogators were regarding him with the same glassy expression.

'I swear,' he protested. 'I never killed Harkup. I never touched him. He was dead when I got there.'

Bliss got to his feet. Mickey was a tall man. Bliss took the opportunity to loom over him. 'All right, son,' he said, his voice like two bricks being dragged together. 'Maybe you're telling the truth, maybe you're not. But let me assure you, if you are lying, if you think you can take Scotland Yard for a ride, I'll come down on you so hard you won't be able to see straight till Christmas. I'll throw the bloody book at you!'

Ding!

The loudest ding, in fact, of the whole interview. Book's finger was on the bell, and if he had discovered Bliss in bed with his wife, he could not have looked more shocked. His expression had barely changed by the time the whey-faced constable had taken Mickey to the cells.

'Do you believe him?' asked Bliss, sheepishly.

'Bent as a dog's hind leg,' said Book.

The door rattled open. Sergeant Morris had a file of papers in his hand and an expression of extreme self-satisfaction on his face.

'Some news for you, sir,' he said. 'We just got the chemist's will through, sir. The daughter doesn't get a bean.'

'Then who does?' asked Bliss.

'The char,' said Morris, narrowing his eyes as though he had just passed on a dead cert for Epsom.

'Mrs Dredge!' exclaimed Book.

'All roads lead to Archangel Lane,' said Bliss.

'Come back with me then,' said Book. 'Do you have time to queue? I'm planning a casserole.'

Archangel Lane was good in a crisis. It enjoyed them. It treated everything from an eight-stick incendiary to a drunken marital fistfight outside the Bull as the subject for a sermon. Like the broadcasts of the Home Service, other people's sins could inform, educate and entertain. There was a divide, however, between audience and players. Half the population of the lane was fixed; the rest changed with the frequency of the chorus of *Chu Chin Chow*: the errors of the latter enriched the conversations of the former. The death of Mr Harkup had disturbed this ecology, however: the principals of a show are not expected to kill themselves.

The body had been taken away, but the presence of Mr Harkup persisted. Mrs Acres polished a card table in which he had once expressed polite interest. Mr Toovey banged nails into the replacement heel of one of his brogues (the chemist had brought them in for repair the previous week: perhaps, thought Mr Toovey, he could make use of them at the funeral, if the family thought them proper for the afterlife). Only the butcher's shop seemed free of him. Enid sat reading *Black Lamb and Grey Falcon* and dreamed of the sun sparkling on the Adriatic, until her employer asked her to wrap up a passable cut of pork shoulder. The recipient, Mrs Trickett, whose boarding house had lost a chimney to the V2 that had hit Inkerman Street, watched the girl fumble the work, rolled her eyes and asked Mr Wellbeloved to finish the job.

A long line of customers waited outside the shop. Book and Bliss were closer to the back of the queue than they might have wished.

'Our cat brought home a pigeon the other night,' said Bliss. 'Mrs Bliss was sorely tempted.'

Book wrinkled his nose. 'We had plenty of pigeons in the war,' he said. 'Nothing wrong with a bit of pigeon.'

'Yes,' said Bliss, 'but now it's all over, don't we want to aim a bit higher?'

Book waved an expansive arm. 'We are all of us in the gutter, but some of us are looking at the starlings.' He had the sudden urge to bang a silver-topped cane on the cobbles. The man behind him sighed audibly.

Up ahead, Mrs Spain, thought by some to be a lady of flexible morals, emerged carrying a generous parcel of mince. A birdlike man in a grey muffler was next in line. The queue shuffled forward.

'Oh, bugger this,' rasped Bliss. He pulled out his warrant card and, waving it in the air, barged his way to the front door of the shop.

'Wait your bloody turn like the rest of us!' barked a ruddy-faced lady. Book was surprised by her language: he had seen her on Sundays, handing out leaflets from the Society for Promoting Christian Knowledge.

'Sorry, madam!' insisted Bliss. 'Urgent police business.' He piloted Book through the shop door, shooed the birdlike man out into the street and flipped the sign in the window from open to closed. The birdlike man pressed his nose against the window. Bliss waved him away.

Mr Wellbeloved did not object to the invasion. He greeted Book and Bliss like Christmas visitors. Even Enid mustered a smile.

'Afternoon, sir!' beamed Wellbeloved. 'I kept your stewing steak to one side.'

'You are a prince amongst men!' said Book.

Wellbeloved tapped his nose theatrically. The gesture drew Book's eye to a dry patch of pale residue at the corner of the butcher's mouth.

'You've got something,' said Book. 'Just there.'

Wellbeloved put a finger to his lip. 'Powdered egg,' he said. 'Bit of a rushed breakfast.' Before he could find his handkerchief, Enid had reached in with hers, removing the offending material.

'How's Sheila?' asked Book.

'Well, sir, well,' said Wellbeloved. 'She's driven up to Sheffield.'

'Her family are Sheffield people, yes?' said Book.

'They are, sir,' beamed Mr Wellbeloved. A cloud came over his face. 'Terrible about George Harkup,' he said. He chewed at an uncharitable thought and let it out. 'Mind you, old Baseheart won't shed any tears, will he?'

'Oh?' said Bliss.

'They never got on, sir,' said Wellbeloved. 'Many a run-in during the Blitz. Harkup was a stickler for the rules. Always on at Mr Baseheart for being too slack. Chinks in the blackout curtains, that sort of thing.'

He was proffering a package of greaseproof paper, wrapped as neatly as an anniversary gift.

'Bless you, Eric,' said Book, handing over his coupon. 'Anything for Dog?'

Mr Wellbeloved produced a large and gnawable bone. 'I spoil you!' He grinned.

'You do!' agreed Book.

Inspector Bliss flipped the sign, pushed open the door and waved his warrant card in the direction of the queue. If this was intended as an apology, it was not accepted. Book smiled weakly at the birdlike man: buyers of studies in Greek rhetoric were as rare as hen's teeth, and best not offended.

'So,' said Book, 'where are we with the murders?' He and Bliss were moving down the street, ignoring the disapproval of the queue.

Bliss flinched. 'Murders? Plural?'

'Sorry, murder.'

They had reached Harkup's shop. The place might have been locked and shuttered for half a century.

'You haven't taken anything away, have you?' asked Book. 'From the chemist?'

'Only the chemist,' said Bliss.

'What about his ledgers?'

'No,' said Bliss.

'Don't suppose you have the key on you, do you?'

The inspector sighed inwardly. 'Ten minutes,' he said.

The lock was stiff. The door rattled and juddered as Bliss pushed it open. Book handed over the bone and parcel of meat to his friend and began examining the frame of the front door. 'No sign of forced entry,' he said.

'Nor round the back,' said Bliss. 'Harkup let his killer in. He must have known them.'

'Perhaps,' said Book. He abandoned the door and opened the account book on the glass-topped counter. His fingers danced over the pages.

'He let them in,' said Bliss, 'they whacked him with a blunt instrument, then poured Prussic acid down his throat and he croaked.'

'Probably quite literally,' said Book.

Bliss juggled Book's shopping as he extracted his notebook from his pocket. 'Dr Calder thinks Harkup died between six and ten. And an awful lot could have happened in those four hours.' He turned a page with one hand. 'Mrs Dredge says she saw the chemist at approximately six o'clock.'

'We only have her word for that,' mused Book. 'But Mickey Hall did say he saw her leaving around that time. With something in her coat that she wanted to keep hidden.'

'She's about to inherit the whole collection,' said Bliss. 'A strong motive for killing him. But not for robbing him.' He put the notebook away. 'And why take just one piece? Why not just grab the lot?'

'Because then it would look like a burglary,' said Book, 'and whoever did this wanted to make it look like a suicide.'

Book tapped at the page of the ledger, then searched the cabinets for the corresponding stock. 'He's down on morphine. Just as Merula said.'

Bliss returned the parcel and the bone to their owner. Book accepted them like a crown and sceptre.

'Mrs Dredge has motive and opportunity,' said Bliss, tackling the door again. 'Mickey Hall has motive and opportunity. And Merula?'

'Mickey says the bundled-up stranger was a man.'

'Well, he would, wouldn't he,' said Bliss, 'if they were in it together. Maybe they knew Harkup was going to disinherit them.'

They had crossed the street and were at the threshold of Number 158, under the gaze of the stuffed fox and the bust of Edgar Allan Poe.

At first, Book noticed nothing amiss in the shop. The kettle droned sweetly from the kitchen. Dog was in his basket and, having already detected the bone, looked upwards imploringly. Jack was behind the counter with an expression of self-satisfaction that barely changed even once he had registered the presence of the inspector.

Then he noticed. It was like seeing the arms restored to the Venus de Milo; the Leaning Tower of Pisa straightened; the universe split from side to side.

'What have you done?' he asked, his throat a dried-up lake of dread.

'Tidied up,' breezed Jack. 'You said you wanted things cataloguing so I thought I'd make a start.'

'That shelf,' said Book, forcing out each word. 'Is that in . . . *alphabetical order?*' He had read about a coven of French Satanists who stole consecrated communion wafers and fed them to the cats of Paris. Now, however, he understood the true meaning of sacrilege.

'You've only done this wall?'

'Yeah, sorry,' said Jack, sounding like someone who'd timed the meat and the vegetables for the arrival of his guests, and found them complaining about the width of his julienning. 'It takes time to do it properly.'

'Thank God,' gasped Book. 'Now put them all back.'

'Put them all back?'

'Catalogue it, I said, not desecrate it,' he snapped. 'I told you. I have a system.'

Bliss flashed a pained look at Book and said his name in gentle admonition. He also gave Jack a discreet sympathetic smile that told him to back down and be generous.

Book took the cue. 'Least said soonest mended, eh?' he murmured. He moved towards the counter and gave Jack a gentle tap on the shoulder. Neither Bliss nor Jack could see that his eyes were still fixed on the alphabetised shelves as if they were a Fascist lightning flash daubed on the wall.

Jack wanted to please his employer and had wounded him. Perhaps, he thought, the old coin might repair the damage? He fished it from his pocket and offered it on the palm of his hand.

'Ah. You've found something?' said Book. There was, thought Jack, something childlike about the speed of this switch of attention.

'It's been cleaned,' he said. 'Recently. That residue you can see? Remains of silver polish.'

'Meaning?' asked Book.

'Meaning,' said Jack, 'it got into the ground recently.'

Bliss made a scoffing sound. 'But it's from 1665. The year of the Plague.'

'Very specifically the year of the Plague,' said Jack. 'Not a year or two before.'

'Quite too horribly convenient,' said Book, plucking the coin from Jack's hand. 'Where better to hide a tree than in a forest? Eleven skeletons in a plague pit from the seventeenth century. Then a twelfth from 1946.'

'Bloody hell!' breathed Bliss. 'Murders. Plural.'

'Yes,' said Book.

'Linked?' asked Bliss.

'Oh, I should think so,' said Book, his eyes glittering. 'Top of the class, Jack! Really, I should give you the afternoon off. In fact I will. Go right now. Go to the Bull, where the late Mr Harkup so loved to play dominoes. Take Nora. She's good at this sort of thing. There's still an hour before afternoon closing. You could learn a lot.'

'This sounds like work,' said Jack.

'Don't worry,' said Book. 'I'm sure the Inland Revenue won't see it that way.'

The Bull was a traditional London pub. Conversations about religion were not permitted. Conversations about politics were not permitted, though a discourteous reference to Sir Stafford Cripps was considered within the limits of propriety. Spouses who wished to give each other a black eye were kindly requested to delay the first punch until they had vacated licensed premises. Questions about the beer-to-water ratio, or the substances beneath the pie crusts under the hot lamp, were not encouraged by the management. Nor was swearing, unless in reference to Mussolini, Hitler or Henry Hall, who had once popped in on his way to the Savoy Hill studios and claimed, quite falsely, to have discovered a fly in his gin. The incident was a landmark in the life of the landlord, Mr Gash, and served only to confirm his suspicions about the leader of the BBC Dance Orchestra. A euphonium player who lived above the junk shop told him that Mr Hall had got the job because he was the only gentile who'd applied, and Mr Gash was inclined to believe it.

On the question of the age of his drinkers, Eddie Gash was more agnostic than the law. A pub was no place for anyone who was still reading the *Dandy* (Mr Blyth, who had been gassed in the trenches and needed all the small pleasures he could get, was the only exception to the rule). The girl in the public bar, however, looked like a five-pound fine in a pinafore dress. Mr Gash had never visited the Istanbul restaurant – he considered parsley an unnecessary imposition on a meat – but he had seen her running in and out of the place with a cloth on her shoulder, and sometimes cursing at old Yusuf in a language Mr Gash did not understand. She was not, as far as he knew, old enough to do more than dishes.

'We don't allow kids in here,' he said.

'I'm not a kid,' said Nora, drawing herself up to her full height, which did not entirely help her argument. 'I'll buy a drink if that's what you're worried about.'

'That would make it worse,' said Mr Gash.

'She'll have a lemonade,' said the man beside her. Mr Gash had never set eyes on Jack before, but the lad was clearly of an age to order a glass of mild. They were both, he thought, a little peculiar. As he turned his back to take the bottles from the shelf behind the bar, he could see them muttering to each other about who was going to pay.

'Get Mr Book to advance you some of your wages,' hissed the girl. 'I'm not subbing you again.' She snapped a couple of coins down on the counter.

'Keep the change,' said Jack. Nora scowled. Mr Gash looked doubtfully at the little stack of coppers.

Nora scanned the paraphernalia behind the bar, looking for a prompt to draw Mr Gash towards the subject of domino nights at the Bull. She noted a shell souvenir from Saltburn; a bust of Queen Victoria; a tiny painted portrait of a greyhound in a scarlet vest. This, thought Nora, was the most likely key to his confidence. Soon his qualms about her age vanished beneath a series of well-informed questions about the crime families she suspected were responsible for doping and race-fixing at Catford dog track. From here it was easy to move to the morality of gambling, and then, with admirable speed, to the games and pastimes pursued at the Bull.

'Monday and Thursday nights,' said Mr Gash. 'Just for matchsticks, mind. They sit over there. Mr Wellbeloved the butcher. Mr Baseheart the ARP warden. Mrs Acres from the junk shop. Mr Quillian the tailor. Mr Toovey the cobbler.'

'It's like happy families,' said Nora.

'And Mr Harkup, God rest his soul,' sighed Mr Gash. He looked sharply at Jack. 'You with the coppers, then?'

'In a manner of speaking,' said Jack. The landlord did not object to the unhelpful vagueness of the answer. On the contrary, he seemed to enjoy it.

'I was in the force myself, back in the day. Saw a few suicides then. Old Harkup didn't seem the type to do himself in. But then, do they ever?'

'I know!' enthused Nora. 'We had a teacher. Life and soul. Drowned herself in a weir over a man. And not a pretty one, neither.'

Jack corrected the course of the conversation. 'How was Mr Harkup when you last saw him?'

'Well, that's the thing, you see,' said the landlord, running a cloth idly over the woodwork. 'I'd seen Mr Harkup just the day before. Marched in here in the middle of the day. He was a man of very regular habits. So it was a bit queer. Seemed to have a lot on his mind. Said he was sitting on a secret. Obviously eating him up a bit.'

'Did you get it out of him? This secret?' asked Nora.

'Not at first. More than my life's worth, he said. His very words. And the next day . . .'

'Dead,' said Nora, slapping the bar with her hand.

'So did he tell you the secret?' asked Jack.

'Yes, son. Eventually. He did.' Mr Gash leaned in. 'It was hardly the crime of the century. But Mr Harkup was a very upright citizen. So particular. He loved rules and regulations. Which was why he was so cut up when he thought one of his pals was cheating at spotties.'

Nora was blank. 'Spotties?'

'Dominoes!' said Eddie Gash.

★

The casserole was good that night. Jack watched Book chop celery, pour stock slowly into flour, then add the meat to the gathering gravy. He was sorry when a customer entered the shop to ask some questions about Shell Guides to the Home Counties; sorrier still that he had to spend time ordering them from the publisher. The smell of the stew bubbling inside the stove drifted from the kitchen. The two hours it took to cook were like a holiday.

Trottie appeared when the meal was ready. She arrived in her street clothes, having returned from an afternoon of complex errands. She did not describe them in any detail, but it was clear that they had taken her from the Portobello Road to Clerkenwell to the streets around the British Museum. A bottle of some unknown honey-coloured liqueur was discovered behind a row of Danish textbooks. Book poured three glasses and said that his first taste of alcohol had been on the scarlet fever ward: Jimmy Turley, a dreary, long-faced boy from Sussex, had made him drink surgical spirit for a bet. Trottie also knew Jimmy Turley. She recalled him being sick into a plant pot and hiding it from matron. Matron, it seemed, was from the same order of beings that contained pterodactyls, the Big Bad Wolf, and ancient sea squids that are glimpsed through the porthole of a submarine. Jack sank back in an armchair, sipped his drink and considered that he had not spent an evening so warm and convivial since before he was sentenced. Then, on reflection, he saw that he was wrong: he had never spent an evening so warm and convivial.

The clock struck ten. Trottie switched on the wireless. Dog gave a satisfied sigh. 'He loves Dame Myra Hess,' said

Book, forgetting that prison interrupts a person's access to piano recitals on the Home Service. 'I think she goes at it too hard. But you can always hear her at the back.' He got to his feet and disappeared into the shop. The dishes had been delegated. Jack and Trottie cleared the table and got to work at the sink.

'That was smashing,' said Jack. He submerged his hands in the soapy water. He was a little tipsy.

'Better than what you're used to?' asked Trottie.

'Oh yes,' said Jack. He passed her a plate. 'So what was that about scarlet fever?'

'That's what brought us together,' said Trottie. 'Me and Book. We met on the ward. We were both about twelve, I suppose.'

'And you fell for each other right from the off?'

Trottie laughed lightly. 'It wasn't quite like that, no.' She put the dry plates back on the dresser. 'Did you have a profitable day?'

'Not sure. I put my foot right in it. Tried tidying up Mr Book's bookshelves.'

Trottie winced.

'Don't think I did too much damage,' said Jack. 'Then I was out and about with Nora. Detecting!'

'It's certainly put some colour in your cheeks.'

The shop bell clattered. Book had left the shop. Taking Dog for a last walk of the day, Jack assumed. 'So, go on, then,' he said, scrubbing away at the casserole dish. 'You didn't fall for each other straight away? When did you know?'

Trottie said nothing. Jack stopped and looked up.

'You'll forgive me, my dear,' she said, 'but we'll have to know each other rather better before such confidences are exchanged.' Jack dissolved into apologies, but Trottie waved them away. 'Really, Jack,' she said, 'don't worry. I do hope we'll become fast friends. But it's complicated, that's all.'

She did not elaborate. 'Love is where it falls. Isn't that what they say?'

Gabriel Book knew the secret geography of London. It had been mapped by men who had died long before he was born. It had its own landmarks. Certain stretches of Hyde Park, close to the barracks, where cigarettes made red dots in the darkness. Certain pubs in Fitzrovia, where chaps sat in a row at the bar, and called each other by names unknown to their wives and sisters. Certain corners of the London Library. Who had decided these things? Who had decreed that the upper circle of the Criterion Theatre, in the hour before a matinee, should be a space of urgent and serious nods and glances? Or a particular bench on the Embankment? Or the upstairs dining room at Kettner's, where the lampshades were such a forgiving shade of apricot? Book did not know. He merely followed his desires along its ley lines and fox tracks, until he found what he wanted.

There it was, in a narrow alley between the National Gallery and Leicester Square. A man, detectable by the glow of his cigarette, hovering by a wall broken by bombs and bursts of London Pride. The lamp above was not bright: better that way. Book walked towards him, as if heading towards the square. One never knew for sure. B Division also had it on their map. One had to ask a question, an innocuous question; one that would sound plain and innocent if repeated in court. One did not wish for court, where an acquittal was only marginally less ruinous than a conviction. Not everyone was a Gielgud. Some had ordinary professions; dependants who might be killed by shame.

'Got a light?' asked the man.

Educated, thought Book, but not public school. A faint hint of the Midlands, perhaps? The light showed a fair moustache, above a mouth of the kind that was easy to imagine kissing.

'I don't smoke,' said Book. It was not true, but it did not matter. These were just words. Their tone and tenor was important, but not their sense. They might have been reciting the alphabet or reading the street signs aloud.

'Are you sure?' asked the man with the fair moustache. 'I have rooms.'

He seemed slightly nervous, as if he were new to this kind of conversation in this kind of place. But two streets away, in a bedsitter on the third floor back, Book discovered that he was no greenhorn, no faintheart, nor one of those husbands who, at the critical moment, would weep and speak of their children in Walthamstow. If anything, thought Book, as he watched him move in the low orange glow of the electric fire, the man with the fair moustache knew the geography better than he.

CHAPTER FIVE

Inspector Bliss and Gabriel Book were rarely the bearers of good news. It was more usual for them to be relaying intelligence of a stabbing, a drowning, an unexpected demise resulting from sudden contact with a poisoned hatpin. Mrs Ada Dredge was, in this sense, a fortunate woman.

Her home did not speak of other instances of luck. It was a battlefield on which she had been fighting a quiet war with circumstance. The rug had been patched. Cheap little engravings were framed on the wall with no care for symmetry: they hid the holes in the plasterwork. The tea service was clean and unchipped, but one mismatched cup and saucer showed that the rest was lost or broken. Dust was not in evidence. Mrs Dredge cleaned more diligently for herself than she had done for Mr Harkup. Perhaps, when in the flat above the chemist, her mind had been elsewhere.

It was the inspector's turn to eat the cake; also to raise difficult subjects. He set his cup down on the kitchen table and cleared his moustache of crumbs.

'And were things more than formal between you and your employer?' he asked.

'I resent that question, Inspector!' huffed Mrs Dredge.

Her pale cheeks were turning pink. 'I won't deny that there was a degree of affection between George – between Mr Harkup – and myself. If you've been doing for someone all those years, how could there not be?'

'Well, that's my point, Mrs Dredge,' said Bliss. 'Is that all you were doing for him?' Mrs Dredge conveyed her affront.

Book was hovering in the door between the tiny kitchen and the parlour. He had long ago perfected the art of keeping a discreet distance from a police interviewee, while raking their domestic environment for evidence. Mrs Dredge's star exhibits were ranged on the sideboard: a Box Brownie snapshot of George Harkup, smiling sweetly on a picnic rug during some trip into the countryside. A studio portrait of a clean young airman, smiling before the storm. Two more objects struck Book as significant: beside the fire was lodged a pair of brown leather boots, which were certainly too big for Mrs Dredge.

He poked his head around the kitchen door.

'Dear lady,' he ventured. 'What my friend is trying to suggest—'

'I know full well what he's trying to suggest!'

'What he's trying to elucidate, then, is whether this affection took any more tangible form.'

'What's it got to do with you?'

'Harkup left the lot to you, love,' said Bliss. 'The shop, the goodwill, his whole estate. All yours.'

Mrs Dredge was astonished. She clapped her hand to her mouth with the same expression she would have made if *In Town Tonight* had stopped the traffic and asked her to tell Home Service listeners about the life and vicissitudes of a

London charlady. She shook her head. She moved her jaw, soundlessly.

'Well, I never saw that coming. Everything?'

'Everything,' said Bliss.

Mrs Dredge gave an involuntary titter.

'Is your son at home, Mrs Dredge?' asked Book. He was looking at the photograph of the clean young airman.

Mrs Dredge was brought back to earth by the question. 'He's upstairs in bed.'

'A late riser?' asked Bliss.

The remark annoyed Mrs Dredge. 'A war hero,' she snapped. 'His Wellington came down over Holland in '44.' Bliss expressed his regret but Mrs Dredge sniffed it away. 'Nothing to be sorry for, Inspector. He survived, didn't he?'

Now the good news had been delivered, it was time for Bliss to produce the concomitant bad stuff. 'We don't think Harkup took his own life, Mrs Dredge. We think he was murdered. Now we've seen his will, can you understand why that leaves us in a rather difficult position?'

Her eyes widened. 'You never think I topped him?'

'The fact remains,' said Bliss, 'you're now in a rather sticky position. The new will was properly signed and witnessed.'

'But I don't know anything about that!' she said.

'But you could have done,' pushed Bliss. 'You could have seen a draft when you were cleaning and then decided to speed things up a bit.'

'By knocking off Mr H?'

'Yes,' said Bliss.

'This is barmy,' she spluttered. 'It's her you should be

talking to. Merula. And him. That Mickey Hall. The mechanic. Have you nabbed him?'

'He is assisting us with our enquiries,' Bliss conceded. 'In fact, Mr Hall has been most helpful. He told us he saw you leaving the chemist's shop on the night of the murder. He said you were carrying something. And trying your very best to conceal it.'

'I told you,' she said. 'Bandages for Alf. I wasn't trying to hide them.'

'Your son lost a leg, didn't he?' said Book. This was not a line of attack. His tone was warm and quiet. He saw Mrs Dredge's lip tremble. She nodded. He was moving into undefended territory.

'How do you know?' she asked.

Book lifted one of the brown boots from beside the parlour fireplace and turned it over in his hands. 'One is worn and creased,' he said. 'But this one is completely smooth. His prosthesis must need constant attention.' He returned the boot to its battered brother. 'Painful, I imagine. Very, very painful.'

'Yes,' said Mrs Dredge.

'Painful enough for morphine?' asked Book.

'More than enough.' She turned her cup on its saucer. 'You'd think it would stop, wouldn't you? When it was all healed. But it's like he's got hot coals in him that won't be cooled.'

'Why couldn't you just ask Mr Harkup to help?' asked Book.

Mrs Dredge sighed deeply. 'I couldn't. Alf needs more than he's ever given by the doctor. So I nicked some extra.

Never thought Mr Harkup would notice. But he did. And he assumed Mickey Hall must've done it. So I let him. I couldn't tell him it was me. He was a stickler, you see. For form. For the rules. How could I tell him I'd had away with drugs from his own shop? You've no idea what it's like.'

'So you dropped in on the pretext of getting bandages,' said Book, 'and instead stole more morphine?'

Mrs Dredge nodded silently.

'But Mr Harkup was alive when you left?' asked Bliss.

Mrs Dredge erupted. She put her hand across her heart. 'I swear on my son's life!' Book thought she was about to weep again, but then realised that the sound he could hear, the deep rolling start of a sob, was coming from the room above. It stopped, then came again. A low, ragged moan. The sound of a boy in pain, calling for his mother.

Mrs Dredge got to her feet. Her chair scraped on the lino. She checked her eyes for tears. 'Please excuse me, gentlemen,' she said.

Bliss also rose. They would let themselves out. Mrs Dredge moved to the curtained door that led from the parlour up to the bedrooms.

'So,' she said. 'When do I get it?'

'Beg pardon?' asked Bliss.

'The money,' said Mrs Dredge. Her eyes were dry.

Bliss shrugged. Mrs Dredge vanished upstairs. They heard the mumble of voices, and the sound of a man weeping out his pain.

'Not her, then?' asked Bliss, as they closed the front door.

'No,' reflected Book. 'Life has hardened Mrs Dredge, but it hasn't made her a killer.'

'Then who did it?'

'Did them,' corrected Book. 'Two murders. But only one murderer, I think.' He put a hand on Bliss's shoulder. 'You're going to need help, Inspector.'

Eric Wellbeloved had seen enough blood for one day. The sawdust took most of it up. A mop and a bucket of water thrown across the tiles would do the rest. The specials were rubbed from the window and his hand was on the sign when he saw Mrs Acres looking at him, imploringly, through the glass. Most shopkeepers would have told her to come back tomorrow, but Mr Wellbeloved had a reputation for good humour and generosity that he wished to keep. He had once overheard Mrs Acres tell Mrs Trickett that his cheerfulness had kept her going through the Blitz; that he was the life and soul of the air-raid shelter. Mr Wellbeloved had cherished the warm feeling this gave him, and held it within himself, like an ember. Every now and then, he did something to keep it glowing.

He pushed open the door. 'You all right, Mrs Acres?'

'Lost my ration book, didn't I?' she said. 'Left it in the library. Someone handed it in. People are kind, really, aren't they? Despite what you read in the papers. I don't suppose . . . ?'

Mrs Acres did not need to finish the question.

'Will sausages do you?' asked Mr Wellbeloved. He pulled four fat ones from the cabinet and wrapped them up in paper. 'Go on,' he said. 'I'm all cashed up, and besides, it's been a shocking couple of days, ain't it? You go home and get those in the frying pan with a few onions.'

Mr Wellbeloved thought Mrs Acres might cry. He would not have minded seeing her tears. She nodded gratefully, pushed the package deep into her bag and backed out of the shop, almost colliding with a man who was standing on the step.

Gabriel Book had his hat in his hand. He wore a serious smile, the kind that people make when they are about to offer their condolences.

'Oh, I'm sorry, Mr Book,' said Mr Wellbeloved, 'I was just closing.'

'That's all right, Eric,' said Book softly. 'I'm all out of coupons so I can't ask you for anything more this week. But I would like to ask you a question.'

'Nothing wrong with that steak, I hope?'

'No, it was excellent. I wanted to ask you something about Sheila. How is she?'

Mr Wellbeloved gathered up his knives and plunged them into the hot-water sink. 'You asked me that before, Mr Book,' he said. 'She's in Sheffield with her sister.'

'And what day did she drive up there?'

Mr Wellbeloved mustered his last smile of the working day. 'Tuesday,' he said.

'When Trottie borrowed her car on a Thursday?'

The days of the week were shuffling in his head like the wooden bricks he'd had as a child. He was trying to arrange them in an order that would satisfy Mr Book; one that would make an even line connecting Archangel Lane with Sheila's sister's place in Sheffield. He thought of that second-hand Daimler parked outside that little house near the colliery, as it had been during Christmas 1938; how the neighbours had stopped to admire it; the pride he had taken in telling them it belonged to Sheila, and the message that conveyed about their prosperous life in London. Sheila had been different in those days. There'd always been a hand on his shoulder; a kiss at bedtime. Later, of course, she was as cold as canned meat.

Mr Wellbeloved looked past Book. He could see, caught in the light of the shop, a knot of uniformed constables out on the cobbles. His stock of smiles was now exhausted. Mr Wellbeloved's mouth fell. His shoulders followed. However, as the first constable entered the shop and moved towards him, his arms jerked suddenly upwards. The officer reeled back, having been cracked beneath the chin with the hinged section of the counter. Book also gave way: the butcher, a cleaver in his fist, barged past him and out into the lane.

But really, what could Mr Wellbeloved do? Six police officers were waiting for him. Book's inspector friend was there. The hard-faced sergeant stood beside him, holding an object that he realised was a pair of handcuffs. A black police car blocked the entrance to the lane. Wellbeloved tried to envisage a version of the next two minutes in which he swung the cleaver in the air, made it through the phalanx of officers, leapt over the car and reached the lights of the Strand. His imagination, however, would take him no further. Would he drop the blade down a drain? Jump on a bus? Attempt to mingle with the crowd? If he couldn't see it in his mind, what chance was there of making it a reality?

Book had emerged from the shop. He was standing on the step, shaking his head. He was not smiling.

Mr Wellbeloved heard a harsh sound. It was loud and

metallic and nearby. It took him a moment to realise it was his cleaver slipping from his fingers and hitting the cobbles of Archangel Lane.

Eric Wellbeloved had never been inside a police station before. His record was as clean as one of the marble slabs in his shop. The business of arrest and questioning baffled him. The forms. The fingerprints. Saying his full name aloud for the first time since school. Though the interview room was frowsty and undusted – butchers are not tolerant of dirt – he found the arrangement less intimidating than he had expected. Book was a familiar presence. Bliss gave him a packet of cigarettes. Mr Wellbeloved lit one clumsily and took a drag. His first words in the room were a confession.

'I didn't mean to do her in,' he said.

It felt good to talk about Sheila, even if it was to Inspector Bliss. He had expected his questions to be simple brutalities of the *where were you on the night of the fourteenth* variety. Instead, Bliss asked about the history of his marriage. Wellbeloved suspected this was a technique. He was being softened up. He found, however, that he did not care, and gave a long account of his courtship of Sheila. He recalled how grateful she had been when he'd first taken a serious interest in her. He had expected some opposition from her family, but found her mother-in-law almost too welcoming. ('It's a good trade,' she had said. 'People will always want meat.') The engagement was short, but long enough to learn of Sheila's near miss at marriage with a man named Walter, whose name made the event an easy subject for mockery. This spoiled their big day in only one respect: Eric's brother was sacked as best man after making a crack about soiled goods.

'We rowed a lot, though, me and Sheila,' he said. 'We started on the honeymoon. Small things. But they got bigger.' Though the flat on Archangel Lane was larger than her family home in Handsworth, Sheila did not like living above the shop. Worse, she seemed embarrassed and disgusted by his trade and the way her husband carried it with him; his shopkeeper's professional smile, the smell of chops and carcasses that carbolic could not quite eradicate; the smell of carbolic itself.

'Enid didn't mind, though. She wasn't a snob. She loved the smell of a ham roasting in the oven.' He could remember the moment she'd told him so, and how sad it had made him feel: Sheila had never said such things, even at the beginning. The memory of it filled his eyes with tears.

'It's an old tale,' said Bliss. 'An old fool and a young beauty. But most men content themselves with an affair. Or a divorce.'

'Most men haven't had a knife in their hand, man and boy, Inspector,' he said. 'I've worked the abattoirs. I was an apprentice at Smithfield. A blade is second nature to me, you see. I work quick. When the moment came, I didn't even think about it.'

'So you did it in cold blood?' said Bliss.

'No, Inspector,' said Wellbeloved. 'I was angry with her.'

'Why?' asked Bliss.

'Because she looked down on me.' Mr Wellbeloved wiped his eyes and sniffed loudly. 'When did you know, Mr Book? If you don't mind me asking?'

'I suspected right away that something was off,' said Book. 'And that was confirmed when I found that some of those old bones weren't so old – though you'd made an effort to age them.'

'Gravy browning,' said Wellbeloved. 'Sheila uses it on her legs. Couldn't afford to get her nylons.' The idea was painful. He drew deeply on the cigarette.

'Your knife marks are also very distinctive,' said Book. 'They were on the bone you gave me for Dog.'

Inspector Bliss produced his notepad. 'So for the sake of a future with Miss Enid Clegg,' he said, 'you sent your wife to meet her maker.'

'After which you found yourself confronting the murderer's oldest dilemma. Getting rid of the corpse.'

'No bother for a man who was trained at Smithfield, surely?' said Bliss.

'Unfortunately, Inspector, people can tell the difference between the bones of hogs and those of *homo sapiens*,' said Book. 'So I think that, after removing the flesh from your unfortunate wife – *flensing* her – you still needed to dispose of her skeleton. So you thought of caustic soda. Freely available at any chemist's. Alkaline hydrolysis. Is that what you were going for?'

Bliss had his pencil in his hand: he was ready to take down all the details. Mr Wellbeloved did not divulge them all. Some were too personal; too shaming. He did not mention that 'We'll Gather Lilacs' had been playing on the wireless when he delivered the killing blow (Sheila had never liked the song: it made her think of Walter, who was a great admirer of Ivor Novello). He did not say that he had imagined her body as a flitch of bacon; something that could be carried over his back. He did not describe tipping the caustic soda into the bath; how her flesh had bubbled into nothing, turning the tub into a tureen of human effluvia. He did not speak of watching it drain away, leaving her bones marooned around the plughole.

'George Harkup asked if I was getting rid of a body,' he said. 'I told him it was for the drains. We used it at Smithfield. Not everything just flushes away. But it didn't work properly. There was so much of her left. So many bones. I didn't know what to do.' He stubbed out the cigarette. His face was twisted in panic.

'And then I saw Mr Baseheart in the Bull. He'd had a couple and he bought me a pint and took me in the corner of the snug. There was some big secret he wanted to share. He told me how he was going to be the toast of his archaeology club. How some chap who'd lorded it over him would soon be laughing on the other side of his face. Then he made some joke about raising a glass to the Luftwaffe for having brought it all to light. All the skeletons. Old bones from the olden days, lying in a hole on Inkerman Street. Under a tarp so the dogs wouldn't run off with them. I asked if he'd told the coppers.'

'Which he hadn't,' said Bliss.

'No,' said Wellbeloved. 'He was tapping his nose, saying he wanted to keep it hush-hush so he could make some big announcement at their meeting.'

'So you knew you'd have time to get in there first. Add your bones to the pile.'

'Wasn't the only thing you added, was it?' Book had the

Charles II coin in his hand. He was turning it between his fingers. 'You're a good improviser, Eric, but you're not an imaginative man.'

'No call for it in my game,' he said flatly. 'Meat is meat, ain't it?'

'You rather over-egged it by planting the coin in the plague pit. That rang my alarm bell straight away. So, armed with a description of our suspect, my wife conducted a short but instructive tour of the local curio shops. I suppose there was no time for you to go further. Or to order one in the post. But even if there had been, well, anyone conceiving such a clumsy clue would never stray far from their own neighbourhood.' He tossed the coin in his hand and placed it on the table in front of Bliss.

'You were already in the frame when I noticed the clincher,' said Book. 'In the queue at the butcher's. Enid dabbed that powdered egg from your mouth. A gesture of uncommon intimacy which you barely acknowledged. You told me Sheila had gone to Sheffield. Well, Eric, it may surprise you to learn that they do have telephones in Sheffield. I rang her people and they said the last they'd heard from her was a letter at Christmas. But at that stage, you thought you'd got away with it, didn't you?'

'Yes,' said Wellbeloved. 'And then I got the note.'

'What note?' asked Bliss. This was new.

'A threat, I presume,' said Book. 'From Mr Harkup?'

'He said he wanted to talk to me on an urgent matter,' said Wellbeloved, his voice falling. 'He said there would be no need to report me to the authorities if we could sort the matter out between ourselves. How did he know? Did he see me? Was it the soda? How did he know?'

'He didn't know,' said Book, with a shrug. 'The letter was about dominoes.'

Mr Wellbeloved seemed to be gasping for air.

'Dominoes?'

'Old Harkup was a stickler for the rules, wasn't he? He thought you were cheating. The authorities? That was Mr Gash at the Bull.'

Mr Wellbeloved knitted his fingers together, as if in prayer. 'No,' he said. 'It was a threat. A threat about Sheila.'

Book said nothing. In the silence, Eric Wellbeloved's little universe turned inside out.

'Did you go to see Mr Harkup intending to kill him?' asked Bliss.

'No, to buy him off.'

'With cash?'

'With beef. I was scared. Scared of what he might say. What if he wouldn't listen to reason? So I kept him talking. But he wouldn't budge. Then I took my chance. Got hold of him and poured the poison down his throat. That place was full of it. But all the names! Prussic acid was the only one I'd heard of. It seemed the right thing. But it was horrible.' He shuddered at the memory.

Book removed his glasses and pulled his chair closer to the table. He appeared unmoved by Wellbeloved's expression of horror. 'Well, that's very interesting, Eric,' he said, wrinkling his nose. 'Because before he was poisoned, George Harkup was struck over the head. And the weapon left a bloody residue in his hair. Dr Calder at Bow Street here analysed it for me. Cow's blood. But you don't seem to know about that. And you would know, if you had murdered Mr Harkup.'

Eric Wellbeloved had lost his bearings in a thicket of lies. He attempted to cut a new path away from the thorns and quicksand. 'No, I remember,' he said. 'I did hit him.'

Book shook his head. 'Did Enid do it? Was it her idea from the start?'

Wellbeloved knew how to smile. He knew how to jolly people along; tell people to keep their chin up; tell them it might never happen. He did not, however, know how to lie. The thorns were in his skin. The ground beneath him was turning to porridge. He buried his head in his hands.

'Enid found me. After Sheila . . . died. And then she took charge. I didn't know what to do. But that girl was so calm. Methodical.'

'And everything looked rosy, I suppose, until that note arrived?' said Bliss.

Book settled his glasses back on his nose. 'After which Enid went round and clubbed Mr Harkup over the head with a leg of beef. And to make it look like suicide, she poured Prussic acid down poor Mr Harkup's gullet. Mickey Hall saw her go in. All wrapped up, and with something bundled in her arms. The meat, I suppose.'

A thought occurred to Book. 'Did you sell it?'

'People like beef,' said Wellbeloved.

'I like beef,' said Book. 'I like beef casserole.'

Wellbeloved knitted his hands together. His long-lashed eyes were wet and submissive.

'Can't we just say I did it?' he begged. 'I mean, I'll swing, won't I? But Enid.'

His abjection, thought Book, had a touch of travesty.

Bliss shuffled his papers on the table. 'The law must take its course.'

'I'm sorry, Eric. I truly am,' murmured Book. 'But I'm even more sorry for Sheila. And for George Harkup.'

Book watched the shape of Eric Wellbeloved through the frosted glass door of the charge room. Confession had stunned him into obedience. He would go quietly.

The entrance hall of Bow Street was busy with its customary Friday evening crowd. Book noted a pair of working girls interrupted in their business, surly and unmoved; a drunk with a torn shirt and a long explanation about why the landlord of the Kemble's Head deserved a punch in the bracket; a middle-aged clerk in a three-piece suit, his eyes glued to the floor with shame. Sergeant Morris had brought him in. Book did not recognise the clerk, but he knew the expression on Morris's face. *Another one off the street.*

'Mrs Book thought you might want this.'

Jack had appeared. He was unscrewing a Thermos of tea and looking warily around the room.

'Mrs Book is very thoughtful. And sandwiches, too, I see. What's in them?'

'Fish paste,' said Jack.

'Thank goodness for that,' said Book, unwrapping the paper.

'Wish I could have sat in with you on that one,' said Jack. 'Seems like you heard quite a tale.'

'I'm pushing my luck as it is,' said Book, sucking fish paste from his thumb. 'Particularly with laughing boy over there, waiting for his chance to collar me.'

'What about your letter from Churchill?'

Book sipped tea from the Thermos cup. 'It can't save me from everything, Jack. They got Ivor Novello for his petrol coupons.'

The door to the charge room opened. Bliss emerged, then Wellbeloved, flanked by the bodies of two constables. Morris abandoned his nervous clerk: the sergeant wanted to see the killer off in the van. Eric Wellbeloved flashed a smile at Book. It was the one he had used on his customers for years, to cheer them up and hide his secret troubles.

As he passed through the doors into the gloom of the yard, the butcher stumbled. His body felt passive and clumsy. He had seen it a thousand times in the abattoir; the strange drunken resignation of beasts. Few ever panicked or struggled, unless, through human error, the rhythm of the process was disturbed.

In this instance, Enid Clegg provided the disturbance. There she was, caught in the headlamps of the prison van, the whey-faced constable at her side, and clearly under arrest. She had planned a trip to the pictures that night. She was wearing peach-coloured lipstick and the tight tartan skirt with the pleats. Eric tried to turn his brain into a camera. The night was foggy: the headlamps made thick beams like air-raid searchlights. Perhaps, he thought, he could keep this picture in his head and recall it as they took him to the gallows. He had heard they were quick at their work, like slaughtermen.

The whey-faced constable was disinclined to put handcuffs on ladies. And what could Enid Clegg do, in the few short yards between the car and the station? When she saw Eric Wellbeloved, the question was answered. She ran to him; threw her arms around him; kissed him passionately. Inspector Bliss sighed his disapproval. Two constables moved to dislodge the couple from each other's arms. Perhaps the humanity of the moment – the tears, the apologies, the hot asseverations of loyalty – blunted their instincts because, as Enid planted one last kiss on the lips of her lover, she reached down, yanked the truncheon from the belt of the whey-faced constable and brought it across his face with a crack. The second constable took the impact on his neck.

'Run, Eric!' she exclaimed. 'Run for it!'

She scarcely knew whether he would do it. To deny her, however, would have been to end their affair – their beautiful, impossible, unstoppable affair – on a note of discord. Therefore he ran. He ignored Book, standing at the station door with a packet of sandwiches in his hand, yelling at him to stop. He ignored the shrieks of police whistles, the clatter of boots on the pavement. He ducked down a side alley, thanking austerity for the dead streetlights; thanking providence for the fog.

When he broke out into the glare of the Strand, he did not stop running. A bus screamed to a halt in front of him. He mouthed an apology at the driver and skittered on over the road. He was at the mouth of Archangel Lane: he ran into it, and past his own shop, where the lights were still burning. Who would pay the bill, he wondered? He could hear the blasts of the police whistles. Perhaps, thought Eric

Wellbeloved, it might be best just to sit outside the shop and wait for them to arrive. Then he imagined being brought back to the station; cuffed and defeated, pushed into the back of the van; Enid observing him, and thinking, perhaps, a little less of him. Therefore he ran.

There was only one way to go: Archangel Lane led into the void of Inkerman Street, where, at the beginning of the week, he had carried Sheila's browned bones and hidden them in the earth.

A barricade of boards and corrugated iron separated the lane from Inkerman Street. He found the gap with some difficulty and lost his footing as soon as he was through. It had rained the previous night. The water had drained into the pit. He could see the tarpaulin that Baseheart had used to cover the skeletons, floating on a bed of mud. Most of Inkerman Street was rubble, but the remains of a few buildings still stood. In the broken frame of the Crown and Anchor, a little campfire was burning. On the other side stood the wreck of a tenement block where some of his best customers had once lived. He staggered through the doorless entrance. Broken furniture in the hallway suggested scavenging after the blast. Kids, he supposed.

On his way upwards, his foot went through a rotten board on the stairs, but the banister, still bolted firmly to what remained of the wall, saved his neck. He tightened his grip and gave the broken board a hefty kick. Something to deter his pursuers.

He reached the third floor of the building without mishap and pushed open the door of one of the flats. The main room had lost its windows, and the bomb had blown a hole through to the next apartment, but the place was relatively intact. Among the rubbish strewn on the floor was a reproduction of Constable's *The Hay Wain*. It was ripped and scorched, but he recognised it, and remembered the owner. He'd dropped her round a packet of liver and lights, in that quiet tight-sprung winter of the Phoney War. The lady had had a parrot and had tipped him.

He could hear police whistles down below. The search party had reached Inkerman Street. Voices were shouting out to each other, passing on warnings about obstacles, calling his name. He heard someone slip over in the mud and swear. A growling, grinding sound then cut through the night: a motor was being started. The passage of a great pale wall of bone-white light revealed that someone had stirred Brenda from her slumbers. Fastidious Mr Baseheart, though no longer an official employee of the state, had come to its aid in another matter. An anti-aircraft searchlight, his pride and joy, was being used to hunt a murderer.

Eric Wellbeloved dived back to the wall. He could see the glare of Brenda bleeding through the gaps in the brickwork. A roosting bird, disturbed by the light, clattered its way through an empty window frame and flapped off into the darkness.

It was then that the butcher heard a voice.

'Where are you going to run to, Eric?'

Gabriel Book. Very close. On the landing of the floor below.

'You can give up today or you can give up tomorrow, Eric. But it's inevitable.'

'You're not stringing me up!' bellowed the butcher.

He waited for the reply. It did not come. Something cracked and splintered on the landing outside. Wellbeloved heard a gasp, the sound of a body in motion; a fall of brick dust. For a moment he thought he had heard the last words of a favourite customer. Then Brenda hit her target. White light streamed into the flat. Wellbeloved saw a smashed sideboard, broken crockery, a tall lamp, its spine broken; Gabriel Book, standing in the doorway, his raincoat grey with dust.

'No,' said Wellbeloved, in a small, level voice. 'You shan't do that to me. I've seen beasts go. It's not always kind.'

He jumped through the hole in the wall. Book backed out onto the landing. Eric was already up ahead. The landing stretched beyond the staircase. The butcher pelted on until he reached the door at the end. He turned back to look at Book, twisted the handle, and pushed it open. The door swung on its rotten hinges over the gaping space beyond. A great chasm of air created when the V2 had sliced off the side of the building, now illuminated by the glow of the searchlight.

Eric Wellbeloved clasped the broken frame of the door. He looked squarely at Book. A droplet of sweat fell from his face. He was going to jump.

'What about Enid?' said Book. 'Are you going to leave her to face the rope alone?'

The butcher steadied himself. Something inside him seemed to relax.

'You're right.' He sighed. 'She did all this for me.'

'Yes,' said Book.

'To be with me.' Wellbeloved nodded, as if he were gathering his energy for something. 'Can't leave her to face the music, can I? If we're going to go, we should go together.'

'That's right, Eric,' said Book. He smiled at the butcher. But the butcher did not smile back. He was shaking. He was wet with sweat. Book watched it gather on the fold of fat above the collar of the butcher's shirt.

As Eric pitched backwards through the gaping doorway, his hand reached out, and scrambled, briefly, at the brickwork. It was hard to say whether this represented a conscious act of will or a burst of animal instinct. Eric himself, of course, would have been best placed to answer the question.

Book saw him sail through the air, his wheeling arms caught briefly in the beam of the searchlight. He did not scream.

Brenda's moving parts were stiff. Jack was a novice. By wrenching the handles downwards, however, he managed to pin the body of the butcher in the light as it made landfall on the tarpaulin. The canvas was not enough to save his life. Wellbeloved's neck snapped as he hit the ground. It did, however, produce a dreadful coda: the mass of the tarpaulin folding around him like a shroud and delivering him into the mud of the pit.

Book, standing three storeys above, watched the corpse slip from view, and gave the only help he could. An epitaph. He spoke it quietly, under his breath, and over the ruins.

'For him the hemlock shall distill.
For him the axe be bared.
For him the gibbet shall be built.
For him the stake prepared.'

That night in the bookshop, Jack Blunt told his friends his name.

As the shops were all closed, Book made dinner with ingredients supplied by the Istanbul. Yusuf mopped his brow with a tea towel and handed over a bag of rice and a metal tray loaded with meat and vegetables, which he then covered with the same tea towel. A bunch of parsley was placed on top, with deference.

While Book kept an eye on the oven, Nora and Trottie listened to Jack's account of the drama in Inkerman Square. They were an eager audience, but not quite as eager as Jack was a storyteller. He had the feeling that they had heard many such stories before, and were humouring him for being quite so strangely thrilled by a chase through the fog to bring a murderer to justice. When he reached the end of his tale, Trottie paused and raised her glass to Sheila Wellbeloved and George Harkup. Lost people of Archangel Lane.

Jack had never had rice outside a pudding. They had finished eating and Nora was perched, cross-legged, in the armchair she favoured for reading about real and fictional acts of violence. Trottie was embedded in the battered leather sofa. Book was beside her, engaged in the opening of a tin of fruit. Dog sat at the feet of his master. There was an air of expectation, as if they had reached the moment at which Jack was required to give an account of himself. The fire was warm. There was food in his belly. He told them the story.

'Jack Blunt,' he said. 'Brought up in an orphanage. Made a few acquaintances of the wrong sort.'

'Oh,' said Nora, leaning forward.

'Yeah,' said Jack. '*Oh*. I was the driver for a smash-and-grab up Mayfair way. They got away with a pile of mink coats. I got away with two years. Missed the war. Some of it, anyway. Then I got a letter from the Prison Reform Society. And on my last day, a postcard giving me an address for a job. This address.'

Trottie put her palms in the air. 'Well,' she said, 'there we are. No need to mention it again. We're not the prying kind, Jack.'

Jack frowned. 'I might be, though,' he said. 'Why am I here?'

'Altruism!' said Book, bending the lid of the tin and showing the contents like a boy with a nest of blackbird eggs. 'Pineapple chunks. Haven't had these since before the war. What a treat.'

Jack would not be distracted. 'What do you mean, altruism?'

Book stirred the contents of the tin with a fork. 'I suppose I could have put up a little card in the newsagent's window. But trying to give a second chance to someone felt like the right thing to do.'

'But you don't know me from Adam,' said Jack. 'I mean, bloody hell, I'm grateful and all that. It's nice here. I mean *really* nice. But why did you pick me?'

'Book's,' said Book, 'is a raft on the great turbulent sea of life.'

'You mean,' said Jack, 'books *are* a raft.'

Book knew he was being teased. 'Don't dwell on it, Jack. Just accept it. A second chance.' He cleared his throat to deliver a quotation. 'You only live once, but if you do it right, once is enough.'

'Shakespeare?' guessed Jack.

'Mae West,' said Book. He popped a piece of pineapple into his mouth and held out the tin to Jack.

He plucked; he ate. And just for a moment, everything in the world was sweet.

DEADLY NITRATE

CHAPTER ONE

Hearts were breaking on Archangel Lane. Tony was breaking Madeleine's heart. Madeleine was breaking Tony's. You could tell because Madeleine's wide blue eyes were wet with tears; or, rather, her left eye was wet with a single tear that gathered, then rolled slowly down her cheek. Tony did not weep, but wore his wound visibly. He gazed at Madeleine with a stoic expression appropriate to a handsome young man who has loved madly and devotedly, then received the bitter intelligence that his lover's husband had not, as previously thought, perished during the Fall of Singapore, but had in fact spent four years in a Japanese POW camp and even now was on his way to London to reclaim the young bride he'd left minding the cake shop.

'We must simply be brave, mustn't we?' said Madeleine, her yellow hair catching the cold white light. 'Heaven knows it will be hard. It will be beastly. But we're strong people, Tony, you and I. And what we feel for each other – well, it will endure. It will endure. So I shall stay in my shop, and you in yours. And all I ask is that you don't grow to hate me.' She rested her cheek on his shoulder.

'Why would I hate you, Madeleine? You mean everything to me.'

He might have said more. He intended to say more. Pages of the stuff. How war demanded sacrifices, but peace demanded them too; how he would always love her but would now teach himself to be content with friendship and the knowledge that life was damned impossible and damned, damned unfair.

He was interrupted, however, by a loud, sharp bang like the sound of a discharging pistol. The bang spoiled the moment, stopped the scene, and abolished Tony and Madeleine.

'What the hell was that?' yelped the woman with the yellow hair.

'Cut!' yelled a voice from above.

The camera operator stopped turning and returned the jib to its first position. The boom man rested his arms. The sparks cut the power to the spot lamp, returning unaugmented daylight to Archangel Lane. Billy Green, the youngest member of the crew, keen as mustard with trousers to match, put down his clapperboard. The woman who had been Madeleine was demanding his attention.

'What was that, Billy?' she asked.

'Just a car backfiring, I think, Miss Dare.'

Miss Dare did not look reassured. 'Sounded like a pistol! Didn't it sound like a ruddy pistol, Stew?'

The handsome young man appeared supremely unruffled: this was, in fact, an important part of his job. He took her hand and kissed it. 'You all right, my love?'

'Just tired,' she said.

'Of course, darling. You must be.' He narrowed his warm brown eyes in sympathy. 'Tell you what, how about a proper dinner after this? Like we used to before the war?' Women in Odeons and Essoldos all over the country would have fainted to receive such an offer. Sandra Dare stayed upright. To her, Stewart Howard was her fiancé, not a vision projected at twenty-four frames per second, to be consumed while draining a carton of Kia-Ora. But she seemed no less delighted.

'Sandra? You okay?' Another man was moving into her light. Jesse MacKendrick had risen from the canvas chair emblazoned with his name to assess the happiness of his leading lady. He was young for a director, and perhaps he felt it: the horn-rimmed spectacles and intense artistic frown seemed calculated to dissuade the onlooker from thinking that he looked more like a university athlete than one of the *Sight and Sound* crowd. A more assiduous man might have chosen a tank top that was slightly less tight, or decided to carry his belongings in a bag that was less obviously something you would take to a locker room.

Jesse's ministrations were not received with gratitude.

'Yes, yes,' snapped Sandra. 'Don't fuss, Jesse.' She popped her lips together. 'How's my pout?'

He examined it through a frame of thumbs and index fingers. 'Could do with a dab.'

A make-up lady streaked forward with a finger of lipstick. Jesse's face crumpled in annoyance. 'No, no, no. Miss Dare only wears Victory Red! Elizabeth Arden.' He scrabbled in the box of cosmetics, pulled out the correct shade and passed it to Sandra.

'Don't fuss,' she muttered, applying it to her lips. 'Let's get on.'

Jesse took back the lipstick and returned it to the make-up lady. He pinched the bridge of his nose and gathered his thoughts about the scene. Stewart Howard watched his efforts with bemused scepticism. When Jesse was ready, he returned to his place beside the camera and clapped his hands to regain the attention of the crew.

'All right!' he exclaimed. '*Ad astra per aspera!* We must have bodies, we must have celluloid, we must have light. And we must have quiet!'

A hush descended on Archangel Lane. Everyone knew the routine. The sparks pulled a switch for the lamps. The camera operator gave a thumbs up. Billy Green rushed forward with his clapperboard. The camera began to whirr.

'Rolling,' intoned the operator. 'And speed.'

'*Lovelorn in London*, scene twenty-eight, take three,' declared Billy, bringing together the jaws of his board.

Jesse pointed a finger, like God posing for the roof of the Sistine Chapel. 'Action!'

Tony and Madeleine were back. 'We must simply be brave, mustn't we?' said Madeleine, her yellow hair catching the cold white light. 'Heaven knows it will be hard. It will be beastly. But we're strong people, Tony, you and I. And what we feel for each other – well, it will endure. It will endure.'

The inhabitants of Archangel Lane, the ones who were happy to spend hours being shushed on their own front doorsteps, knew Tony and Madeleine well. They knew their colleagues, too; the boiler-suited army that dragged cables over cobbles, changed signage on the shops, turned Archangel Lane into a blowsily exaggerated version of itself; the extras and bit-part players who now walked among them like uncanny impostors you might meet in a fever dream.

The premises once occupied by Mr Harkup had been a beer-off shop since April. Now, in August, they had been transformed into a fishmonger, with a pavement stall displaying a prop flounder on a bed of crushed glass. Mr Wellbeloved's butcher shop, shuttered for six months, was now staffed by an actor in an apron much cleaner than any worn by Eric. (Some thought this was in bad taste, with the trial just over and the unseemly debate in the press about whether Edith Clegg should go to the gallows.)

The surviving members of the Archangel Lane dominoes club were replaced by simulacra. Mr Hilliard the tailor was represented by a man wearing a tape measure and a gummed-on moustache, who, when questioned, did not know the difference between a shawl lapel and a notch lapel. Mrs Acres, told that the stock of her junk shop would not 'come over' on camera, was obliged to watch her modest arrangement of planters, tallboys and umbrella stands be augmented by an ormolu clock and a preposterous stuffed bear. This, however, was less upsetting than coming face to face with the Mrs Acres of the screen, whose teeth were, at best, Dickensian. Still, the money was nice.

Mr Gabriel Book had made his own surrender. It came in the form of a tin of bottle-green paint, used to lick the confusing apostrophe from his sign. As the ladder had gone up, he had crossed himself.

He was unable to watch the morning's scene from his own doorstep: his own doorstep was in this morning's scene. He and Dog hovered with the other onlookers outside the Istanbul restaurant, which was keeping the production supplied with hot water and bacon rolls. The smell of the latter confirmed Dog as an unswerving admirer of the British film industry.

'What do you think?' asked Yusuf.

'Head-scratcher, isn't it?' said Book. 'Mrs Trickett thinks they should just keep on doing it behind his back.'

'He'll find out, though, won't he?' said Yusuf. 'He's no fool.'

'Divorce, perhaps?'

Yusuf frowned darkly. 'Madeleine is a Roman Catholic, Mr Book.'

'Mrs Spain said she should simply run away with Tony to Rio de Janeiro.'

Yusuf shook his head. 'And leave the shop behind? Good business, that. And what would the husband do?'

Book shrugged. 'He could make his own choux pastry.'

'After four years in a POW camp?' sniffed Yusuf. 'I doubt it.'

Book sighed gently. 'Nice to see a bit of crème pâtissière again, isn't it? Trottie's window is full of it, now it's playing the part of a cake shop. Pity it's all made of plaster.'

On the set of David Lean's *Great Expectations*, the extras had salivated, wide-eyed, at the pork pie in Mrs Gargery's larder. Barbara Markham and Linda Bruce knew this agony. They had been there under the lights at Denham in their bonnets, trying to walk like Victorians. *Lovelorn in London* was the ground of similar hunger. It was not, however, provoked by anything actually edible. Madeleine Brownlow's cake shop was all gong and no dinner. Its green marzipan domes, sugar mice and maids of honour had been constructed in the workshops of Ladyhurst Studios, SE13. Barbara and Linda had watched dispassionately as a pair of overalled men removed the proper contents of the window – rolls of wallpaper, pots of paint, packets of paste and plaster – and replaced them with confectionery moulded from the same ingredients.

Barbara and Linda had no lines. The path from background nodding to a foreground cough-and-spit seemed as inaccessible as a trip to Timbuctoo. Their job was to stand inside the shop and settle a fake slab of Battenberg on a mirrored cake stand in the window, as the camera moved outside. It might have been easy under other circumstances. But these circumstances involved Stewart Howard.

Stewart Howard figured in their conversations and their dreams. He was the leading man of their Unconscious. His portrait, clipped from the pages of *Picture Review*, sat by their bedsides like a votive object. They knew the way his hair fell at his temple. They knew the line of his shoulder inside a suit. They knew the cords of muscle that you saw, all too briefly, when Sandra Dare tore his shirt in *Madonna of the Purple Mountain*. They imagined themselves at his home in Buckinghamshire, in some unspecific arrangement that involved them lying on his patio like sunned cats, sipping gin and orange. In this bright and cloudy version of reality, Sandra Dare had taken holy orders, been killed by TB, crushed by the bus to Elstree, or choked to death on the olive in her Martini glass. The details were not important. Whatever tragedy befell her, Barbara and Linda would help him recover; make him forget her. It wouldn't take long.

'Do you think he likes Battenberg?' asked Linda.

'Bit pink and yellow for him,' said Barbara.

'I think he likes something dark with a soft centre.'

'Rum barrel?'

'Definitely liqueurs.'

Trottie Book had been listening to these conversations for several days. She knew Stewart Howard's favourite cocktail (an old-fashioned), favourite authors (Graham Greene, C. P. Snow), favourite pastime (messing about in boats). She knew that Barbara thought Stewart Howard's finest hour was in a submarine at 20,000 fathoms, and that Linda preferred him on horseback in the Argentine. In the face of this, she had taken the opportunity to pursue all the small tasks open to a small business owner who is being paid to pause trade, many of which involve disappearing into stock cupboards. One yielded an orphan roll of a good quality Belgian paper. Attractive, but only useful now as drawer liner: the factory in Antwerp had been bombed out of existence.

'Here it is,' she said, placing the roll on the glass-topped counter.

Barbara and Linda gazed upon it with religious awe.

'And this is on his bedroom wall?' asked Linda.

'Maroon and lily-green,' purred Trottie. 'I said to him, Stewart, Stew I said: you're just like this paper, you're so strong and modern. He handled this very roll.'

It was a magical idea.

'Can I touch it?' asked Linda.

Trottie chewed her lip. 'I shouldn't really. But since you're working in my cake shop . . .' Both girls tittered at the joke. Linda extended her hand towards the paper and made contact with its smooth surface. Barbara, watching her friend's fingers move over the pattern, seemed to be holding her breath.

'This is the last thing he sees when he gets into bed,' said Linda.

'Yes,' confirmed Trottie.

'And the first thing he sees when he gets up in the morning,' added Barbara. 'With his hair all disarranged and—'

'It's fourteen shillings,' said Trottie.

Linda withdrew her hand. Barbara made a strange noise, something like a sigh of anguish.

'Tell you what,' said Trottie, with a conspiratorial smile. 'It's a bit irregular, but I could let you have a sample for, well, sixpence, say? Then you could keep a little reminder of him, wherever you go.'

The news pleased Linda. She giggled as if someone had placed her feet in a bag of feathers. The effect on Barbara seemed more pronounced: she turned very pale and gave an involuntary twitch.

'Smashing,' she gasped.

Jack had not been comfortable in Norfolk. Partly this was due to the lie of the land. A man who has spent over two years behind high brick walls cannot but feel discombobulated in a county composed mainly of sky. Belborough Hall looked over this nothingness: clouds with a thin underlay of marsh and reed beds, and, somewhere beyond, the brown mass of the North Sea. The owner, Lord Belborough, had 5,000 acres of parkland, an excitable cocker spaniel, a daughter with a mole on her forehead that required an urgent trim, and in his library, a First Folio on which he had given Book first refusal.

Lord Belborough's letter had arrived at 158 Archangel Lane with no warning.

'Could be worth a fortune, Jack,' said Book.

'Why are you sending me, then? What do I know about Shakespeare?'

'Nothing, I hope.'

'Why?'

'I don't want to let him know how deeply interested I am.' He waggled the letter in his hand. 'Terribly cheap paper,' he said. 'Second-class stamp. I love a bargain, don't you? God bless the mansion tax.'

An expert, as it turned out, was not required. Jack's suspicions about the quality of the merchandise were aroused by the Belborough family's apparent unwillingness to let him see it. He arrived bright and early, having put up in a pub in Cley the previous night. A tour around the grounds was offered, during which Lord Belborough's daughter and Lord Belborough's dog were both more friendly than he might have wished. Lunch followed, at which Lord Belborough produced a bottle of amontillado he claimed to have liberated from Barcelona before the anarchists moved in. By the time Jack was permitted to enter the presence of the text, he had consumed several generous schooners. Even in this poor condition, however, he was quite capable of discerning that Belborough's book was doing worse. It was grey-green, brittle and blooming and quite clearly of more interest to students of mycology than of English literature.

'I may be drunk,' said Jack. 'But I'm not that drunk.'

The journey home – the long, slow journey home with nothing to look at but cloudless blue – was tiresome, but consistent with his visit. The day was hot. The carriage was closed. One of his fellow travellers planned to surprise his London relations with a selection of ripe local cheeses. Another man delighted the company by reading aloud all the most amusing paragraphs from that week's *Punch*. He did not subscribe to the orthodox view that it was not as funny as it had once been.

Book had instructed Jack to take a taxi from Liverpool Street back to Archangel Lane. He had been thinking of the security of the First Folio more than the comfort of his assistant, but after four days in East Anglia Jack decided that fifteen easeful minutes in a clean and quiet hackney cab was rather less than he deserved. He did not, however, expect to find his employer waiting for him at the end of the lane, waving as though he were late for a party.

'How was Norfolk?' asked Book, paying the driver.

'Flat,' said Jack.

'And Lord Belborough's First Folio? Good?'

'As his teeth.'

'Oh dear.'

Jack thought that Book might have been more disappointed; instead, he seemed oddly giddy. He took Jack's arm, and his suitcase, and guided him forwards.

'Are you all right, Mr Book?' Jack asked.

'Thought I'd better prepare you.'

'For what?'

The lane ahead was crowded with people. Jack's impression was that some kind of public meeting was taking place. It was the shouting postman, however, who caught his attention first. He was not the man who usually delivered the mail to Archangel Lane – a Somme veteran who did not let one crackling lung prevent him from singing 'Mademoiselle from Armentières' at the top of his voice at 6 a.m. – but a compact, hard-boiled-looking figure with thick eyebrows and a gigantic paintbrush moustache. He was giving a speech.

'Life and death!' he exclaimed, in a surprisingly high-pitched and forceless voice. 'The whole world is here, in this little patch of London town.'

The words were addressed to an earnest young man in horn-rimmed spectacles and a tank top. He seemed unimpressed. 'Are you going to do it like that?'

The postman tried again. 'Life and death!'

'You know,' said Jesse MacKendrick, raising his hand, 'I think we'll just lose the line. I'm already worried about the moustache. You'll be super in the background, though.' He patted the postman on the back and darted away, scribbling on his script. Jesse gave a signal to Billy Green to yell out the start of a ten-minute break. It took the clapper boy a moment to comply: Billy had just popped a boiled sweet into his mouth from the little pouch he wore attached to his belt.

'Watch your back, chaps!' Two men in long brown jackets pushed past Jack and Book, carrying what appeared to be an old-fashioned gas streetlamp. A serious young woman followed them, clipboard in hand. Outside Mrs Acres' junk shop, a technician adjusted the barn doors of a spot lamp. Jack put his hand up to his eyes: a white light was dazzling him.

'What in hell?'

'Close,' said Book. 'Hollywood. Or rather, the closest England can get to it.' He gestured towards the new colonisers of Archangel Lane. 'We're going to be in pictures! Just the exteriors are being done here, you understand. The rest is at Ladyhurst. That's the studios. The *sound stages*. You see, I know all the jargon now.'

Prison had more obvious forms of hardship – physical confinement, rotten food, the unceasing undercurrent of violence – but for Jack, the absence of a silver screen and a kiosk selling New Berry Fruits had been one of its hardest deprivations.

'Who's the star?' he asked. Book had no need to answer. Stewart Howard walked by, flipping open a silver cigarette case, offering Book a friendly hello and lavishing Jack with the extravagant wink he employed to make fans at gala nights and church fetes feel special without having to touch them or inhale their air.

'That's—' began Book.

'Yes, I know,' said Jack.

'He's passed me by entirely, I'm afraid,' confessed Book. 'He plays the hero. The idealistic young bookseller in love with the girl next door.'

'Did you not see him in that submarine picture? He went

mad and tried to throttle everyone. It was dead sweaty. Who else?'

'Patience!' warned Book. 'You have arrived halfway through this picture. And you haven't laid eyes on the leading lady yet. Who is also Stewart's fiancée. His real-life fiancée.'

Stewart Howard was sauntering towards the bookshop, a cigarette now smouldering at the corner of his mouth. He extended his hand – Stewart Howard's actual hand, the one that had held the spanner that had done for the periscope of HMS *Carthage* in *Ship of Shame* – and pushed open the door: the same door through which Jack passed several times a day when going out to buy a pint of milk or a packet of biscuits. Stewart, however, did not pass through. He was holding the door open, graciously, for his co-star.

'Sandra Dare?' said Jack, more loudly than he intended.

'She's using my room,' said Book. 'Decanted my things so she could do her mascara. Sip her Vichy water. Or whatever these people do. It's a strange feeling, seeing your private study colonised by make-up boxes and bouquets of white lilies. Particularly if you once had a cigarette card of the coloniser.' He cleared his throat. 'Before the war, of course.'

Sandra crossed the threshold of the bookshop. Stewart followed her inside. For them, even this simple process carried grace and luminosity. It was impossible not to stare. They made everything around them seem less ordinary.

'I hope we're not causing too much disruption!' The earnest young man in the tank top was approaching Book as if he were an old friend.

'Not at all,' said Book. 'It's an education.'

'Larry Olivier calls film an anaemic little medium,' said Jesse. 'He's such a crashing snob.'

'For he today that sheds his blood with me shall be my brother; be he ne'er so vile!' declared Book, in a passable imitation of a knighted actor addressing the troops from a rough wooden cart parked somewhere near Agincourt. He frowned. 'Though he says "ne'er so *base*" in the film. Not vile. I wonder why? Perhaps it sounded less insulting to the Americans, given they had been so decent as to join the war. But where are my manners? Jack, this is Mr MacKendrick.'

'Delighted,' said Jesse, offering Jack an unnecessarily tight handshake.

Nora was sidling towards them: she had come to welcome Jack home, but the man in the spectacles and the tight tank top also stirred her interest.

'So, you're the director?' she asked.

'And the writer,' confirmed Jesse, mistaking her incredulity for awe.

'I thought you'd be older,' she said. 'With a monocle. And a riding crop.'

'You mustn't believe everything you read in the film magazines, young lady.'

Nora narrowed her eyes. 'I've seen you before . . .'

'Mr MacKendrick had a lot of green Penguins from us last summer,' explained Book. 'And sold them back to us at a very reasonable price – for which you, particularly, Nora, should be grateful.'

'Oh yeah! You look different.'

'It's the shorts,' said Book.

'I'm not wearing shorts,' said Jesse.

'That's why you look different,' said Nora.

Book decided to treat Nora's impertinence as a factual observation. 'Yes,' he agreed. 'You were a very busy bee as I recall. Always running about the place, weren't you, Mr MacKendrick?'

'Jesse,' said Jesse.

'Jesse,' repeated Book, a little flatly. They had now formed a little awkward knot of people who did not quite know whether to continue the conversation or bring it to an end. This minor social problem was solved, however, by the arrival of a fourth person, whose sly intercession produced a physical reaction in Jesse, of the kind given by people who have discovered mouse droppings in the bread bin.

She wore a tight red tweed twinset and a tighter red smile. Her hair was parted like Wallis Simpson and her eyebrows were shaved and redrawn in the fashion of the previous decade. She smiled the smile she gave to waiters, coat-check girls, her mother, and other victims.

'Hello, Nerina,' said Jesse, almost separating his teeth. 'Hunting for column fodder?'

'Always!' trilled Nerina. She waved her little spiral notebook like a pearl-handled revolver.

'Well, the bins are round the back.'

She gave a silent laugh. 'Aren't you going to introduce me?'

'This is Mr Book,' said Jesse.

'Oh, the apostrophe man,' she said, looking him fully up and down. 'I saw they subbed your sign.'

'I'm trying not to look,' said Book. He eyed her notepad, which was already open. 'Would you by any chance be a member of His Majesty's press?'

'The Girl with the Poison Pen,' said Jesse. 'That's what they put under your byline, isn't it?'

'Nerina Bean,' said the Girl with the Poison Pen, offering a hand. '*Picture Review*. If you have juicy titbits, my door is open.'

Book smiled warily. 'I'll bear that in mind.'

Barbara and Linda were not cruel girls, but Trottie was grateful that the universe had not granted them the ability to kill with the power of their minds. If it had, she was sure that Sandra Dare would be experiencing tortures that would make some of the spikier pages of Dante's *Inferno* look like a day out in the Cotswolds. Their contrary feelings about Stewart Howard seemed no less ferocious; though, if he were to perish in their care, it would be from other causes.

'He looked at me this morning,' said Barbara.

'You didn't say,' said Linda.

'I wasn't sure, but I am now. He's got to be subtle with her around, hasn't he?'

Trottie coughed to attract their attention. She had snipped two neat samples of wallpaper from the maroon and lily-green roll, about the size of a playing card. She laid them down on the counter with sensual slowness.

'Oh, it's lovely,' cooed Barbara. 'And he definitely has this in his bedroom?'

'Up to his ceiling,' said Trottie, 'and right down to the skirting board.'

They paused in reverence. Barbara's breathing was loud and quick.

'Does Stewart tell you any gossip?' she asked.

'Does Stewart talk about *her*?' added Linda. 'The *fiancée*?' She could not bring herself to say the name aloud.

Barbara had more questions. 'Does he say: "I don't like her anymore. She's too old for me"?'

'No,' said Trottie.

'Does he say: "She's so old it's like kissing a leg of mutton"?'

'No,' said Trottie.

'Does she say: "She's a fascinating bitch"?'

Linda winced. Trottie smiled glassily. Even Barbara seemed to acknowledge that this remark had crossed a line.

'No,' said Trottie, crisply. 'He says he was very excited about *Lovelorn in London* from the moment he saw Mr Mac-Kendrick's script. And that he's very much looking forward to married life.'

It was a disappointing answer. Linda and Barbara frowned as if some heresy had been uttered.

'Though,' Trottie continued, throwing the girls a Stewart-shaped bone, 'he also says one must keep an open mind and who knows what fate may throw one's way.'

This was much better. Linda was by the pool again in Buckinghamshire, sipping that gin and orange, watching Stewart execute a perfect dive into the pool.

'Hear that, Barb?' she said. 'Who knows what fate may throw your way.'

Barbara, however, seemed unable to hear anything. Her little handbag fell, spilling its contents. Her eyes rolled back in her head. She pitched backwards onto the carpet.

Trottie had never in her life done anything to make a teenager faint and fall to the floor.

'Heavens,' she said. 'That girl has it bad.'

At first, Linda was unperturbed. Barbara had once fainted against the barrier outside the Odeon, Leicester Square, crushing the little bunch of hyacinths that she had intended to give to Stewart. Her present insensibility, however, was different. The colour had ebbed from her face. Something inside her was twitching, as if her body was trying and failing to exhale bad air. Linda fell to the floor and shook her friend by the shoulders.

Trottie leapt around the counter. She tore open the collar of Barbara's blouse, placed a hand on the girl's forehead, tilted her head back and lifted the tip of her chin to open her throat to the air. Nothing.

Linda loosed a low moan of panic.

The shop door clattered.

'Home is the hunter!' declared Book. Jack's suitcase was in his hand, until he dropped it. Then he was on his knees, trying to help the girl lying motionless on the floor. But there was no help to be given.

CHAPTER TWO

Before the inspector's car could enter Archangel Lane, the streetlamp had to be removed. An ambulance was the true obstruction, but its crew was busy inside Trottie's shop, and no one wished to disturb their solemn work. Two men in overalls made the space passable by plucking the prop from the ground like a great painted wooden flower and settling it down on the ground outside the butcher's.

The police car, unlike the lamp, had not been hired in for the day. It contained a working radio, a driver and Inspector Bliss, who, at this moment, also resembled a phenomenon of the screen – a cartoon character, possibly a dog, who props open his red eyes with matchsticks.

As the car came to a halt, Inspector Morris opened the door.

'Is this a sad one, Morris?' asked Bliss. 'I've been up all night with the razor-blade case.'

Morris had no good news. Bliss cast a weary gaze over the extinguished spot lamps, the motionless camera and jib, a group of extras standing listlessly outside the junk shop. The ten-minute break had mutated into lunch. A catering table set up for the crew and extras was dispensing hot rolls and tea. Linda, pale and silent, sat nearby in a folding canvas chair, attended by a friendly WPC. The chair had Jesse's name stencilled on the back.

'All right,' said Bliss, 'let's have it.'

'Film-struck girl, Inspector. Dead by the counter of Mrs Book's shop. Suspicious. We've shut down filming for the time being.'

'Any witnesses?'

'Yes, sir,' reported Morris. 'Mrs Book herself, and a young friend of the victim.'

Bliss indicated Linda. The WPC was pressing a mug of tea into her hand. The girl seemed baffled by it, as though someone had just asked her to hold their theodolite.

'Is that the friend?' asked Bliss. Morris nodded. 'And have the parents been informed?'

'Yes, sir. She and the family didn't get on. Her friend said that's why she spent so much time at . . .' Morris came to a halt. The shop door had opened and two officers were emerging, carrying a body on a stretcher. It was Barbara, swaddled in a clean white hospital sheet.

'. . . so much time at the pictures.'

Morris cast his eyes to the cobbles. Bliss removed his hat. They watched the body being loaded into the ambulance. Over by the catering table, Linda began to sob. The WPC put a friendly hand on her shoulder. Bliss felt relieved that this part of the job was delegated to others.

Book, standing in the doorway of the wallpaper shop, observed the ambulance backing out of the lane. He threw a sad smile at Billy, who was crossing the cobbles, clipboard in hand, making for the door of Book's Books.

'Have you told them?' asked Book.

'Doing it now,' said Billy. He replied as if Book had given an order, not asked a question. The bookshop door rattled shut.

Book turned to Bliss. 'Good afternoon, Inspector,' he said. 'It seems we're at home to murder.'

For a moment, Billy Green stood inside the empty bookshop, collecting his thoughts. He could hear voices through the partition that separated the two businesses: Trottie's words were not completely intelligible, but he understood that she was describing Barbara's breathlessness, the movements of her body before she lost her battle with gravity.

Above his head, a floorboard creaked.

He did not go upstairs immediately. First, he moved to the back kitchen of the bookshop, where a trolley, property of Ladyhurst Films, had been parked. It was piled with a great stack of letters addressed to Stewart, or Sandra, or Stewart and Sandra. Beside this was a chocolate box of scandalous luxury. This was Sandra's favourite kind of confectionery: soft centres in a heart-shaped, velvet-lined repository of off-the-ration pleasure. The accompanying correspondence did not look so sweet. Billy had been in his job long enough to detect, unopened, the difference between a request for a photograph enclosing a stamped self-addressed envelope and a lunatic's tightly argued offer of marriage, destined for the fire. Using his clipboard as a tray, he gathered the contents of the trolley and made his way up the stairs to the makeshift dressing room above. He did this slowly, carefully, without disturbing a floorboard. A generous observer would have said that he paused outside the door before knocking. A more suspicious person would have called it eavesdropping. Certainly, Billy stood in silence long enough to recognise the tone of the conversation on the other side of the door and absorb some of its details. This was Sandra and Stewart unsurveilled by public or colleagues, and he knew the rocky territory.

The topics were familiar. Stewart asked if Sandra would mind if he cried off the premiere of *Caravan* the following week: Stewart Granger, he said, was convinced he had stolen his name and was always unpleasant to him. Sandra said that this was quite impossible; told him to think of the event as an unpleasant but necessary piece of work, like dumping the ashes.

'Anyway,' she continued, 'Jean Kent says he has sardines for lunch and she can't bear to kiss him in the afternoon.'

'Jean Kent has a soft spot for me,' said Stewart.

'Jean Kent just married an Albanian stuntman so I'd watch your step there. We might need a bit of *quid pro quo* from the Gainsborough lot when this one hits the Odeons.'

'We don't need them,' said Stewart. 'The fans will buy it. They love us, don't they? Both of us.'

'Don't take it for granted, Stew. You know what they shouted at the test of *Brief Encounter*? "Why doesn't she just kiss him?" Only they didn't say "kiss".'

'Relax, darling,' said Stewart. 'It'll be another smash. We're the nation's most blissfully engaged couple.'

'And what a long engagement it's been,' said Sandra.

A silence followed. Billy saw a shape move at the bottom of the door. His heart lurched. Had one of them detected his presence on the landing? He took a few noisy steps on the floor to suggest a sudden arrival and tapped at the door with his foot.

'Sorry to bother you,' he called.

Stewart whipped the door open. His eyes were cold. 'What do you want, barley-sugar boy?'

'Well, there's this lot,' said Billy, dumping his cargo and extracting the clipboard. 'And then Miss Dare will be giving an interview to Miss Bean.'

'The fire-breather of *Picture Review*?' said Sandra.

Stewart shrugged. 'She's always been rather sweet to me.'

'She's the very devil,' growled Sandra. She was staring at her reflection in a mirror propped on the table where Book's papers were usually stacked. She was not quite happy with what she saw.

'Remember the ashcan, darling,' said Stewart. 'You have good news for her. Our three-picture deal. A *Picture Review* exclusive.'

'And I have to do that before the end of lunch?'

'No,' said Billy, looking at the clipboard. 'Mr MacKendrick says we're all going back to Ladyhurst.'

'We are?' said Stewart.

'Yes,' confirmed Billy. 'I'm afraid there's been a bit of an accident.'

One floor below, the scene was under examination. On the rug in front of the counter lay the principal exhibit: a little blue handbag, from which the contents had fallen as its owner began her descent. Nora and Jack peered at these items over the shoulders of Book and Bliss, who were hunkered down like a pair of bomb disposal experts trying to decide which wire to cut.

'Melancholy, isn't it?' said Book. 'Evidence of a little life, spilled on the floor.'

They noted a compact; a few copper coins; a cheap lipstick from Boots the Chemists; a handkerchief, tied with a piece of string like a *bouquet garni*, to gather up some loose collection of small objects; a tiny stapled booklet formed from sheets of tissue paper, each one bearing a photograph of Stewart Howard's face.

'What are these?' asked Bliss.

'You kiss your excess lipstick onto your favourite star,' said Book. He indicated the bundled handkerchief. 'This interests me. May I?' Bliss nodded his assent. Book pulled a pair of tweezers and a pencil from his pocket, teased open the string and lifted the edges of the linen to reveal the contents. Four chocolates. Handmade, globe-shaped, with those secret squiggles that told the initiated what lay inside their shells.

'Very carefully wrapped,' he breathed. 'Tenderly, I would say.'

'They're still on the ration,' said Jack, remembering the sad day in 1941 when Cadbury ceased production of the Dairy Milk bar.

'They look expensive,' said Book. 'But there are only coppers in this purse. Trottie? Did they have money, these girls?'

'Very little,' said Trottie, quietly.

'So they didn't buy them. I haven't noticed the production providing fancy confectionery.'

'No,' said Nora. 'The fans bring stuff like that. Letters and presents. Sad little things they've knitted. Homemade biscuits all done up with ribbons. Billy hands them on to them. I saw him with a box of chocolates earlier on. Big heart-shaped thing. If I was him, I'd have eaten a few myself.'

'Billy brings his own sweets,' said Book. 'He keeps them in a little pouch on his belt.' He nudged one of the chocolates with his tweezers and examined it through a magnifying glass.

'Ah,' he said. 'Puncture marks.'

He rose carefully to his feet. Bliss, Nora and Jack moved with him.

'Barbara was breathless, yes, Trottie?'

'Yes,' she said. 'And twitchy.'

Book's eyes flashed with horror.

'Strychnine!' he exclaimed.

Stewart Howard and Sandra Dare were accustomed to deferent knocks from visitors and were in the habit of turning them away. A tall man with a loud voice, tearing open the door, pointing a finger and bellowing into the room was a novelty for them both. He had brought an entourage with him: the dark-eyed girl from the Turkish restaurant, the wiry young man with keen blue eyes who had turned up on the lane before the break, and a small plainclothes policeman entirely given away by the cut of his raincoat.

'Put that down!' yelled Book. 'It's poisoned!'

Stewart had a little orb of chocolate between his thumb and forefinger.

'Don't be absurd,' he said. 'They're by Royal Appointment.'

'I'm afraid it's true, sir,' said Bliss.

Stewart realised that this was not a strange kind of joke. He dropped the chocolate like a hot coal. It rolled across the bare floor. Sandra recoiled, upturning a pot of face powder.

'You didn't have any, did you, Miss Dare?' asked Bliss.

She shook her head. Her hands were shaking too, as she screwed the lid back on the pot of powder.

'What about you, Mr Howard?' asked Bliss.

'No,' said Stewart, rubbing his fingers on his trouser leg.

'Good,' said Bliss.

Book picked up the chocolate box and examined it like a dealer assessing the provenance of a rare antique. It was an object that reminded them all of better times, and how distant they still seemed, when peacetime chocolate came in plain and pleasureless slabs. The purple velvet shivered against Book's fingers. Even the crinkle of the black lining paper triggered a sensation of nostalgia. The underside of the lid bore the impression of some rectangular object. A card? A label?

Six of the chocolates, he noticed, were missing.

'Have you received chocolates like this before, Miss Dare?' he asked.

'Yes, of course,' replied Sandra. 'My fans know they're my favourites.'

'And they can afford them?'

'They're not all penniless shopgirls,' said Sandra.

'There's a valve king who sends some on the third of every month,' said Stewart. 'Fortunately, I'm not the jealous type.'

Book sucked his teeth. 'It seems reasonable to assume, then, that you were the intended victim.'

'Intended victim?' exclaimed Sandra. 'What does he mean, *intended* victim?'

'We're investigating the death of Barbara Markham,' explained Bliss. 'The chocolates missing from this box were in her bag. Well, all but one.'

Sandra absorbed this dread intelligence. 'My God,' she breathed. 'I've been sent some strange things in my time. Macramé. Fig jam. A sepulchral urn, filled. But poison! Why would anyone want to kill me?'

'Billy,' asked Book, 'who gave you this box of chocolates?'

Billy had his hands buried in the pockets of his mustard-coloured trousers. 'Nobody. They were just with the usual mail. I always deal with it.'

'So anyone could have got at them?'

The boy nodded. 'And Barbara and her friend presumably did,' reflected Bliss.

Some kind of elastic seemed to snap inside Stewart. 'Jesus Christ, Billy,' he growled, twisting his fist against the palm of his hand. 'We might both have been killed. What were you thinking of?'

'Sorry, Mr Howard,' said Billy. 'But you said to bring everything that comes in.' His tone was ambiguous. He sounded abject. He also seemed ready to assign the ultimate blame to his employer.

'Don't answer me back!' snapped Stewart. 'I think I need to find myself a new assistant.' He moved towards Sandra and wrapped her up in his arms. She was grateful for the gesture. They were no longer film stars, performing their elegance in public. They were two frightened people.

'I'm sorry to ask such a brutal question, Miss Dare,' said Bliss, 'but do you have any idea who might want to kill you?'

Sandra could not answer the question. She shook her head. Tears pooled in her eyes. She drew herself close to Stewart. 'I'm so terribly sorry, Inspector,' she said. 'This is simply more than I can bear.'

'Can't this wait?' asked Stewart.

'Of course,' concurred Bliss. Book nodded in agreement, though, as he departed, the box of chocolates went with him.

The circus was leaving Archangel Lane. Lamps and cables were hauled away; costumes shunted on rails. The extras formed a line outside the junk shop: some were handed their fee in small brown envelopes, others told to await the bus that would take them back to Ladyhurst. Billy sat outside the Istanbul restaurant, reading his clipboard and playing idly with a box of Swan Vestas. From the window of Book's study, Stewart watched the production mobilise, and smoked the last of his cigarettes. Sandra, having dried her tears and fixed her mascara, read over the script, committing the evening's speech to memory. The schedule was tight. Money was tight. A long evening at Ladyhurst awaited her.

In the shop below, Jack told Nora about the oppressive features of Norfolk. The land. The sky. The sea. Miss Belborough's mole.

'How's business been while I was away?' he asked.

'Booming,' she said, indicating a pile of fresh orange Penguin novels.

'*Goodbye to Berlin*. All the Stewart Howard fans are mad for it.'

'In the film version, is he?'

'That's what I'm telling them.'

'And you must be making something from the film people. How much are they paying?'

'Twenty guineas,' said Trottie.

'Per week?' asked Jack.

'Per diem,' said Trottie. 'For ten diems.'

An immaculate Lagonda drew up outside the shop, a uniformed chauffeur at the wheel. Stewart and Sandra descended to meet it, passing through the bookshop on their way. Stewart thanked Jack and Nora for their forbearance and promised them tickets to the premiere of *Lovelorn in London*. His fiancée, hidden under headscarf and shades, ignored them and sailed out into the lane.

Sandra found Book on the doorstep, thinking quietly about murder. She broached the subject herself; expressed her sorrow at the death of Barbara Markham.

'And you're filming again tonight, I hear?'

'Can't leave those cameras idling, Mr Book.'

The chauffeur, noticing her presence, stepped out of the car and opened the passenger seat. Sandra settled herself inside.

'What about the people in front of them, Miss Dare?' asked Book. 'They might appreciate a few idle hours.'

'Not if they're paying for them,' she said. 'Anyway, it's not the most ghastly part of the job.'

'Oh?' said Book.

'Have you met Miss Bean?' asked Sandra. 'She's a phenomenon of the business. Arrived in the early days. Like that plague of locusts in the Book of Exodus.'

Book followed her gaze. Nerina Bean was approaching like a small tornado in a fox-fur wrap. Sandra marshalled the appearance of graciousness. 'Is it time for our *tête-à-tête*, Nerina?'

'*Picture Review* has loved you all its life, Sandra,' said Nerina. 'We'll always make time for you.' Her little notebook was already in her hand. Perhaps it was never out of it.

'Well,' said Sandra, 'if you'd be so adorable as to climb inside, we could do our interview here.'

Book opened the passenger door on the other side. Nerina smiled her thanks as he withdrew. The car was now closed like a confessional.

Book found Stewart inside the shop, being importuned by Nora.

'Would you mind signing this?' she asked.

'It's a Christopher Isherwood book,' said Stewart. 'I didn't write *Goodbye to Berlin*. I'm not that sort of chap.'

'Doesn't matter,' said Nora, proffering a pen.

'I'm afraid Jesse and I are taking Miss Dare for an early dinner. Or a late lunch. To take her mind off things. If that's appropriate.'

'It's going to be a little later,' said Book. 'Miss Dare is giving an interview to *Picture Review*. She might need a bit of a stiffener afterwards. Where are you taking her, if I may ask? Wheeler's is rather good.'

'No. Camille's. On the Strand.'

'Oh. Excellent choice. And they're not sniffy if you turn up between services. Don't have the halibut, though.'

'Oh, why?'

'I don't think it's halibut.'

Nora grinned. She had now gathered an armful of Isherwoods, clean and bright and unfingermarked.

Nerina Bean had been in the game since before the pieces were carved. Her first paragraphs had described the habits of creatures as unknown to the present generation as the Corn Laws or Mother Bailey's Quieting Syrup. She had shared a lettuce leaf with Lya de Putti, who survived a plane crash but choked on a chicken bone. She had transcribed the last words of Nita Foy, who leaned on an electric radiator in a dressing room at Twickenham and went up like the torch of the Columbia lady. She had repelled the winter offensive of Syd Chaplin, whose spot of bother at Elstree had caused him to disappear into the background of his half-brother's movies. All forgotten. Pitch a story to *Picture Review* about any of these figures, and you might as well ask them to hold the front page for the discovery of a bed of fossil oysters.

When Sandra told the chauffeur to stretch his legs and find a cup of coffee, Nerina was pleased. 'Try the Istanbul,' she said, knowing that the service was slow, and Yusuf's unwitting assistance might yield a double-page spread.

'How delightful to see you, Nerina,' said Sandra. She smiled brilliantly. Politeness would be her Maginot Line.

'You know my motto,' purred Nerina. 'If you've nothing nice to say, come and sit by me. And here you are. Sitting by me.'

'But I do have something nice to say,' smiled Sandra, lowering her sunglasses. 'About *Lovelorn in London*. It's the first in a new three-picture distribution deal!'

'With whom?'

'J. Arthur, of course. Stewart and I have just signed. Isn't that marvellous?'

'Marvellous,' agreed Nerina. 'The sun never sets on the Rank empire.' Her sharp little pencil hit the paper. 'And you're shooting interiors at – ah – Ladyhurst, aren't you?' She smiled sweetly. 'Not exactly MGM, is it?'

'Well,' said Sandra, firmly. 'It'll do the job.'

'Still, you must know the old place like the back of your hand. Made plenty of pictures there in the past. Like that one where you played the simple crofter's daughter who married a duke.'

It was a leading question, but where was it leading? 'Yes,' Sandra confirmed.

'And the one where you played a simple fisherman's daughter who married a jute magnate.'

'Yes.'

'I always forget what jute is,' said Nerina.

'It's a kind of fibre,' said Sandra, tightly. 'People make bags with it.'

Nerina held eye contact with her subject. Her pencil was poised. 'What was the first film you made there, Sandra? At Ladyhurst?'

'I don't know,' said Sandra, drily. '*Springtime for Mary*, I think.'

'About the simple blacksmith's daughter who—'

'All right.'

'I think it was quite a bit before that, you know. Well, I can check the date later. Oddly enough, I've been offered the chance to see it again. That film. I love those old intertitles, don't you? *Came the dawn* and all that.'

'What film?' asked Sandra, losing her insouciance.

'Oh, Sandra . . .'

'But who has a print? That film is so—'

'*Old!*' howled Nerina. 'Yes! You know, I think *Picture Review* readers would be very surprised to learn that not all Sandra Dare's pictures were talking pictures. And that you used your real name in those days. You did the right thing there, darling. It would have looked terrible in lights.'

'Please don't say that name, Nerina.'

'Deirdre—'

'Yes,' interrupted Sandra. 'That one.'

A thought came to Nerina Bean. 'Maybe we could put you in a special feature on silent stars who survived the coming of sound.'

It was at this moment Sandra Dare recalled that the Maginot Line, despite comprising 1.5 million cubic metres of French concrete studded with gun turrets, was circumvented in a few days by a panzer incursion into Belgium. A different form of warfare was required.

'Perhaps you should concentrate on the present, Nerina,' she said. 'Do you know that someone is trying to kill me?'

Nerina blinked. Nerina swallowed. This was a story as big as a dirigible; the sort on which one might retire or dine out forever. 'I saw them taking that girl away,' she said. 'I assumed it was an accident.'

Sandra shook her head. 'Poisoned chocolates, meant for me. That poor, sad girl intercepted them. One moment full of wide-eyed excitement about the beguiling world of motion pictures, the next gasping her last on the carpet. How's that for an exclusive?'

Nerina worried that she might actually be salivating. 'So tragic,' she breathed. 'And what an angle!'

Sandra flashed her a look of admonition. It was as insincere as the apology it produced from Nerina, and both knew it. The star threw the hack a few more facts. She described the shape of the chocolate box, the texture of the paper, the moment when Stewart had, quite unsuspectingly, played the confectionery version of Russian roulette. Nerina's notebook grew dark with details. 'As for whodunnit,' said Sandra, 'you'll just have to use your skills to root out the truth. Just as you did when you broke the story about John McCallum popping the question to Googie Withers.'

The car door opened. Stewart had dragged the chauffeur out of the Istanbul restaurant and was inviting Nerina to conclude the interview.

'I was just leaving,' warbled Nerina, shimmying out from the back seat. 'Congratulations on the new contract, Stewart.'

He thanked her with genuine politeness. 'I hope you got what you needed.'

Nerina seemed almost shell-shocked. 'Sometimes, you know, I sit in dressing rooms, thinking: how am I going to squeeze good copy out of *that*? Not an anxiety I ever feel in the presence of your fiancée.'

The gleaming Lagonda drifted out of Archangel Lane. As soon as it had vanished, a rather less glamorous vehicle stuttered in to occupy the same space – the bus hired to take a cargo of background artists back to the set on the other side of the river. Most were loitering in front of the empty butcher's shop. Billy moved among them, asking them to extinguish their cigarettes and claim their seats.

The last to board was the craggy postman with the high-pitched voice. Stripped of his moustache and peak cap, he looked a small and unsensational being. Billy, standing in the aisle of the bus with his clipboard, told the driver to start the engine. The noise prevented him from hearing the conversation between the postman and Nerina Bean. Best that he did not know the details. Plenty of extras sold little stories to the press. Most of them were harmless. As for the rest, nobody paid him enough to worry about it.

If you were to look for Linda Bruce and Barbara Markham in the canon of British cinema, you would not find them on any credit roll, nor written up in the *Kinematograph Weekly*. And yet they are there. Both girls are present in the bandstand number in *Shilling Serenade* and the pickle factory prelude to *Old Ma Cabbage's Jungle Adventure*. The David Lean *Great Expectations* condemns them to the cutting-room floor, but they have a close-up each in the Sandra Dare and Stewart Howard vehicle *Phyllis I Vow to Thee*, which must be considered their most substantial work in the medium.

Unless, of course, we include their contributions to the letters pages of *Picture Review*.

> Dear *Picture Review*,
> You have asked your readers to name the most charismatic rising star on the British screen today. I have three suggestions. Peter Arne, who was so good as the young officer in *For Those in Peril*; Trevor Howard, whose small role in *The Way Ahead* drew the eye so strongly. But if you will excuse the pun, way ahead of both is Stewart Howard. He has one scene in *Moonlight Departure*, as the wicked young Resistance fighter who betrays Eric Portman. He positively blazes. There is more of him in *Blonde in the Navy*, as the surly rating who spills Sandra Dare's drink. I do hope his parts will get bigger and we will see him 'go off' in many more pictures.
>
> Linda Bruce, 6 Pollard Road, Hendon, NW9

Of all the British screen stars
The one I love the best
Is Mr Stewart Howard
He sure licks all the rest!
We saw him in the moonlight
As that young French vagabond.
We saw him in the navy
Tipping Horlicks on a blonde.

> I'd like to watch him rising
> Much higher on the bill.
> His talent is enormous
> So I'm very sure we will!
> *Barbara Markham (Miss), 23 Blondin Avenue, W5*

For Linda Bruce, those two letters, printed side by side in September 1944, were proof that she and Barbara had detected something shining in Stewart Howard long before Sandra Dare put his name above the title but below her own. They had seen his star quality in the curl of his lip as he stood with Eric Portman beside a hayrick, deep in Vichy territory.

Linda carried the clipping in her handbag everywhere she went. She had shown it to the WPC assigned to look after her after they carried Barbara's body from Archangel Lane. (Disappointingly, Constable Chivers had never heard of Stewart and preferred the Palais de Danse to the movies.) She showed it to Inspector Bliss when the WPC brought her into the back kitchen of the bookshop to go through the events of the morning. The conversation was painful, but the place was comforting, and far preferable to the hard space of Bow Street station. A friendly dog allowed her to stroke him, before padding back to his basket. Trottie made tea, put extra sugar in her cup, and returned the sixpence she had taken from her. The dark-eyed girl from behind the counter asked her if she wanted to exchange the copy of *Goodbye to Berlin* she had purchased the day before for a fresh copy that bore Stewart Howard's signature on the title page. Linda had started reading it on the way home to South Hendon. It had made her feel funny on the bus.

Although it turned on the same events, the conversation in the bookshop was different from the formal statement she had given earlier in the day. It was more like being at home with Dad, except the inspector with the moustache and the red-haired bookseller had asked questions and listened to her answers.

'So when you get something on the letters pages of *Picture Review*,' asked Bliss, 'they print your whole address?'

'If you ask them to,' said Linda. 'Makes it easier for like-minded folk to find each other.'

'Sandra Dare fans?'

'Some,' she replied, trying not to sound too sour. 'And the other big names too. There's a hairdresser I know who's potty on James Mason. But, you know, Stewart was our favourite. That's why we got jobs as extras.'

'To get close to him?' asked Book.

'Babs was so pleased to be on set. I thought, when she was sick, she was just excited. Breathless with it. She thought he'd looked at her, you see. Directly at her. Can you imagine how that made her feel?' She choked back a tear.

Trottie nodded sympathetically. 'You're doing very well, my dear,' she said. The concern in her voice was genuine, but she was also braced for questions about a certain roll of maroon and lily-green wallpaper.

Inspector Bliss had no desire to punish the girl, but he was obliged to do more than offer reassurance.

'So you admit to taking the chocolates, Miss Bruce?'

Linda's brow creased with remorse. 'I'm awfully sorry. We couldn't resist them. We just saw them there on a trolley in the bookshop. I mean. Come on. Chocs! It's been years. I can barely remember them.'

'And what did you do with the note?' asked Book.

'Note?'

He held up the lid of the chocolate box. The velvet contained the clear impression of a rectangular object. 'There was obviously an enclosure of some sort. There isn't now. What did you do with it?'

'I didn't see any note,' said Linda.

Book sniffed. 'Where was the trolley?'

'Over there,' said Linda, indicating the front of the shop. 'Near your dog's basket.' Book crossed the room and fell on his hands and knees.

'You opened the box,' he mused. 'Maybe the card fell out.' He could see nothing on the floor, or behind the bookshelf. Dog, he noticed, was looking up at him. 'Dog,' he said. 'If you weren't a dog, I'd say you looked a bit sheepish.' He snapped his fingers. Dog rose to his feet, a little resentfully. He knew that this was not an invitation to a walk. As he rose, he revealed the presence of a letter, slightly chewed, in the warm space of his basket. Book plucked it out, brushed off the canine hair and cast his eyes over it.

As he read, he called out to the back of the shop. 'Linda, do you have back issues? Of *Picture Review*, I mean.'

''Course! January '35 onwards.'

'Would you be so kind as to let us have them? A loan, you understand?'

''Course.'

Book stuffed the letter in his pocket and rejoined the group. He pulled up a chair and sat beside Linda as if they were both in the cheap seats at the Regal. 'What he's got, Linda? Stewart Howard. What makes him a star? Is it background and breeding?'

'Oh no,' said Linda. 'You don't need to be from money.'

'You're his biggest fan. You must know all the gen,' said Book. 'Who are his people?'

'He never says very much about them. So nobody bothers his mum, I suppose. He tells a funny story about a Hollywood studio wanting to sign him up and say his name was Carlos and he came from Guadalajara. But he's a London boy. He was born near the Peek Frean Factory, London Bridge way. He says the house always smelled of biscuits.'

'So he wasn't born into wealth, like Mr MacKendrick?'

'Oh no,' said Linda. 'I suppose it's easier for people like him. He didn't work his way up from tea boy.'

'And what about Sandra? People adore her, don't they? Didn't she once wake someone up from a coma?'

'He would've woken up anyway, probably,' said Linda.

'She's been so successful for so long. And she had a Hollywood period. Not many British stars get that.'

'Didn't work out for her, though. It was a flop, that film. They cast Vincent Price as her dad. She's older than he is.' Linda took a noisy mouthful of tea.

'She's been married before, though, hasn't she? I vaguely remember the pictures in the paper. Bald chap with a moustache. Rich.'

'Stinking rich,' said Linda. 'From tinned oranges.'

'And what happened to him?'

'He died,' said Linda. 'Quite quickly, I think. When they were in America.'

Book rose to his feet. 'Thank you, Miss Bruce,' he said. 'You've been very helpful.' Book was looking not at Linda, but at Inspector Bliss. It was a request for him to ask the WPC to escort the girl away. Bliss took the hint.

As the shop door closed, Book produced the letter in triumph. He cleared his throat.

'"Oh Stewart",' he read. '"Oh Stewart, my love. There's so much I want to say to you. From that moment on the submarine, I knew. Your look of concentration. Your strength."'

'*Ship of Shame*,' enthused Bliss. 'Good picture, that one. Very dramatic. Makes you think about what you'd do if you lost pressure and were idling on the seabed near Malta.' His review stopped suddenly. 'Hang on, where did you get that?'

'From the dog basket,' said Book.

'So the poisoned chocs were meant for him!' Bliss tore the letter from Book's hand and began to read. '"To the stars we strive, despite adversity. We were destined to love each other. We imagine we control our passions. But they direct us. They drive ordinary people to extraordinary actions."' He put the paper down. 'Like injecting strychnine into strawberry creams?'

Now Trottie took the letter. '"So, Stewart, my own best darling, I implore you not to try. Follow your heart. Break off your engagement. And we can be together. You and I, my sweetest boy. In life or in the cold, cold tomb of death. And if one proves impossible, I'll take the other – joyously."'

'That seems pretty clear,' said Bliss. 'If the writer can't have him, nobody will. So we're looking for a film fanatic?'

'Well,' said Book, 'that would be the obvious explanation.'

'The girls, do you think?' Bliss was gnawing at an idea.

'Kill their idol?' snorted Trottie.

'*I'll take the other – joyously*,' repeated Bliss. 'Maybe Linda brought the poisoned chocs and Barbara took them without her noticing.'

Trottie pulled a face. 'Where would she get the money? You saw what was in her handbag, Inspector. That cheap little lipstick.'

'All right,' said Bliss. 'What do we know about this movie lot? What do we know about Mr Stewart Howard?'

Book steepled his fingers. 'He's proof that smouldering Latin looks sometimes occur spontaneously in Bermondsey. He and Sandra, they've bound their careers together. The nation's sweethearts. But who knows the truth of it? He's an actor. And he's young and ruthless and rather over-rewarded and appears to be hopelessly in love with someone else.'

'Who?' asked Trottie.

'Himself,' said Book.

'Then there's the Honourable Jesse MacKendrick,' said Book. 'He lived in rooms on the lane last year. Just for a few weeks. Young toff. Slumming it for the summer. You remember him, Trottie?'

'Ran up and down here like a billy goat. Always pounding the streets in his plimsoles.'

'Where did he stay?' asked Bliss.

'He rented at Mrs Trickett's, so he can't be that fussy.'

'He left when it got cold,' said Book. 'Went straight back to Daddy's place. In Wiltshire, I think. I'm sure I looked it up. And then, we must assume, wrote his script about the private lives of the proletariat.'

'Good neighbour, was he?' asked Bliss.

Book shrugged. 'Didn't pay him much attention, to be honest.'

'He was obviously paying attention to you,' said Trottie. 'He gave his hero a bookshop. Stopped short of the specs and the beard, thankfully. Wallpaper didn't stir his interest quite so much. I'll try not to take it personally.'

'And Miss Dare?' asked Bliss. 'I remember her orange man. Italian national. That'll be why she went to the States. If they'd stayed he would've been interned as an enemy alien. I suppose they preferred the Californian sunshine to barbed wire at Ascot racecourse.'

'That makes me think better of her,' said Book. 'I thought she was just running away from the bombs.'

'What about Billy?' asked Trottie. 'He's a bit of a mystery. Disappears off into corners sometimes. He has sweets that he doesn't like to share.'

'Yes,' said Book. 'I've noticed that. Mind you, he probably has to take his pleasures when and where he can. While the job lasts. And you're right, Trottie, he is the odd one out here.'

'Why?' asked Bliss.

'We know absolutely nothing about him. But he's the man with the clipboard. Name a person on the production, from the biggest star to the humblest carpenter, and he knows where they are. He'll have booked the car that took Stewart and Sandra to dinner. He'll know that they're at Camille's in the Strand, and that Jesse MacKendrick is waiting for them. He'll know when Miss Dare is required back at the studios in Ladyhurst, and that the scenes Jesse has chosen to shoot this evening do not involve Mr Howard. Who will, presumably, find something else to occupy him tonight. So. I think I know what I need to do.'

'What?' asked Trottie.

'Take Jack to dinner. He needs feeding up, that boy. Where is he, by the way?'

'I'm here,' said Jack. He was standing in the doorway, holding a small green handbag that was a perfect match for Trottie's dress. His smile looked a little effortful.

'Thanks so much,' said Trottie, taking the bag from him. 'I hope it wasn't too difficult to find.' Jack shook his head.

'You're going out too then, dear?' said Book.

'Yes,' said Trottie. 'I have something Russian lined up.' She planted a kiss on his cheek and disappeared through the partition. Book moved to pull down the shutters of the shop, and would have done so, had he not seen one of his favourite customers through the window.

'I'm not too late, am I?' said Jean Goodwin. Her husband was following behind, sweaty and ill-tempered.

'What the devil's going on here?' he huffed. 'Bobbies swarming around like the ruddy Cup Final.'

'An accident, I'm afraid,' said Book.

Jean's brow furrowed. 'Nothing to do with Sandra Dare, I hope? I heard she was in the neighbourhood.'

Gerald let out a weary sigh. 'Oh, so that's why we're here!'

Jean winced but kept her gaze on Book. 'Always been a fan.'

Book waved his hand gently. 'Miss Dare is perfectly

sound, I'm happy to say. As for books – *The Scarlet Pimpernel* was the last one you took, wasn't it? I trust you enjoyed it.'

'Oh, very much,' Jean replied with a warm smile.

'And I promised you the sequel, didn't I?'

Gerald tapped his watch pointedly. 'I'm due at the golf club at a quarter to.'

Book put a hand to his temple. '*I Will Repay*! That's the sequel to *The Scarlet Pimpernel*.' He began burrowing into his stock.

Gerald Goodwin watched him with a bemused air. 'Got anything on how to cook? That's what she needs, what?' Jean flushed, looking down at her shoes.

Book located the novel and began looking for a paper bag. 'How are your feet, Mrs Goodwin?' he asked gently.

'Much better, thank you,' Jean murmured.

'I'll wait in the car,' said Gerald, sulkily.

'That'll be just a bob,' Book said, handing her the Orczy. 'And I popped another one in there. Compliments of the management. That's me.'

Jean's eyes widened slightly. 'What is it?'

'Just a little play. Ibsen. *A Doll's House*. Thought you might find it enlightening.'

CHAPTER THREE

Jack was quiet on the way to Camille's. His employer found himself talking to fill the silences. There had been several such moments in the months since Jack had moved into Archangel Lane. Book knew that they were harbingers of something painful; something that it was possible to put off but not avoid. When he imagined a moment of total frankness between them, a knot of fear moved in his gut. *Jack's not ready*, was his thought. Trottie said it, too. They said it to each other, and almost believed it. It was a matter of finding the right time. But the time never seemed to come. There was always too much to do; too many distractions; too much police work.

When Book pictured the moment of revelation, he imagined himself with Jack and Trottie, sitting by the stove in the back kitchen. Sometimes Jack was an image of forgiveness and generosity; sometimes he banged his fist, shouted and slammed the door behind him. The scene took place in some indeterminate future where everything had been cleared to one side. No bodies, no Bliss, no case to be cracked. How could he broach the subject now, on a day when a girl had dropped dead in Trottie's shop, and their lives were crowded with suspects? Barbara Markham's corpse was in the way. In some recess of his heart, Book knew the truth of his feelings: the obstruction suited him.

A bus halted on the street. The side bore an advertisement depicting Sandra in a silver evening gown, accepting, with radiant gratitude, a light from her fiancé. The ad, Book noted, was for a brand of cigarettes that neither actor smoked. Sandra and Stewart looked smoothly happy. A grey cloud of contentment wreathed their images.

'They smile a lot, don't they, these film stars?'

'It's their job,' said Jack. 'We sell books. They sell whatever that is.' The bus ground its gears and moved off.

'Why is Sandra marrying Stewart, do you think?' asked Book.

Jack's reply was quick. 'To show she's still here. To show she knows what the audience wants. Stewart Howard's just arrived at the top, hasn't he? And Sandra's been there for years. She can only stay there for so long.'

Book accepted the answer, and it made him sad. 'What a brutal business this is. It captures people in time. And then they change. And it mocks them for it.'

They found Stewart at a corner table of the restaurant and they found him alone. For this, Stewart blamed Camille, whose extravagant attentiveness had proved too much for Sandra. She had not cared for his reminiscences, his professions of loyalty, his weepy reflections on their mutual survival of the Blitz. She had taken strong exception to a long anecdote which placed her, Camille and Lew Stone's Novachord player drinking moonshine in an air-raid shelter at 3 a.m. She had cried off before the *hors d'oeuvres* had been brought to the table. Jesse had volunteered to motor her to Ladyhurst, where she planned to lie on her divan and learn her lines.

Stewart, hungry and unrequired, stayed put and surveyed the room. He received a glance from an acceptably attractive young woman who was dining with her mother. She looked again. Stewart wondered, with no special strength of feeling, what it would be like to go to bed with her. He imagined asking daughter and mother to fill the empty spaces at his table. Not because he felt any keen desire to have them there, but just to watch their reactions.

The arrival of Book and Jack halted these thoughts. They seemed to have been sent by fate to keep him out of trouble. Camille was also pleased: he did not even need to alter the order. Jack found that the bread on the table was good; so was the Bordeaux red. Book decided to get the difficult bit done first. After the initial pleasantries were over, he took the dog-bothered letter from his pocket and placed it on the table in front of Stewart. Stewart read it with an ashen face.

'You've no idea how draining it is, Mr Book. Gladhanding. Scribbling one's autograph. Failing to recognise someone whom you apparently met at a village fete ten years ago. And the smiling. Great God, the smiling.' He slid the letter back across the table. 'That madness is simply the next step. They can only love one so much. And there's only one way to go from there.'

Camille appeared, bringing his fastidious dicky-bowed presence and a cloud of adjectives to the arrival of *filet mignon*, green salad, *escalope de poulet, pommes sautées*. 'Miss Dare's favourite,' he twittered, 'was always the spring chicken.

But that was before the war, of course.' Book wondered whether the remark contained some cryptic unkindness.

As the staff receded, a curious incident occurred. Instead of his knife and fork, Stewart's hand went first to his spoon. The error was momentary, a tiny fumble. Its meaning, however, was all too clear to his companions.

'Well,' said Book, attacking his steak. 'A crazed fan is only the most obvious theory. But we don't like to be obvious, do we, Jack?'

Jack was thinking about Stewart's mistake. 'What? Oh. No. No we don't.'

'So,' said Book. 'If I might repurpose the inspector's earlier question, can you think of anyone who might want to kill you, Mr Howard?'

Stewart exhaled loudly. 'Take your ruddy pick, Book. There are quite a lot of angry ladies out there. Not to mention their husbands. Savile Row tailors. Producers. Directors. Writers. My ex-agent. My ex-ex-agent. Uncle Tom Cobley and all.'

'And what about prison?' asked Book.

Stewart stiffened. 'What?'

'What about somebody from prison?' Book peered at the letter again. 'This is an ambiguous hand. It's hard to say for certain if it's the work of a man or a woman.'

'Mr Book, I don't know why you think—'

'You were about to eat your dinner with your spoon,' said Book.

Jack moved in with a conspiratorial smile. 'It's a dead giveaway,' he said. 'And it takes one to know one.' Stewart grinned coyly. Much to his surprise, he found he was not at all offended. Instead, he felt an odd little thrill of pride. He and Jack, it seemed, were members of a secret brotherhood. They had once lived on bread and water. They had once not been trusted with knives. Now they were dining in a place with linen tablecloths and French menus and old boys in penguin suits who called them 'sir'.

'I was younger than you,' said Stewart, cutting carefully into his chicken. 'It was nothing too terrible. But I shouldn't like it to get into the popular press.'

'I should think not,' said Book.

Stewart looked carefully at Jack. His eyes; his hands moving his cutlery. 'What did they get you for?' he asked.

'I just went for a drive,' said Jack.

'Where?'

'Through a furrier's window in Mayfair. You?'

'Went to the bank to make a withdrawal.'

'With a stocking over your face?'

'I feel sorry for young lads today,' said Stewart. 'What are they supposed to do? Use gravy browning and draw a seam with a kohl pencil?'

They both laughed. Book felt a little left out; a little old.

'I'm a Bermondsey boy, Jack,' said Stewart. 'Rough as a sailor's arse. My lot lived in a tenement near the Pool of London. No shoes, no coal in the winter. Dad drank his cash and then beat us with his braces. But we were happy.'

'Were you?' asked Book.

'No,' said Stewart. 'We were absolutely bloody miserable. Prison was an improvement in some ways. Regular meals. Board games. And nobody was allowed braces. In case they hanged themselves, of course.' He drained the last of his wine. 'So, you think it could be something to do with that? With prison?'

Book shrugged. 'As you've indicated, it's a wide field.' He nodded to the waiter, who swooped in to refill everyone's glasses. 'I tell you what, though, why not take on young Jack here as your new factotum? No harm in having a strapping young fellow like him keeping an eye out. And if you're planning to give Billy the boot then you must be looking for a new assistant.'

'I've already got a job.' Jack frowned. 'In the bookshop.'

'Oh, I'm sure we can spare you for a few days, Jack. Nora can hold the fort.'

It would be wrong to say that Stewart looked enthusiastic about this plan, but he seemed unable to formulate a refusal. 'You know, Mr Book, you should all come to Ladyhurst. You could help us get the details right.' He leaned forward. 'And keep an eye on things.'

'We'd be delighted.' Book put down his knife and fork. 'Thank you for this. It's very generous.'

'I'm a film star,' said Stewart. He pushed his plate away. 'Do you want to go on somewhere else? It's still early. How about a Thames sunset and a Walsingham sour on the rocks?'

Book demurred. 'But you must go, Jack,' he said, with a hard imperative smile that indicated this was not an offer but an order. At least, Jack reflected, he knew he would not be paying for his own drinks.

An orange August evening embraced London. Book retreated from it. He walked alone along the Strand, turned left towards the river, disappeared down the stairs at Charing

Cross and boarded the first northbound train. At Baker Street he changed to the Metropolitan Line. He was heading for Wembley Park. He often headed for Wembley Park. He had never visited Wembley Park.

The line had new carriages. It was good to see something fresh in London; something that did not require a lick of paint or wooden supports. The carriage had a luggage rack, fluorescent lighting tubes running along the aisle, illuminated glass panels that told the passenger to push the button to open the door, and a man sitting alone in a bay of four transverse seats. He was in his mid-twenties, with dark eyes and neatly parted hair to which he had applied just enough Brylcreem to stop it falling into his eyes. Book settled opposite him. He gazed out of the window, keeping the dark-eyed man in his peripheral vision. Was he doing the same? The doors opened and closed at Finchley Road. The train was now fast to Wembley Park. It would rush through Kilburn, Willesden Green, Dollis Hill and Neasden. The possibilities of these twelve minutes of unbroken privacy were familiar to Book.

The train ran above ground on this part of the line, but the evening was dark enough for him to check the man's reflection in the window. He seemed to be looking in his direction. Book turned. The man locked eyes with him. Book's pulse raced. He thought of moving his mouth along the parting in the man's hair; tasting his Brylcreem.

It was at this point that Book saw the plainclothes police officer. He was, in truth, as obvious as Inspector Bliss, but Book had failed to notice him board at Finchley Road. Book froze. He stayed frozen through Kilburn, Willesden Green,

Dollis Hill and Neasden. He watched the sunset catch the windows on the backs of terraced houses. At Wembley Park he stood up and pushed the button. The doors rattled open. He stepped out on the platform. The dark-eyed man and the plainclothes policeman also got to their feet, but they did not leave the train. They were talking to each other, shaking their heads. As the train moved away, the plainclothes policeman stared straight at Book. The dark-eyed man was laughing.

He had only once been caught. It was before the war, in the Cave of Fancy, a basement bar in Fitzrovia with no alcohol licence and no effective lights. The working bulbs were all directed at the tiny cabaret stage, upon which the resident act, Miss Lanchester, would belt out the Victorian songs she sourced from the stacks of the British Library. 'Fiji Fanny', 'Please Sell No More Drink to My Father', 'If You Peek in My Gazebo'. On special nights she shared her avant-garde dance piece inspired by the work of the Austrian sexologist Krafft-Ebing, in which she portrayed Case 74b of Zurich, a Swiss nun engaged in an obsessive search for the foreskin of Jesus. That night she was howling. The troglodytes of the Cave sat in the gloom, kissing, applauding, sipping from blood-warm bottles of White's lemonade.

The police arrived before the foreskin was located. A low collective moan of dread went through the room. There were one or two truncheon blows, but most of the clientele came quietly. The drive to the station was short. Book remembered the other men huddled in the back of the Black Maria. A willowy clerk with a waistcoat and watch-chain, but no shirt. A nervous student. A docker.

The desk sergeant had not been kind. The pansies in his garden abhorred the shade, he said. But their sort seemed to like it. He had rounded on Book with unnecessary pleasure. 'Right, sir,' he leered. 'It is *sir*, is it? Let's find you on my list. Name. Occupation. Marital status.'

Book did not reply. He was ready to die of shame.

'Come on, sir,' said the sergeant. 'Don't be shy.'

'Engaged,' boomed a commanding voice. It did not belong to Book. It was the property of an imposing woman in a beret and red neckerchief, who stood with both her palms planted on the sergeant's desk.

Booked stared at her in total astonishment.

'Who are you?' asked the policeman.

'Medical Officer Strotford Perry,' declared the woman. 'Late of the Garibaldi Brigade. And I don't mean the biscuits. I can pull out shrapnel, I can strip a Tachanka in under two minutes and I once took a bullet south of the Ebro. Which I wouldn't recommend, even to you, Sergeant. And I never, ever leave a man behind.'

She indicated Book. 'Chap here. I'm getting married to him next Saturday and the Chief Constable's daughter is the one of the bridesmaids. So if I were you I'd just admit the error right away and cross him off your list. What say you?'

Book felt like something between a silent film heroine rescued from an encroaching saw blade and an umbrella retrieved from lost property. He did not complain. He held the woman's hand and remembered long-vanished days before the Great War, when they had gazed up at the vast grey skies from the window of the scarlet fever ward and plotted a daring escape.

'Saturday all right for you?' said Trottie, as they stood on the steps of the station. 'Forecast is good.'

'Quite all right, Trottie,' said Book.

'Well then. Kiss me.'

In the blue glow of the police-station lamp, he did.

Trottie was already in bed when Book returned from Wembley Park. He lit the small lamp by the counter, which was enough to allow him to find what he wanted – the most recent volume of the *Varsity Sporting Record*. He took off his shoes before he climbed the stairs to his study. It seemed cavernously empty. The smell of Sandra's powder and perfume was palpable. The events of the evening had unsettled him, but a little whisky did the trick. Almost. There was an item on which he wished to lay his hands, but it did not seem to be in its proper place on the shelf. He frowned, sank the drink, and went back to the landing, the *Varsity Sporting Record* in his hand. Trottie, he saw, had switched on her bedside lamp. She was not yet asleep. Book stepped softly into the room.

'Don't worry,' she said. 'You didn't wake me up.'

'How was your evening?'

'He killed himself at the end.'

'That bad?'

'I've never got to grips with Chekhov,' she said.

'Nor me,' said Book. 'But I like all the tea-drinking.' He put the *Varsity Sporting Record* on the eiderdown and began brushing his teeth. Trottie picked it up and flicked through it.

'I thought you were the sort who ran away from the ball,' she said.

Book cleared his throat. 'Football is all very well for rough girls but should not be played by delicate boys. Not my observation.'

'I know,' she said. 'You cleared your throat. You always clear your throat before you quote. Anyway, I have good reason to remember all the Oscar Wilde quotes.'

'Oh?' said Book.

'Particularly the one about the wallpaper.'

'I fear it's apocryphal,' said Book. He looked at himself in the mirror. 'Must be nice to have apocrypha.'

Trottie tapped the *Varsity Sporting Record*. 'What's your interest in this?'

'I was looking for Jesse MacKendrick, but there's no sign of him.'

'Gave up running for the movies, I suppose,' said Trottie.

Book gargled and spat in the little sink. 'We're invited to the studios tomorrow,' he said. 'Jack has a new job. As Stewart Howard's stand-in.'

'Just as well,' said Trottie, settling her head against the pillow. 'They'll try again, won't they? Whoever it is. Murder by chocolate having failed.'

Book was ready to get into bed. 'Budge over, then,' he said. As he negotiated the quilt he noticed a small blue box file on the bedside table. It was tied with soft cotton legal tape.

'Oh,' he said, 'so that's where you put it. I've been fretting about that. Since we moved all my stuff to accommodate the stars.'

'Then fret not, dear. And recall our Solemn Pact.'

Book unpicked the tape and lifted the flap on the file.

He checked the contents. Letters on blue paper, some airmail. Cabinet photographs. A battered pocket notebook. A cardboard ticket illustrated with a pair of *putti* flying around the words 'Cave of Fancy' in baroque letters. He looked at them wistfully.

'Where would I be without you?' he asked.

Trottie looked at him sleepily.

'I think we both know the answer to that, my love.'

It was time to put out the light.

The river terrace of the Walsingham Hotel offered some of the best views in London. The lights of the Thames barges; the tallowy disc of Big Ben, like the man in the moon come down too soon; Stewart Howard in profile, at the cocktail bar.

'Set 'em up, Barberini,' he said, lighting a cigarette.

'Your usual, sir?' The barman, an attractive Italian with a streak of grey in his glossy hair, was one of those hotel ghosts; so professional that he barely disrupted the surrounding atmosphere.

'Yes,' said Stewart. 'Actually no. I shan't be a creature of habit. I have a guest.'

'Evening,' said Jack.

'Good evening, sir,' whispered Barberini.

'I'll leave it to you,' said Stewart.

At the end of the bar, a young couple drank comets and shared a bowl of peanuts. The man was lobster-pink, sheeny, making some long and shifting point about government bulk-buying. 'It was necessary during the war, of course,' he said. 'But these Socialists won't stop. Eventually the whole system, built up for centuries by private firms, will be destroyed. And where does it leave the British farmer?' The young woman looked quite content to leave the British farmer exactly where he was, even if Clement Attlee was plotting to send him the way of the kulak: she was gazing across at Stewart as though he were the breakfast buffet.

'She's noticed you,' said Jack.

'They always notice me,' said Stewart. 'Girls. Doesn't mean anything. It's like when kids point at dogs on the street and say, "Dog".'

Barberini placed two ruby-red drinks on the bar.

'What's this?' asked Jack.

'Blood and sand,' said Stewart. 'Barberini's little joke about my profession.' He raised the glass at the barman. 'I spit in your milk!'

Jack took a sip. It was sweet and strong. 'You're getting married soon.'

Stewart nodded. 'You may have seen it in a column by Nerina Bean. But let me tell you this, Jack: I've never gone down on one knee to anyone.'

Jack decided to treat this as a fond joke. 'Sandra popped the question, did she?'

Stewart's expression was glacial. 'Most of the questions were from her business manager.'

'Oh,' said Jack, feeling far beyond home territory. 'You have an arrangement, then?'

Stewart gave a bitter laugh. 'I shouldn't drink so much, should I? Yes. An arrangement. But we all have those, don't we? You have one with Book. Book has one with Mrs Book. If we're talking about unusual marriages.'

Jack did not reject the idea. In fact, he wanted to hear more. 'Why do you say Book's marriage is unusual?'

Stewart took a first sip of his drink.

'You're like him,' he said. 'Book.'

'How?'

'Because you *read*. So go on. Read me.' Stewart turned on his bar stool to align himself with Jack. Was he supposed to put a hand on his head and feel his bumps? Jack locked his gaze with Stewart's and gave it his best shot.

'Well,' he began. 'You come here because you think this is the sort of place film stars go. It's always in the *Picture Review*, cluttered up with mink and diamonds. But you don't like it here. You hate it. And you hate that drink.'

Stewart pursed his lips. 'It's like a pudding from the war.' He put the glass down on the bar.

'So you're thinking,' continued Jack, 'why can't I be the chap I was – before I knew the camera loved me? Which is a terrible thing to know.' He drained the cocktail. There had been no sugar in prison. No orange juice. Certainly no cherry liqueur. He would enjoy it while he could. For a moment Stewart looked irritated, as if Jack were a parrot that had bitten him unexpectedly. Then he raised his glass.

'Absolutely right. It's not all it's cracked up to be. Being in the motion pictures.'

'I wouldn't mind a bit of it,' said Jack.

'Be careful what you wish for, son. I've got someone sending me poison. And even the bits that are supposed to be nice, you can lose your taste for those.' He pushed his drink away and asked Barberini for two sours. 'I was a bit stuck when I met Sandra. Typecast. Not officer material, they said. Always the problem kid. Sandra changed that. She pulled strings. Whispered in ears. And producers started to cast us as lovers. And we were lovers by then, of course.'

'Do you love her now?' asked Jack.

'When I don't hate her.' He lit another cigarette.

'But you want to be your own man?'

'Of course.' He sighed. 'But it's impossible, isn't it? We're a pair. Like Hope and Crosby. Fred and Ginger. Karloff and Lugosi.'

'It's all an act, then? You and her. The golden couple?'

'Film is for dreamers, Jack. When you sit there in the dark, there has to be space for *you* there. In that kiss. In those scenes in the moonlight. Standing by the rail of a ship. If you've just read in the fan mags that the screen lovers have broken off the engagement, and can't bear to be in a room together, then there's no space to dream.'

Barberini placed fresh drinks on the bar. They were not the last of the night. Jack was not used to such plenitude. Some of the details of the evening escaped him. He remembered Stewart walking him back through the lobby of the hotel and having a quiet conversation with the general manager, a serious man in little round spectacles. He remembered hugging Stewart goodnight. But did they walk through the revolving doors together? Or did Stewart return to the desk and book himself a room for the night? And was that the woman with the lobster-pink husband, waiting by a potted palm? It was hard to be sure.

Somehow, he found his way home to Archangel Lane. It took him several attempts to get the key in the lock, but he persevered. Dog, curled in his basket by the stove, did not look overly censorious. Perhaps this was why Jack felt able to sit by him in the armchair, while his head cleared. Perhaps this was why he found himself scrabbling in his pocket for a photograph and holding it up to Dog. It was a monochrome portrait of a young man, handsome, alert, with a sandy military moustache.

'See him?' said Jack. 'That's my dad. Only picture I've got of him. You know what?' Dog, it seemed, did not know what. 'I saw him somewhere else today. Does that surprise you? I saw him when I was sent upstairs to fetch a handbag. In Trottie's room, in a frame. A fancy silver frame.' He stuffed the photograph back in his pocket.

'My dad,' he whispered. 'My bloody dad.'

Trottie liked breakfast. She liked it best, however, at breakfast time, and did not consider 5.30 a.m. to fall within its ambit. She might have remained in bed, finding the cold spot with her feet, luxuriating and dozing, had she not detected that her husband was frying bacon on the stove in the back kitchen, and found her hunger in conflict with her torpor. She pulled on her dressing gown and followed the hot smoky smell downstairs, failing entirely to see Jack, already dressed and surprisingly fresh after four hours' sleep, standing on the landing above, watching her descend. Neither did she register him sneaking into her vacated bedroom.

The failures of observation were not all hers. As Jack made a quick study of her shelves, peered into her bedside drawer and rifled through the documents in a scratched tin box stowed on her dressing table, he did not notice a pair of eyes upon him. When he did, his heart skipped a beat.

'Not a word, mate,' he hissed.

Dog stared back at him from the door with a look that did not constitute agreement. Jack was holding a creased piece of paper in his hand. It was a marriage certificate. He read it. He read it again, calculating years and months. The dates matched. His heart pounded.

When he went down to the kitchen, Jack found himself unable to eat the eggs that Book had prepared for him.

'I had a bit of a night,' he said.

'Did Stewart?' asked Book, moving the eggs to his own plate.

'I'd put money on him still being asleep. He got proper hammered. What are the ingredients in a Walsingham sour?'

A car horn honked from the lane. Stewart Howard was parked outside in a pristine grey sports car. His eyes were hidden behind shades, but he appeared quite unhammered and unsour.

Jack opened the front door.

'Say, kid,' drawled Stewart, 'do you wanna be in pictures?'

Ladyhurst Studios, as any film nut will know, is a series of large grey faceless hangars built on a drained water meadow at the limits of south London. It is not Pinewood or Shepperton. Throughout the thirties, Hollywood used it to make pound-a-foot melodramas for the domestic British audience they were obliged by law to serve, and independents used it to make art or agreeable nonsense on a budget. During this time, the same uniformed commissionaire stood sentry at the main gate on Doggett Road. As the studio buildings had been erected on a site between the hospital and the greyhound track, Gerry Mayne spent much of his time directing people to the correct location for their X-ray or bunion removal. He was there as Stewart arrived with two men perched in the back of his car; men whom Gerry regarded as objects of suspicion.

'Not banned, though, are they?' said Stewart.

'We're not critics or gossip columnists,' Jack promised.

'We're antiquarian booksellers, do you see?' said Book, helpfully.

'We don't ban those, Gerry,' said Stewart. 'The movie is about one. Actually, it's about *this* one. And I know we're being extra vigilant. But they're with me and I can vouch for them.' He smiled one of his smiles.

The commissionaire lifted the barrier and waved them on. That little Petula Clark, he thought, had been at Ladyhurst the previous week. Even she was less cute and persuasive. Stewart motored through the checkpoint and into a parking space directly beside the sound stage. As he set the handbrake, he felt Book reach over and slip a piece of paper into his jacket pocket.

'What was that?'

'It's the address of Barbara Markham's parents.'

Stewart read the paper and nodded quietly. 'I'll go and see them.'

'No. There's the inquest first. Just write them a kind letter.'

'I will. Thanks, Book.' He tucked the paper back into his jacket and swung his legs from the car.

Lovelorn in London was preparing for another long day of work. Extras, some already in costume, had gathered by the tea urn. Billy Green was checking through pages of script. He said hello to Stewart, who, not wishing to seem unreasonable in front of his guests, treated the boy to a perfunctory greeting. They had reached the great barn door of the main sound stage.

'You boys,' said Stewart, 'are in for the biggest surprise of your lives.'

He pushed open the wicket gate. The studio beyond was as dark as a cave. Stewart jumped into the gloom and asked his friends to follow.

'Go on. It's better this way. More dramatic.'

Book and Jack shuffled into the space beyond the door. They heard a thud and brief electric twang as Stewart threw down the switch that flooded the sound stage with light.

They were on Archangel Lane. *An* Archangel Lane. One taken from life and reconstituted in plaster, wood and canvas. The Istanbul restaurant, Mr Quillian's tailor's shop, Harkup's old pharmacy, redressed as a fishmonger – these were present as painted images on a cyclorama suspended from the ceiling. The cobbles were entirely correct, though needed a lick of brown paint where white plaster of Paris had been exposed.

The bookshop itself was the outstanding marvel. Ladyhurst's Number 158 was grander, wider, larger. It had no ceilings; its bookcases extended upwards until they stopped. It was, however, quite possible to walk through the front door and stand by the till, examine the papers on the glass-topped counter, and remove individual volumes from the shelves; except those that, on close inspection, turned out to be a row of disarticulated spines glued to a black piece of cardboard.

'It's amazing!' exclaimed Book, shaking his head in wonder. 'It's absurd. Ridiculous. A bizarre exaggeration of reality. But it is wonderful. What a thrillingly peculiar life you lead, Mr Howard.'

'It's an imitation of life,' said Stewart.

'Well,' said Book, peering at the furniture, 'that's certainly an imitation of my armchair. And Dog's basket!'

'Is Dog cast yet?' asked Jack.

'Yeah,' said Stewart, 'but she's not much cop. No screen presence. Can you think of a good replacement?'

'I can,' said Jack.

Book ran his hands over the cash register. It was nicer than the one at home. He stabbed a button with a little flourish of his hand, causing the drawer to open with a noisy shudder. He was surprised to find it full of money.

'Scads of cash. Your Tony is a better bookseller than I.'

'Not real, though, is it?' said Jack.

'Fake,' said Stewart. 'Like everything here.'

They were no longer the only people on the studio floor. A group of technicians was bustling through the wicket gate. One began testing a battery of arc lamps.

'Well,' said Stewart. 'I'm glad you had a chance to look before the hordes arrive. Let's nip to the canteen and I can get you a cup of tea before we start. Lots to do today.' There was a gap between the cyclorama and the wall. Behind the painted version of the Istanbul restaurant was an unobtrusive door. 'We can cut through here,' said Stewart.

The door opened onto a stairwell. This, too, was sunk in

gloom. Again, Stewart found the switch. This time, however, there was no wonder to behold.

Sometimes, when confronted by the sudden sight of a corpse, the mind takes a moment to compute what it has been shown and comes up with a more pleasant alternative. A body is read as a bundle of clothes, or a waxwork, or a living person who has chosen an unconventional place to sleep. This case, however, was unambiguous.

The figure was smallish. It was lying face upwards on the stairs that led down to the basement. Its skull had clearly made a sudden and ferocious impact with the concrete: dark blood had collected around it, but not enough to drip from one step to the next. One hand stretched upwards, as if trying to reach for something on the landing above. Book noticed a series of inky smears on the palm; some aide-memoire, perhaps, smudged into illegibility. He also registered the clothes. A navy-blue postman's jacket with red piping on the cuffs and lapels. The most eye-catching feature of the corpse, however, was its luxuriant grey moustache.

'It's one of the extras,' said Jack.

'No,' said Book. 'I think not.'

He reached down and pinched the grey moustache between his thumb and forefinger. It peeled away like a sticky label.

The face beneath was unmistakable.

'Nerina Bean,' breathed Book. 'The Girl with the Poison Pen.'

CHAPTER FOUR

There was no popcorn, but there was a picture. From their red velvet seats, Book, Bliss and Jack watched the scene unfold.

The screen showed a street in London. They would understand that from Tirana to Texas to Tierra del Fuego and think it a good fit with a view of England garnered from *Mrs. Miniver* and the lids of biscuit tins. It was busy. Rather busier than reality, where a peak-capped postman did not always have to dodge the butcher's bicycle to salute a nanny on the other side of the pavement. It was hard to tell whether the rest of the street was similarly full of people and incident: the shot was a tight one from the bay window of the bookshop.

'It was then that I knew,' said a voice from the screen. 'We had fallen in love over the pages of a book. But was that love strong enough to thrive, out in the teeming world?' The voice belonged to Billy Green. The face, however, was that of Sandra Dare, beautiful and pensive and fully inhabiting the consciousness of a widowed pâtissière in the throes of romance.

Until her expression changed, like someone snuffing out a candle.

'Could we try it without him reading in?' she asked. Madeleine's internal monologue was over; Sandra's eyeline was now thrown somewhere beyond the camera. 'I can do it to time, Jesse. I know it's in VO but I learned this bloody speech.'

'Absolutely, Sandra,' said the voice of an unseen Jesse MacKendrick.

Sandra looked no happier. 'I'm so sorry, Jesse. Could I beg ten minutes? A ciggie will sort me out.'

'Cut!' declared the director. The screen flared and shrieked. When it settled again, the camera was back in its first position. Billy Green was in the frame, the clapperboard in his hands.

'Scene forty-nine, take nine!' he yelled and scurried out of the shot.

'Action!' called Jesse.

The scene played out again, and postman hailed nanny in the endless time-trap of cinema.

The screening room at Ladyhurst Studios was cramped. When Book rose to his feet he was caught in the beam of the projector. The confected version of Archangel Lane moved over his body.

'Kill the sound, please,' he said.

The hiss of the speakers ceased. The clatter of the celluloid through the machine was faintly audible through the open door of the projection booth. It was a pleasant sound.

'The work of last night,' said Book. 'Captured on the set and printed fresh for the morning.'

'The rushes,' said Bliss, from the dark.

'I know,' said Book.

Bliss squinted at the screen. 'Can we stop the film and take a proper look?'

'No. It would burn in the projector. But I think the difference is pretty obvious, really. You'll see in just a moment.'

Take eight ran through the mechanism. Take nine followed. The black and white nanny smoothed her uniform, gazed into her empty pram and began to push it down Archangel Lane. The butcher's boy wheeled down the street, sticking out his legs.

'And here comes postie,' said Book, pointing at the screen.

The postman, bag on shoulder, envelope in hand, waved a hand in the air.

'Oh,' said Bliss. 'I see what you mean. He's lost six inches. Just while Sandra Dare went off for a gasper.'

'So. Between takes eight and nine, Nerina Bean gets her screen break. And an hour later – is that right?'

Bliss nodded. 'Certainly no more than two, Dr Calder says.'

'She's on the cutting-room floor. Well, the basement steps.'

Bliss was solemn. 'She hit them with tremendous force.' He had Dr Calder's typed report in his hands.

'But did she fall, Inspector, or was she pushed?'

The screen was now filled with Sandra Dare's close-up. Book looked like a tourist at Mount Rushmore.

'If only we could step through the screen,' he mused. 'Beyond a door behind that set is a flight of stairs, where I think Nerina Bean is already dead.'

The last of the film snickered through the projector.

Sandra Dare's face yielded to a bright white oblong. The projectionist brought back the house lights.

Jack had said nothing throughout the strange little movie show. As the lights went up, Book thought he saw him put something back in his pocket.

'I know who he is,' said Jack.

'Who?' asked Bliss.

'The postman. He was in the lane yesterday. He's here this morning. I saw him in the yard just now, having a sandwich. Should I go and fetch him?'

Jack delivered him faster than any telegram. The postman's scenes having been completed, he was dressed in more conventional street clothes and his face was unencumbered by a grey caterpillar of false hair.

'This is our postman,' announced Jack. 'Mr Burt Masterson.'

'*Kurt* Masterson,' he corrected. The name suggested the boxing ring, the saloon bar brawl, the reeling-in of 12-foot marlins. The voice did not.

'Normally I do landlords.' He curled his lip with a suddenness that made Book wonder if he was having a stroke. '*I've seen a glass pushed in a bloke's face and I've laughed, see?*' He made a noise in his throat that he considered rich with Cockney cynicism.

'Very good,' said Book. 'Robert Newton should watch his back. But you're not auditioning now. We're investigating the unfortunate death that occurred here last night. The second one on this production, in fact, after Miss Barbara Markham. And two looks like carelessness. Whose, though?'

Kurt Masterson was not laughing. 'You the police?'

'Inspector Bliss is the police. I'm just helping them.'
'With their enquiries?'
'With the fiddly bits.'
Bliss smiled magnanimously.
'Now,' began Book. 'Kurt Masterson. Not your real name, I take it?'
He seemed genuinely surprised. 'How did you know?'
Book ignored the question. 'You went home early last night. Why?'
'Well,' said Kurt Masterson, 'I was made an offer I couldn't refuse, wasn't I? I knew the lady. Nerina Bean. I read her column, always do. She gave me a fiver. Just to borrow the uniform, mind. Said she would go on for me and no one would clock it.'
'And why,' asked Book, 'did she want to pose as you?'
Kurt looked at the floor. 'She said she was writing a story. "The poisonous secret at the heart of *Loveless in London.*"'
'*Lovelorn,*' corrected Bliss.
'If you say so. They'll change it. Too negative, isn't it?'
'What was she up to?' asked Book.
'She wasn't specific, but she said she needed one last bit of proof. I didn't think it would do no harm. I was barely in the shot. She did it once before, you know. Dupont banned her from his set and she sneaked back on disguised as a rabbi. That was before my time. But I remember the lovely write-up she did in *Picture Review.*'
'Sell a lot of stories to the press, do you, Mr Masterson? About actors here?'
'No!' he protested. 'Well. Nothing nasty. Just whether someone likes mink or feathers. Where they drink.'

'Or how much?' asked Book. A note of disgust had crept into his voice. He took Dr Calder's report from Bliss and began to read it. Kurt Masterson no longer seemed to hold his interest.

'All right, thank you,' said Bliss. 'We'll come and take a statement later.'

Kurt Masterson seemed disappointed. 'That it?'

'That's it,' said Bliss, getting up to open the door.

'I was a red herring before, once,' said Kurt Masterson, wistfully. 'Arthur Wontner tapped his pipe and looked beady at me, but I never done it. I was just in the wrong place at the wrong time.'

'Thank you,' said Bliss, closing the door firmly.

Book had his eyes on the official description of Nerina's injuries. He read the names of vertebrae and cranial bones.

'Why was she here?' he mused. 'Why go to the trouble of bribing him and dressing up in his costume?'

'The extra security. She couldn't just hang around like in the lane, could she? So I suppose she needed a disguise. As that chap said, she'd got form in the area. And the title of that article is suggestive. Maybe she was on to the poisoner – and the poisoner knew it?'

Book returned to the report. A section at the bottom of the page was not typewritten but rendered in Dr Calder's own hand. 'These ink marks on Miss Bean's right palm. They were from something she was holding. Evidently she was sweating a lot from the exertion of the stairs and the heavy costume. They're reversed, of course, but if you unreverse them, you get this.'

He held up the paper. Bliss read the broken fragment of two words.

'... *ty Wins*.'

'What do you think, Jack?' asked Book. Jack had said nothing since bringing Kurt Masterson into the room.

Jack pursed his lips. 'I think I need to get back to work,' he said, getting to his feet. 'I'm standing in for Stewart.'

'It's not a proper trade, you know,' Book teased.

'Yeah,' said Jack. 'Like being a part-time detective.'

The door closed behind him. Bliss blinked, unsure how to read the moment.

'He's an orphan,' said Book, forcing a smile. 'Now. Shall we question some suspects?'

Linda Bruce was as good as her word. She arrived at nine o'clock, in a taxi from South Hendon, bearing a suitcase loaded with ten years of *Picture Review* back numbers. (When Stewart Howard was on the cover, she explained, she bought two copies.) Nora heaved them from the car and set them down on the carpet in Trottie's shop. Linda sat with Dog in the back kitchen.

'Make yourself a cup of tea,' said Nora. 'Give us a shout if the bell goes.'

The archaeology began.

The work of Nerina Bean, they discovered, ran through the publication like a seam of graphite. Her byline picture never quite kept up with her age, but the pose was always the same – sitting on a cinema seat with a notebook in her hand. In early numbers, her column came with a testimonial from Rebecca West: 'Miss Bean writes, not so much badly as barbarously, as if she had never read anything but a magazine, never seen a picture but a moving one, never heard any music except at restaurants. Yet she is full of talent.'

The cast and crew of *Lovelorn in London* could also be tracked through its pages. They noted Jesse's fast and recent emergence as a serious British talent, usually pictured holding a loop of film up to the light. The earliest photograph of Stewart – featuring Sandra Dare and a malted bedtime drink – got his name wrong in the caption. A month later he was a pull-out pin-up. The run did not go back far enough to mark the birth of Sandra's stardom. The first extant article was an interview with Nerina from 1935, when her magnitude was firmly established.

> *Miss Dare's dressing room at Elstree is not a wholly private space. I've heard it whispered that Mr Walter Mycroft – production chief of British International Pictures and proof that physical and professional stature are not the same thing – would prefer the traffic to be thinner. But I adore it this way. Miss Dare is a darling, a wit, a woman of the world. We sat among lilies and talked of Elinor Glyn and chocolate cake and sex.*

Nora and Trottie were more interested in stargazers than stars. *Picture Review* split its letters between the front matter and the back pages among the adverts for elocution lessons and rejuvenating cream. The rhythm of flicking between the two places soon became as reflexive as the act of shelling peas. Nora, accustomed to reading prose with a gunshot in every chapter, was not impressed.

'"In *Love Story*, Stewart Granger plays a molybdenum

prospector who is losing his sight. I noticed that in one of his scenes with Pat Roc, he raised his left eyebrow. Have any readers seen him raising the right?"' Nora rolled her eyes and pulled out another plum of banality. "'I think John Mills has lovely hair and his nails always look so neat."'

'Book thinks there's something here,' said Trottie, her eyes combing a series of questions about Phyllis Calvert's enthusiasm for eighteenth-century furniture. 'Clues.'

Nora flicked to the back of another issue. 'We like those,' she said. 'Trouble is,' she added, lowering her voice, 'all these people sound like psychopaths.'

'Any names coming up a lot? Regular correspondents?'

'Name and Address Supplied is a very reliable contributor: "I tried to give myself a mole like Margaret Lockwood but Mum says I look like a tart."'

'I've seen Barbara and Linda twice.'

Nora brightened. 'Writing about what?'

'Soviet experimental cinema,' said Trottie. She turned a page. 'Oh no, sorry, Stewart Howard's trousers.'

Nora was ready to mock again. Instead she frowned. 'Hang on. Here's one that comes up more than once. Saying nice things about Sandra Dare. Apparently, nobody can compete with her for looks, talent and sheer screen charisma.' She indicated the page. '*Basilisk*. That's a pen name, I suppose?'

'I went to boarding school,' said Trottie, 'and even we didn't have any Basilisks. Maybe Linda will know?' She called out her name. Linda appeared through the partition with a ginger biscuit in her hand, Dog following behind hopefully.

'Do you know a Basilisk?' asked Nora. 'Sandra Dare fan who writes in to *Picture Review*. A lot.'

Trottie had found another example. 'It says here she elevates the art of screen acting to new heights. Oh. But they're less keen on Stewart. "Mumbling shop boy" isn't very nice, is it?'

Linda bristled. And bristled more when Trottie found another letter from the same correspondent in a recent edition. '"The public's infatuation with Dare and Howard is beyond me. Miss Dare should be striking out alone. Of course, there is always difficulty when one reaches for the stars. But the difficulty as I see it is Stewart Howard."' She put down the magazine. 'Well, what a horrid Basilisk.'

'They obviously don't like Stew.' Linda shrugged. 'But you really think they might be the one who sent the chocolates?'

'I don't know,' said Trottie. 'Is it too much of a stretch to go from disliking a film star to lacing their sweets with strychnine?'

'Some of the discussions can get very heated,' said Linda. 'At the meet-ups. People have strong views.'

'Meet-ups?'

'Oh yes,' said Linda. 'We get together and have chats and that. Sometimes the studio sends a star down to open a fete or make a personal appearance. That's how I first met Barbara. At the Uxbridge Odeon to see Stewart get out of his car and wave. Some girl tried to rip the pockets off his trousers. He sews them up now.'

'But you never met a Basilisk?' asked Trottie.

Linda wrinkled her nose. 'How would I know if they never used their real name?'

The magazines were spread across the floor. Linda began to gather them up, inspecting each one for wear and tear.

There was only one lift at Ladyhurst Studios, and that was for props. Sandra Dare was not the first star to swallow her pride and trudge upwards to dressing rooms in a long corridor high above the sound stage. Gloria Swanson, it was said, had persuaded the management to convert a section of the ground floor scenery store into a place to learn her lines and drink champagne, recumbent. But the film had been a horrible flop – made as a prestige production, sold as a B-picture – and the space had been returned to its former use. The story was now a warning to those who thought themselves too famous to use the stairs.

Sandra did not appreciate the climb, but she was a pragmatist. *Lovelorn in London* did not require a large cast. She enjoyed the quiet at the top of the building. She could lie on her divan in her yellow silk kimono, undisturbed by the chatter of chorines. Undisturbed by anything but her own thoughts.

'It's me.' Stewart was outside the door. Sandra thought about not letting him in, then relented.

'She's dead?' she asked. 'You saw her?'

'She was on the stairs. Like a broken doll.'

Sandra slipped another cigarette into her mouth. 'How awful. I mean, *she* was awful too. But still. How awful.'

Her hands were shaking. The lighter sparked uselessly. Stewart interceded. The flame rose and she inhaled gratefully.

Stewart took her hand. It was a tender gesture and it was appreciated.

'If it was murder,' said Sandra, 'there'll be a lot of suspects.'

'Half the British film business.'

'All of it.'

'It's true. Everyone hated her. You hated her.'

Sandra could not contradict him, so she changed the subject. 'What did you do last night?'

'Had a drink with that boy. Nice kid. Went to bed early. Did some film-star duties.' He could tell she was not listening. 'You know, answering fan questions. What's your ideal night out? What do you like for breakfast?' He had, he reflected, answered them all, while her husband lounged in the smoking room, listing things he didn't like about Clement Attlee. He might have worried that Sandra would detect his innuendo and punish him for it, were she not, in her own way, as oblivious as the lobster-pink husband with the unhappy bride.

'And you were just shooting here?' he asked.

'Take after take, Stew. Simple stuff, really, but . . .' She was looking at her reflection in the dressing-room mirror. One bulb, Stewart noticed, was missing.

'I met a man once,' she said. 'At the White House, would you believe? Roosevelt had a party. So much dazzle. So much light. All those boys in white naval uniforms.'

'That's who this chap was? A sailor?'

'No, darling. He was an old bird with hair like a Brillo pad. An astronomer. He knew about stars. The real ones, I mean. Did you know that the stars we see in the sky aren't really there? Most of them, anyway. The light takes so long to reach us that they're just echoes. But some of these stars don't go quietly. Towards the end they get bigger. Bigger, Stew. They give out more and more light and heat till nothing can eclipse them. Nothing.'

She smiled wolfishly. 'It takes so much effort just to stand still these days. And I don't want to stand still, Stew. I want to move fast. To explode. Light up the town. Like I used to.'

Sandra thought of the cameras and the studio lamps, of her multiplied image, fixed on a strip of celluloid, struck by the beam of the projector and thrown, enormously, upon the screen. She thought of her body converted into light, its brightness outlasting the world.

At first, Book had been charmed by the film studio version of his home. Now, he felt mocked by it: its bigness, its crudeness, its foolish illogic. He looked at the shelves in the shop – Tony's shop – and wanted to tear them down. He looked at the absurd Dickensian bullseyes in the windows and felt like kicking them through. Billy's copy of the script for *Lovelorn in London* was open on the counter. He picked it up and read. It pleased him more than the ill-tempered conversation in the room.

Book and Bliss had walked into the shop unannounced and found the clapper boy sitting in Jesse's folding canvas chair. He held a matchbox in his hand and was scratching something against the rough little strip on its side. It was a needle.

'Got to keep them sharp, haven't I?' he said. 'These things are expensive.' Bliss had never seen a diabetic's kit before.

Billy unrolled the little pouch and showed him the glass phial, the syringe, his store of barley sugars.

'Everyone knows I have this, Inspector, it's not a secret.'

'So nobody round here would have batted an eyelid to see you with a syringe. Or a box of chocolates for Miss Dare.'

Billy's cool evaporated. 'Why the hell would I have wanted to poison Sandra Dare?'

'Well, that's just the thing, Sonny Jim,' said Bliss. 'Miss Dare was not the target. They were after her fiancé. Which puts a rather different complexion on things, eh? Particularly with Mr Howard threatening to fire you.'

'Yes. But not till after the business with the chocolates.'

'He treated you badly, though, didn't he?' pushed Bliss. 'Belittled you? Insulted you?'

'You need to develop a thick skin in this business, Inspector. I've dealt with bigger egos than Stewart Howard. If I'd wanted to get my own back I'd have pissed in his tea, not poisoned his chocolates.'

Bliss stifled a chuckle. He liked this boy. 'You can account for your movements last night?'

'We shot right through.'

'No tea breaks?'

'Yes of course we had tea breaks.'

'So, theoretically, you could have pushed Nerina Bean down that stairwell?'

'Yeah,' said Billy. 'And theoretically I could have won the pools and rung up Veronica Lake for a date. But I didn't.'

Book looked up from the script. He betrayed no sign of having kept an ear on Billy's interrogation. 'What's this?' he asked, waggling the document.

'Tomorrow's pink page,' said Billy. Book and Bliss looked blank. 'Mr MacKendrick's rewrite of scene thirty-four. Just a little one. But in this business, the details matter. You don't want actors bumping into the furniture.'

Bliss smiled broadly. 'I'm a details man too.'

He passed the page of script to Bliss. 'I'm terrible at the pictures,' said the inspector, running his eyes over the paper. 'I always know whodunnit straight off. Irritates the marrow out of Mrs Bliss.' Book looked as if he might say something disobliging.

'Why not take her to a western?' asked Billy.

'And watch all those cowboys getting shot in the chest and falling forwards? I don't think so.'

'Do you ever go home, Billy?' asked Book.

'If I try hard, Mr Book, I can remember the daylight. Can I go now?' Billy held his hand out for his diabetes kit.

'We'll have to get this tested,' said Bliss.

'For insulin?'

'For strychnine, lad.'

Jesse MacKendrick was a more co-operative witness. He did not even seem to realise that he was being questioned. He demonstrated the soundproofed door between the studio floor and the staircase, establishing to everyone's satisfaction that nobody on set would have heard Nerina Bean scream, had screaming been Nerina Bean's thing. He described his curtailed dinner at Camille's with Stewart and Sandra, and the unwelcome familiarity of the maître d'. (Having eaten Jesse's steak, Book could vouch for the accuracy of this account.) He put times on the tea breaks during the evening shoot, the first of which, he said, had allowed him to go to his desk and make a small alteration to scene thirty-four.

Bliss nodded. 'A pink page.'

'Yes,' said Jesse. 'You can check with my secretary.'

They had reached the part of the concrete staircase where Nerina had met her end. All three avoided putting a foot on the actual step that had broken her skull. Jesse listed the functions of the rooms on each floor above them — dressing rooms at the top, wardrobe, offices.

'What's down below?' asked Book.

'Film vault,' said Jesse. 'Nice place if you like asbestos.'

'The treasures of British cinema,' said Book.

Jesse produced a short, humourless sound. 'Not really.'

'Oh? What then?'

Jesse leaned on the railing. 'Well, a film opens in Leicester Square. Then it goes across the country. Then to the second-run houses and the fleapits. And when it's so scratched that every scene looks like it's happening in Antarctica, it comes here. Back home. And it's taken up to the tank on the roof, where it's put out of its misery. Gets dissolved in sodium hypochlorite.'

A demonstration became inevitable. Jesse bounded up the stairs. Perhaps he had forgotten his own athleticism. Perhaps he had remembered it and was using it to punish Book and Bliss; to remind them that he was twenty-two and directing a feature film, and they were a pair of middle-aged men scuffed and battered by war. When they reached the top, he threw open a hatch to the roof and invited them upwards into the sunshine.

The flat summit of the sound stage was like a wide grey

netball court suspended above south London. Its bitumen surface felt pliable in the rising heat of the day. Book and Bliss saw the light shining on the Kentish hills, the red brick lines of Lewisham, the Eiffel height of the Crystal Palace transmitter. In one corner of the space was a metal tank about the size of a bathtub. Its lip was fixed with a mount intended to hold a spool of 35mm film as it was paid through a chemical solution. A tap protruding from the side allowed the tank to be drained. Beside this apparatus was a tea chest piled with empty film cans.

'Why up here?' asked Book.

Jesse rattled the handle of the mechanism. 'The fumes, Mr Book, the fumes. This is where it happens. In goes some old tat starring a terrible provincial comic. And out comes something useful. Waterproof paint. And silver halide.'

Book let out a soft laugh. 'What an odd little cottage industry.'

'It's valuable,' said Jesse. 'More valuable than what's on the films.'

Bliss reached into the tea chest, picked up a dented film can and read the label. *Jack Spratt's Parrot Gets His Own Back.* 'Seems like a lot of effort to go to,' he said.

'Oh, it's a simple process. The chemical solution does the work.'

'No, I mean making a motion picture. The stars and the lights and shooting all the scenes, and then just melting it down for scrap?' Bliss returned the can to its place. More titles were visible. Most were baffling. *How Pimple Saved Kissing Cup. Dr Trimball's Verdict. Mary Find the Gold.*

'British cinema is mainly stupid, Inspector,' said Jesse. 'It's never been *about* anything. That needs to change. And when it does, I'll make movies that won't end up here.'

Something noisy was happening on the stairs. A huffing, clattering presence resolved itself into a portly police constable, his blue serge uniform damp with sweat. A drama, he reported, was unfolding on Lewisham High Street and Inspector Bliss had been cast as the leading man. 'Smash-and-grab,' gulped the constable. 'Tray of wedding rings missing, lead cosh left behind.' A B-picture business, Bliss reflected, but a job was a job, and he was firmly under contract.

As he descended the stairs, he called back to Book: 'Keep an eye on the beautiful people for me, would you?'

'They are beautiful,' replied Book. 'But what else are they?'

He turned to Jesse MacKendrick. 'I'm so enjoying this tour, Mr MacKendrick. I wonder if I might take a look at the dressing rooms? I've always wanted to see those mirrors with the light bulbs round them.'

'They're really not very exciting,' said Jesse.

'It's just the thought of sitting in the chair and thinking: *Cicely Courtneidge parked herself here*. Indulge me.'

'Indulge yourself,' said Jesse, with a bemused smile. 'I have a film to shoot.'

The cement yard outside the sound stage was as hot as California. The chief electrician had opened the barn door to let air flow into the studio. Now he leaned on the brickwork, mopped his brow and reminisced about the quota quickie days when one picture rolled in the day and one shot through the night, and the space was thick with the smell of sweat and beer and orange peel. Sandra, meanwhile, had created a little oasis of canvas chairs and folding tables, where she presided, Cleopatra-like, her eyes shaded expensively. Jesse was giving her notes. Stewart, also hidden beneath dark glasses, turned his face to the sun. The background artists knew their place. When Book gazed in their direction, only Kurt Masterson – hurt and glowering – seemed to be in focus.

As Bliss and his constable crossed the yard towards their car, several heads turned. For a brief moment, the make-up woman assumed these were new faces to add to her list. Stewart also watched their progress. A police uniform always drew his eye. As the black Wolseley drove away, he also spotted Book. Stewart rose from his chair and stalked towards him.

'Solved it already?' he asked.

'No,' said Book. 'The inspector's off on a 999 call. A clobbered shopkeeper needs his attention.'

'It's all down to you, then?'

'For the moment,' said Book. 'So maybe you could tell me what you were doing last night? If that doesn't seem impertinent.'

Stewart played the game. 'Oh, after drinks with your Jack, I went to bed early. But I couldn't get off. I spent a lot of time staring at the ceiling. Contemplating mortality, as you might imagine.'

'Any witnesses?' asked Book. 'Sorry to sound so official.'

'Of course not!' he scoffed. 'I'm an engaged man.'

'I had heard something of the kind. I read it in *Picture*

Review. And again, I'm awfully sorry to use this sort of language, but was she – ah – *blackmailing* you? Nerina Bean, I mean.'

Stewart shook his head. 'About prison? I don't think she ever got a sniff of that. Incredible, isn't it? In a business where most people are as discreet as the Pathé rooster. I suppose I'm just lucky that way.'

He winked at Book and made a noise like a camera, then strode through the door to the sound stage. Book caught a glimpse of Jack, under the eye of the lighting cameraman, lamps being adjusted around him. Book, however, was not left alone for long. He could see a black cab turning at the studio entrance, Gerry the commissionaire shaking his head in despair, and the unmistakable figure of Trottie marching down the tarmac drive towards the studio. Clutching a thick brown envelope and wearing an expression of triumph, she even drew Sandra's attention. Jesse also noticed, as a man with a headache notices someone about to start hammering a nail into a wall.

'Oh! Mrs Book!' he exclaimed. 'Didn't expect to see you here today.'

'Mr Howard said we should visit.' Trottie smiled. 'And I brought something for my husband.'

'Lunch?' Jesse ventured.

'No,' she replied. 'Some back numbers of *Picture Review*.' She slapped them into Book's hands. 'We found your trail.' Book pulled a magazine from the envelope. The relevant pages had been marked with narrow strips of paper. Book pored over one, nodded, then turned his attention to the next.

'Yes,' he murmured. 'It's a pattern, isn't it? I thought I saw something earlier too. In that note. A repeated phrase. *Basilisk*, eh?'

Jesse blinked. 'What?'

Book's eyes remained on the page. 'It's a mythological creature. Could kill you just by looking at you.' His eyes flicked towards Sandra. 'Rather the way Miss Dare is looking at me now. Would you excuse me, Jesse, just for a moment? If there's time for you to show Mrs Book the set, I'm sure she'd be most grateful.' Book gave his wife a kiss of gratitude and made for Sandra's little enclave.

'We've rebuilt your husband's bookshop here,' said Jesse. 'I hope it'll amuse you.'

'Wallpaper didn't suit your story, then?' asked Trottie.

'Well, no. Because Tony desires pleasure. But he's afraid of it. He's repressed. That's Freud, you know.'

'So I understand,' said Trottie.

'And wallpaper simply doesn't give us that,' Jesse continued, warming to his subject. 'Wallpaper is about covering things up. So I thought, well, cakes. They're freighted with pleasure. Simply freighted.'

'Is that in *Cakes and Their Relation to the Unconscious*?'

'That's *jokes*, isn't it?' said Jesse.

'Oh yes,' said Trottie. 'You're quite right.'

Sandra Dare had not enjoyed Book's first intrusion into her personal space. The pointing, the shouting, the lack of ceremony. As he loomed over her, fell into Jesse's chair and pulled it towards her, grinning like a split turnip, she concluded that she liked him no better when he was friendly.

'Miss Dare,' he beamed. 'Skirts gathered ready for the pursuit of art?'

'I suppose so.'

'Well, before you rush off, perhaps I could check some details?'

Sandra tilted her head. 'How exactly do you help the police, Mr Book?'

'I check details.' He pulled the chair even closer. 'You must be relieved to know the chocolates weren't intended for you.'

'Naturally. But also terribly worried for Stew.'

'Of course. Perhaps we could discuss the events of last night? Now, I've no need to ask where you were, Miss Dare, because I've seen the rushes. I know you were doing the scene where you look through the window and think about the resilience of your love.'

Sandra nodded. 'Yes.'

'And I also know that Nerina Bean was among the background artists.'

Sandra gave a start. 'Nerina? She was on set? In the shot?'

'Yes. And then moments later, she was on the stairs.'

'Well, I know about that.'

'And then at the bottom of the stairs.'

'Yes,' Sandra said tersely.

'And perhaps she was killed because she knew who'd sent the poisoned chocolates?'

'Is that what you think?'

'It's a working hypothesis.'

Book smiled in a way that suggested to Sandra that he might be about to go for her neck. She knew an accusation when she heard one. 'Wait a minute, Mr Book. I love Stewart. You can't think I tried to kill him. We're everything to each other.'

'Everything to the box office,' he replied.

Sandra paused to consider the perverse disconnection between the pleasantness of Book's tone and the unpleasantness of his meaning. During this pause, Billy Green appeared, hauling two more canvas chairs, brought to accommodate his director and the newest visitor to the set.

Trottie settled beside her husband.

'This is nice,' she said.

Sandra was undelighted. She looked at Trottie as if she were a scullery maid she had caught trying on her new gown. She snapped her fingers in Billy's direction. 'Be a darling and fetch me a coffee, would you? Black.'

'Me too, Billy,' added Jesse. 'Good strong one.' Billy disappeared at the speed of mustard. The make-up woman arrived with a tray of cosmetics and took out powder and brush: Sandra offered up her face.

'Mr MacKendrick has just shown me around the set,' said Trottie, cheerfully. 'Apparently sometimes an éclair is just an éclair.'

Billy reappeared with two cups of coffee. Jesse received his eagerly and took a large and enthusiastic sip. He reacted as if he had swallowed a mouthful of lemon juice. 'This stuff's horrible,' he blurted. 'So bitter.'

Disgust gave way to a sudden surge of terror. He leapt to his feet, dropping the cup to the ground and knocking over the folding table and its contents. He spat. He clutched at his throat. His face twitched. His whole body twitched. 'Get me some water,' he cried.

Sandra staggered upwards. The make-up woman recoiled. Book recoiled. Billy ran for a jug of water. Trottie, however, stayed seated, observing coolly as Jesse dropped, flailing and coughing, to his knees. She then reached towards the make-up woman's tray, grabbed a tube of mascara and yanked off its cap with the certitude of a Yugoslav partisan pulling the pin from a grenade. She moved behind Jesse, locked his head in the crook of her arm and pinched his nose. Jesse's mouth gaped open. He moaned in discomfort and incomprehension.

'What the hell are you doing?' Sandra yelled.

'Saving his life. I think,' said Trottie. She squeezed the mascara down Jesse's throat. 'Eat it!' she bellowed. 'Swallow it now! Get it down you. Quick as you can!' Jesse obeyed. He champed desperately. Black make-up caked his lips and oozed between his teeth. When Billy arrived with a jug of water, Trottie took it from him, pinched her patient's nose again and tipped the contents into his mouth.

Jesse MacKendrick, late of Shinstone Hall, near Cricklade, and St Biddulph's College, Oxford, squealed and retched on the ground. He looked like a fish coughing up tar. Importantly, however, he was not in the least bit dead.

Trottie exhaled. 'Perhaps someone could call an ambulance? Just in case I've got this wrong.'

CHAPTER FIVE

Bliss was passing the police box on Morley Road when he saw the ambulance racing in the opposite direction, its siren clanging as loudly as his own. A voice from the brand-new dashboard radio confirmed that Ladyhurst Studios was its destination.

He leaned forward to address his constable. 'This jeweller. He's all right, is he?'

'Fit as a flea,' said the constable. 'He took the cosh from the thief and whacked him back with it. It's the culprit we're looking for.'

'Stop the car, would you?' said Bliss. The constable brought the Wolseley to a halt. There, by the war memorial, was a man, lying semi-conscious on the pavement. A woman with a basket of shrimp under her arm had him pinned to the ground with one foot. A rosy-cheeked child, presumably her son, was holding a flat wooden tray like a fairground prize.

'Right, constable,' he said, 'you deal with this little problem. I'll motor back to the studio.' The constable could summon no grounds for objection. He clambered out of the Wolseley and relinquished the driver's seat to the inspector, who executed a noisy U-turn and drove back the way he came.

Bliss arrived at a curious scene. An aftermath of some sort, clearly, but of what? The ambulance was parked in the yard, its doors yawning open. The extras, Kurt Masterson among them, formed a small crowd of perturbation. Jesse lay sprawled on a stretcher, attended by Sandra Dare and two members of the ambulance crew. His face was blotchy and smeared, as if he had fallen in a pond while sweeping a chimney. Jack and Stewart stood with their arms folded. Mr and Mrs Book were also present. They were crouched among an assembly of scattered objects – overturned chairs, broken crockery, a sports bag that had lost half its contents – and appeared to be examining a pool of black liquid on the ground.

'Is he hurt?' asked Bliss.

'It's largely cosmetic,' said Book.

'What's that stuff on his face?'

'It's largely cosmetic.'

'Mascara,' said Trottie.

The picture became a little clearer. 'Oh!' said Bliss. 'Charcoal.'

'I believe that's all mascara is,' said Trottie. 'And petroleum jelly.'

'Bit of a risk, though, Mrs Book. Charcoal's good for strychnine. But I'm still waiting for the report on what was in Barbara Markham's chocolate. It could have been anything.'

'Mr MacKendrick twitched,' said Trottie. 'Strychnine gives you the twitches.'

'Great presence of mind, my wife,' said Book.

Bliss crouched to examine the broken cups. 'Was it in the coffee?'

Book chewed his lip. 'Everyone else seems to have drunk it and they're fine.'

'Just in the cup, then? Added afterwards?'

'You'd think so, wouldn't you?'

The crew lifted the stretcher into the ambulance. Its upward motion forced Sandra to release her grip on Jesse's hand. She spoke to him softly: 'All my thoughts, dear Jesse.' The director seemed dazed. Although he had managed to keep his horn-rimmed spectacles in place, his struggles had spread the black residue all over his face. He looked like a silent film comedian who had forgotten to let go of a stick of dynamite.

'My bag,' he said, weakly. 'Can't do without that.'

'Allow me,' said Book. The bag was on the ground beside a toppled canvas chair. Book lunged down, swept up its loose contents and passed it into the back of the ambulance just as the doors were closing. As the vehicle moved off, Sandra waved as if she were in a film about the American Civil War. Stewart moved towards her and wrapped a tender arm around her shoulder.

'More poison,' said Sandra darkly.

Stewart's Adam's apple moved in his throat. 'Was it meant for me, do you think?' The question went unanswered. The production had other problems to tackle: Billy was already moving around the yard, distributing copies of a revised schedule. The afternoon was cancelled, but tomorrow was another day.

★

The Ladyhurst train was fast from Lewisham to Charing Cross. Trottie was grateful for its speed: Jack stared at the gasometers and the backs of houses and barely spoke a word. Book seemed untroubled by his silence. He was reading a film script, which had somehow joined the back numbers of *Picture Review* in the large brown envelope.

'Did you take that from Jesse MacKendrick's bag?' asked Trottie.

'I suppose I must have picked it up in the rush and confusion,' said Book, not expecting to be believed. 'I'll return it tomorrow.'

Trottie could see his eyes scudding over the blocks of dialogue. She turned the cover to read the title.

A Plea for Christiana.

'A hit, do you think?' she asked.

'What would I know?' asked Book. 'He's clearly written it for the divine Miss Dare. And she's in every scene. Though it's not her usual sort of part. Christiana Edmunds is a bit older than Madeleine Brownlow. And this scene in the condemned cell, well, there's not much sweetness or glamour in it.' He turned the last page. 'Who knows? It might be the making of her.'

They went their separate ways at Charing Cross. Jack walked down to Embankment Gardens to hear the band. 'I won't be late,' he said. 'Looks like another early start tomorrow.'

'Who'll call the shots, I wonder, if Jesse is too sick?' asked Book.

'He'll be fine,' said Trottie. 'He was fine when he got in that ambulance.'

'Anyway,' said Jack. 'There'll be someone only too happy to step into his shoes. It's that kind of world.'

They watched him walk towards the river.

'You off to another Russian play?' asked Book.

'No,' said Trottie. 'Dinner with a friend.'

'I might see if Yusuf has room for one,' said Book, a little wistfully.

When Book returned to the shop, Dog appeared to have been left in charge. A volume of *Notable British Trials* (William Hodge, 1911, inscribed to 'Mother dearest') had been left on the armchair in a position deleterious to the health of its spine. A copy of *Harry Craddock's Savoy Cocktail Book* (Simon and Schuster, second edition, 1933) was propped up on the counter.

'What's happening?' he asked. He had the trial book in his hand.

'They're starving a baby to death in Penge,' said Nora, emerging through the partition that divided Book's Books from Strotford Supplies. She was carrying two dusty bottles of alcohol. 'The whole family was in on it. They killed the mother, too. That's south London for you.' She squinted at the Craddock, poured two measures carefully into a glass, and agitated the cloudy result with a pencil. 'Here's mud in your eye,' she said.

Book plucked the glass from her hand. 'I'll have that, thank you. Your uncle would kill me. I've already found a body today and I've no wish to discover my own.' He drained the drink in one gulp and banged the glass on the counter.

'Awful case, the Stauntons,' he said. 'In closed little groups of people, I suppose even the most dreadful deeds can come to seem acceptable. And how the names of those killers stay with us. Dr Crippen, Dr Cream, Madeleine Smith. Like a catechism.' He was climbing the library steps, scanning the shelf for a half-remembered title. 'Nora,' he said. 'Would you do me a favour? Film almanacs.'

Nora was staring resentfully at the empty cocktail glass. 'You mean those daft mags about Margaret Lockwood's mole? That girl took them home to Hendon.'

'No,' said Book. 'Older than that. Yearbooks. From the teens. When we still called them the "flickers". There's a stack of them somewhere. Look between William Friese-Greene and *How Green Was My Valley*.' He paused, thinking of picture houses with bench seating and peanut shells on the floor. 'I saw a can of film today. An old one. Stuffed under a chaise longue in a dressing room. It made me nostalgic for those early days.'

Even from the top of a ladder several feet above her head, Nora's lack of enthusiasm was palpable. 'Come on,' said Book. 'I'm hoping to bring this one to a conclusion tomorrow. What would you say to a day in the public gallery at the Old Bailey? Neville Heath is due up any day now. We could go for tea at Fortnums after.'

Nora said nothing. Book did not look down. He was reassured, however, by the sound of rummaging; and he had found what he wanted. Another in the *Notable Trials* series. A fair copy, dust jacket partially chipped, bearing a photogravure portrait of a Victorian woman with placid black eyes.

'Hello, Christiana,' said Book. He opened the volume

and something fluttered out like a sycamore leaf. Book descended the steps and picked it up from the carpet. It was a blank piece of notepaper that had been used as a bookmark. Embossed above the address and telephone number was a Latin motto, wound around a heraldic symbol. A beast with the combed head of a cockerel and the scaly body of a dragon rampant. Its mouth and its tongue were both forked and curled.

Book read the motto aloud. '*Ad astra per aspera* . . .'

The shop bell jangled. Jack had returned from the park.

'We have to talk, Mr Book,' he said. His mouth was tight.

'We will,' said Book, gently. 'When the filming is done.'

Jack did not like this answer. 'I don't finish until ten. I'll be dead beat.'

'I think,' said Book, 'that the schedule may change. Cinema is an unpredictable medium.'

It was the final day of shooting on *Lovelorn in London*. This is not what it said on Billy Green's clipboard. A glance over his shoulder would have shown several more days allocated to the bookshop set, followed by a week of location work at Camber Sands, where a POW camp was already under construction. None of this, however, would happen. An East Sussex landowner would collect a cheque for inconvenience he did not fully experience; seventeen perfectly good RAF uniforms would be distressed for no purpose; the Imperial Japanese Army rack at Angels and Bermans would remain undisturbed. The iris was about to close on Tony and Madeleine.

Jack was accustomed to standing still. He had done it in

prison for years. Finding the light was also easy for a man who knew how the sun moved across the wall of a cell. Trottie possessed no such discipline. She wandered carelessly over the set, inspecting props and knocking walls to check their solidity.

'It's barmy,' she exclaimed. 'And the staircase doesn't go anywhere.'

'It's all right,' said Jack, holding his position by the cash register. 'These people never go upstairs.'

Trottie seemed unsatisfied. 'Rooms in films never have ceilings. Why's that, eh?'

'It'd stop the light getting in.' Billy, swooping in to reposition some of the props she had disturbed, provided an answer. Book was by his side, and an astute person might have wondered whether the clapper boy was now in his employ, or perhaps vice versa. They had the air of two people who had been in conclave for an hour before the start of the working day. They exchanged nods, glances and single words.

'So,' said Book, approaching Jack as if he were something in the sculpture gallery of the British Museum. 'How's the life of a stand-in?'

'Static,' he replied.

The lighting cameraman pulled out a tape to measure the distance between actor and lens. He placed one end in Book's hand, told him to hold it steady against Jack's face, and walked back to the rig. Book took advantage of the unexpected intimacy. 'Billy and I need you to do something for us,' he said, smiling mildly in the direction of the cameraman. 'I hope we can rely on you. I'm so sorry for the last few days, Jack. I can see that you're angry with me and I will do something about that. Once this case is closed. I promise.'

Jack said and did nothing. At this moment, that was his job.

At the bookshop door, Sandra Dare was being prepped for action. Sunglasses shielded her eyes from the glaring lamps. A make-up artist retouched her lips. Stewart slouched nearby, listening to notes from his director that he clearly found unnecessary, perhaps even insulting. Book decided to add himself to their conversation.

'Mr MacKendrick!' he exclaimed. 'Good to see you hale and hearty. Fully recovered, I hope?'

Jesse gave a weary smile. 'Yes, thank God. When I went into the picture business, I never thought it would be so bad for my nerves. No wonder so many directors start the day with vodka in their grapefruit juice. It's absolutely exhausting.'

'More exhausting than running?'

Jesse gave an involuntary shudder. 'Much more. Near the end though, now, aren't we?'

'Yes,' said Book. 'We are.'

Jesse glanced down at the script and crossed something out with a pencil. 'I'm so sorry, Mr Book. Would you excuse me? I need to keep my head clear for this next sequence. It's a bit complicated. I'd get in there now, Stew. Douggie looks like he's got what he wants.' He smiled at Book, retreated to the pool of gloom around the camera and began bending the ear of the operator.

Stewart gave Book one of his winks and slid towards the

bookshop counter. He pulled off his shades and handed them to his stand-in, who gave up his place to its proper occupant.

'Good luck, Stew,' said Jack.

Trottie remained exactly where she was. 'So,' she said with a blithe smile, 'what's the story so far, Mr Howard?'

Stewart gave her the smile he used for girls and film hacks. 'Well, we've been having this passionate affair of the intellect, Madeleine and me. But then this telegram comes – the telegram of doom – and what do you know? Her husband's been found in a Japanese POW camp. Turns out for him, the Death March didn't live up to its name.'

'Oh, bad luck,' said Trottie.

'Yes,' Stewart agreed. 'And he's on his way back to Blighty, with his ribs sticking out but still very much a going concern, love-wise. So she tells me she has to leave me.'

'And what do you say?' Book asked.

'Nothing, of course,' Stewart replied. 'Writers never want to write those bits. They just prefer a nice clear reaction shot. And something swelling on the soundtrack. Nice bit of Spoliansky if we're lucky.'

'Positions, please!' Billy called out.

'But credit where it's due,' Stewart continued. 'Jesse listened. So instead of standing there catching flies, I gird my loins and go stoically back to work.'

'Like Uncle Vanya,' Book observed.

'I'm sure that's what Jesse had in mind,' said Stewart. 'Ask him.'

'I might,' Book replied. He and Trottie moved to the margins. Stewart mumbled lines under his breath. Across the set, the make-up woman bustled around Sandra. She stepped into her light, breathed deeply, loosened her lips. 'What a to-do to die today. What a to-do to die today . . .'

Jesse addressed his cast and crew. 'So, everyone. I know we're working under very difficult circumstances. But I wanted to thank you for your forbearance. I hope none of you think I'm asking too much. As you can see, I'm not demanding anything of you that I'm not demanding of myself.'

The crew, by and large, did not appreciate these remarks. The operator had been on the *Ben-Hur* chariot race; the lighting cameraman had tried and failed to extinguish Nita Foy on the floor at Twickenham. Even Billy Green rolled his eyes. Ladyhurst was not Agincourt.

'So let's run this one right through,' continued Jesse. 'Right to Madeleine's exit. And we'll stay on Tony for that last close-up as he hears the door bang and knows that it's all over. She's handed over her money. It's in the till. That's that. Account settled. And for Tony there is only the consolation of work. Got that, Stew?'

'Loud and clear,' said Stewart.

'Right,' said Jesse. 'Let's make that movie magic happen.'

'We're rolling,' reported the operator.

Billy stepped into the frame. '*Lovelorn in London*, scene thirty-four, take one!' He barrelled out again.

On the call of action, Tony and Madeleine were conjured back into existence. It seemed almost an act of cruelty. There they were, Tony with his hand crooked against Madeleine's cheek, Madeleine with her eyes bright and sorrowful. They gazed at each other. They knew they were saying goodbye.

'And now the telegram is here,' he said. 'The one I think we always knew would come. Is this the end of the affair?'

She turned from him. 'Don't use that word, Stewart. You know it hurts me. I shall—'

'She said Stewart!' Stewart Howard was looking straight into the lens. He turned back to his co-star. 'You said Stewart.' His voice was dull and cold.

'Cut!' barked Jesse.

Sandra muttered and pawed at the floor with her foot. 'Damn, damn, damn,' she muttered. 'Sorry. Sorry, Stew. Sorry, Jesse.'

Jesse barked from the gloom. 'Let's go again. First positions, please!'

'Rolling,' declared the operator. 'And speed.'

Billy rushed in again. '*Lovelorn in London*, scene thirty-four, take two!'

When the clapper boy returned to his place behind the camera, he felt a hand on his shoulder, a mouth close to his ear. 'You can handle this one, can't you?' whispered Jesse. 'I've been watching you, Billy. You have talent. You have an eye. I just need a breather. All right?' Jesse did not wait for an answer. He called action and disappeared like a ghost.

It was not a lie. Jesse just needed to stand outside the set. Just for a moment.

Just to clear his head. Just to escape the little whirr from inside the camera; the heat of the lamps. He stepped over the margin of the bookshop, where the edge of the wooden scenery met the smooth floor of the sound stage. The cyclorama of Archangel Lane soared above his head. He walked towards it. The nearer you got, the less substantial the picture seemed. What looked like bricks and mortar were just daubs and lines. Abstraction. He closed his eyes. He inhaled the smell of the paint. He could hear the scene rumbling on. Tony and Madeleine, their world splitting.

'There's still time, you know.'

Jesse opened his eyes. Book was beside him.

'Time for what?' asked Jesse.

'To do the right thing. To stop the filming.' Book was also looking at the cyclorama, as if the answers were written on its surface. 'I've known for a while. About a certain secret relationship in your life.' His voice was gentle.

Jesse swallowed. 'We're not,' he protested. 'She isn't—'

'Not with Sandra,' Book interrupted. 'With strychnine.'

Jesse fell silent.

'I read those grave little paragraphs in the *Varsity Sporting Record*,' said Book. 'How you took it as a stimulant to get you through those last agonising yards of the race. Rather reckless, really. Your father wasn't very pleased, was he?'

'No,' said Jesse. 'So I got into trouble. So what?'

'And then there's Christiana Edmunds. The name of your new heroine. A household name, once. Fell in love with her doctor. Believed he was in love with her, too. Pure fantasy. But she thought she'd help him escape his wife by bringing her a box of poisoned chocolate creams. Which the wife spat out just in time. And Christiana's poison of choice? Strychnine, of course. Bit of a leitmotif, isn't it?'

The voice of Sandra Dare bled from set. 'Don't use that word, Tony. You know it hurts me. I shall think of our time together as something bright and precious. And so I think it's only fair that I settle my account here.'

Jesse knew the next bit of business. He had typed it, while his secretary waited to put it on the mimeograph machine. Book knew it too: had read it, while Bliss was giving Billy a hard time about diabetic needles. Madeleine would open her purse and place a note and a few coins on the counter (the script did not specify an exact amount). She would then deliver her final speech. The speech they could now both hear from the set next door.

'I've had a lot of time to think. Too much, I dare say. And I think we've been living in a kind of dream. It's time for that dream to end. You stay here with your books. I must go back to my husband, Tony. I simply must.'

There was a brief pause, then the sound of Sandra's heels clicking slowly across the floor.

Jesse listened. Book leaned in towards him, his face as close as a lover's. 'I know you didn't mean to kill poor Barbara Markham. That might save you from the gallows. But you couldn't make the same argument about what's happening here, could you? This is your very last chance, Jesse.'

The bookshop door opened. The bookshop door closed. Sandra Dare stepped into the space beyond the set. She saw two figures were silhouetted against the cyclorama and identified them immediately. The tall one in an attitude of confrontation was Book. The one with his head sunk against the backdrop was Jesse. He punched the canvas. It shivered above them.

'Oh damn you, Book,' he wailed. 'Damn you, damn you, damn you!'

Jesse had made a decision; more, perhaps, with his body

than his mind. Like the decision a runner makes when he hears the starting pistol.

Billy's voice rose from the set. 'And cut! Thank you, everyone.'

Another voice rang out, sharp and startled. 'What the hell was that? It was bloody painful.' The voice was Stewart's.

'Ah well,' said Book. 'Too late now.'

Jesse was fast. Nobody outran him at school; at St Biddulph's, only Leonard Sanditon had managed it, and that was with a glass of chemical assistance. Sharing the recipe – 2 egg whites, a shot of brandy, 1 milligram of rat poison – was the price of Jesse's silence, but by the end of Trinity term it had ceased to be Leonard's secret and become his own, for others to keep or betray. That cocktail won him six cups in one year. He had even been allowed to keep one of them.

Sometimes, however, Jesse could be too fast. As he ran into the bookshop set, he stumbled on the base of a wooden flat. It was the kind of error that would have lost any man the race. He did not quite collide with the camera rig but staggered against the arm of the boom operator and was obliged to use Billy to prevent himself tumbling to the floor.

The crew, however, were oddly uninterested in his entrance. They were looking at Stewart, whose hand was raised, almost as if he were asking a question in the classroom. Something was protruding from his index finger. Something tiny and slender and sharp. A pin. He pulled it from his skin and, obeying pure instinct, sucked his finger.

'It was on the cash register,' he said, his voice tight. 'It went right into me as I pressed the button.' A thought came to him like a crack appearing in a frozen lake. He yanked his finger from his mouth. He moved his tongue around and spat on the floor. His gaze darted wildly around the set. It landed on Billy.

'Oh my God. Oh my God. *You.*'

Billy understood the accusation. He did not deny it.

'I have a name, Mr Howard.'

Sandra was standing in the doorway of the shop. She ran to her fiancé, took his hand, sought the little red puncture mark on the tip of his finger.

'I can see it,' she said. 'Just like the chocolates.'

Stewart was drowning in cold panic. 'Is this what happened to that girl?'

'No. Barbara Markham swallowed strychnine.'

Book had returned to the set. He was standing by the camera, taking the space that had, until a few minutes earlier, been occupied by the film's director. 'This time,' he explained, 'the poison was on a pin. So that it would go straight into the bloodstream. If Jack hadn't followed my instructions perfectly and swapped it for a clean one.'

Stewart pulled his hand from Sandra. A little drop of unpoisoned blood had gathered on his finger. The tiny wound made him think of his mother, sewing under the lamplight in their flat in Bermondsey. He wished himself back there, in her company.

'The pink page told me where to look,' said Book. 'But it was Billy Green who found it. You should be grateful he was so diligent, Stewart, considering how bloody rude you are to him.'

Stewart winced. He began to gather some words of

apology, but both Book and Billy seemed already to have forgotten him. Jesse, marooned between the camera and the counter, was now the object of their interest.

'You, Mr MacKendrick,' said Book, 'should also thank Billy. One less name on the charge sheet next to little Barbara Markham.'

It was clear from Jesse's face that something more than the production of *Lovelorn in London* was in a state of collapse. Book thought of Alice at the end of the story, the courtroom dissolving into a flurry of playing cards. For Jesse, Sandra Dare, standing on her mark, the light still finding drama in the architecture of her face and body, was the only solid object in the room.

'It was for you, my love,' he whispered. 'All for you!'

Sandra's eyes creased in horror. 'What?'

Perhaps, he thought, if he made his case with sufficient strength, she would understand. 'It was so we could be together. And I could make you a bigger star than ever. Not in cheap trash like this. But in a real film. A masterpiece.'

Disgust electrified Sandra. 'What the hell are you talking about?'

'He's been obsessed with you for years, Miss Dare,' said Book. There was no note of triumph in his voice. 'He used to write to *Picture Review* under a pseudonym. Basilisk. It's his family crest.' He pulled out the notepaper that had escaped from the copy of *Notable Trials*.

'*Ad astra per aspera*. Through hardships to the stars. The MacKendrick family motto. You got to the stars, didn't you, Jesse? Or at least, the only star that mattered to you.'

Jesse knew he had lost his case, but he kept on making

it. 'My family has money. So much money. I could have financed our picture, Sandra. But he was spoiling it. *Him.*' He fixed Stewart with an expression of simple and intense contempt. The true attitude of the son of the park gates to the son of the biscuit factory.

'And what better publicity,' said Book, 'than a tragic widow overcoming her grief? Tackling the role of a lifetime alongside the brilliant young writer who consoled her?'

Sandra had played through her shock, her loathing, her horror. It was time for pity. 'You poor fool, Jesse. You're absolutely lost.'

In the Empire, Leicester Square of his mind, Jesse could see the movie playing. *A Plea for Christiana* was a plea answered. Even the usherettes were applauding. He could see Korda telling him to come by Sunday; Caroline Lejeune raising her thumbs over her glowing review in the *Observer*; Sandra eclipsing the night.

'A whole new career, my darling,' he murmured. 'Playing your own age. No make-up. A true character part to show your real range. Elevating the art of screen acting to new heights.'

Sandra regarded him with an expression of total disbelief. 'No make up?' she seethed. 'Are you out of your mind? I'm Sandra Dare!'

The remark rang in the dead air of the studio. Jesse looked around, hoping to see a sympathetic face. He did not find one.

'So he did it?' asked Jack. 'He killed that poor Barbara?'
'Yes.'
'And Nerina Bean?'

'No,' said Book. 'Not the Girl with the Poison Pen. Jesse has a cast-iron alibi for that one. He was in his office, his secretary by his side, passing him the carbon paper. Typing out a way to murder you, Stewart.'

Stewart bristled. 'Then who did kill her?'

'Where was she found?' asked Book.

'On the stairs.'

'Which lead where?'

'Props store,' said Stewart. 'Offices. The vault.'

Book nodded vigorously. 'The vault, yes. The scrag bin of British cinema. Piled with forgotten films. And one film in particular. Unseen for decades, but recorded in an old movie almanac back in Archangel Lane.'

'What film?' demanded Stewart

'*Kitty Wins the Calcutta Sweep*.'

'Kitty does what? What the hell's that?'

'It's the film I found in your dressing room, Miss Dare. Under your daybed.'

When the details of what followed were processed by the apparatus of justice – the police statements, the inquest, the cross-examination of witnesses – consensus was hard to reach. The toppling of a studio light was one source of difficulty. This was an old klieg lamp, lit by a bank of mercury tubes, brought unexpectedly out of retirement, and its fall produced gloom, confusion and a cloud of toxic vapour.

Trottie, running to telephone the police, was certain that Jesse had kicked it over deliberately to clear his path to the studio door; Jack thought that it had been felled by a junior member of the crew attempting to get out of his way. Stewart had no opinion on the matter. He could recall deciding to throw himself forward and tackle Jesse to the floor. He remembered Jesse kicking back, kicking hard, and in doing so, propelling himself into the bookcase that formed one of the walls of the set, and bringing the whole thing crashing downwards. Book's principal impression was the sight of Jesse, flat on the floor in a chaos of broken props, the leading man of *Lovelorn in London* hanging on to his ankles.

'You never loved her, Stewart!' he was shouting. 'Not like I did!'

And Book remembered looking for Sandra Dare, and looking fruitlessly.

She knew it was a dead end; but it was full of lilies and good luck cards and the sweet smell of powder and grease. An unopened bottle of champagne lolled in a sink of cold water. On the chaise, a battered but comforting thing, was her gold lighter – a relic of her tinned orange years – and a packet of cigarettes. They were her favourite brand, not those cheap ones she smoked in the adverts.

Sandra thought of panicking. She tried it for a moment, pacing the dressing room, screaming silently, banging a fist on her temple, but it brought no satisfaction. It did not, she reflected, watching herself in the dressing-room mirrors, even appear particularly sincere. She knew it was over. She knew that the film would not be completed. She knew that she would never work again. She knew she was box-office poison.

Was a prison cell smaller than a dressing room? If visitors

brought flowers, did they let you keep them? Who was she kidding? She'd seen those films. Turned plenty of them down. They took away your make-up, your compact, your pins and every ounce of self-respect.

There was a photograph of Stewart on the dressing table. It was not a film still, but a studio portrait. He looked heroic, as if he were on deck, gazing at the clear horizon. She remembered the afternoon with the photographer, and the night afterwards. It was the night they'd made their bargain.

She turned the picture to the wall. She did not want to bear his gaze. Or her own, for that matter. There was no escape, however. The mirrors were bolted to the wall and could not be turned.

She sank on the chaise and stretched out, like a corpse on a catafalque. Her hand dropped downwards and made contact with something cold and metallic. The cause of all this misery. She sat up and dragged the tin of film from its hiding place. The archaic stupidity of the title appalled her. Had anybody under thirty even heard of the Calcutta Sweep? It was as ancient as broughams or Zeppelins or Hall's Distemper boards; a bygone from a world long burned.

She ran a finger over the lid. Perhaps, she thought, there was time to obliterate it. This was the only copy in existence. If this was the death of her career, the death of everything, perhaps this film could also be killed.

'Sandra?' The voice belonged to Book. Unmistakable Mr Book. Relentless as a wasp at an August picnic. He was outside the dressing-room door. She saw the handle turn, pointlessly.

'I remember making this,' she said. 'The summer I left

home. I was so green. In those days we shot outside. Even the interiors. Sets open to the daylight. I used to think – won't they notice the leaves of the houseplants moving in the breeze? Nobody ever did.'

'Unlock the door, Sandra,' said Book. 'You can tell me all about it.'

Sandra recognised a soothing professional tone when she heard one. She would not be soothed. 'But I don't want to talk about it, Mr Book. I don't want anyone to talk about it. I wasn't Sandra Dare back then. I was someone else.'

'Deirdre Piddock,' said Book.

Sandra brought her fist down on the film can. The lid loosened. 'You see?' she exclaimed. 'How that name brings everything down? Even here? Even now. It was so long ago, Mr Book. The film was lost. Then Nerina discovered it. And I discovered her.' She pushed open the lid, revealing a glossy dark coil of celluloid inside.

'Were you hunting her?' asked Book. He sounded like a priest; the dressing-room door had become the screen of the confessional.

'It was pure chance. I was just going back to the dressing room. She was running up the stairs from the vault, with her prize in her hand. Her big winning ticket. I opened the door coming the other way. And there she was. She looked ridiculous, with that stupid moustache. And then I recognised her. And I saw what she had in her sweaty hands. There it was on the label, plain as anything. The master print.'

'And you tried to get it off her?'

'Pulled as hard as I could. And over she went. She hit that step like a fairground coconut. A horrible, horrible accident.' She drew a cigarette, placed it between her lips, snapped the gold lighter, and inhaled the delicious heat of good American tobacco. Her eyes lingered on the reel of film. A cursed object. A sacred object. Her past, caught in a coincidence of light and people and chemicals.

'Accidents can be forgiven,' said Book.

Sandra detected movement from outside the door. Book, she realised, was not alone. 'This business will forgive you a lot of things, but not getting old.'

'Are you *smoking*, Sandra?'

There was a new urgency in Book's voice. Sandra allowed herself to feel amused by it.

'When nitrate stock burns,' said Book, 'it makes its own oxygen.'

Sandra could hear whispers. Trottie was with him. A pair of Books. She inhaled again; looked into the mirror; watched the smoke curl from her mouth.

'I was sorry to see it go, Mr Book. Silver nitrate. I mean, I knew it had to, after that terrible fire in Scotland. Those poor kids. But we never looked better. That stuff made us shine. It had a quality. Like starlight, real starlight.'

'Sandra. If that film catches, that'll be it for you. It would be a terrible way to die. Trottie and I won't escape unscathed.'

Sandra gazed at the film; its black glossy coils.

'And neither will Stewart,' said Book.

Confusion flickered across her face. 'Stewart?'

'Yes, Miss Dare,' said Trottie. 'He's here too.'

'Darling, it doesn't have to be like this.'

She knew it was his voice. But it sounded different. It sounded like it had when he loved her.

'Darling,' he said. 'Please.'

Sandra felt tears pricking her eyes. 'She would have told them all my secrets, Stew. That I was making pictures when Lenin was in office. That would have extinguished me. And I told you. I want to go on and on. Light up the town. Explode.'

Book spoke again. His tone was warm. It had lost its calculating edge. He had stopped acting. They had all stopped acting.

'That script Jesse wrote,' he said. 'I've read it. It's about a woman who makes a terrible moral error. But faces her fate with dignity. Inspector Bliss will be here soon. You'll be under arrest. But before he arrives, we could save you a little bit of humiliation. Let's go up to the tank, Sandra. Bring that film. That one with you as a seventeen-year-old. With your whole life ahead of you. Before this business made you what you've become. What do you say?'

Sandra looked in the mirror again. What she saw did not horrify her.

'Oh no, Mr Book. I always had it in me. I've always been a star. I think that's what the camera saw. And why they've always loved me. Just give me a moment, would you?'

She picked up her lipstick. Victory Red. The colour suited her.

The stateliness of Kitty's funeral belied its urgency. When Sandra unlocked the dressing-room door and walked out, bearing the grey steel tin like a chalice, the police were already at the gates of Ladyhurst. She knew how to do these things. Where else should she be but at the head of the procession? She had played a simple crofter's daughter who became a duchess. She might have played the title role in *She* and lived forever inside the fire of a Saharan mountain, had Zoltan not got cold feet about the location costs and canned the movie.

Stewart followed her like a consort. Mr and Mrs Book came on behind. The seriousness of the business took them by surprise. They ascended the steps to the flat roof of the studio, where the south London morning spread around them, dazzlingly wide. Sandra led them to the tank and the dirty grey liquid inside. Trottie found the store of sodium hypochlorite and topped up the chemical bath. With exquisite ceremony, Sandra passed the tin to Stewart. She lifted the dark coil of film like Cleopatra lifting the asp from its basket.

She held it aloft for a moment, then dropped it into the tank.

'Boom!' she whispered.

They stood, watching the reel unspool, observing silver seep from celluloid. It was like seeing a black pearl dissolve in milk.

Sandra looked up. Inspector Bliss was standing in the doorway at the top of the stairs, flanked by a pair of constables. As the officers approached, she turned to Stewart.

'Watch out for those people, Stew,' she said.

'What people?'

'The public, darling. The bloody public.'

She held up her wrists for the cuffs.

Bliss had no intention of restraining her, but the gesture gave him pause. He was in a scene with Sandra Dare, and she had assigned him a role. Then he thought of the stairs, and her heels, and the humiliating consequences of a trip. Some things were best left to the screen. He made his arrest, reading Sandra her rights as undramatically as he could. He asked Book, Trottie and Stewart to remain at the studio until they had given a statement. He did, however, allow Sandra her exit.

As she vanished down the staircase with her police escort, she turned back to give Stewart one last look. Book and Trottie gazed at her. She was magnificent. It was all they could do not to applaud.

'Will they hang?' asked Stewart.

'Jesse MacKendrick undoubtedly,' said Book. 'But I'm sure the jury will be kind to Sandra Dare, if she persuades them her role was accidental.' He turned to Stewart. 'And now you're a free man, Mr Howard.'

Stewart gave a bitter laugh. 'I suppose so. But at what cost?'

For a moment, Book thought that Stewart was going to produce a calculation; one that would involve the poisoning of Barbara, the breaking of Nerina Bean, the execution of Jesse MacKendrick, Sandra Dare in a cell at Holloway. Instead, Stewart tapped the tip of a cigarette on his silver case and slid it into his mouth.

'Mind you,' he said. 'A tragic ex-fiancée. A broken-hearted leading man. Suddenly single . . .'

He was feeling in his pockets, looking for a light.

'I don't suppose . . . ?' Book and Trottie shook their heads.

'Ah well,' he said. 'Sandra has one. Present from her husband. I suppose it's still in her dressing room.' He walked back to the door with a carelessness that surprised neither of them.

The sun was bright in the sky. Trottie and Book moved to the edge of the great white cliff of the sound stage, and watched Sandra Dare again. The view was higher than the highest crane shot. They saw her cross the cement yard. They saw her climb into the police Wolseley as if it were a Leicester Square limousine taking her from the premiere to a Quaglino's supper. The crew and the extras gathered round the car. As it moved off, she may have waved at them.

Jack, they noticed, was among the little crowd.

'You and I have a scene to play, Book,' said Trottie. 'A difficult one. Soon. Do you know your lines?'

'I've been rehearsing them for weeks,' he said.

It took place the following morning. The rest of the day had been filled with distraction: Nora required a briefing on every detail of the events at Ladyhurst, down to the last drop of strychnine. Book was only too happy to supply them. He was still doing so when Jack went to bed. Trottie noticed Book's anxious eyes following him to the staircase. Had he left it too late?

At about seven the next morning, Book heard the door of the shop snap shut. He scrambled out of bed. Had Jack left without saying goodbye? Not quite. There was his suitcase, on his bed, packed and ready. And there was Dog's basket, empty.

Jack and Dog both favoured the Embankment for a morning walk in good weather. It was an agreement they had struck in the spring and by which they had abided through the summer. A short cut down the service road of the Walsingham, a stop at Cleopatra's Needle to admire the river, and back to the Strand via Charing Cross station. The morning editions carried photographs of Stewart and Sandra. The piles of folded newspapers repeated their image like the frames on a strip of film.

'If you think I'm doing the wrong thing,' said Jack, 'you only have to say.'

On the way back to Archangel Lane, Dog said nothing.

Nora, however, was not so silent.

She was sitting on the step of the Istanbul restaurant when she saw Jack. A delivery had arrived: a crate of vegetables, which, like everything concerning her Uncle Yusuf, came with a generous garnish of parsley. Nora was supposed to be checking the contents against an invoice half buried in the potatoes. The newspaper, however, had swallowed her attention.

Dog sniffed around the crate in hope.

'Was it really an accident, do you think?' she asked. 'Nerina Bean?'

'We'll never know, I reckon,' said Jack. 'Thing about Sandra, she's a really good actress.'

'You're not so bad yourself,' said Nora. She dug into the crate, found an apple and took a noisy bite. 'What's going on between you and Mr Book? What are you hiding from him?'

Jack turned the question in his mind. He answered by reaching into his jacket pocket and producing his most precious treasure. The creased cabinet photograph of the young man with the sandy military moustache. She squinted at it.

'I've seen him somewhere before,' said Nora.

'In Trottie's room,' said Jack. 'On the dressing table.'

'Who is he?' she asked.

He did not reply. He gave Nora a tight smile and crossed the street.

Jack opened and closed the door of Number 158 as gently as he could. Dog padded over to his water bowl, which was empty. Jack filled it from the tap. He ran his fingers over Dog's flanks and listened to the sound of him drinking. The house was quiet. Perhaps Book and Trottie were still asleep.

They were not. They were sitting on his bed, waiting for him.

'Go on, then,' said Trottie.

There was a look in Book's eye that Jack had not seen before. A kind of nervous tenderness. Hope and fear. He recognised it because, at this moment, he felt it too.

'Jack,' Book began, 'there's something we need to tell you. I'm sorry we didn't say it before. We wanted to let you settle in, you see. And it's a rather delicate matter.'

'It's about our relationship.' Trottie handled the word carefully. It sounded strange and technical.

'Ah,' Jack said. 'I think I've guessed.'

This was not the expected answer. Book's face now held more hope than fear. 'Is it that obvious?' he asked.

'I wasn't sure at first,' said Jack. 'But yeah. I found the photograph.'

Book was blank. 'Photograph?'

'My dad,' said Jack. The words were now coming easily to him. This would not, perhaps, be as difficult as he had anticipated. Everyone had their reasons. Everyone had a history. Nobody chose their families. Everyone deserved a second chance. 'You have a photo of my dad,' he said. 'In your room. Just like the one I have.'

Jack reached into his jacket pocket and produced the creased cabinet portrait of the young man with the sandy military moustache. He handed it to Trottie like a passport, as if it would move him from one territory of life to another. He then pulled open his bedside drawer. Its only contents were wallpaper lining and the marriage certificate he had found on Trottie's dressing table.

'I have this, too,' he said. 'I was going to give it back to you today. I know I shouldn't have taken it. But when I saw you had the picture . . .' If this was a case, he was ready to close it. 'Marylebone. 20 September 1921. Strotford Perry and Eric Percival Banks. Your first husband. Is that him in my photograph? Is that Eric Percival Banks?' He took a deep breath.

'Trottie?' he asked. 'Are you my mother?'

A long moment passed. Jack was not blind: he could see what she was going to say.

'No, my dear. Not at all. I'm so sorry.'

Jack winced in confusion. If not this, then what?

They told him. At first he was baffled. Why was Book talking about his school days? His father? Some Harley Street man who'd ordered him to take up hunting and walk around with a gun? Why was Trottie saying nothing about her first husband, her first marriage? Instead, she was describing how to extract bullets from the bodies of wounded anarchists, and a journey from Spain on a British cargo ship that had brought her to a police station where

Gabriel Book required treatment for a wound from which nothing could be extracted, because his heart was the cause of it.

And here Jack understood. In Book's description of the hare-eyed men with whom he'd shared a ride from Fitzrovia to Bow Street; in Trottie's account of a register office wedding, and rice thrown by veterans of the International Brigades; in the way they both spoke of love and trust and pleasure and discretion.

'And you're happy with this . . . arrangement?' he asked.

'Book has his life,' said Trottie. 'I have mine. It suits us very well. I'm amazed more people don't do it.' There was steel in this; a challenge. Grow up, it said. Know when you're well off.

It might have worked. Jack might have unpacked his suitcase, put his good shirt back in the wardrobe; exchanged apologies and sympathetic words. He might even have accepted a consoling lie about the photographs; been persuaded that these images were of different men. But Book spoke.

'I knew him,' he said. 'Your father. I knew him. Before the war.'

Book waited.

'Knew him?' repeated Jack.

The phrase burned in the air.

Knew him. The weight of it. The heat of it.

Knew him. Like Adam knew Eve.

Was the building on fire? Jack grabbed his suitcase as if it were. He was frowning, looking down at the floor, muttering apologies, telling them that this was impossible; the whole bloody thing was impossible.

Book and Trottie heard him stumble down the stairs. They heard the harsh sound of the bell, the door being slammed shut. They heard the silence that followed.

SUCH DEVOTED SISTERS

CHAPTER ONE

Trottie did not want Captain Victor Orr to die. She wanted him to stop talking and stop touching her. When the end came – painfully, burningly, at cocktail hour, with an expensive view of London – she had already resolved never to see him again. But it had been a day of surprises.

The first had occurred at eleven o'clock in the morning, when she'd seen him peering through the window of her shop. He was looking at his own reflection, checking the neatness of his moustache, affecting to examine a pyramid of paint tins. Victor liked what he saw, but he preferred what he had once seen, in the mirrored walls of Piccadilly before the war. So did Trottie. She remembered the dance floor at the Allegro, after-hours poker at the Shim Sham, and one night in an air-raid shelter on the first Friday of the Blitz, and the memory made her wistful.

'What would you say to a day at the races?' he asked, his foot in the door. 'I fancy something in the two thirty.'

A taxi waited in the lane, its engine running.

'It was awfully nice to bump into you yesterday, Victor,' said Trottie. 'After all this time. But I have a shop.'

'Come on, be a sport. You used to be a sport. Fate has brought us back together, so why resist it?'

'I have a shop,' said Trottie, less insistently.

'Have a flutter, then, too,' said Victor. 'There's a fast train from Waterloo in fifteen minutes. Come on. For old times' sake.'

'Oh Victor, you're an unspeakable reptile.'

'Is that a yes?' He was doing something with his eyebrows that Trottie had seen, many times, from much closer.

'I suppose it is,' she said, reflecting on the dangerous power of nostalgia. 'Just wait there a moment. I have a coat that needs airing.'

In previous decades, Ascot racecourse had been the place to mix with the cream of London society. In 1946, cream was on the ration. Men in pre-Munich morning suits grumbled about the mansion tax. The fullest, newest skirts were worn by women who claimed to be actresses. Punters at the bar spoke of the recent visit of Princess Elizabeth and prayed that her presence had conferred some restorative magic upon their little stretch of Berkshire.

Victor ordered sandwiches and a bottle of hock. 'We had some great days at the gee-gees before the smash-up, didn't we?'

'You're thinking of someone else, Victor. I was a Plaza de Toros Monumental sort of a gal.'

'I never brought you here?'

'The Embassy, yes. The cabmen's caff at Hyde Park Corner, oh yes. But our joint pursuits were rarely equestrian.'

'Then we should make up for lost time,' said Victor.

Trottie glanced down at the names on her card. 'What was your tip?'

'Riddle-Me-Ree.'

'I'd go for Winter Sea.'

'Why?'

'It's the name of a gloss paint.'

The bell clanged; the gates juddered open; hooves pounded the turf like rolling thunder. Small men in silk too bright for wallpaper sank low and held their animals to the course. Love Letter folded at the first hurdle. A grey gelding, Moroxite, surged forward. Gay Lussac, Miss Blighty and Winter Sea ran neck and neck, with a chestnut mare named Clemenceau galloping behind. At the final bend Moroxite stumbled, opening the course for Winter Sea, and for Victor, who, five minutes after the finish, was grinning his way from the bookie's booth back to the bar, patting a thick wedge of notes.

'Put your coat on, Trottie. I'll bag us some champagne for the car.'

A taxi from Ascot to the Strand was a ridiculous extravagance. Trottie decided that there was room in the day for the ridiculous. She settled in the back of the cab and allowed Captain Orr to fill her glass, knowing that she was a fox-fur away from looking like a cartoon in the *Daily Mirror*.

'Nice win, sir?' said the driver.

'To the victor the spoils,' exclaimed Captain Orr.

'Where are we going, sir? Home?'

Victor made a noise like a seal falling off a cliff.

'No fear,' he said. 'Take us to the Walsingham!'

★

Most of the great buildings between Charing Cross and the Aldwych – the Adelphi, Shell Mex House – have their backs to the water. The Walsingham puts its best face south and shares its lights with the river. Trottie saw them as the taxi crossed Waterloo Bridge. In the dark of an October evening, the grand hotel looked its grandest; an art deco ocean liner moored on the Thames.

The car cut right down the Strand and then left into the little access road that met the main entrance. A uniformed employee swooped forward to open the taxi door. Victor drew a note from his jacket pocket and pressed it on the driver, not even pausing to tell him to keep the change.

'Tally-ho, sir,' said the driver, and tapped his cloth cap.

Trottie had visited the Walsingham before, though not as often as she might have liked. To judge by the reaction of the staff, Victor was a frequent patron. The doorman smiled and saluted. The man behind the front desk greeted him by his rank, and though not obviously delighted by his arrival, permitted himself to be drawn into a discreet conversation. His younger female colleague moved to the far side of the desk and busied herself with a ledger.

'Chap to chap,' Victor said. 'Could you see your way to it?'

'It won't be possible, sir,' said the general manager. His voice had a quiet, cool music.

'But I'm here frequently, old man. Frequently.'

'And it's always a pleasure, Captain. When the bill is settled promptly.'

Victor unpeeled a five-pound note and laid it on the counter.

'Winter Sea.'

'Beg pardon?'

'In the two thirty.'

'Miss Wicking,' said the general manager. He said no more than that, but his young female colleague knew she had been asked to surrender the ledger. His eyes fell to its pages.

'504 is available. It has the same view.'

'Oh, I doubt that, Mr Kind,' said Victor, glancing in Trottie's direction. The general manager understood this remark, but his response was undetectable to the human eye. Trottie also understood it, and decided, in that moment, that she would be spending the night at home in her own bed, however pleasant the view from Room 504. The Walsingham and Archangel Lane were reassuringly proximate.

'No luggage?' asked Mr Kind, his round-rimmed glasses catching the light from the chandelier.

'It's being sent on,' lied Victor.

The banknote remained on the desk.

'Advance payment will not be necessary,' said Mr Kind.

Victor did not pick up the money.

The River Bar of the Walsingham had always been a battlefield. In the gilded twenties, when its glass and chrome fittings were first installed, the theatre critic of the *Chronicle* sat at its bar to receive a vengeful slap from Tallulah Bankhead. In the thirties, a hunger march halted on its terrace, where drinkers and demonstrators stared at each other in mutual incomprehension. During the war, fittings disappeared behind sandbags and scaffolding, and every cocktail raised under its reinforced roof felt like a shot fired in the direction of Berlin.

Now, a full year after the end of hostilities, the bar – the whole building – seemed poised between two worlds. The barricades had been dismantled, revealing glass cracked, here and there, by kisses from the Luftwaffe. The clientele spent their money, but did so carefully, under an income tax regime their grandfathers had thankfully not lived to see. The age of deference seemed dead: the staff were now disinclined to respond to fingers snapped across the room. Who knew if Attlee's brave new Britain had space for grand hotels built for old-time plutocrats? Claridge's, the Savoy, the Ritz, the Walsingham – what would these names mean to the coming generation? While the jury decided, ice cubes rattled, vermouth flowed, cocktail sticks slid through olives and the pianist played on.

Trottie had not entered the River Bar since the night the Second Republic had fallen to General Franco. The company on that occasion had not been simpatico, and a fusillade of Walsingham sours had proved small consolation for the death of Spanish democracy. On her return with Victor, she found the crowd unchanged. A red-haired man with a silver watch-chain shared a bottle with a woman who was not his wife. A hawk-like figure whom she faintly recognised – a minor playwright or composer, perhaps – nursed something in a tall glass and smoked with his fingernails turned away from the audience. A woman in a blue gown stood close to the wall and made conversation with the cigarette girl. (Both moved to one side as Victor, a man now past the base camp of inebriation, stumbled as he passed.) Trottie looked down on the pleasing clarity of the chequerboard floor. Later that evening, its black and white grid would structure her memory of who had been there, what they'd said, how they'd fallen.

They moved to the only free table in the room. Trottie's progress was surer than Victor's: during the drive through Berkshire, she had not emptied her glass in such haste. Behind the bar, a young waiter in a smooth white uniform turned a cocktail shaker into a silver blur, the action causing a curl to tremble at his forehead. Beside him was an older man with a streak of grey in his glossy hair, who, on seeing Victor, brought over a bottle of champagne and two glasses.

'Barberini!' exclaimed Victor, his voice warm and comradely. 'How's the new boy working out?'

'Splendidly,' said Barberini. 'Mr Guzili is a master in the making.'

'Where was he before?' asked Victor. 'Have I seen him at White's?'

The question was hostile: Mr Guzili had been seen at White's by no one. A flicker of his eyes, however, showed that the waiter knew he was being discussed. He popped the shaker open and poured its contents into two rocks glasses. Barberini watched with an approving eye.

Guzili's customers, however, were not happy.

They appeared to be sisters. They had the same black eyes, the same regal posture. One wore a pained expression with her immaculate black Schiaparelli gown. The other – slightly taller, sleeker, and redder of lipstick – displayed the sort of glare a servant might learn to fear. No patrons sat behind them. From their high stools they were able to survey the entirety of the room and see it reflected in the mirrored wall behind the bar. This, it occurred to Trottie, was exactly what they were doing.

'Not enough lime juice,' said the sad-eyed woman.

'Too much ice,' judged her sister.

'And I did not like the way you shook it.'

'*Tepër i dhunshëm . . .*'

Guzili gave a plausible nod of assent and withdrew his work to the other end of the bar, where Barberini was refreshing the ice bucket.

'They think I'm too violent,' he reported.

'It's a violent art,' said Barberini.

'Well at least I didn't waste any gin on them.' He poured one of the cocktails down the sink beneath the bar.

The older man allowed himself a smile. 'You're a quick learner, Guzili.'

Victor's dexterity, however, was failing him. In the middle of a story about a school friend who had escaped the Japanese by hiding inside a washing basket in a brothel in Malacca, he lifted his glass of champagne and missed his mouth entirely. He frowned at the wet patch on his trousers, as if some passing patron were responsible.

'Do forgive me,' he declared, far too loudly. 'I seem to be in a state of advanced refreshment.'

Trottie felt the prickle of self-consciousness. 'I'll fetch a cloth,' she said. But it was not necessary. The woman in the blue gown had darted towards her and was pressing a large napkin into her hand. Trottie thanked her, passed it to Victor and turned her head away in embarrassment. When she saw Jack Blunt staring back at her from the other side of the room, she did not thank the universe for the coincidence. She had not seen the boy for weeks. The last she'd heard of him was the door banging as he left Archangel Lane in anger. When their eyes met, she sensed that anger again.

She offered a brief excuse to Victor, which he did not appear to hear, and crossed the bar.

'Lovely suit, Jack.'

'Jermyn Street,' Jack replied, paying the cigarette girl for a packet of Dunhill Royal Yachts, and betraying no surprise at Trottie's presence.

'Are you meeting someone?' she asked.

'I'm at work.'

'Oh,' she said, noticing him look over her shoulder towards the bar. 'I'm glad you've fallen on your feet.'

'I don't have long,' he said, wincing slightly. 'What do you want?'

His coldness was painful. 'Jack, this is silly. We miss you. We both hoped you'd found a safe berth in Archangel Lane. A home.' The word did not fall well.

'Home? With some bloke who had the eye for my old man? And a wife who – well – is that your latest one? That feller with the moustache?'

She did not follow his gaze. 'That's Captain Orr. He's an old friend. From before the war.'

'Dreamboat of the officers' mess, eh? Looks to me like he's listing.'

At that moment Trottie became aware of a murmur of dismay from somewhere behind her. She turned to see that the red-haired man and his guest were on their feet, fussing and frowning. As he attempted to dab himself down, Victor's elbow had caused further damage: the chequerboard floor now bore an upended ice bucket, and a puddle of fizzing liquid decorated with fragments of green glass.

Jack shook his head. 'You don't half pick 'em, Mrs Book.' He gave her a look more of judgement than commiseration and began walking towards the bar. Trottie saw that the cigarette girl was now regarding her with an expression of pity. Perhaps, she thought, it would be best to slip quietly down the stairs, past Mr Kind and out into the evening. She had drunk her fill of champagne and embarrassment. The commotion flaring around Victor changed her mind. She felt obliged to intervene.

'Get your hands off me!'

The accent was Irish and angry. Trottie saw a young woman in the black uniform of a chambermaid. Her hair was dark, its tight curls barely tamed by her starched cap. The Peter Pan collar of her blouse was disarranged. She held a wet cloth that she had clearly been using to mop up the spilled champagne.

'I won't have it! For shame!'

The nature of her complaint was obvious. Victor wobbled visibly. His face was flushed and furious; his right arm tensed as if he was going to slap her. The chambermaid returned his angry stare, then looked to the bar with an imploring expression. She was appealing for help from Guzili, who in that moment seemed quite unable to give it.

It was Jack who broke the impasse. He tucked the packet of Dunhills into his jacket pocket, plucked the cloth from the chambermaid's hand and interposed himself between the woman and her aggressor. Placing a hand on Victor's shoulder, he pushed him down with quiet force into the seat that had been vacated by the woman who was not the wife of the red-haired man. Jack flourished the cloth and began dabbing it across Victor's thighs.

'Oh dear, sir,' he said, 'you've had a mishap. Wet trousers are against the dress code, you know. This is the Walsingham, Captain Orr. So why don't you go back to your room, take off those trousers and have a lie down?'

Victor bubbled with anger. 'I've never been so insulted—'

'Oh,' interrupted Jack. 'Surely you must have been. Chap like you.'

Victor was unable to translate his anger into words: his mouth moved helplessly. The chambermaid registered his humiliation and seemed pleased, but did not stay to savour the feeling. She flashed a dark look at Guzili and disappeared from the bar.

It was now Trottie's turn to intercede. She sailed towards Victor, slipped her arm through his and yanked him upwards. Captain Orr took a deep breath. Knowing that he had been rescued from further ignominy, he was now doing his best to pretend that the last two minutes had not happened. The patrons seemed happy to collude. Conversation resumed over the chrome-topped tables. The minor playwright or composer drained his glass.

'Girl can't take a joke,' muttered Victor.

Trottie piloted the captain to the bar, where Guzili had begun a second attempt to serve his two dissatisfied customers.

'Let's have a couple of those,' declared Trottie, as cheerfully as she was able. 'I love those. What are they?'

'Walsingham sours,' said Barberini. 'For the two ladies.'

Victor's eyes fell upon the women at the end of the bar. He recognised them. 'Ladies?' he exclaimed. 'Their Royal Highnesses, you mean!' He tapped his nose. 'These drinks are on me, chaps.'

Barberini set up two more glasses and gave one of those inscrutable nods of assent used by waiters all over the world in the presence of a drunken bully. Guzili became a human whirlwind, gathering up ice, lime juice, brandy. The silver shaker rattled. Victor smiled disarmingly down the bar. 'May I say you're looking superbly Balkan tonight? I salute the House of Scutari!' He bowed his head and chopped his right arm across his chest. The princesses did not seem remotely fazed. They acknowledged his gesture graciously.

Victor, still smiling in their direction, dropped his voice. 'Whichever commissar lives in it now. Take a good look, Trottie. That's what happens to you if you get dethroned by the Reds.'

Trottie did take a good look. The two women were a picture of European exile; carriers of an imperious attitude for which even the River Bar had little use. Their proper place was at the opening of a minor parliament, draped in ceremonial ermine, or on a long veranda, being served tea from a silver samovar. Such places were not to be found on the Strand. The most surprising aspect of the view, however, was that Jack was part of this royal tableau. Not sitting with them at the bar or joining them in conversation, but standing beside them, as if awaiting orders. In what capacity was he employed? Trottie burned with questions.

The willowier of the two sisters waved two fingers across

her mouth. Jack produced the packet of cigarettes. She took them and reached into her reticule with the apparent intention of recompensing him. Trottie did not quite see how the accident occurred, but a moment later, shillings and coppers were bouncing on the tiled floor and the least royal people on the public side of the bar were helping to scoop them up. Even Victor assisted. He was so determined to erase recent history that he passed the coins to Jack as if they had never met.

'Look after the pennies,' said the captain, 'and the pounds will look after themselves.' He turned back to the bar and slipped a hand into his pocket to pay for the round of drinks. Barberini watched him peel a pound from a wedge of notes.

'Had a bit of luck on the horses,' drawled Victor. 'You know Ascot?'

'Very well, sir. How was the going?'

'Good to firm,' Victor replied, with an unsubtle sideways glance at Trottie.

Trottie felt Jack's eyes on her. She also felt that she wanted to die. Victor now had an arm at her waist. His breath was hot and alcoholic. 'After this, shall we . . . ?'

'I don't know, Victor,' said Trottie. 'Perhaps we should call it a night.'

'You're no fun anymore.' He pitched a sulky gesture in her direction and then beamed at the princesses, sparkling glass in hand.

'Here's to Joe Stalin's next stroke,' he boomed, and took an enthusiastic sip. Trottie followed suit. At this moment, a drink was exactly what she needed. The princess with the red lipstick returned the toast.

'Tinkety-tonk,' she declared. The glass, however, did not reach her mouth. She was staring at Captain Orr.

Victor was trying to speak; or to smack his lips, it was hard to tell. His eyes were wide and helpless, and his jaw seemed suddenly to have been put beyond use. He felt something hot and forceful reaching from his throat, through his chest and into his gut. He gulped, but air declined to enter his body. His mouth was wet with something. Brandy? Lime juice? Blood?

The rocks glass slipped from his hand and landed with a dull clunk. Victor followed it. His bar stool pitched backwards. As he fell, his winnings escaped from his pocket. He was more or less a corpse when he hit the chequerboard floor. The banknotes fluttered around him like confetti.

An Archangel Lane evening could be gloomy, once the shops had closed their shutters. Down on the ground, the Istanbul restaurant was the strongest source of life and brightness. Above, flats and rented rooms displayed light of varying magnitudes: flickering fires, electric bulbs shaded and naked. A gentle glow was usually visible through the windows of Number 158. Tonight, Book's Books was an impluvium of darkness.

Nora had spent the afternoon minding the shop for her employer, who was in Brighton on the trail of a signed three-decker *Great Expectations*. The day was cold and cheerless. Turning on the lights would have fixed the problem, but sixpences were in short supply and Nora recognised the usefulness of a deterrent. She had lost some of her enthusiasm for the clientele of the shop: with Jack gone, there was nobody with whom she could be rude about their tastes and tics. As the light faded, she put a candle on the counter and gave her attention to work of her own that she did not, as yet, wish anyone to read over her shoulder. She was so engrossed that she forgot to shiver. When Book's key turned in the lock, she hurried to pack her papers away, and, in the process, extinguished the candle.

'Why are you sitting in the dark?'

'Sorry, Mr Book,' she said, fumbling for the matches.

'How was Brighton?'

'Exhausting.'

'Took your time, didn't you? I thought you'd be back for lunch.'

'The major wouldn't budge on the price. I suppose that sort of intransigence is what got him through Mafeking. And besides, I had a couple of other errands to run.'

'What's that you've got there?' asked Nora. Book was holding a foolscap file, tied with legal string.

'Paperwork,' he said. He snapped the light switch. Nothing happened. 'Has there been a power cut?' Nora began an explanation, but Book had already taken her light and was using it to explore the interior of the cupboard under the stairs. She heard him rattle the little handle on the meter.

'Nora . . .'

'I never did it,' replied Nora, with suspicious speed.

'Never did what?'

'Made shillings out of ice and put them in the meter.'

Book scraped at the mechanism with his fingernails.

'What's all this corrosion, then?' he asked.

'That's rust,' she answered.

Book emerged from the cupboard wearing a withering expression worthy of the headmistress of a provincial boarding school.

'Cold, isn't it?' said Nora.

'Yes, it is,' said Book.

Nora knocked her foot against a box of mixed paperbacks. The candlelight briefly revealed an illustration of a Regency lady looking coquettish on top of a horse.

'We could burn a few,' she said.

'No, we couldn't.'

'Not even the Georgette Heyers?'

'Really, Nora,' said Book, scrabbling for something on a shelf above the sink. 'For someone so new to the pleasures of reading, you're fast becoming a terrible snob.'

'It feels quiet without him,' she said.

Book did not reply. He had located a battered tin of Harrogate toffee that produced a promisingly metallic rattle, and was back in the cupboard, using the candle to examine its contents.

'Where was Moses when the lights went out?' he said. 'Looking for his emergency store of shillings, I've always assumed.' He paused. 'Except this is a pfennig.'

'Oh,' said Nora.

The tin rattled again. 'And this is a guilder.'

'Oh.'

'And this is a button.'

Nora leaned forward to inspect the coin. 'It's a very nice button.'

'Nora,' said Book. 'Remind me, what is the cover price of a green Penguin crime novel?'

'A shilling,' said Nora.

'A shilling,' echoed Book.

A shadow moved across the front door of the shop. Someone was outside, peering through the glass. The beam of a battery torch created a looming silhouette like the villain from a German Expressionist film. The case of the vanishing shillings was abandoned.

'Who is it?' hissed Nora. 'Do we owe any money?'

'I paid the rates last week,' said Book.

'Vengeful husband?'

'I hardly think so,' said Book.

'Burglar?'

'Possibly,' said Book. 'Though I fear he's in for a disappointing evening.'

'Did you lock the door?'

Book shook his head. Nora dropped to the floor and reached out for a defensive weapon. A leather-bound folio, something dusty and possibly philological, seemed the obvious choice. She grabbed it in both hands and took up a position in the shadows beside the counter. Book followed her lead, keeping the toffee tin in his grip. If this was a burglar, he might perhaps throw its contents in his face.

A thought occurred to him. 'Nora,' he whispered. 'If this is an authoritative-looking chap with a jaw and an eye patch, then please don't hit him.'

'An eye patch?' hissed Nora.

'Like James Joyce,' said Book. He braced himself and, with a sharp yank, flung open the door.

It was not a burglar. Nor the author of *Ulysses*. It was Sergeant Morris, surprise making his face look more than usually equine. His torch illuminated Nora, the heavy green volume raised above her head, her black eyebrows knitted in concentration.

'Ready to commit an affray, miss?'

'She was just browsing,' said Book.

Nora lowered the heavy green volume and put it back on the table.

'Why are you in the dark?' asked Morris.

'For want of a shilling,' said Book. He shook the toffee tin and held it to the beam of Sergeant Morris's torch. A dirty silver bob revealed itself. Book plucked it out and delivered it to the slot in the meter. The lights flickered back to life.

'Look, Sergeant, I hate to seem inquisitive, but why are you here?'

'There's been a chap killed at Walsingham,' said Morris, enjoying the weight of the information. 'Poisoned. Dead on the floor of the River Bar under a pile of pound notes.'

Nora's eyes lit up. 'That's just our sort of thing.'

'Don't get too excited,' sniffed Morris. 'Inspector Bliss has need of a book.'

'Well of course he has,' said Book. 'G. Book, Esquire.'

Morris let the joke die and flipped to the relevant page of his notebook. 'There's some foreign royalty involved, it seems,' he said. 'The inspector asks if you've got anything on the Balkan rules of revenge. Specifically, the *Kanun of Scutari*.' He pronounced it as if it were the name of a pub on the wrong side of the Thames.

Book raised an eyebrow. 'How too, too ridiculously obscure.'

'Do you have it?' asked Morris.

'Almost certainly.' Book was already scanning the shelves. Morris jotted something down. 'And 504, he says.'

'504?'

'With a river view. All right for some, I suppose. Mrs Book has already checked in.'

Book blinked. 'Why?'

'She's one of the suspects,' reported Morris. He watched Book's eyes widen.

CHAPTER TWO

It was a pity that Captain Victor Orr could not appreciate the spectacle of his final departure from the Walsingham. It might have compensated for the indignity of being left on the tiles, contorted and dead, as Dr Calder peeled back his eyelids, explored his ragged throat with a swab, then left him waiting while she gave the same careful attention to the dirty glassware on the bar.

Her investigations produced the Platonic ideal of a fingerprint.

'Looks like one of those clues,' she said. 'We like those.'

Inspector Bliss nodded his approval. He was examining the contents of Victor's pockets: his winnings, his wallet, his comb, a little black address book. The address book contained something that did not please him: the name of Mrs Strotford Perry. He watched his photographer move in on Victor's body. The flare of the bulb was returned by mirrors, chrome, and the countless bottles ranged above the bar.

'Do people really say, "What's your poison?"' asked Bliss.

'No idea, Inspector.' Calder shrugged, sampling an abandoned sour with a pipette. 'I don't get out much.'

'What do you mean?' sniffed Bliss. 'You're at the Walsingham.'

Dr Calder looked down at the body on the floor. 'So's he.'

'Well,' said Bliss. 'Let's take him on somewhere else. The night is young.'

The photographer packed away his camera and flash bulbs; the whey-faced constable gathered Victor's belongings and placed them in an envelope. The body was settled on a stretcher and borne through the doors of the bar and down the grand staircase. The stiff sheet that covered his face shone white against the black lacquer of the walls. Dr Calder carried her bag of forensic tools and specimens like a ceremonial object. Inspector Bliss followed, his hat pressed to his chest.

The survivors of the River Bar outrage had been asked to remain on the premises until they had spoken to the police. Most of the residents retired immediately to their rooms. Visitors and staff with homes to go to loitered in the lobby as Bow Street constables moved among them, taking addresses and telephone numbers. Trottie took up position on a sofa beneath a voluminous potted palm and watched their movements. The cigarette girl did her duty by the front desk, content with the sales from captive customers with nerves to calm. The woman in the blue gown paced by the stairs. The red-haired man and the woman who was not his wife dealt with the consequences of the unexpected extension to the evening: each took their turn in the telephone booth, explaining their absence. The minor playwright or composer was nowhere to be seen. Trottie tried to remember whether he'd left the bar before or after

Victor had crashed from his stool. She crossed the floor, casting a subtle eye over people who had made no impression on her before the evening's fatal turn. A Canadian couple muttered in low tones about the absence of violence in Metis Beach, Montreal. A large man wearing a turban read the *Tatler* and ate cucumber sandwiches in silence. Two women in matching pearls conducted a loud conversation about poisonings in the operatic canon, congratulating Leonora in *Il trovatore* for keeping poison in her ring that acted at the precise speed required to save her from being ravished by the count.

When Victor's remains reached the floor of the lobby, a hush descended. The turbaned man put down his magazine and stood up in respect; others followed. The eyes of the cigarette girl and the red-haired man turned to Trottie: they remembered that she had arrived in the River Bar on the dead man's arm. She removed herself from their gaze.

It was at this moment that Inspector Bliss became aware that the general manager was not in his usual position behind the desk but standing beside him. Mr Kind moved with a frictionless ease. He was like smoke.

'Not the main entrance, please, Inspector,' he implored.

Bliss shrugged. 'I'm sorry we can't be more discreet.'

'I was thinking about the revolving door,' said the general manager. 'May I suggest the service corridor?' Mr Kind did something very subtle with his eyes, which seemed to have the effect of conjuring a uniformed page boy into existence from the air. The page's buttons were bright and shiny. He indicated the way to a door beside the entrance to the main restaurant.

'Thank you, Mr Kind,' said Bliss. 'Nothing to stop you reopening the bar tomorrow, I think.'

Edmund Kind watched him go. Murders, he reflected, were rare at the Walsingham. The most celebrated case had been before his time; that of a French actress who had shot her husband on the Palm Court, perhaps with some justification. Deaths on his watch had been mostly prosaic. Heart attacks, suicides. The Walsingham rarely asked for payment in advance. Any plausibly respectable person might book themselves into a room with a bottle of pills about their person and be sure of escaping the bill.

He returned to the desk, where Miss Wicking was assisting the two ladies with an interest in opera. 'You've spoken to the policeman, haven't you, madam?'

'We gave him our address,' said the older of the two. '*Addresses*. But we just thought we might be of some help if we stayed the night. Made ourselves available. So we wonder whether you have a free room?'

Miss Wicking consulted the ledger. Mr Kind might have saved her the bother: he knew the state of the Walsingham's capacities like a master mariner knows the condition of the sea. His attention, however, had been commanded by the arrival of a man whom Mr Kind had not set eyes upon for several years, but knew as surely as his own brother.

In he spun, his long grey coat flapping around him. It was cold outside. As he emerged into the warmth of the lobby, his honey-coloured spectacles misted with condensation. A page boy came to his aid and took his bags – a large suitcase and a small attaché – allowing him to remove his glasses and wipe them clean with a handkerchief. Replacing them on his nose, he beamed at the detail and the dazzle of Walsingham art deco.

'Good evening, sir. Do you have a reservation?'

Book's gaze fell upon the general manager. He too could not disguise a flicker of recognition. His reply was measured and steady. 'My wife has.'

'Your wife?' echoed Mr Kind.

'Yes. Mrs Book. Have you seen her? I'm afraid she may be rather distressed.'

'Rather,' said Trottie, who was sitting on a black velvet sofa, half concealed by a potted palm. She leapt to her feet and rushed to embrace her husband. In the lobby of the Walsingham this counted as an unusually strong display of public affection.

Mr Kind masked his surprise and gave a discreet nod to the page boy.

'504, Freddie.'

Book indicated the attaché case. 'I'll keep this one, thanks,' he said. 'But take the other, by all means.' The page scurried away. Mr Kind extracted himself with a technique close to evaporation.

'What's happened, darling?' asked Book. 'What's this about a corpse? And why have I been scouring my stacks for books on Balkan blood feuds?' Trottie looked at the cigarette girl, who looked quickly away. The man with the red hair also pretended not to show any interest. The potted palms provided cover. Trottie ushered Book to the black velvet sofa and dropped her voice to a whisper.

'I'm not proud of myself,' she began. 'There was

champagne. A day at the races. Winter Sea in the two thirty. Cocktails. More cocktails. And then . . .'

Book creased his brow. 'Trottie, we live our own lives. That was always the agreement.' He held her hands. 'Who was he?'

'Victor Orr.'

'Or?'

'With two "r"s. Army captain. Married. But not when I knew him before the war. We used to go dancing. He liked jazz. I last saw him in '41, at Aldwych station during a raid. We were trying to sleep on the same platform. And then, the other day, he made a pass at me in . . .' She hesitated.

'Where?'

Trottie flushed. 'Please don't make me say the F word.'

'Foyles?'

She nodded.

'Oh, Trottie.' Book winced.

'And then this morning he turned up at the shop. With a taxi waiting. And he invited me to Ascot. I just fancied a good time.'

'Nothing wrong with that.'

'But he turned out to be the most awful boor,' said Trottie. 'Really, Book, it was shaming. You know when you meet someone, and you get a bit giddy, and perhaps have a little drink with said someone, and then the light changes, and you think: *what am I doing? Why am I here?*'

Book concurred, thinking of the flattering effect of a modest fire in a little room. 'Where is he now?'

'The morgue.'

'Ah. One last night on the tiles.'

'And there's something else—' Trottie began.

A hothouse plant, no matter how luxuriant, is not an impenetrable barrier to the gaze of a Bow Street detective. The eyes of Inspector Bliss were piercing the verdure. He swerved towards his friends and perched on the end of the velvet sofa.

He gave Trottie a grim smile. 'I'm sorry you didn't have a better evening, Mrs Book. Should I offer my condolences?'

'I'd rather you didn't, Inspector. I wasn't close to the victim.'

Bliss nodded. 'Are you ready, Book?'

Book frowned. 'For what?'

'To interview royalty. They're up in their suite, ready to give us an audience.'

'Us?' queried Book. 'Bit irregular, isn't it?' He felt he had lost the ability to judge the circumstances under which the inspector was prepared to raise the rope and allow him into the restricted area of an investigation.

'I don't care,' said Bliss, with a shudder. 'They terrify me. I'm not going in there alone.'

'But they've given statements? Fingerprints?'

'Morris did all that. I may be a coward, but I'm not a fool. Seems they talked a lot about revenge. One of them was banging on about a rule book that would explain everything.'

'The *Kanun of Scutari*,' said Book, with relish. 'Our primary text.' He rested the attaché case on his knees and flipped the lid to reveal an exquisite folio in red Morocco leather. The binding glowed with intricate gold inlay and the cover bore a painted miniature of an Ottoman pasha in a jewelled kaftan.

'Looks expensive,' said Bliss.

Book nodded. 'Cosway-style levant binding, gilt and inlay, late nineteenth century.'

'Is it expensive enough to pay for our suite?' asked Trottie.

'Don't worry about that, Mrs Book,' said Bliss. 'The late captain sorted that out. I thought it might be useful to keep the reservation. It's a nice room. You're next to the princesses.'

'What are they like, the sisters of Scutari?' Book asked. 'Apart from terrifying.'

'Glamorous,' said Trottie. 'In a disappointed and stateless kind of way.'

'I remember them when they arrived here,' said Book. 'They were always in the court and social. In white uniforms and Sam Browne belts like something out of a comic opera. I suppose they thought they were in with a chance of getting the throne back after the war. Their brother certainly thought we should be backing him instead of the partisans. You don't hear much about him these days, do you?'

Bliss tapped the cover of the *Kanun*. 'Will this help us find whodunnit?'

Book passed it into his hands. 'It's a book of customary laws for remote mountain communities without a magistrate or justice. The village elders consult the text and tell you how much raki to provide at your daughter's wedding, what to do if your bees escape and build a nest on your neighbour's land. That sort of thing.'

Bliss looked discouraged.

'Or who you're allowed to kill if someone kills your cousin.'

Bliss brightened, until he opened the cover and examined the frontispiece. The text was dense and curlicued and intractably Albanian.

'What language did you think it would be in?' asked Book.

Bliss frowned at the pages. 'We have three native speakers on the premises. Unfortunately, they're all suspects.'

'Who's the third?' asked Book.

'He's a rather good-looking cocktail waiter,' said Trottie. 'Mr Guzili.'

'Well, don't worry too much,' said Book. 'Some dutiful Teutonic scholar had the sense to publish a translation in German.'

'Oh well,' said Bliss. 'You certainly speak German.'

'In his sleep sometimes,' Trottie added.

'So where is it?' Bliss asked. 'This translation?'

'Nora's looking for it now,' said Book. 'It must be somewhere in the law section. Or social science. Or etiquette. Or propping open a door.' He waved away his own doubts. 'Time for our royal appointment?'

Bliss swallowed like a man who has heard that the dentist has run out of ether, got to his feet, and ushered Mr and Mrs Book in the direction of the lifts.

Book turned to his wife. 'You said there was something else.'

'Yes,' said Trottie. 'The princesses have been giving gainful employment to one of the capital's dispossessed.'

'Really?' said Book. 'Anyone we know?'

Trottie had the distinct feeling that he already knew the answer.

From his place behind the desk, Mr Kind watched the doors of the lift bump closed, the indicator needle rise. Miss Wicking was transferring her notes to the card system employed by the hotel to preserve the likes and dislikes of favoured guests. He watched, pleased by her diligence. A hotel depended on its staff. They were moving parts in a beautiful machine.

Jack had little experience with princesses; had never spoken to anyone who had sat on a throne more regal than the one in the smallest room. Perhaps his ignorance of the fatal entanglement of post-Ottoman constitutional monarchy and Italian Fascism had brought him favour with the Royal House of Scutari. Certainly he was in no danger of asking awkward questions about the whereabouts of their nation's stock of gold bullion, or the fate of the silver Mercedes that Hitler had sent their brother as a birthday present. Nor were their Royal Highnesses Princesses Ruhije and Nafije of Scutari overly inquisitive about Jack's history and background. They were faintly puzzled by his account of his months behind the counter of a bookshop, but enquired no further. They were pleased by his claim to have worked as a bodyguard for a film star. (Ruhije held a high opinion of Stewart Howard's performance in *Ship of Shame*.) His time in prison – about which they guessed almost immediately – did not trouble them. Quite the opposite.

'Can you use a gun?' asked Ruhije. She conducted the interview from the piano in the Walsingham's royal suite and considered a wistful Balkan melody appropriate accompaniment.

'I prefer fists,' Jack replied.

'Our last man did not take this view,' said Nafije.

'Who will I be fighting?' asked Jack.

'Our enemies,' replied Ruhije, adding a line of musical notation to a manuscript sheet.

Jack did not learn why the previous occupant of the job had left so quickly. The precise nature of the royal enemies also eluded him, though he soon learned that they might attack from any quarter, using any method. His first assignment was a shopping trip to Fortnum & Mason, where the princesses held an account. Jack was obliged to place himself between his employers and the doorman, in case the latter's long coat hid an offensive weapon. They also visited Madame Tussauds, where Ruhije gave loud opinions on the moral character of various members of European royalty and Nafije gazed at the freshly made effigy of the freshly executed Neville Heath, and commented on the cobalt blue of his eyes.

The bulk of Jack's duties, however, made him a sentry on the door of Suite 503, watching the staff come and go. Sometimes they stopped to talk as they wheeled the linen cart or room-service trolley up and down the corridor. He was on speaking terms with one. The Irishwoman with tightly curled hair, who seemed to take shifts all over the building. On his first night, he had spotted her with an armful of clean sheets, following behind the head of housekeeping. The previous evening, she had turned up at the door of the royal suite with a cargo of sandwiches and soda water. He had tried to engage her in conversation.

'They eat a lot of smoked salmon, don't they?'

'Never on the ration, was it? Nor were oysters and caviar. Funny that.' She had watched Jack, almost in admiration, as he popped a sandwich into his mouth. 'Won't they sack you if they catch you doing that?'

'All part of the job. They might be poisoned. What about you? Any weapons concealed about your person?'

She had laughed at that. 'Do I look like an assassin?'

'What's your name?'

'Rosa Luxemburg.' Jack knew it was a joke. He could not quite remember who this was, but he had once seen a book about her, shelved between *Spartacus* and *The Canals of Germany*.

'What's your real name?'

'Eadie Rattle.'

This, he decided, was probably not a joke.

These were the only words they had exchanged before their painful encounter over the wet trousers of Victor Orr.

After her departure, the captain's violent end, and the arrival of the authorities, Jack had escorted his royal employees to their suite and endured the peculiar experience of seeing Sergeant Morris sitting in its opulence, notebook in hand, asking questions about the progress of the evening. Nafijc and Ruhije treated him like someone who had come round to fix the radiator: they could not quite compute why they were obliged to give him an account of themselves. After he had gone, they shrugged at each other, exchanged their cocktail frocks for something casual in pale pink satin and rang down for olives and potato crisps. Jack returned to sentry duty, in which capacity he saw three familiar figures emerging from the lift.

'Hello, Jack,' said Book. Jack said nothing. Inspector Bliss smiled weakly.

Trottie took the attaché case from Book's hand. 'I'll put this somewhere safe,' she said. 'Perhaps we might have a drink later? Catch up?' It seemed a vain hope. She disappeared into the next room along the corridor. Jack knocked on the door of the royal suite and closed it behind him. After a few moments he emerged.

'They'll see you now.' He did not look Book in the eye.

There were two sofas in the room. Princess Nafije sprawled upon one, smoking a cigarette, too sunk in elegant ennui to acknowledge the entrance of Book and Bliss. Princess Ruhije occupied the other, alert and cool. She moved a hand to indicate that the visitors should be seated. The command led Book and Bliss to a low cushioned stool by the fireplace. They settled upon it, their legs splayed like frogs by a garden pond.

Nafije peered at Book. 'I am sorry for this pouffe,' she said. It was the first indication that she knew the visitors had entered the room. Smoke rose from her lips. 'You remember the great banqueting table, Ruhije? Chairs made from birch as silvery as the snow on the mountaintops. Upholstered with damask so soft that—'

'No need to apologise,' Book interrupted, with a good-natured smile. 'We've been in more awkward positions than this, haven't we, Inspector?'

'That we have, Book,' confirmed Bliss.

Ruhije's gaze flicked between the two men. 'So. Which is the policeman? You or this Book?'

Bliss cleared his throat. 'He's taking notes for me. Helping with . . . um . . .'

'Pitman shorthand,' said Book, beaming as he extracted a notebook and pencil from his jacket. 'So useful.'

Nafije arose from the sofa and took a close look at Book. 'Tall and red-headed,' she murmured, the smoke curling around her. 'Like the poppies of our homeland.'

Bliss cleared his throat again. He was not in the room to indulge the reveries of a crownless blow-in from one of the obscurer sections of the *Almanach de Gotha*. 'I realise that this will be very difficult for you, your . . . Royal Highnesses. But if there's any detail you can recall, however small, it may help us explain the tragic death of Captain Orr.'

Nafije stubbed out her cigarette. 'That is easy. I killed him.'

Bliss's jaw dropped. 'You did what?'

'It is true. I switched the glasses. He drank the poison meant for one of us. We have a routine, my sister and I. To cause a distraction.'

'It is a habit,' said Ruhije. 'A necessary precaution.' She hitched up her soft silk skirt to reveal a small pearl-handled revolver concealed in her garter. She snapped the elastic. 'Do you think I am the sort of person who spills coins from their reticule?' At that precise moment, both Book and Bliss found it hard to say what sort of person she was.

Nafije nodded gravely. 'This was the third attempt on our lives since we left New York. There was a steward on the *Berengaria*. "Can I turn over your room, madam?" So transparent.'

'And that Salvation Army woman outside the opera,'

Ruhije sneered. 'Shaking her box. She denied everything, of course. It's quite exhausting.'

Book leaned forward, pencil pressed against page. 'Who wants to kill you, do you think?'

Ruhije rolled her eyes. 'The Communists, of course! The benighted adepts of the cult of Marxist-Leninism. Their secret police have agents all over Europe. Ready to strike. They send us threatening letters. Awful, poisonous words. They watch us. They hunt us.'

Book frowned. 'Why would they bother? They have your palaces. Your estates.'

Nafije sank back on the sofa. 'Our summer house on the Adriatic. There is a lake there. When the rising sun touches it, it is like the blush on the cheek of a newborn—'

Even Ruhije was tired of nostalgia. 'In the spring,' she said, 'our country was proclaimed a people's republic. The National Caucus of Labour Committees drafted a new constitution in an afternoon. They had a little ceremony at the steps of the palace. They burned the old one signed by our brother. And then they took his crown and prised out the rubies with a knife. But they are not satisfied. They want – what's the expression? – a big finish.' She loosed a dry laugh.

'So that's why you need a bodyguard,' said Bliss. Ruhije nodded.

Book looked down at his blank notebook. 'And – ah – how are you finding him?'

Ruhije's lips became a thin line. 'As he failed to prevent an attempt on our lives, I would say he has not covered himself in glory.'

'Don't the Communists also have your other sister?' Book adopted the insouciant smile he reserved for his most provocative remarks. The question was an ice cube dropped down the back of Ruhije's neck.

'We do not speak of her.'

'Senije, yes?' breezed Book. 'The youngest. Renounced her title and gadded off to the International Lenin School—'

Ruhije's voice rose sharply. 'We do not speak of her! She betrayed her birthright. Her country. Her family . . .' Nafije began to weep quietly. Without a word, Ruhije thrust a silk handkerchief into her hand.

'Thank you . . .' Nafije whispered, dabbing at her tears.

Bliss watched the performance: this kind of melodrama was not to his taste. 'Of course,' he said, 'if this does turn out to be the case, then your swapping of the drinks will not be without consequence.'

Ruhije assumed an expression of martyrdom that Andrei Rublev would have asked her to turn down a notch. 'We are used to being pilloried. We will take whatever comes to us.'

'Right,' said Bliss, flatly. 'In your statement, you mentioned something about this murder being written about in the *Kanun of Scutari*. What does that mean?'

Nafije answered first. 'It means that a killing like this follows certain customary principles.'

'It means,' added Ruhije, 'that the first thing you must do is arrest that cocktail waiter.'

Bliss frowned, flipping through his notes. 'Ismail Guzili?'

'Certainly,' said Ruhije, deciding to forgive his error of pronunciation.

Book did not hide his bafflement. 'Why?'

'He's from the mountains,' said Ruhije. 'These people know the rules of revenge. They're obsessed with them. You must arrest him.' She crossed to the piano and opened the lid.

'And you must bring in any others on the staff,' Nafije added.

Bliss raised an eyebrow. 'Other . . . mountain men?'

'Yes,' Ruhije confirmed, as if it were the most modest and obvious proposal in the world. Bliss and Book exchanged glances. The inspector got to his feet. 'Well, thank you so much. This has been most helpful.'

Ruhije's eyes narrowed. 'So you will do as we say?'

'No, I will not,' said Bliss.

'Why?'

'Because, Princess, I am not your subject. And in this country, a man is innocent until proven guilty. Whatever altitude he was born at.' Bliss smiled a polite proletarian smile and led Book from the room. Jack was waiting outside. Book did his best to make eye contact with him, but his best was not enough. Jack stared ahead, like a guardsman on Whitehall. From inside the royal suite came the sound of the piano. Book could not place the tune, but even through the door it sounded plangent and Mitteleuropean.

'Never really thought of myself as republican,' Book mused, pressing the button to call the lift.

'It's the war, Book,' said Bliss. 'It changed us all. I never thought of myself as a Jew.'

For a few moments, they stood listening to the rumble of the cables. 'Did you ever come here?' asked Book. 'In the Blitz?'

Bliss fixed him with a sceptical look.

'They had to let you in if there was a raid on, you know,' Book continued. 'Even without a tie. We used to come down to the Lower Bar. It was known as "The Fruit Cellar". That was quite the mixed grill.'

'Don't you start,' said Bliss. 'Did it have damask chairs?'

'It was too dark to tell,' said Book.

The door shivered open and they stepped inside.

'Book,' said Bliss. 'How did you know about the other one?'

'The other what?'

'The other princess. The one who threw her lot in with the Reds?'

Book put a hand to his temple. 'I'm not sure. I suppose I must have read about her in the shiny papers.'

Bliss was not entirely convinced. 'Well,' he said, 'if you find the article again, do say. Might be useful.'

The Walsingham had regained its composure. There were, as far as anyone knew, no more corpses on the premises. The doors of the River Bar remained closed, but the cleaning staff were the only uniformed presence. The men from Bow Street now moved more subtly around the building, knocking on the doors of guest rooms and staff dormitories. Sergeant Morris led the work. He was accustomed to the mainly grim and dull routine of taking witness statements, but the prospect of asking uncomfortable personal questions of Trottie and Jack did not bore him. Mrs Book's day at the races, he concluded, had been against the spirit, if not the letter, of her marriage vows. He enjoyed reminding her that the story might require reiteration at the inquest. He found more bracing pleasure in quizzing Jack on the break with his former employer.

'You seem very angry, Mr Blunt,' he said.

'I'm always like this, Sergeant, if people ask about things that are none of their business.'

The chambermaid, however, proved Morris's most difficult interviewee. Eadie Rattle answered each of his questions with a contemptuous one of her own.

'Do you often get into arguments with guests, miss?'

'Arguments?' hooted Eadie. 'Would you call that an argument?'

'An altercation, then.'

'Between his wandering hands and my stockings?'

'Would you say you had a fiery temperament, miss?'

'*I* wouldn't say it. Why don't *you* say it and see what happens?'

After the interview Eadie thundered from the room and made for the walk-in basement cupboard where cleaning supplies were stored. She had no particular duties to perform, but among the Walsingham staff this was widely considered the best place in the building for a silent scream.

She distracted herself by sorting through a disordered heap of hand soap and carbolic that some careless person had placed in a single box. As she did so she noticed a shadow fall across her. Guzili was leaning on the doorframe, a look of sorrow in his puppyish eyes. Eadie liked these eyes. Today she was determined to resist their effect.

'You did nothing,' she said flatly, without greeting him.

'What did you expect me to do?'

'Nothing.'

The word burned angrily. Guzili decided to offer no further defence. 'Was he the one from last week?'

'Yeah. Came at me in his silk dressing gown, with everything pointing north.'

'His name is Captain Orr, apparently.'

'Not anymore,' she spat. Her hands went back to the box of soap. 'They gave me a warning,' she said. 'Apparently shouting at customers isn't the Walsingham way, no matter how lecherous they are.'

'I'll talk to Mr Kind,' said Guzili. 'He likes me. He'll listen.'

Eadie shook her head. 'It was Mr Kind who gave me the warning. Another black mark, and I'm out on my arse.'

Guzili twitched with frustration. He slammed his fist against the woodwork. 'I hate this place.'

Eadie did not appreciate the expression of feeling. 'I was doing all right here, you know. I thought I was. I'd even started to hope we were in with a chance of getting unionised, getting rid of the bloody tronc system. Those boys in the pot room, they were all behind me.' The idea seemed to dissolve as she described it. 'Oh, what's the bloody point?'

Guzili took a step closer, his hand reaching for Eadie's shoulder. He wanted to comfort her, to close the distance between them. Perhaps, he thought, if he kissed her, it would change the weather of the conversation.

It did not. 'My dad was right about you, Ismail,' said Eadie. 'I should have listened to him.'

She pushed past him and back into the corridor. Anger buzzed in his throat. He resisted the temptation to hit the wall again and pushed his head against the shelf in front of him. His forehead came into cool contact with a row of bottles filled with a pale honey-coloured liquid. He thought of his only meeting with Eadie's family. Tea at their pleasant little cottage in Brixton, everyone smiling and making an effort; Eadie's mother asking about the partisans; Eadie's father asking about his prospects; the whisky coming round. Guzili thought it had gone well. It *had* gone well, in that bright domestic space, with thin frayed curtains and tea on the hob. It was the Walsingham that soured things.

His eyes levelled with the row of bottles. He listened to the sound of Eadie's feet on the concrete floor of the basement, and the distant clang of a door.

The cold night air comforted Eadie Rattle. So did the caress of nicotine. She put her back against the enamel brick wall beside the staff entrance and stared at the dark body of the Thames. It looked like oblivion.

She was halfway through her smoke when she noticed she had company. A second smoker, shielded from her by the grey mass of the bins.

'Oh,' she said. 'It's you.'

Jack Blunt exhaled and gave her a friendly little salute. 'It's me.'

'Ta for . . . you know.'

'Don't mention it. Happens a lot, does it?'

Eadie gave a dry laugh. 'Goes with the job. An octopus round every corner. Still. Wouldn't have killed him for it.'

She felt Jack studying her. 'Somebody did,' he said.

'Yeah,' she said. She looked at him closely. Her curiosity was piqued. 'So,' she said. 'Which side are you on?'

'Sorry?' Jack's brow furrowed.

'Which side are you on?'

Jack hesitated, unsure where this was going. 'What are the options?'

'Well,' she began, stubbing her cigarette against the wall, 'there's the management of this hotel, who treat their staff like muck and give a girl a mouthful just for standing up for herself. And then there's the workers.'

Jack offered her his packet of cigarettes. 'Oh,' he said. 'Well, the workers.'

Eadie slid one out. 'Very glad to hear your expression of solidarity. But it's deeds, not words, that count, brother. Don't you agree?'

'Erm . . . yeah,' Jack replied, hoping that she wasn't about to ask him to buy some literature or attend a meeting in a backroom in Holborn.

'Then why don't you take me to the cab stand and buy me a nice cup of Bovril?'

'I can't,' he said. 'I gotta get back.' The apology was genuine.

'To their Royal bloody Highnesses, I suppose,' spat Eadie. 'How does it feel, working for those parasites?'

'Is that what they are?' Jack asked, half curious, half evasive.

'What would you call them?'

Jack felt for the appropriate word. 'Sad, I suppose. Yeah. Bit sad.'

Eadie snorted, shaking her head. 'Speaking for myself,

I'd line them up and shoot the buggers.' She gave a great gleaming smile, as if she was thinking of a week at the seaside, with a fish supper wrapped in paper on the pier, and the red flag flying on Blackpool Tower.

CHAPTER THREE

Sergeant Morris and his constables worked their way through the Walsingham in a vertical direction. As night thickened, they reached the male staff dormitory in the eaves. The atmosphere was different at the summit. The dorm had the air of a genteel doss-house. Men who work long shifts ensuring the linen is clean and the spoons are polished have lost interest in such matters by the time they retire to bed. The whitewashed walls were naked, except for dirty thumbprints, clusters of picture postcards and pin-ups torn from *Picture Review*, for those who wished to say goodnight to Sandra Dare before they put out the light.

Each bed was flanked by a metal locker. Morris had no qualms about searching them under the eye of their owners. He pulled the catch on Barberini's as Barberini watched from his bed, sneering between drags on a cigarette. The paucity of the contents told a story about the narrow frame of the barman's life: a Catholic Bible, smoking paraphernalia, some boiled sweets. The shelf above carried a memorial card for those lost in a disaster at sea. All Italian names, noted Morris. Guzili's locker was marginally more interesting – a copy of *The Savoy Cocktail Book*, marked with little strips of paper, and a dog-eared edition of *Wow* magazine, its cover carrying an image of a woman in pursuit of a beach ball and the promise of the thrilling story of how Carruthers avoided the cannibal pot. As Morris opened its middle pages, Guzili appeared in the doorway.

'Careful, officer,' said Barberini. 'My friend borrows his jazz mags from the maître d'.'

'You can't shock me, sir,' said Morris. 'I've been to the Windmill Theatre. Seen those gents with the newspapers on their laps. Brought a few into the station, too.' He moved to Guzili's bed and yanked up the mattress with deliberate carelessness. Underneath he found a book, inside which was a propaganda leaflet depicting the royal family of Scutari. They were dressed in matching tweeds and feathers for a hunting expedition in the mountains. They carried rifles on their shoulders. Above them, in dramatic graphic montage, a red hammer and sickle subdued the white royal eagle.

Morris held it up to the light. 'Been jazzing with this, sir?'

'Oh no,' replied Guzili. 'That lot put me right off.'

Morris squinted at him. 'You hate your royal family, do you?'

'They're not my royal family. Haven't been anybody's royal family since 1940, when they left us at the mercy of that chap. Hey, Barberini, what was his name?'

'Mussolini, mate,' said Barberini, stretching on the bed behind a copy of the *Chronicle*.

'I knew you'd know, mate,' said Guzili.

Morris, unamused, slipped the leaflet inside *Wow*. 'Right-ho, sir. I'm confiscating this as evidence.'

Anger flared in Guzili's eyes. 'You enjoy this, don't you?'

'It's just our work, sir. Keep your temper, eh?' Morris looked to the constable standing outside the door and rolled his eyes. 'I suppose they usually take out all that aggression on ice cubes,' said the sergeant, loudly enough to know that they would hear him. The two policemen began walking back down the corridor. They did not see Guzili spit on the floor as they went.

The corridor was narrow and comfortless, making it difficult for two people to pass. Porthole windows – those, at least, that were not painted over – looked out onto the night. It was the Walsingham at its most maritime.

Sergeant Morris had not expected to see his superior and his questionable friend at this level of the hotel.

'Anything interesting?' asked Book.

Morris produced the copy of *Wow*. 'I don't know whether this would interest you much, sir,' he said, proffering the magazine, 'but this other one might be your sort of thing.' Book ignored the remark and took the leaflet from his hand. He inspected the image of the royal sisters – of whom there were three.

Bliss peered at the cover. 'That's the missing one, yes?'

'Senije,' said Book. 'Spent the last years of her teens in Moscow learning how to blow up railway lines and commandeer telephone exchanges. Then she came back west and toed the line for a bit. Did some royal duties. Anyway, she left with the rest in '40, but now she's cheerfully unburdened herself of her styles and titles and is assumed to be back home, working for the revolution. Running a collective farm, I shouldn't wonder.'

'I should start reading the *Tatler*,' said Bliss. 'Amazing what you can pick up.'

Book waggled the revolutionary pamphlet under Morris's nose. 'Where did you find this?'

'Under the bed of Mr Guzili.'

'Good work, Morris,' said Bliss. 'Take this lot back to Bow Street and let's get this case in order. Statements typed, charge sheets ironed and ready.'

The idea pleased Book more than it pleased the sergeant. Morris tapped his helmet and trudged back to the staircase. Book had already stuck his head around the dormitory door.

'May we?' he enquired.

Guzili leaned against the wall. He was cool but offered no objection. 'You're the guest,' he said. Barberini looked up from the bed. He was in short sleeves and braces, like a corporal in barracks.

'You think it was one of us,' he said, rising from the bed.

'I don't think anything yet, Signor Barberini.' Book studied the photographs pinned to the wall. Among a cluster of film stars was a postcard of a White Star liner. It was marked with a date: 2/7/1940.

'Well I've got it narrowed down to two,' said Guzili. 'A member of the Royal House of Scutari. Nafije or Ruhije.'

Book could see that he was serious. 'Right-ho,' he said. 'Method?'

'Poison. Something slipped into his cocktail glass after he tried it on with Eadie Rattle.'

'This was the chambermaid, yes?' said Bliss. 'Where was she when Captain Orr coughed his last?'

'Gone already,' said Guzili.

'So what's the motive?' quizzed Book, his hands deep in his pockets. 'Any idea why anyone would want to kill Captain Victor Orr?'

'Are you kidding?' said Guzili. 'That captain, he's always here. With different women. Usually in the same room. 504.'

'Oh, really?'

'River view. Noiseless bedsprings. Duchess rate for favoured patrons. And Captain Orr has been coming here for years. Once a week.'

'Without a squeak,' added Barberini.

'You're very well informed.'

'No secrets at the Walsingham,' said Guzili. 'We see all the dirty linen because we have to clean it.'

'Some might say,' ventured Bliss, 'that it is the duty of a grand hotel to ensure that the private life of a guest remains private.'

'And some might say, Inspector,' returned Barberini, 'that in a grand hotel, people are usually at it like cod in a bucket.'

Book smiled tightly. It was a vulgar observation, but it was probably true.

'Ah,' said Bliss. 'So it *was* a crime of passion, then?'

'No,' said Barberini. He was warming to his theme. 'I reckon the captain was something in intelligence, during the war.'

'How do you know that?' asked Book. He was interested.

'They're a type,' said Barberini. 'Friendly but tell you nothing. With a drink, they always have what the other person is having.'

'And why would the princesses want to kill a British spy?' asked Bliss.

'Because British intelligence gave Scutari to the Communist partisans,' said Guzili. 'And the captain recognised the princesses. Revenge is a very powerful motive, don't you think, Mr Book?'

Book nodded, and imagined a lake kissed by the Adriatic sun, with the house above it, where men in boots and bandoliers trod dust into the carpets.

Gabriel Book was not immune to nostalgia. Long ago, a pleasant aunt had given him the *Essays of Elia* as a birthday present. He had felt instant kinship with Charles Lamb, a man watching the eighteenth-century London of his childhood vanish and wondering why the other men in the office were so indifferent to its passing. Did they not mourn the loss of the chimney sweeps' ball? Did the old lamplit names of Drury Lane stir nothing in them? 'That I am fond of indulging,' wrote Lamb, 'beyond a hope of sympathy, in such retrospection, may be the symptom of some sickly idiosyncrasy.'

Book shared the affliction. Sometimes the ghosts of the past were more substantial to him than the hard outlines of the present. 'You have an old soul,' his wife would say, when she found him, sitting by the fire, or putting out the lights at the end of the day, caught in the web of some other moment. The Walsingham Hotel was thick with those webs.

'I give it ten years,' said Bliss, as they descended the stairs to the lobby.

'What?' asked Book.

'The grand hotel. The Walsingham. They'll knock them down and build a massive Lyons Corner House.'

Bliss did not have an old soul. He liked new things, untroubled by history. But he was also a man of routine. When Book bade him goodnight, he knew that the inspector would call at Bow Street before returning home to his wife. Dr Calder would have some chemical news for him.

The Walsingham sailed uneasily into the night. The River Bar was dark, there were police constables posted by the exits, and most of the guests had retired. Room service was understaffed and overworked. Miss Wicking sat behind the reception desk, dealing with calls coming from the rooms above. Mr Kind padded about the lobby, silent as a cat. He adjusted a flower arrangement; removed a forgotten coffee cup; passed a polite moment with the woman in the blue gown. The events of the evening, she said, had made her nervous. Mr Kind ordered her a cup of something calming, and did not add it to the bill. As Book and the inspector came down the grand staircase, he noticed her eyes flick in their direction. 'I suppose it is time to go to bed,' she said, finishing her drink.

Across the lobby, Book watched Bliss disappear through the revolving door; noticed him wince at the deference of the uniformed man who wished him goodnight. It was not, he reflected, an awkwardness much in evidence at Bow Street.

'I can say a proper hello now.'

Book turned round. The general manager was standing in the middle of the lobby, as if waiting for a request.

'Edmund Kind,' said Book, enjoying the sound of the name.

'Good evening,' said Mr Kind. His politeness contained the embers of something.

Book smiled gently. 'More than Kind, I used to say.'

'Oh, well, that's too kind.' Mr Kind gave a soft chuckle. The past seemed close. Perhaps it was the quietness of the lobby, or the flawed light cast by chandeliers that had lost a few prisms to the war.

'They closed it, you know,' said Mr Kind. 'The Lower Bar.'

Book was aghast. 'The Fruit Cellar? No! What a shame.'

'For redecoration, apparently. Though when they'll actually start the work, I've no idea. The management seems to prefer it mothballed.'

'You mean it's all still there? The mural and everything?'

'Oh yes,' smiled Mr Kind. 'We could take a look, if you like.'

They had arrived at one of those moments when the past opens itself up to the present. The sort we experience when we see a former acquaintance across a tube carriage, or in the cinema queue; or find ourselves near a place we once loved and wonder if we should drive through to see if the village green is quite so broad as we remember.

Book hesitated, glancing towards the stairs. 'Well, I really should be going back upstairs.'

'Of course,' said Mr Kind. And said nothing more.

'But I suppose a quick peek wouldn't do any harm, would it?'

Mr Kind glanced behind him. 'Would you look after the

desk for a moment, Miss Wicking?' She nodded, the receiver clamped to her ear.

'Shall we?' asked Mr Kind.

Mr Kind turned his key in the lock and pushed open the door. The Lower Bar was dark and silent, like the control room of a lost submarine. Most of the chairs were stacked at the edges of the room; the shelves were empty except for a pile of old menus and a forgotten bottle of Angostura bitters. The wall behind the bar retained the conversation piece installed in the first months of the Blitz; a mural of Hitler and Mussolini receiving a kick in the backside from a large disembodied high-heeled shoe, painted by a *Daily Sketch* cartoonist who had gone on to be crushed by a German tank at Dunkirk.

'But will the lights work?' asked Mr Kind. 'That's the question.'

'I don't remember there being any,' said Book.

'We never put them on,' said Mr Kind, fumbling for the switch near the doorframe.

'The blackout, I suppose,' Book mused.

'Oh no. They were just terribly unflattering.'

'Oh well,' said Book. 'Let's leave them off, then.'

The lamps behind the bar, Mr Kind discovered, contained a couple of functioning bulbs. They gave off just enough light to prevent the visitors bumping into the few items of furniture that remained. The removal of a dust sheet revealed a comfortable sofa and a table with a scratch that the gloom could not hide. They settled at it and listened to the empty sound of the room.

'Kim Strang is dead,' said Mr Kind. 'Did you hear?'

'Kim Strang. He used to keep his Max Factor in a gas-mask box.'

'Well, he'd been in Egypt, hadn't he? Needed to keep that tan up.'

'What happened to him?'

'Walked into the sea at Shoreham, I'm sorry to say. Someone had his letters. Dreadful, really.'

'Dreadful,' Book echoed.

Kind's gaze fell upon Book's hand. 'And you're very married, I see.'

'Very, very married,' confirmed Book.

'Congratulations,' said Mr Kind, and meant it.

'Thanks,' replied Book, looking his old friend in the eye. 'And thanks for your help with the other matter.'

'Not at all,' said Mr Kind. 'Old pals should help each other out. I was pleased to hear from you. Surprised, too, of course. But pleased. What does Jack know?'

Book exhaled. 'That my wife and I have an arrangement. That I knew his late father.'

'Nothing more?'

'That was difficult enough for him to take. There was a dreadful scene. He was terribly angry with us both. Not fair on Trottie, of course, but I fear I deserved it rather. Sometimes life can make one feel an awful coward, can't it?'

'Oh it can,' said Mr Kind. 'Discretion isn't the better part of valour.'

'No,' said Book. 'That would be valour. He walked out on us that very night.'

'And floated here. I'm glad we could find him a berth.'

'Well,' said Book. 'I'm very grateful. He needs a home. He needs something to occupy him. Otherwise, who knows, he might be tempted back into bad company.' He lowered his voice, as if the room might contain a hidden microphone. 'And I must confess another motive. It allowed him to keep an eye on the other bodies floating around. The regal Scutari ones.'

Mr Kind also lowered his voice, without quite knowing why. 'Why do you want to keep an eye on them?'

'It's possible that they were the intended victims.'

'Not the captain?'

'It's a working hypothesis.'

Mr Kind now saw a truth that had eluded him. He had assumed that his friend was at the Walsingham to attend his wife in a moment that demanded a heroic amount of decency. He had assumed that his relationship with Inspector Bliss had been that of detective and witness.

'Are you with the police now, Gabriel? You always were a dark horse.'

'It makes up a substantial part of my charm.' Book grinned.

Mr Kind shook his head. 'And how does that work? Christ, isn't that dangerous? One false step . . .'

'I am all too aware of that, Edmund.'

Both possessed a repertoire of near misses; both had friends who might have died of shame, had they not chosen some other method first; both knew the ice-cold feeling of turning to the back page of the *News of the World* and seeing a familiar name. Your former schoolmaster; your clergyman cousin.

'So,' said Mr Kind, 'you should probably not be found in a half-lit basement with—'

'With a terribly handsome old friend? No. Perhaps not.'

The lights behind the bar flickered suddenly. For a second the room was sunk into complete darkness.

'Problem with the grid?' Book asked.

Kind shook his head. 'The Walsingham isn't connected to the grid. It has its own oil-powered generators. We bring it in by the barrel. Everything depends on it. Even the plumbing.' The light flickered again, this time for longer. 'It was always a bit of a selling point during the war. We kept going even when the rest of the Strand went dark. But what's a grand hotel without power and hot running water?'

'Well,' Book said thoughtfully, 'I suppose it's just a big building full of people who are rather cold and rather hungry – and very, very rich.'

The light failed again, like an omen.

'I'd better get back,' Kind said.

'Me too,' Book agreed.

They did not move. Book reached out, took Kind's hand and gave it a gentle squeeze. 'It's good to see you again,' he said.

'I knew you were on Archangel Lane,' said Mr Kind. 'I've often thought of coming by the shop.'

'You should,' said Book.

This time the light stayed out for a full three seconds.

In Room 504, Trottie also received a taste of darkness. It almost made her drop the glass she had pressed against the wall adjoining the royal suite. Since she knew no Albanian, her eavesdropping had produced no new information, though she had reached a secure critical position on Ruhije's relationship with the piano keyboard. Her patience was rewarded when Jack entered their room. She could not hear all that passed between them, but it was clear that the princesses were milking him for details about the staff and the guests. They seemed particularly interested in the chambermaid who had been caught up in the regrettable incident involving Victor Orr and a wet cloth.

'What is her name?'

Jack's reply was too quiet to catch, but it seemed to produce a bloom of anxiety from Nafije. 'Why did you help her?' she demanded. 'You are supposed to be protecting us.'

'She may have revolutionary tendencies,' said Ruhije. 'Please find out.'

The conversation seemed to have come to an end. When a knock came at the door, Trottie feared that she had been detected. The person responsible, however, turned out to be her husband.

'Good evening, my love,' he said, with telegraphic cheerfulness.

'Where did you get to?' she asked.

'I was talking to the staff,' he replied, closing the door behind him. 'The ones who served your cocktails tonight.'

'Ah,' she replied. 'Well, it was only really the older one.'

'Barberini?'

Trottie returned the glass to the washstand. 'If you say so. He was in charge. Those princesses wouldn't drink the stuff made by his mate. He poured a whole round down the sink. Ice, fruit and all.'

He noticed that Trottie had laid out the attaché case on the little writing desk by the window. He flipped open the catches and extracted the *Kanun of Scutari* and a foolscap folder stuffed with papers. He began reading the documents.

'And could he have tampered with the second round?' Book asked.

'Oh yes. Nobody was looking. Because of the brouhaha.' Trottie opened the curtains and looked out over the Thames. The night was clear and bright.

'Brouhaha?'

Book's brain was chuntering away like a comptometer. Trottie decided that if she was going to supply a detailed account of the evening, she might as well do it in comfort. She kicked off her shoes and sank back on the bed. 'One of their Royal Highnesses dropped her reticule. Loose change all over the tiles.'

Book nodded slowly. 'Yes, I've heard about that. And after the brouhaha?'

'I dragged Victor back to the bar and he gave the toast. And then there was a furore.'

'A brouhaha and then a furore? The plot thickens.' He was looking at a typewritten document: Trottie could see a photograph gummed to the first page. It appeared to be one of the princesses.

'People were recoiling in pure horror,' she said. 'It was burning his neck out, Book. You could hear it crackle.' She shuddered.

Book put down his papers, settled beside her on the bed and put an arm around her. She leaned into his warmth.

'I'm sorry you had a beastly time,' he said softly.

Trottie sighed. 'I just wanted to get stinko and wake up somewhere with clean sheets and three-egg omelettes. I wanted *something*. So I wanted him.'

She closed her eyes, her cheek resting on his neck. It might have been the moment for a kiss, but there was no kiss.

'I do love you, Mrs Book,' he murmured.

'Ditto,' she replied. Then, after a moment: 'Book?'

'Yes?'

'We never really talk.'

'Talk?' There was something in his eyes that looked a little like fear.

'About . . . the arrangement.'

'What's to talk about?' Book smiled, hoping that he had not sounded too much like a man avoiding a difficult subject.

'Well, to see that all's well. That we're both all right with—'

A large and fragile body seemed to stretch before them. They had built it themselves, as shipwrecked people might build a life raft. They occupied it; they were both undrowned. But Book feared the sea more than Trottie.

'I could have been making love in this,' she said, running a hand over the eiderdown. There was pain in her voice, and Book wondered if he was competent to read it.

The bedside lamp flickered, went out and stayed out. The room, however, did not succumb to total darkness. The winter moon was bright over London and had light enough for Room 504.

'Has anyone told Victor Orr's poor wife?' The question

was fair and pertinent, but it was also about the case: for Book, the most comfortable territory in the world.

'It's not like she's expecting him to come home,' said Trottie.

'Do you know who she is?'

Trottie sighed. 'I didn't really know who he was. Still, I suppose he did get us a night here. Isn't it magnificent?'

The moon seemed near, as if it might descend into the Thames. Mr and Mrs Book gazed up at it. Another moment for a kiss. There was no kiss.

'No clouds tonight,' Book said. 'Nowhere for the stars to hide.'

'We never really had a proper honeymoon, did we?'

'No. Bit of a diary clash. The Luftwaffe also had their hearts set on Eastbourne.'

'The beach was very pebbly, anyway.'

'And covered in barbed wire,' Book added. He drew her close; she moved with him. They did not look at each other, but both gazed together at the pattern of the night. 'Does it worry you, though? Disappoint you?' His voice was soft.

'What?'

'The absence of landmarks. Declarations. Grand gestures.'

She considered the question carefully. The war had demanded pragmatism; it had left room for little else. Was their marriage a form of civil defence? A matter of make do and mend? It did not seem so to Trottie. She thought of the alternatives and felt no joy. Victor Orr, for instance. He had been a man for grand gestures. He was lavish, reckless, the sort who would kiss you in front of waiters and railway porters. He was not Trevor Howard in *Brief Encounter*, offering to whisk you away to South Africa. Nor was Book the suburban husband who knew all about crossword puzzles and nothing of desire.

'Oh no, Book,' she said. 'In fact, I'm going to make one now. Let's order a bloody huge bottle of champagne.'

Book was pleased with the answer, but the question had entangled him in the past and he could not quite unhook himself. The ghosts within him were moving. He was thinking of a man. A handsome man. Anyone would say so, if they had observed his warm brown eyes and the neat line of his military moustache. They might also say that he was troubled, if they had seen him as Book saw him in memory, sitting alone in a busy railway station buffet, surrounded by travellers, some anxious, some trying to hide their anxiety, and the portrait of the Führer framed above the counter. There were many reasons to return to this moment. It was one that, as Book entered it, full of jittery optimism, suitcase in hand, he had entirely failed to understand. It was the moment that divided one half of his life from the other.

At first, he did not see Felix, the restaurant was so crowded. The room was full of families, none of whom were travelling lightly. Everyone had slightly more luggage than was comfortable; every case bulged. He saw a mother failing to jolly her two miserable children about the surprise holiday she said their father had booked; a woman giving a mournful lecture to her dog about the difficulties of long train journeys. When Book spotted Felix, alone at a table, his eyes on his cup of coffee, he rushed towards him with a kind of breathless pride.

'I have our papers,' he said, putting down his case. 'Stamped and signed. And tickets.' He reached into his jacket pocket, but Felix stopped his hand.

'Can't you do anything discreetly, my love?'

Felix glanced around the room. A man was standing nearby. There was something about him that Felix did not like. It was his unhurried quality: he had no luggage, nor did he betray any sign of waiting for anyone to arrive. He had no party badge or armband, but the well-fed face beneath a greasy grey hat seemed to bear the invisible mark of the swastika.

An announcement rang out on the tannoy. 'We have five minutes before it leaves,' said Book. 'Platform six. We'll be in Paris for breakfast. There are no Nazis in Paris. But there are croissants. So it's all going to be fine.'

Several passengers began to gather themselves. The woman with the dog concluded her lecture and moved for the door.

Felix shook his head. 'I can't come with you, Book. For the same reason that you must leave.'

Book was looking at the floor. He had noticed something that, in retrospect, he felt he should have seen at once. 'Where's your suitcase?'

Felix's silence was answer enough. Book put his hands on the table, as if to steady himself. The future was coming unstuck. Some new bleak version of tomorrow was emerging. It was not the one that they had been planning, just a few hours before, under the skylight of an attic room on Motzstraße. Book had woken first, and watched Felix sleep, and the dawn turn the sky pink. He had lit the little stove and made a breakfast from their two last eggs, the heel of the previous day's loaf and the remains of a salami. He had run to the British consulate, hoping that a long-owed favour had been returned in paper and red ink, then run to the Potsdamer Bahnhof in a state of elation. This had now drained away, leaving icy, ashen panic. He wanted to remonstrate with Felix. Persuade him to change his mind. Plead with him.

'*Es ist so überfüllt,*' said the man with the grey hat. '*Darf ich hier sitzen?*'

Book knew what was being asked. There was an empty chair at their table. He could not stop him taking it.

'*Natürlich,*' said Book, smoothly.

The man pulled the chair about a foot away from the table, turned slightly away from its occupants, and sat down. He settled his saucer in the palm of his hand and took a small sip of coffee. The tannoy burst with another announcement about platform six.

Felix fixed his eyes on Book. 'Oh. And I must return this to you, my dear fellow.' He reached into his pocket and produced a little volume of poetry in plain calf binding. 'I love a good book,' he said. 'A beautiful book. And how easy it is to picture myself, on some winter evening in the country, lying with this particular book. It moves me so much. But I'm afraid I cannot keep it. I know its frailties. Some books get burned, you know. And I should not like to be responsible for the loss of this one. Because it is so dear to me that I know it by heart.'

Felix pushed the little volume of poetry across the table. Book took it. His hands, he noticed, were trembling slightly. Could the man with the grey hat see? Book did not look.

His gaze was on Felix, who was quoting the poem from memory.

'*Henceforth, wherever thou may'st roam,*
My blessing, like a line of light—'

Book finished the stanza, hoping his voice would not break, as his heart was breaking.

'*Is on the waters day and night,*
And like a beacon guards thee home.'

The tannoy called the train again. For a moment, the two men sat in silence. Book got to his feet. His fingers closed around the handle of his suitcase. Every movement felt like an unravelling. He withdrew his eyes from Felix and his body from the room.

Felix watched the door of the restaurant swing shut. The noise of the people in the room had gained a new and unwelcome volume. His eyes fell to his coffee cup, which was empty.

'Tennyson?'

The man in the greasy grey hat was staring at him.

Felix nodded. The man drained his coffee and put the cup and saucer down on the table.

'You should read German poets,' said the man.

When he rose, the chair gave an unpleasant screech.

CHAPTER FOUR

It was nearly midnight when two Bow Street constables arrested Ismail Guzili. Bliss, ringing from his desk, let them in on the reason: a searing dose of hydrochloric acid inside the residue of the cocktail; the waiter's fingerprint upon the glass, big and clear as a headline in the *Express*. They took Guzili from the dormitory and did it with commendable subtlety. Only Barberini, shaking his head and cursing quietly, and Mr Kind, who escorted them down the service staircase, knew anything about it.

After the arrest, Edmund Kind stood at his post and tried not to think of the captain of the *Titanic*. Thankfully, the Palm Court orchestra were not on the premises: there was no danger of a spontaneous outbreak of 'Nearer, My God, to Thee'. It was, however, hard to dispel the feeling that catastrophe was approaching the Walsingham, out of the darkness. Mr Kind had a suspicion about who was responsible. The engineer had come to his office, partly to describe his own competence and the good order of the hotel's systems, partly to produce evidence of sabotage by persons unknown; several bottles that had been hidden, rather inexpertly, in the waste bin by the furnace. The engineer brought one to the reception desk. It had contained boiled linseed oil, a product found in abundance in the basement cleaning stores. As Mr Kind half listened to a lecture on the dangers of fuel dilution, the name of a member of staff came swiftly to mind. A noisy name.

He picked up the telephone to ring housekeeping, but did not complete the call. Something peculiar had appeared in the lobby: a distinguished-looking Labrador, which added an agreeable shade of honey to the monochrome restraint of the Walsingham. The dog was not alone. He was the herald of an impishly small young woman in a knitted green suit and matching beret, carrying a scuffed nineteenth-century folio under her arm. She planted the book on the reception desk like a Covent Garden boy bringing a tray of lettuce to the kitchen.

'Delivery for Mr Book,' said Nora. 'Would you see that he gets it?'

Mr Kind looked down. The cover was busy with embossed Gothic German script. It appeared to be a bound collection of pamphlets and papers.

'How's your Albanian?' asked Nora, winking as if this were some kind of euphemism.

'Weak, miss,' said Mr Kind.

'That'll sort you out, then.'

Nora noticed a bowl of complimentary peppermints on the reception desk. She picked one out and popped it into her mouth. 'You do *know* Mr Book? He is a guest here?'

'Oh yes,' said Edmund Kind. 'I know him.'

Satisfied, Nora took a handful of mints and dropped them into her pocket. 'Good,' she said. With that, she clicked her tongue at the Labrador and both disappeared from the lobby.

Mr Kind flicked through the folio. His eyes were drawn to an engraving of a mermaid perched beneath a cliff; the illustration of an alembic producing what might have been gold; a programme from a Viennese production of *Fidelio*; a thick run of pages in which the word 'Scutari' was prominent. The latter, he assumed, were the object of Book's interest. He gave a vague nod to Miss Wicking and called the lift, hesitating slightly before he stepped in.

The lift did nothing out of character between the ground floor and the fifth, but as Mr Kind moved down the corridor, the lighting became increasingly low and fitful. It was as if the nervous system of the building was expressing its unease. He wondered how long it could last without breaking down completely. He put a hand on a nearby radiator. Cold.

He turned a corner and saw Jack on duty outside the royal suite. He had been given a chair and was trying to read the newspaper in the imperfect light. Jack stood up as the general manager approached. Perhaps, thought Mr Kind, the boy expected the shine on his shoes to be inspected. He offered Jack a faint smile. 'I'm doing the rounds. Explaining about the . . . situation.'

As if on cue, the lights flickered again. Mr Kind was aware of a brisk rattle, the sudden and violent opening of the door to the royal suite, and a shiver of salmon-pink satin. Ruhije stood on the threshold, her revolver pointed directly at his chest, her finger on the trigger, her eyes looking ready to find the next Archduke Franz Ferdinand.

Mr Kind had devoted decades of his life to the cultivation of professional unflappability, but inside he felt distinctly flapped. His heart was pounding. He would have liked to take cover or use the book as a shield. Instead, he looked at the princess and inclined his head.

'Be so good as to move around a little less silently,' Ruhije said. 'It arouses suspicion.'

Kind cleared his throat. 'I do apologise, Your Royal Highness. It's my training, you see.'

Ruhije raised an eyebrow but did not lower the gun. 'It's mine too.' She looked him up and down, then hitched her skirt and replaced the weapon in her garter. As she did so, the lights shivered off and on.

Ruhije cast a critical eye upwards.

'An engineer is investigating,' said Mr Kind. 'I do apologise for the inconvenience.'

Ruhije shrugged. 'We are accustomed to hardship.' Her gaze shifted to the object in Kind's arms. 'What are you carrying? Show me.'

Mr Kind opened the volume to reveal the pages he thought might be of most interest.

'This is the *Kanun of Scutari*,' she said, her tone sharpening. 'Why do you have this?'

'I'm taking it to Mr Book, in the next room. He's helping the police.'

'This is most interesting,' she said. 'Continue.'

'Well,' said Mr Kind, 'he's a sort of expert witness, and he's staying here with his wife, who I believe—'

'I meant continue on your way,' Ruhije interrupted,

closing her eyes impatiently. 'Goodnight.' With a swish of satin, she turned and closed the door. The sound of the piano began almost immediately.

Jack flashed Mr Kind a sympathetic grin. The general manager adjusted himself, continued down the corridor and knocked on the door of Room 504. Trottie seemed pleased to see him, just for a moment.

'Oh,' she said, her face falling. 'I thought you were a bottle of . . . How dispiriting.'

Mr Kind smiled pleasantly. 'A book for Mr Book,' he said.

Trottie took it carelessly, glancing over her shoulder.

'What is it, Trottie?' came Book's voice from within.

'It's that book you wanted, dear,' she said.

'Very good,' Book replied. Mr Kind shifted the weight on his feet and peered over Trottie's shoulder at the other occupant of the room. He saw Book at the writing desk, making notes on a pile of hotel stationery. Beside him was a large volume bound in green leather and a foolscap file of the sort for storing official documents. An attaché case lay open on the floor. When Trottie noticed Mr Kind trying to get a better view, he averted his eyes.

'The radiator's on the blink up here,' she said.

'An engineer is investigating,' said Mr Kind, dutifully. 'I do apologise for the inconvenience. Is there anything more I can do for you?' The radiator gave a digestive gurgle.

Trottie looked down to see if Mr Kind's foot was actually in the door, but no; the general manager was a being of ghostlike subtlety. 'Well,' she said, remembering that she was staying in a grand hotel, even if she owed the room to a murdered acquaintance, 'tracking down our champagne would be nice.'

Mr Kind nodded graciously and evaporated.

'Extraordinary man,' said Trottie, closing the door. 'Smells nice, though.'

'Gardenia,' said Book, without looking up.

'Nora seems to have found your translation,' said Trottie. Book accepted it with relish. He placed it side by side with the original text and devoured it like a new dish at a Chinese banquet.

'Room service isn't up to much, is it?' Trottie muttered.

'I think there's trouble below. With the generator.' Something in the text caught his eye. 'Oh!' he exclaimed, making more notes. 'Now that's very helpful.'

Trottie watched him scribble. 'You don't need champagne, do you, Book? Just anything with footnotes.'

'And a bibliography,' said Book. He smacked his lips. 'Maybe an erratum slip.'

She cast an eye over his work, and found her attention drawn by a handwritten letter in an elaborate and angry-looking script. She picked it up and took it to the bed to read.

'Rather colourful, this, isn't it?' she said. 'Did the inspector give it to you?'

Book looked up to see his wife's eyes dancing over the page.

'No,' he said, and said no more. Trottie was too absorbed in the text to pursue the matter. She read the letter aloud, with more relish than was entirely necessary.

Princesses!

Gargoyles of feudalism! We lopped you from the crumbling escarpments of the house of our oppressors. Now the people of Scutari, their will as irresistible as the granite truths of Marxist-Leninism, occupy the rooms in which you once pursued your lives of sordid decadence.

We have expelled you. But the people remember your crimes. And they have dispatched me to demonstrate that the justice meted by the dictatorship of the proletariat is inescapable. I do not act alone. There are many in Britain who support our just and proper cause. We are everywhere.

She might have reached the end, had not Book shushed her so fiercely.

A violent altercation was happening in the next room. They heard the low, fast rumble of argument, the door of the royal suite clattering. Then the light disappeared. This time there was no flicker, no sense of a current struggling to complete the circuit, just the sudden arrival of complete darkness and, a second later, a loud and sudden report, sharp and hard as a gunshot.

Trottie sat bolt upright on the bed.

'What's that?'

From the other room, a cry reached them. It was Nafije.

'Oh God. Oh my face! I'm hit!'

For a second, the lights returned, giving Book and Trottie just enough time to exchange a wide-eyed look of shock. Darkness then drowned the room again. The curtains were closed: the moonlight did not come to their aid.

Book leapt from the bed, found the handle, tore open

the door and stumbled out into the corridor, where an unscreened window made the gloom more navigable. He saw what he took to be the shape of Jack, banging on the door of the royal suite.

Inside, Nafije was howling in pain. Then came the voice of Ruhije: 'One more step and I'll—'

A gunshot cut through the air.

Eadie's voice roared out. Had she been hit? Or had she fired the shot herself?

Book ran forward and launched himself at the door with all the force he could muster. His body slammed against the woodwork and he burst through it like a chorus girl jumping out of a cake. The room was a space of hot breath, noise and confusion. Ruhije was shouting in her own language. It sounded like a warning. Nafije screamed again: a sound of helpless pain and panic.

As he barrelled forward, Book collided with a heavy object in the middle of the room. He went crashing down with it to the carpet. There seemed to be broken glass on the floor, and something wet and cold beneath his hands.

Book was rising from the floor when another gunshot rang out, ear-splitting in the pitch-black room. He threw himself down and a hot bullet whistled over his head. In the brief flash from the discharge, he saw a room-service trolley lying on its side, its contents spilled, and Her Royal Highness Ruhije of Scutari, pistol in hand, her face a mask of fear and fury.

When the lights sputtered back to life, Mrs Trottie Book had the surest overview of the carnage. From the threshold of the royal suite, she saw her husband marooned on the floor, surrounded by culinary debris. Jack was standing over him. Ruhije was upright, breathless and defiant, her revolver now levelled in Trottie's direction. (The architrave of the door, Trottie saw, bore a ragged bullet hole.) Nafije was backed against the fireplace, one hand at her face, nursing the painful impact of a projectile. Her left cheek bore a great red welt.

The nature of her injury was explained by the presence of the fifth person in the room. Eadie Rattle stood beneath a patch of broken plasterwork, flushed and breathless. In her hands she held a bottle of champagne as Al Capone might have held a machine gun. The last of its contents frothed on the carpet at her feet.

'That's my champagne!' exclaimed Trottie.

'Indubitably,' said Book, from somewhere near the skirting board. He held a fat cork between his thumb and forefinger.

For a moment, everyone held their positions in this tableau. Eadie broke the spell. The bottle slipped from her hands, bounced on the carpet and came to rest in a field of scattered ice cubes. Something was wrong with her. She clutched at her shoulder, where a crimson patch was forming on the white cotton of her collar. Wincing and cursing, she crumpled to the sofa.

'Oh ruddy hell,' she seethed, clenching her teeth. 'It hurts!'

Trottie lit up with anger and directed it at Ruhije. 'You shot her, you bloody Carpathian lunatic!' Book scrambled to his feet, retrieved the napkin that had been wrapped around the bottle of champagne and passed it to his wife, who used it to dab Eadie's wound. Jack stared at the scene, suddenly seeming very young and helpless.

Ruhije muttered her defence: 'I thought she had a gun.' She then disappeared into her bedroom. This provoked another tirade from Trottie, who relented only when Ruhije rematerialised bearing a bowl of water and a compact Army field medical kit stamped with the eagle insignia of Scutari. With a regal flick of the hand, the princess ushered the Books out of her way and got to work. Her skill was as obvious as it was surprising. The lights, still feeble and unstable, did not help her task.

'Am I going to die?' asked Eadie.

'It's just a graze,' said Ruhije, applying antiseptic.

'Fortunately for you, Your Royal Highness,' said Book.

His sonorous tone prompted Nafije to begin a curiously formal apology. 'This is a very regrettable incident. Miss—'

'Eadie Rattle.'

'Miss Rattle, we live under the constant threat of assassination. The black mantle of death hovers over us like the London fog. Sometimes, out of fear, we make mistakes. I implore your forgiveness.' She inclined her head graciously.

Trottie was unimpressed by the performance. 'You shouldn't forgive them,' she said, hotly. 'You should press charges.'

The remark seemed to annoy Eadie as much as the bullet did. 'Don't tell me what to do,' she snapped. 'I've had enough of it. I've simply had enough of it.' Her eyes flashed with anger.

'We understand, dear,' Trottie said softly.

'Do you?' scowled Eadie. 'I've worked a long shift today. It began with a pass in the River Bar, and then I got fired.'

'Fired?' Jack had come to life.

'Been given my cards, haven't I? Someone sabotaged the boilers – tipped linseed oil into them. Mr Kind has been gunning for me for weeks. He gave me a mouthful for standing up to that bastard with the moustache. And he knows I'd gladly see this place sink into the Thames, so naturally he put me in the middle of the frame. And now I've been bloody shot! Shot!' She flinched: Ruhije had pulled a small syrette from the medical kit and was holding it up to the light from the chandelier, clearly intending to jab it in Eadie's arm.

'Morphine tartrate,' Ruhije explained.

'Oh no you don't,' said Eadie, recoiling. 'There's a poisoner in this building. How do I know it's not you?'

'It will ease your pain.'

'I can live with a bit of pain,' Eadie said stubbornly. 'And,' she said, looking Ruhije straight in the eye, 'if you think you're just going to patch me up and watch me get on the night bus and say, "Oh, I quite understand, it must be beastly when your country hates your guts and you're forced to slum it at the Walsingham," then think again, ladies. No wonder you're nervous around the working classes. You damn well ought to be.'

Ruhije did not argue. Nor did Nafije. They knew Eadie was right. Ruhije stayed the needle. Nafije withdrew her hand from her bruised face to reveal an expression of genuine contrition. Something had adjusted in the room; something for which Friedrich Engels had probably coined a long German word.

The chambermaid exhaled, her anger losing its temperature. 'I'll take the morphine now,' she said.

Ruhije injected the dose without a word. 'So, Eadie Rattle. What do you suggest?'

Eadie named her terms. 'I'll stay here tonight. In the royal suite.'

'There are only two beds,' said Nafije.

'Then I'll have the biggest. And when I wake up I'll have breakfast in it.'

Book was sitting at the piano, watching the scene play out. 'I think that's a very modest demand,' he said, 'considering the bullets in the wall. And I know how important the rules of hospitality are in your country. I've been reading up on them.' He lifted a page of music manuscript propped on the lid and dislodged an expensive-looking fountain pen. He picked it up and examined it as if he were considering buying one himself.

'At home, we are obliged to take in those who need shelter,' said Nafije. 'During the war, many British officers parachuted into our territory. None were betrayed.'

Ruhije decided to honour ancestral tradition. 'I'll sleep on the sofa,' she said.

Eadie had achieved victory. 'Right,' she said. 'Who's going to lend me their toothbrush?' She smiled like Lenin receiving the news of the Potemkin mutiny.

Crossing the threshold of the royal suite put Jack together with Trottie and Book for the first time since his sudden departure from Archangel Lane. He did not take the opportunity for a reconciliation. The bullet hole in the doorframe gave him a reason to avoid eye contact.

'Better get someone to see to this,' he said, disappearing down the corridor.

'Have we lost him?' asked Trottie, watching him go.

'We hardly knew him,' said Book quietly.

'I like her,' said Trottie. 'Eadie Rattle. She's sharp.'

'As her nibs.'

'The princess, you mean?' said Trottie. 'Sharper.'

'I remember laughing at them before the war,' mused Book. 'The Scutari royal family. A comic opera monarchy that mortgaged itself to the Fascists, and were surprised when they called in the debt.'

'Odd, isn't it?' said Trottie. 'I've had nights out with people who would have happily put them against the wall and let them have it. But in person? They seem sad and lost. Like old music hall turns.'

She had the key in the door of Room 504.

'It's the Dinaric Alps, by the way,' said Book.

'What?'

'Not the Carpathians.'

Trottie rolled her eyes. 'Clever clogs.'

'Well,' said Book, 'if the shoe fits.'

The latch clicked shut behind them.

Ismail Guzili had never enjoyed the attention of the police. Up to this point, the gendarmes had been his least favourite. He had come to know their foibles and eccentricities while toiling in the kitchen of a filthy hotel in the rue du Marché-des-Blancs-Manteaux, where the *entremetier* had accused him of involvement in a racket selling car magnetos stolen from the garage next door. Now the words '*liberté, égalité, fraternité*' brought the instant feeling that someone was about to hit him with a stick.

Bow Street police station produced the same effect. It was, he concluded, the opposite of a grand hotel, and Sergeant Morris — the opposite of a maître d' — had done everything in his power to ensure his stay was memorable. Nothing was too much for him. Morris had arranged a freezing waiting room; a contemptuous desk sergeant; a grimy holding cell he was obliged to share with a man who reeked of spirits and wanted to assert, in great detail, how he had only knocked his wife about to teach her a lesson, and that after fifteen years of marriage, a woman should know her husband likes his bacon to be crispy. Then, after a long night of this monologue, the sergeant brought Guzili to the interview room, a dispiriting place where natural light seemed to be on the ration. Morris motioned for him to sit, then stood to one side. The hard institutional chair made Guzili realise how quickly he had become accustomed to the plush cocoon of the Walsingham.

Two men were already in the room. Inspector Bliss was standing in the light; another figure stayed back, lost in the shadows. Bliss offered Guzili a cigarette, which he took and lit with deliberate slowness. The brand was perfectly acceptable.

'Are you going to charge me?' he asked.

'Plenty of time for that,' said Bliss.

Guzili exhaled smoke and leaned back as far as the chair would allow. 'I've said it all already. It's in the statement.'

Bliss ignored the remark. 'One thing before we start,' he said. 'Mr Book here will be joining us. He's a specialist.' Book emerged from the gloom. Guzili eyed him warily. He had already registered that Book was not a policeman. Who was he?

'Mr Guzili, it's very important that you use this interview to tell us the truth,' said Bliss. 'If you do not, I cannot be held accountable for the consequences. We know about your affair with Eadie Rattle. She's given us a statement. She was quite nice about you really. Said you were a good man. But in revealing your romantic connection, she's provided a possible motive. A reason for you to kill Captain Orr.'

Guzili snorted. 'Because he made a pass at Eadie? It must happen three times a day. The Walsingham is full of captains.' He turned to Book. 'What business are you in, exactly?'

'The antiquarian book business,' replied Book, with terrible gravitas. He stepped into the light. 'I've read the *Kanun of Scutari*. Have you?'

'I know it.'

'Live by it?'

'It was very important in my village.'

Book sat down at the interview table. A police file was in front of him. He polished his glasses, replaced them on his nose and flicked through its contents. His expression suggested he had noted several points of interest. He closed the file and folded his arms. 'Let's start, then. If I said we were going to give you the third degree, what would you expect?'

Guzili had not anticipated that the threats would start so soon. 'A kicking out by the bins?'

'Snake in the grass,' snapped Book.

The waiter was confused. 'What did you say?'

'Forget the third degree,' said Book, his eyes narrowing. 'Snake in the grass. Come on. I'm waiting.'

Something clicked, like the lid of a stainless-steel shaker. 'Oh. Um. Anisette?'

Book shook his head darkly. 'No, Mr Guzili.'

'Vodka.'

Book slapped the table. 'At last!'

'Crème de menthe. Lime juice.' Guzili stumbled. 'Er . . . lemonade?'

Book's expression was glacial. 'Where's my ice?'

'It went in first.'

'Are you shaking this drink?'

Guzili hesitated.

'This is the Walsingham, Mr Guzili,' pushed Book. 'Are you shaking this drink?'

'No,' Guzili stammered. 'I'm stirring it. I'm stirring it.'

'Attaboy,' Book said.

'Attaboy!' exclaimed Guzili. 'I know that. French vermouth, dry gin, grenadine. Four dashes. Shaken.'

Book moved closer. He lowered his voice to ask the most serious question of all. 'What would you put . . . in a pansy?'

Guzili paused. 'Oh. Um. Angostura bitters?'

'Yes. What else?'

'Anisette?'

'No, no, no, Mr Guzili,' snapped Book. 'That's a pansy blossom. A pansy requires absinthe.'

Guzili's confidence had cracked. 'Look, I'm still on probation. I'm not an expert.'

Book seemed to have secured what he wanted. 'I'll say

you're not. But nor are you a murderer.' His eyes went down to Dr Calder's report.

Bliss leaned forward. 'What makes you say that?'

'Because he left a dirty great fingerprint on the higher part of one of those glasses. And a good cocktail waiter – someone who knows how to mix a third degree – always handles a rocks glass lower down.' Book raised a police station mug to demonstrate his point.

'You set them up for Barberini. That's when you left your print on the glass. I'm sorry if this sounds insulting, Mr Guzili, but you haven't yet acquired the skill to poison anyone in a crowded bar in plain sight. Particularly with just a few seconds between the inciting incident and the crime. But I'm sure you'll get there. In fact, I'd go so far as to say you are already a model employee.'

Guzili raised an eyebrow. 'Going to write me a reference now, are you?'

'Why not?' breezed Book. 'How long had the princesses been staying at the Walsingham?'

'Four days,' Guzili replied.

'And you'd already noticed that they always reject the first drink. So you made it with tap water. Some employers would promote a member of staff so concerned about wastage.'

Inspector Bliss was quietly impressed. Inspector Bliss was also quietly miserable. The case against Guzili had dissolved like an ice cube in a cup of tea. He turned to Sergeant Morris. 'Looks like our friend here is checking out,' he said. 'Would you be so good as to reunite him with his things?'

Guzili rose to his feet with a surly smile. Morris nodded smoothly and delivered him through the door into the hands of the whey-faced constable. Guzili would not be permitted to celebrate his victory in front of Morris.

'Now what?' Bliss asked. 'Anyone could have got the poison into the drink.'

'Anyone but Mr Guzili,' said Book. 'As I discovered late last night, the *Kanun of Scutari* has strict rules about hospitality. It's taboo to harm anyone you consider your guest. Captain Orr was Guzili's guest, strictly speaking. And the *Kanun* is very strict.'

Bliss made a grumbling sound. 'Did it tell you anything else useful?'

'Oh yes. If someone is murdered under your roof, you are obliged to take revenge. If you don't, the blood debt passes down to the next generation.'

'I find it's usually best if people are just nice to each other.'

They trudged down the corridor back to the inspector's office. At the front desk, the whey-faced constable was handing Guzili his belongings: a belt, his wallet and a copy of *Wow* magazine in a plain brown police envelope. As his interrogators passed, Guzili gave them an insolent salute and slapped the envelope against Morris's chest. 'Here,' he said. 'Have one on me. Compliments of the Walsingham.' Morris was obliged to take the envelope. As Guzili turned on his heels, the sergeant dropped the package into the wastepaper basket.

Book pretended not to have noticed the exchange. He had no wish to give Morris more reasons to be hostile. He marched towards the inspector's office with the case file open in his hands. 'Good old-fashioned hydrochloric acid, I see.'

'They can't all be virtuosos,' muttered Bliss. '*Virtuosi.*'

'Where would you find that in a hotel, I wonder?'

'Ah,' said Bliss, 'that's easy. It's what they use to get the limescale off the bath. It's a suicide's favourite, Book. Particularly among the servant class.'

Morris, still stinging, closed the door behind them. Book flopped on a chair and pulled Eadie Rattle's statement from the file. 'So where do we stand? Our chambermaid says she was round the back of the hotel having a Woodbine when Victor Orr hit the floor.'

'That's corroborated by all the others,' said Bliss.

'So,' pondered Book, 'perhaps Eadie administered it, walked out and waited for it to take effect?'

'On one of the princesses?' said Bliss.

Book tapped his nose. 'My sources tell me she's a fully paid-up member of the Communist Party. Red as Lenin's combinations.'

'So she might have wanted them dead?'

'Indeed. On behalf of the new ruling class of Scutari. The princesses certainly think that there's some fraternal feeling between Eadie's friends and the new government of their homeland. I'm not convinced, frankly. Miss Rattle is a revolutionary but she's also a pragmatist. Last night she almost persuaded Ruhije and Nafije to join the cause.' He shuffled the papers. 'Perhaps it's the other princess who should be commanding our interest? There are three of them, like the Chekhov play. But only Senije got to Moscow.'

'So it could be her?' asked Bliss. 'Striking a blow for the workers by assassinating her siblings?'

'This is where we should be looking,' said Sergeant

Morris. He was holding the envelope containing objects retrieved from Victor Orr's body. 'In my opinion, sir,' he added.

'His winnings?' said Bliss.

'His little black book,' said Morris. He extracted it from the envelope and passed it to his superior. Book detected a familiar undertone of malice in the sergeant's manner but did not fully appreciate its quality until he was turning the tiny pages for himself. The book carried names and telephone numbers. Beside these, other data were recorded – asterisks, numbers, adjectives. Book was unsure how to interpret them until he found the name of his wife, accompanied by a date and a place. The date was the previous week. The place was Foyles bookshop.

'He liked the ladies, didn't he?' said Bliss, and regretted the remark immediately.

'Not how I'd put it,' said Book, quietly. 'Still, at least we have his home number.' He indicated a page. 'Here. This must be his wife. She's the only one without a star rating.'

'There's another familiar name in there too, sir,' said Morris.

'Yes, Sergeant, I can see that Mrs Book is recorded here. It does rather jump from the page.'

'No, sir,' said Morris. 'I don't mean her.' He indicated another entry, crossed out but still quite legible.

Bliss read the entry aloud: '*M. Barberini. 2 May 1940. Ascot racecourse. 4 stars. Passionate Italian.*' His brow furrowed. 'What does it mean?'

'Obvious, innit?' said Morris. 'The late captain didn't just like the ladies. He was a bit queer.' The sergeant had acquired an expression of clear-eyed insouciance, which he now directed at Gabriel Book. Morris was a public servant doing his job; pursuing the truth, wherever it might lead.

Bliss looked at the floor. Book, however, returned Morris's gaze. 'Do you mean,' he said, 'that he travelled, as it were, on the 38 bus and the 43?'

Morris was happy to accept the definition. 'He met that Eyetie barman at the races and had relations. It's here in black and white. Ascot was his happy hunting ground.'

'What's the motive?' demanded Book.

'Blackmail, obviously.' Morris sniffed. 'Captain Orr was threatening to expose Marco Barberini.'

'And yet the captain was the married man.' Book wrinkled his nose. 'Seems a little far-fetched, Sergeant.'

'Well,' said Morris, with quiet clarity, 'you never know with married men, do you?'

Bliss thanked Morris for his help and took back the address book.

'Could I make a suggestion?' asked Book, as the door closed. 'It's high time someone interviewed Mrs Orr. And given the sensitive nature of that document, might I suggest that Trottie rings that number? Wives always know. Whatever husbands think.'

CHAPTER FIVE

Eadie Rattle was cold when she woke in the royal suite of the Walsingham. She was also hungry, and her shoulder ached as if it had been kicked by a cow. Ruhije soon fixed the pain with a needle from her medical kit. It was not within royal power to heat the radiators or cause poached eggs to rise five floors to a person in a four-poster bed, but thankfully it was entirely possible for a boy to be sent to a black-market contact who knew where to obtain a hamper of rolls, smoked salmon, madeleines, apricot jam and salty French butter. Eadie breakfasted off the ration and beneath the eiderdown, pondered the theory of surplus value and found she did not care about the crumbs falling on the sheets.

The princesses joined her. Ruhije settled in the chair and ate nothing. She seemed haunted: her eyes kept darting to the door. Nafije sat on the bed and reminisced about the breakfasts of her enthroned years, which seemed to have involved a line of soldiers in white and gold saluting as she ate her yoghurt.

'Do you really miss all that?' asked Eadie.

'I miss being at home,' said Nafije. 'With my own people.'

She dipped a roll into the jam pot and bit off the end. 'And I would also like them to be free.' For a moment, Eadie felt the pull of sympathy; then she recalled Lenin's decision to forgo listening to Beethoven because his music was a threat to cool revolutionary detachment. She smiled anyway.

When Jack walked into the room, he knew he had spoiled a sweet reflective moment. His reason for entering was in his hand: a small blue envelope bearing large angry handwriting. Nafije recognised it immediately. She clapped a hand to her mouth. Ruhije took the letter and opened it; stared at its contents with an expression of horror. Nafije snatched it from her, began to read, then gave a low moan of horror. 'Will they never stop tormenting us?'

Ruhije touched her sister's arm in a gesture of consolation, but she would not be consoled. Nafije shuddered and retreated to the suite's other bedroom. Her sister followed.

'More threats?' asked Eadie, extracting a cigarette from the packet on the bedside table.

'He's a proper nut, that one,' said Jack.

'Any idea who's sending them?'

'Somebody who likes laying it on thick,' said Jack.

He peered at the half-demolished contents of the hamper; watched smoke spooling from Eadie's lips. 'You did all right, didn't you?'

'They ordered in,' she said. 'No less than I deserve.' She blew a smoke ring over the bed. 'Balkan mix, apparently. Got the little gold rings on the end, see?'

'I prefer Capstans myself,' said Jack.

'I'm sure your employers would stand you the odd fancy fag, you know.'

'Don't think they're going to be my employers for much longer,' Jack muttered. 'I'm not much cop as a bodyguard.'

In the next room, a sob rose from Ruhije.

Eadie sighed. 'You promised me a cup of Bovril last night,' she said, twisting the lid back on the jam pot. 'Is the offer still open?'

Jack nodded. Eadie slithered out of bed, revealing that she was wearing one of Nafije's Parisian silk nightgowns. Jack averted his eyes. He always seemed to be on the back foot with Eadie Rattle. It was hard to know whether she was planning to welcome him into the dictatorship of the proletariat or send him off to be re-educated in the countryside.

There was a tall silk screen in the corner of the room. It appeared to have been rescued from a royal palace. Eadie disappeared behind it and, after a couple of minutes, emerged in a neat blue dress. An embroidered shawl covered her shoulders.

Ruhije returned to the room like a pale ghost. She put the new poison pen letter into Jack's hands. 'Go to Bow Street,' she said. 'Give this to the inspector.'

'Any message?' asked Jack.

'Tell him that we summon him immediately to the Walsingham to discuss the security of the Royal House of Scutari. Tell him that we will make an official complaint to His Majesty's government if he does not agree to post a constable on our door and give us an escort wherever we go in this city. Remind him that he and Mr Book talk of the *Kanun* and our rules of hospitality. But we say: what welcome do we receive in their famous London? Wretched food, wretched cold, wretched protection.'

Jack listened carefully. 'I'll do my best,' he said, 'but I'm not sure he'll be able to do much about the weather.'

Death threats had put Bovril off the menu, but Eadie walked out with Jack all the same. The morning light in the corridor was thin and grey. Not a single bulb burned.

'This place is dead,' said Eadie, stabbing at the lift buttons. They took the stairs to the lobby. As they passed each floor, Eadie described a grisly object left behind by a guest. A Winston Churchill mask. An RAF flying helmet covered in lipstick kisses. A piccalilli jar filled with toenail clippings. 'It's not for the fainthearted, the life of a chambermaid,' she said. 'But my dad ran a pub in Balla so I've seen it all.'

They reached the entrance of the River Bar. Jack peered through the window.

'What about the murder?' he asked. 'What did you see of that?'

'Nothing,' said Eadie. 'I was outside. You can't pin Captain Victor Orr on me.'

'I wasn't trying to,' said Jack, more defensively than he had intended. 'Honest.'

'Pity I wasn't there,' said Eadie. 'I would have liked to watch that one go down.' She looked at him sharply. 'Got anything by Marx in that bookshop of yours?'

'We've got *Das Kapital*.'

Eadie tutted.

'All four volumes,' said Jack.

'Now you're talking.' She grinned. 'So why'd you leave?'

'I don't think they're my sort of people.'

'Hmm,' said Eadie. 'Maybe it's time you expanded your horizons a bit, sunshine.'

They stood at the summit of the grand staircase and gazed down into the lobby. Behind the desk, Mr Kind and Miss Wicking were trying to stem the tide of a small revolution. A phalanx of grumbling guests was gathered in the lobby. The staff could barely keep up with the tide of returned keys and demands for remuneration. Miss Wicking's rubber stamp slammed paper receipts like the Anvil Chorus.

'That letter,' said Eadie. 'Will you read it to me?'

Jack obliged:

Princesses!
Relics of the despised past!

I express my disgust on behalf of the masses of Scutari. My gorge rises as I see you in the newspapers. Drinking your cocktails. Eating your caviar. Sharing a joke by the river with Mr Douglas Fairbanks Junior. I spit on your Mr Douglas Fairbanks Junior. I spit on your Henley Regatta. I abhor your decadent bones, draped in the silk of Schiaparelli and Madame de Bavière – which will soon drip with your evil blood.

Vladimir Ilyich declared that the capitalist is no more capable of self-sacrifice than a man is capable of lifting himself up by his own bootstraps. The same is true of the monarchist. You cannot escape your punishment. Nor can you prepare for it. It is as inevitable as the complete liquidation of the bourgeoisie.

Eadie smirked to herself.

'Fiery,' she said.

'The bourgeoisie, eh?' said Jack. 'That's us, I suppose?'

'Oh no,' said Eadie, glancing down into the foyer. 'It's them. Let me know if you fancy that Bovril sometime.'

'I will,' Jack agreed. He descended and disappeared into the street, envelope in hand.

Eadie's eyes moved back to the unhappy knot of people in the lobby. A large man wearing a turban was asking for candles. A Canadian couple who had booked for a week were trying to negotiate an immense discount. Two women in matching strings of pearls were making unfavourable comparisons to the Blitz.

Eadie processed down the staircase with enough grandeur to turn a couple of heads; not least the head of Mr Kind. She saw him attempting to disguise his reaction to her sudden shift from sacked chambermaid to valued guest.

'Miss Rattle,' he said. 'I heard about the unfortunate incident last night.'

'Well, fortune works both ways, Mr Kind. I'm the guest of their Royal Highnesses. I intend to indulge myself a little. And I'm to put everything on their account.'

'I wouldn't spend too much then,' he muttered.

'What?'

'Nothing. Er, Miss Rattle?'

'Yes, Mr Kind?'

'Would you be so good as to come and see me? When you've indulged yourself. At your convenience, of course. I have a proposal to put to you.'

'Certainly, Mr Kind,' said Eadie. 'I think I'll take tea on the Palm Court.'

Mr Kind nodded. 'We're just about managing tea.'

As she turned the corner, she saw a man hovering among the palms. Guzili was in a fresh new uniform. His smooth professional air, however, did not bear close examination.

'Can we talk?' he asked. 'I want to apologise for the quality of the service today. The heating is off. The menu is cold. I'm deeply sorry.'

Eadie was confused. 'None of that's your fault, Ismail.'

'I'm afraid it is,' he said. 'It was caused by the three bottles of boiled linseed oil I stole from your cupboard.'

'Linseed's for polishing.' Eadie frowned. 'I do my newel posts with it. And my dados.'

'Yes,' replied Guzili. 'But I poured it into the generator. I didn't poison Victor Orr, Eadie. But I did poison the hotel. I was so angry. With myself. With that man. And with this place. So I thought: I'll kill it.'

He gave a formal little bow.

'I shall confess this to Mr Kind. You will not lose your job, Eadie.'

Trottie wept when she looked inside Victor Orr's little black book. Not for her own humiliation – self-pity was not one of her vices – but for the years and years of heedless women who would never know that they had been translated into numbers by a man they imagined might have loved them. They were legion. The WAF who accepted a kiss under the ack-ack gun at Croydon. The waitress at Skindles, whose fingers smelled of onions and was persuaded to undress in the tea garden. The trainee teacher who took him to her bedsit and called him by the name of a boy killed in the Blitz.

'It's terribly brutal, my love,' said Book, as he watched his wife flip through its pages. 'Do be careful with it.'

Mr and Mrs Book were in Room 504. They were sitting on the bed in their coats. They could see their breath.

'So Guzili is free?' asked Trottie.

'It wasn't him,' said Book. 'But there's something I saw up in that dorm he shares with Barberini and all those potmen. I'm going up for another look. And I'll need to pop back to Archangel Lane, too. Nora has pulled out some materials for me. The shipping lists. And then I must answer a summons.'

'A royal one, I assume?'

'Oh yes,' he said. He placed a hand on the line of her jaw and kissed her.

'I could do it, you know, if it all seems too awful.'

'No,' said Trottie. 'I want to talk to her. Better this than seeing her at the inquest, or in a courtroom months from now.'

Book gave his wife another gentle kiss, picked up his attaché case and slipped from the room.

Trottie stared at the bedside telephone. What would she say to Mrs Sylvia Orr? Perhaps there was no correct approach. Perhaps she just had to choose her own way of getting it wrong. She looked up the number and raised the receiver. When the call was connected, a female voice answered.

The maid was helpful. 'I'm sorry, madam, Mrs Orr isn't here at the moment. Nor is the captain, for that matter, though I'll not worry myself about him.' Trottie did not give her the news. 'Would you like me to give you the number of the place where Mrs Orr is staying? You may reach her there.'

It took Trottie a moment to realise she was being given the telephone number of the Walsingham Hotel. It scarcely took longer to ask Miss Wicking to put her through to the correct extension, and to hear the voice of Sylvia Orr on the crackling line.

'My name is Mrs Book,' said Trottie.

'Ah,' said Sylvia Orr. 'Perhaps we might meet on the Palm Court? I don't imagine it'll be hard to get a table.'

Trottie agreed. Ten minutes later, she was positioned in a discreet spot by the ornamental fountain, with coffee for two already ordered. She shivered as she waited, perhaps from the cold. There were few other patrons. The man in the turban was making the best of a plate of something ungenerous. On the other side of the room, Eadie Rattle nibbled bread and butter and read the *Morning Star*. The Palm Court orchestra fought the falling temperature with a dutiful rendition of 'Penny Serenade'.

Sylvia Orr was a tall woman with green eyes, a tight roll of rust-coloured hair, and a long blue gown that flowed beneath a thick winter coat. Trottie recognised her immediately. She had spotted her the previous night, talking to the cigarette girl in the River Bar. She had accepted a napkin from her, when Victor proved incapable of keeping his champagne in his mouth. She had noticed her pacing the lobby in the hours after the murder.

'This is not easy for me,' said Sylvia, standing at Trottie's table. She had eyes as distant as the moon.

'Of course,' said Trottie. 'You've just lost your husband.'

Sylvia gave a harsh little laugh. 'Oh, that boat sailed a long time ago, Mrs Book. And you're not the first of Victor's conquests to telephone.'

'If it's any consolation,' said Trottie. 'He didn't.'

'Didn't what?'

'Conquer.'

Sylvia Orr did not seem consoled. She did, however, sit down. 'I used to come here all the time, you know,' she said. 'To watch him. With the latest model. Does that seem strange to you?' The waiter bustled in with coffee. It steamed in the chill air of the room.

Sylvia noticed the little black book on the table. 'I'd been wondering where that was. I looked everywhere. When he's at home he keeps it in his sports jacket in the wardrobe. I used to wake up in the night and imagine it there, hot like a little piece of coal. You've read it?'

Trottie nodded. 'To see oneself here. Assessed. Like livestock.'

Sylvia noticed the involuntary curl of Trottie's lip. 'You think he got what he deserved?'

'Well, not quite,' Trottie said, making careful eye contact. 'But what a pig he was.'

It was a truth as inarguable as the date of the Battle of Hastings. 'Do you know,' said Sylvia, picking up her coffee cup, 'I'd think better of him if it was a real diary. Something with a bit of proper adulterous passion. But this is like – well, you said it – like something from Smithfield. Or the back of the *Racing Post*. It almost makes me sad for him. Almost.'

Trottie's eyes fell to the table. She had not expected Sylvia to be so cool and frank. She had expected her to be angry, and for some of that anger to come her way.

'Don't worry, my dear,' said Sylvia. 'I don't really blame you. Victor had charm to spare. In his day. I grew used to his adventures, numb to them. My marriage grew cold. Life grew cold. So I would come here, where there was light and laughter. Well, usually. And I'd watch him. Keep him under observation. Like a specimen of something. And I suppose I thought that if he was guilty of more than just adultery, then I'd do something about it.'

'Do something about it?' repeated Trottie.

'Yes,' said Sylvia. Her eyes shone. 'Take action. Warn the girl. Or call the police. Well, they came for him in the end.'

'Didn't you worry that he might see you?'

'He hadn't noticed me in years. There was no reason to think he'd start now.'

Trottie trod delicately. 'Was that how you were able to . . . ?'

'What?'

'The poison?'

Sylvia smiled grimly and put down her coffee cup. 'I didn't kill my husband, Mrs Book. I pitied Victor. I didn't wish him dead.'

'Then who did?'

Their eyes fell to the little black book on the table: a gazetteer of possible suspects. Waitresses, widows, Wrens.

'How was his war?' asked Trottie.

'Did his service in Cairo. God knows what he got up to. Must have needed a separate little book. Then a stint in the Balkans.'

'The Balkans?' said Trottie.

'Oh yes. I think he was rather heroic there, to give him his due. He cared about those people. I'm not aware he ever went to bed with any of them. And he hated all those second-rate Mitteleuropean Fascists. The Greenshirts. The

Iron Guard. He had a hope that after the war those countries would become pleasant little independent republics where he could go on fishing holidays and get smashed under the trees.'

'And before the Balkans?'

'Here. The Home Front.'

'Whereabouts?'

'Ascot,' said a voice from the doorway. Book stood in his outdoor coat, his attaché case in his hand. He walked towards the table. 'A town full of interest. The racing, of course. The winter quarters of the Bertram Mills Circus. A Gothic church with a fine rose window. And a sadder history, too. One that we may discuss later, perhaps over drinks in the River Bar?'

Sylvia looked glassily at Book. Introductions seemed unnecessary. 'Bit early for that, don't you think, Mr Book?'

'Well, let's give it an hour, shall we? I've instructed Mr Kind to open the place for us. A little party. Ourselves, the inspector, Miss Rattle. And Jack, of course, too. I should very much like him to be there. And I'm hoping for a couple of royal guests of honour. One of them is about to join me here. Listen, I know this sounds awfully rude, but I might stand a better chance if I was sitting here with her alone. And this is the most discreet table in the room.'

Book had no idea whether Ruhije would come. Form suggested that the Royal House of Scutari believed that invitations were better given than received. He ordered tea and listened to the Palm Court orchestra drag their way through the Al Bowlly songbook. He opened his attaché case and went through the documents inside: state files on three princesses, and an image of a White Star liner, below which was a long list of Italian names. He put these away as the answer to his question appeared through the potted palms in a cloud of black mink.

'Everything's off,' said Book, passing Ruhije the menu. 'Kippers. Kidneys. Kedgeree. And the radiators. They're definitely off.' His eyebrows rose. 'Oh, but there's a selection of cold meats.'

A waiter appeared silently beside them. 'Two of those, please,' Book said, without looking up. 'And do make sure they're properly cold. I abhor inconsistency.'

The waiter nodded loosely and gave a loud and liquid sniff. Ruhije's gaze followed his retreat with disdain. 'The service here,' she muttered. 'It is appalling.'

'Well, call me Marie-Antoinette, but I *was* expecting the lavatories to flush. Still, the heating did come on for half an hour. That was nice.'

Ruhije folded her hands on the table. 'You said it was urgent, Mr Book.'

'In a way, yes.'

Her gaze turned steely. 'Are you any closer?'

'Closer?'

'To finding out who tried to murder us?'

Book picked up a spoon and examined it for smears. 'No one tried to murder you,' he murmured.

Ruhije frowned. 'But the letters, Mr Book. The threats.'

He put down the spoon. 'You sent those.'

Ruhije received the accusation like a lighted match in the ear. She jumped to her feet. 'You are mad! How dare you?'

Book was unimpressed. 'Do sit down, Princess.'

Ruhije began the opening bars of an aria of outrage, but Book would not hear it.

'I might be more of a diplomat than the inspector,' he said, 'but there's only so much of this exhausting hauteur I can take.' He gathered his scarf around his neck. 'And I could murder a bacon sandwich.'

Ruhije sank back into her seat. The Palm Court orchestra was staring at her. They looked like the jury.

'When did you start?' asked Book. 'Sending the letters?'

Ruhije, it seemed, was also exhausted. A great sigh broke from somewhere inside her. 'For a while, it was real,' she said. 'When we fled our country, there were eyes everywhere. We feared to eat or drink. We lived day by day, shoved into stinking cellars and the holds of filthy ships. I can still feel the motion of the seas. Nafije and I would sit together in the darkness with nothing but our furs and a tin of beef.'

The mention of Nafije brought a crack of anxiety into her voice. She was going to make a special plea. 'She knows nothing of this, I assure you,' said Ruhije. 'She is still an innocent in a way, lost in her past like a child in a fairy tale. But the threat was real then. In New York, we were feted. They love royalty there, precisely because they have none of their own. For a time, we fitted the bill. But the invitations dried up. The parade moved on. I realised we had gone from being in danger to something far, far worse. We were irrelevant. What did the new regime in Scutari have to fear from us? Why would they send assassins halfway across the globe to make away with us? Why would anyone bother?'

'Yes,' said Book. 'I did ask you that question myself. The party seems quite preoccupied at the moment, liquidating the landlord class and collectivising the goats and whatnot.'

The cold meats arrived. They ignored them.

'There is glamour in death,' said Ruhije. 'In danger. And it produces sympathy. So I began to write the letters. Both to us and to the authorities.'

Book stirred his tea. 'Some suspected your other sister might be behind them.'

'She is dead, Mr Book,' Ruhije replied. 'The Communists never trusted her. They used a bullet to tell her so. I will not lose another sister. And that is why we go through the world, Nafije and I, an image of tragedy and fascination. And we are fascinating enough to live on credit in places like this. Mr Kind has been very generous.'

Book smiled gently. 'You were probably good for business. Until the poisoning.'

Ruhije's composure faltered. 'I didn't know what to think. Nafije swapped the glasses as always. And then that man – that captain – was lying dead at our feet. My mind raced. Had it all become real? But what else could I do but continue as planned?'

'It was very well done,' said Book. 'You have a nice melodramatic turn of phrase. But once I saw your pen sitting on the piano, I knew it was you. A music nib. Thin downstrokes and wide cross-strokes for writing musical notation. And those references to your wardrobe. I'm not sure if a desperate Communist assassin could tell an *étoile* from his elbow.'

Ruhije conceded the point. She drew closer. Book could

smell her perfume. 'So I have to ask, Mr Book, in the spirit of your British stories, if Captain Orr was indeed the intended victim . . . whodunnit?'

'Perhaps,' said Book, 'we might discuss that over cocktails?'

When the architect of the Walsingham installed a chessboard floor in the River Bar, he hoped to stir memories of the Grand Trianon at Versailles, the Doge's Palace in Venice, and those sunlit Vermeer interiors where Protestant ladies play the lute in harmonious three-dimensional space. In practice, plutocrats with gin fizzing in their blood had often blamed its black and white squares for their turns and headaches. For Book, the pattern induced a twinge of self-consciousness. He had gathered his pieces, and he was ready to play the game.

Refreshments were required. As host, he oversaw their production. He stood behind the bar, a stainless-steel shaker in his hands, moving with zip and vigour and hoping he did not look like someone auditioning for the percussion section of the Gaucho Tango Orchestra. 'I'm not usually a fan of this sort of thing,' he said, over the clatter of ice cubes. 'It's redolent of those thrillers you find at W. H. Smith. However, sometimes it really is best to gather everyone together. Unity of place and all that.'

The company was uneasy. Inspector Bliss, Sylvia Orr and Mr Kind hovered by the window, three pairs of observing eyes. Eadie placed herself in the middle of the composition. Despite the cold, she had removed her shawl; an action calculated, Book thought, to display her bullet wound.

Jack stood near her, on the spot where he had confronted Victor Orr. Ruhije and Nafije perched on their high stools. Trottie was beside them, reoccupying the place where Captain Orr had made his last order. Barberini and Guzili were an awkward presence behind the bar. They shuffled their feet, watching Book pour the contents of the shaker into a pair of rocks glasses. They were servants without a role.

Book watched the golden liquid drown the ice. 'So, on the night of the murder, Mr Guzili here made the first round of two drinks.'

'Yes,' Guzili confirmed, his voice low.

'Which,' Book continued, 'was rejected by the princesses and went down the sink. Now we come to the brouhaha. A new character enters our drama. Captain Victor Orr. Kindly represented here by Mr Kind.' Book pointed at the general manager with a flourish, and drew him to his mark. Mr Kind nodded at the room, unused to being the centre of attention.

'In you come, Miss Rattle,' said Book. 'Tell us what happened next.'

'Well, so there's Captain Whatsit, soaked in Taittinger, saying he's got extra duties for me, which seem to involve me coming to his room and leaving with some money.' She looked hard at Mr Kind. He did not enjoy the experience. 'So I decline, of course. And I'm looking over at Ismail. Hoping he might help me out. Do the decent thing.'

Book turned to Guzili, who was directing his gaze at the floor. 'And he doesn't?'

'No,' said Eadie. 'I'm thinking, is the captain going to hit me? So I tell him where to get off. He says – well, some threat or other, I didn't listen. Then Jack comes to my rescue.' She threw a playful look at Jack. He blushed visibly.

'And what did you do then?' asked Book.

'Went straight outside for a smoke.'

'Thank you, Miss Rattle,' said Book. Eadie withdrew to one of the tables, like a substitute returning to the bench. Book began agitating the shaker again. 'So Mr Guzili then set up more glasses for a fresh round. And soon there will be four Walsingham sours on this bar. Three good ones. One, as we shall see, about to go bad.'

He poured the round of drinks and peered at the result. 'But when, precisely, does one of these drinks receive a dash of hydrochloric acid? Princess Nafije, you told us you switched two of these drinks. Which two?'

Nafije reached forward, swift and practised, and swapped the first and fourth glasses in the row. 'Like this,' she explained. 'One of ours for one of theirs.'

'Very good,' approved Book. 'But you're not drinking yet, are you? Because you want to see someone else drink first. It's only prudent when there are so many assassins about. So you wait a little longer. Until the distraction is over and Victor and Trottie have come up here.' He peered over his spectacles. 'That's you, Edmund.'

Mr Kind moved forward and found his place next to Trottie. He picked up the glass in front of him. Trottie did the same. The drinks looked agreeably effervescent. 'This is the Russian roulette moment now, is it?' she asked.

'This was not a casual murder,' Book said. 'It was very carefully thought out. We know the poison was not in Signor Barberini's shaker. We know that Princess Nafije deserves no reproaches. All Your Royal Highness did was exchange one perfectly safe and effective Walsingham sour for another. In fact, I would suggest that none of these drinks would have produced anything worse than a hangover until the distraction with the coins occurred. That was the moment of opportunity for someone here to poison one of these cocktails.'

'The one that he was clearly about to pick up,' Trottie said.

'Yes,' Book replied simply. 'There was no mistake. Captain Orr had to die.'

Jack had moved to the bar. He was standing behind the princesses, as he had done on the night. 'Why, though?' he asked. 'What had he done?'

Book reached beneath the bar and produced his attaché case. From this he retrieved a printed card bearing the image of a White Star liner, and below it, a roster of names. He held it up for everyone to see. The gesture was theatrical, but there was no hint of pleasure in his voice.

'Do you remember the *Arandora Star*? Not our finest hour, I fear.'

Trottie nodded grimly. 'Yes. She was torpedoed by the Jerries.'

'That's right,' said Book. 'On 2 July 1940.'

'There was a set-to on board, wasn't there?' said Trottie. 'A lot of internees being sent to Australia.'

'Canada,' said Barberini. They were his first words since the start of Book's little gathering.

Trottie took the correction. 'Canada. Fighting amongst themselves.'

Book nodded. 'That's what they said in the *Daily Express*.'

'In Parliament, too,' Barberini added. 'Doesn't mean it's true.'

'Indeed,' murmured Book. He studied the memorial card. 'I do apologise for taking this from the dormitory. It wasn't the only sign of the ship I found there, but it was the one that showed who here is most marked by its tragedy. There are so many names listed here. So many dead. But only one Barberini. *M. Barberini*. Your sister, Maria, I think?'

A strange expression had settled on the waiter's face; it was as if there was some image in his mind that he could not put to one side; something that blocked his view of the room. Book could have made a guess. The mirrored ballroom of an ocean liner, crammed with people. His sister among them, in the chaos and panic.

Book pulled Victor's little black book of secrets from his pocket. 'It's not the first time I've seen her name today,' he said, gravely. 'Here she is, I'm sorry to say, in the pages of Captain Orr's little black book.' He turned its tiny pages and read the entries aloud. '*M. Barberini. 14 January 1940, Ascot racecourse. 16 January, Ascot racecourse. 19 . . .*'

Barberini's lip began to tremble. He was thinking of his sister; but he was not thinking of what she had endured at sea.

Bliss was confused. 'Captain Orr met her at the races?'

Mr Kind shook his head. 'He can't have. There was barely any racing during the war. Certainly not at Ascot.'

The inspector remembered. 'Oh, of course. Ascot was one of the places where they sent the Regulation 18B lot, wasn't it?'

Book nodded. 'English Nazis. German anti-Nazis. Ice-cream men. Spaghetti-house owners. Waiters who'd once said something faintly positive about the cut of Il Duce's jib. All put under barbed wire. All made to live together. Not very fair, that, was it, Mr Barberini? What was the case against you?'

Barberini might have said nothing. He usually said nothing. Some of the River Bar regulars had been there on the day they'd removed him from the hotel. Some even knew that the *Arandora Star* was always sailing in his mind. Book, however, was the first to ask the question; the first to show an interest.

'My parents were born in Italy,' said Barberini. 'So someone here claimed I was a Fascist. They marched me out during service. I was sent up north. Nobody protested. Particularly the man who ran the bar here in the Blitz.'

Mr Kind shifted in his chair. He remembered the moment and the man. He had since been sacked for stealing from the till.

'And your sister?' asked Trottie.

Barberini was standing behind his bar. This was his place. It was his story. He told it. 'In 1938 my father said to her – why not spend the summer with your Italian aunt? Go to the beach and to the *campo solare*. Build fires, get some fresh air. They give you a nice uniform. Like the Girl Guides. Mussolini's Girl Guides. She brought it home as a souvenir. Big mistake. It was enough for the men from 18B. There it was in her wardrobe, sir. So off she went to Ascot.'

Trottie was incredulous. 'She was interned because of a uniform?'

'People do take them terribly seriously,' said Book.

'They do,' said Sylvia Orr. 'It worked for Victor. When he was in his sailor suit, people did what he said. It was charm as much as rank.'

Barberini concurred. 'That's how he got Maria's name on the list for Canada. Turned it on with the lady in charge of typing it up. Added her name at the last minute.'

'Perhaps we should be generous,' said Book. 'Imagine that he was getting her out of the camp to a new life away from the war.'

The idea caused something to crackle inside Barberini. 'No,' he said. His eyes glittered with anger. 'He just wanted a troublesome lover out of the way before his wife found out. That ship was a death-trap. I dream about that. When I'm asleep. When I'm standing here in the middle of a shift. Those people, pushing at those barricades. They couldn't get past them. That's the thing that's in my head, you see? The picture that's always there. Her hands on those things. Great wooden "X"s wrapped in barbed wire. Cutting her hands. Cutting her beautiful hands. And then the sea coming in. And drowning them both.'

'Both?' said Book.

'Maria and the baby,' breathed Barberini. 'His baby.' He was looking straight at Sylvia Orr. She could see the tears gathering in his eyes; the defiance in his voice.

'I knew his name,' he said. 'That was all. But I couldn't find him. The war turned everything upside down. And no one was in any great hurry to help an insignificant wop waiter. Then it turned out I had been serving him Walsingham sours for months. The man who took away my precious Maria. My beloved sister. A regular in my own bar, here with a new friend every week. So I did what had to be done. I prepared ice. Special ice.'

'Where did you get the acid?' asked Book.

'Cleaning supplies. You could kill an army with what's in there. But I didn't need so much. Just a little supply. Kept it in a Thermos under the bar.' He smiled fondly. 'It was her birthday, you see. Maria's birthday. Or it would have been.'

Barberini lifted a glass, checked it for finger marks and placed it on the bar. 'It wasn't so difficult,' he said. 'You can time me if you like.' He found a clean shaker and added the ingredients – whisky, lime juice, bitters, a dash of egg white – and agitated them with the controlled violence of an expert. He pushed open the lid of the shaker and allowed the drink to fall silkily. With his free hand, he plucked an ice cube from a silver bucket and added it to the cocktail.

'Takes a while to learn,' he mused. 'But you never forget.' He examined his work with pride, holding it up to the light. 'And,' he added, 'I took the precaution of keeping some of the poisoned ice. Tinkety-tonk!'

Barberini toasted the company and drained the glass, swallowing the ice cube like a snake eating an egg.

The reaction was immediate. There was uproar in the room. Chairs scraped on the chequerboard floor. Bliss reached out to grab the glass. Guzili got there first. Barberini, however, would not yield it. He was smacking his lips, frowning, shaking his head.

'Just ordinary ice, alas,' said Book softly. 'I'm afraid I switched them.' The remark was offered in a spirit of apology.

Barberini seemed to accept it. He had lost his mastery of the moment, but he did not allow arrest to rob him of his dignity. He placed the glass in the sink, so that it might be washed for the next customer. When Bliss applied the handcuffs, he adjusted his position as if the inspector was straightening his tie. Barberini nodded wordlessly as his rights were read; betrayed no response when Book offered his condolences; ignored the looks of horror and pity from the others in the room.

As Bliss led him away, Mr Kind was the only person to whom Barberini spoke. 'By the way, sir,' he said. 'The linseed oil in the generators. That was me too. I do apologise.' Guzili and Eadie exchanged glances, but Barberini was careful not to look at either of them. He had left them behind. He had left everyone behind. Colleagues, comrades, customers, every sweating blazered fool who had leaned on the bar and talked down to him.

He was thinking of his sister. Not as a lone and terrified figure, watching cracks split the glass of a ballroom wall and dreading the coming rush of the sea. Not as a pair of bloodied hands clasping at a barbed-wire barricade. Maria had been restored to him, untorn, unbroken, undrowned. All that lay between them was a guilty verdict and the quick, smooth violence of a fellow professional. After that, they would be children together again.

As darkness fell that evening, light was restored to the Walsingham. Bedside lamps sputtered back to life in vacated rooms. In the River Bar, bottles glinted again beneath the chandeliers. Mr Kind put a hand on the nearest radiator and felt warmth refilling the system. The guests at his desk were still complaining, still asking for items to be struck from their bills, but the general manager now acquiesced gladly. Life was returning to the hotel. Grandeur would follow. Even the two ladies in the matching pearls failed to annoy him.

As they peeled away, Mr Kind saw Eadie emerge from the Palm Court. She was dressed for outdoors, in a winter coat clearly borrowed from a member of the Royal House of Scutari. He noted the confident movement of her body. Odd, he thought, how the loss of a uniform could change how a person walked across a room.

'Mr Kind,' she said. 'You wanted a word?'

'Ah, yes, Miss Rattle. I was thinking about your position here. Now it's clear that you were not responsible for the incident with the generators, I see that your dismissal was unnecessarily expeditious.'

Eadie looked at him carefully. Mr Kind cleared this throat. 'And I wanted to say, I would very much like to offer that position back to you.'

She looked delighted. Grateful. 'I accept,' she said.

The general manager beamed back. 'Well, that's all very satisfactory.'

Eadie took a step closer to the desk. 'There's a ledger here, isn't there?'

'A ledger?'

'Yes. One where you record all the comings and goings of the staff. Might I see my entry?'

Mr Kind hesitated, but Eadie had spotted the document on a shelf behind the desk. 'Of course,' he said smoothly. He retrieved the ledger and placed it on the counter, opening it at the most recent page. Its columns recorded the names and addresses of staff, their dates of employment, and their reasons for leaving. *Did not keep himself clean. Stole from the kitchen. Married.*

'There I am,' Eadie said, pointing to her name. 'Edith Rattle. Reason for leaving. Oh. Sabotage.'

Mr Kind's smile tightened. 'Well, let us strike that from the record.' He picked up his fountain pen and obliterated the word with a thick line of ink.

'Excellent,' said Eadie. 'Thank you. Now, Mr Kind. I resign.'

Mr Kind's head snapped up. 'You resign?'

'Yes, I resign,' Eadie said brightly. 'Would you write that in, please?'

Mr Kind stared at her, utterly bewildered. 'You can't resign!'

Eadie smirked. 'I believe I just did.'

She was already striding across the lobby towards the revolving door. Just before she stepped through, she flicked a two-fingered salute over her shoulder.

'Up the workers!' she exclaimed, and was gone.

The River Bar revolution would be a more subtle affair, but it would come. Ismail Guzili opened up as light flooded back to the building. His first night as head cocktail waiter would not be a great test of his abilities. Customers were thin on the ground. A pair of couples on their way to the theatre were the only non-residents. Most of the guests, not wishing to shiver in their coats, had gone elsewhere.

The two elegant figures sitting at the bar had come not for a night out, but to mark the end of an ordeal. Walsingham sours were required.

Ruhije examined her drink and gave a slight nod of approval. 'All this is quite correct.' Nafije set her glass down. 'Two more, please. For those people.'

Book and Trottie had arrived. Their bags were packed. A page boy was bringing them down to the lobby. They had decided to pay one last visit to the River Bar. Book noticed Nafije pointing in his direction and understood her meaning. He clicked his heels in acknowledgment of her generosity.

'Missing the war, are you?' Trottie asked.

'Well, I don't know what the etiquette is,' he said, with a diplomatic smile. Nafije was now beckoning him over.

'I think that's the royal summons,' said Trottie. She watched him cross the room to join the princesses. A brief and courtly conversation ended with Nafije handing over a small envelope. With a slight bow of thanks, Book returned to his place beside Trottie. Inside the envelope was a cheque.

'What's that for?' asked Trottie.

'A hundred guineas,' Book replied, gazing upon it with pleasure.

'No, I mean what's it *for*?' Trottie pressed.

'Our copy of the *Kanun of Scutari*,' Book explained. 'As I'm always saying, in our trade, it pays to specialise.'

'It'll bounce,' muttered Trottie.

'Well, if it doesn't,' Book said, tucking the cheque into his pocket, 'I'll send it to the *Arandora Star* Memorial Fund.'

Guzili placed two glasses on the bar. Two perfect examples of the Walsingham sour.

'What shall we drink to?' asked Trottie.

Book raised his glass, meeting the eyes of his wife. 'To us.'

'To the Barberinis,' Trottie added. 'To Marco and Maria.'

Book paused. 'Yes. To all the Barberinis. The lost, the defeated. All the Barberinis. Those who bear the name and those who do not. And let there be no more drownings.' He turned to the princesses. He could not be sure if they had heard his words across the room, but they acknowledged his gesture and raised their glasses.

It was a melancholy moment, a solemn moment. The kind that rarely occurs at the cocktail bars of grand hotels. It was punctured by the sound of a man snapping his fingers across the room. He was on his way to a show at the Trocadero. He was in a hurry. He wanted the waiter to know his place, and to look at him.

'I'm sorry, sir,' said Guzili. 'Have you lost your dog?'

Book and Trottie drank up. They did not stay to listen to the customer huff and splutter, nor to watch Guzili infuriate him further with his brown-eyed smiling calmness, nor to see Ruhije and Nafije amplify the effect with their own glassy stares.

Their luggage was waiting for them in the lobby. Mr Kind, however, was not. Only Miss Wicking stood behind the desk. Book thought of asking her to pass on a message but then thought better of it. It might look odd. She checked them out with no fuss, no ceremony.

'Seems silly to get a taxi,' said Trottie. 'Shall we just walk?'

'Won't we look like we've been kicked out?' asked Book. 'Do you mind?'

'I suppose not. Will you be at home this evening, Mrs Book?'

'I'm planning an early night,' she said. 'You're very welcome to join me.'

The revolving doors spun behind them.

The case was closed, but Book felt little satisfaction. He imagined Barberini in a cell at Bow Street, staring at the wall, knowing the noose would add another name to the death toll of the *Arandora Star*. He thought of 158 Archangel Lane, shuttered, doubtless, by Nora. Dog would be waiting for him, but the attic bedroom would still be empty. As he walked out into the Strand, he felt the ghost of another moment, long ago, when he had moved through the street, suitcase in hand, leaving someone he loved behind him.

He was wrong on at least one of these points. Nora was still minding the shop. The lights were on. The stove was warm. Inside was a dish of something rich and strong from the kitchen of the Istanbul. Somehow, Nora explained, the missing shillings had returned to the tin. She stayed while he ate. She wanted details of poison and peril, but Book suspected that she had detected his sadness and wanted to assuage it.

'Some big news here today, too, Mr Book,' she said. 'Nothing with princesses and frozen acid, but pretty significant.'

'Oh?' said Book, picking parsley from his teeth.

'That lady who drags her husband here.'

'Jean, you mean? Mrs Goodwin?'

'That's her. She was back this afternoon. With no husband.'

'Ah,' said Book. 'That must have been a relief. He was on the golf course, I suppose?'

'No,' said Nora. 'She's given him the elbow. All in the hands of her solicitors, she says. Anyway, she wants to thank you for that play. Said it gave her a few ideas. She's coming back tomorrow for some more recommendations.'

'What's she after?' asked Book. 'Another Ibsen?'

'No,' said Nora. 'Stuff on travel. She's planning to go off somewhere exotic.'

A sound came from the front of the shop. Someone had opened the door. Nora and Book looked at each other and made a silent resolution not to assault this unexpected visitor with a large volume of Albanian customary law.

A man was standing by the counter. It was Jack.

Nora got to her feet and rushed to meet him.

'Hello, stranger,' he said.

'Not as strange as you, mate. Running off without saying goodbye.'

He nodded silently. Jack seemed to have brought silence into the shop.

'Will I see you if I come back here tomorrow?' she asked.

'I dunno,' he said. 'I can't promise.'

Book had not risen. He remained in the gloom of the back kitchen. 'Put the kettle on, shall I?' he said.

Nora gave Jack a thump on the back. The gesture meant goodbye; it meant affection; it meant admonishment. 'Sort it out, yeah, you two,' she said. When she left, she closed the door quietly.

Jack moved into the back kitchen and took over the making of the tea. He scalded the pot, spooned the leaves, added the water. The two men waited together in silence as it brewed, then Jack poured. He passed Book a cup, the china clinking softly as it changed hands.

'I know you run on it,' Jack said. 'You and your unreconstituted dust.'

'I do,' said Book.

'I was talking to Mr Kind,' said Jack. 'He said you and him go back years.'

'It's true. What did he say about me?'

Jack blew on his tea. 'Mr Kind said you were a kind man. He also said you rang him a few weeks ago and asked him about the job with the princesses. And told him to look out for me.'

'Ah,' said Book.

'Things have changed, though. I've got no position now. Apart from one on the Embankment, I suppose.'

'Their Royal Highnesses have let you go?'

'I quit,' said Jack.

'Good for you,' said Book. 'The job here is still yours, of course.' There was a giddy note in his voice.

Jack nodded, but he did not relax. 'So, I've got a position,' he said, slowly. 'And I've got a cosy little room over a bookshop on Archangel Lane. But what am I supposed to do? How can I take them when I have so many questions?'

'Such as?'

'Why me, Mr Book? Why me?'

Book watched the firelight play on Jack's face. How young he seemed; how torn. For a moment, Book said nothing.

The room was pleasant and warm. There was tea in the pot. A colder world might lie on the other side of this question. There was, however, no avoiding it. He rose to his feet and went over to a bookshelf. No burrowing was required; no elaborate memory game. His hand fell immediately on a little volume of poetry in plain calf binding. *In Memoriam.* Alfred, Lord Tennyson.

'Your father gave this to me,' said Book, as quietly as if he were in church. 'The last time I saw him. In 1935.'

Jack's eyes narrowed slightly. 'The last time?'

'He died soon after.'

Jack let this statement settle upon him. It was no extra burden. He had always assumed that his father was dead. Now, however, it had been spoken aloud, and something had changed. It was like having a name for a weight he knew he had been carrying for years.

'I couldn't face looking at this,' said Gabriel Book, the Tennyson in his hand. 'Not for years. Then the war came, and I was busy. Rather busy. It was only a few months ago that I picked it up again. Dared to pick it up. And I found there was a little more to it than I'd thought.'

Book trembled as he found the page. When he read, he read with difficulty, as people do when giving a eulogy. Each word offered to break his voice; to sting him into tears.

> *'O somewhere, meek, unconscious dove,*
> *That sittest ranging golden hair;*
> *And glad to find thyself so fair,*
> *Poor child, that waitest for thy love!'*

Keeping the page open, Book placed the little volume in Jack's hands. Written in faint pencil was a margin note: *Jack Blunt. 27/4/21.* Many aspects of Jack's life were a mystery — a closed book, one might say — but even in the orphanage, he had known his own birthday.

'He was trying to tell me, you see,' said Book. 'Trying to tell me about you. About the son I never knew he had.'

Jack let the book rest in his lap. He reached into his jacket pocket and pulled out his most precious possession, his only real possession. The photograph of a young man, attractive, attentive, with a sandy military moustache. He had given it to Trottie; he had shown it to Nora; now he surrendered it to Book.

Book gazed upon it in quiet wonder. 'It must have been taken around the time you were conceived,' he murmured. 'I knew there'd been someone, you see. Someone before me.' He let out a slow breath, the name slipping from his lips like a benediction. 'Felix.'

'I never had his name,' murmured Jack. His eyes were shining. 'I only had that. Just one picture.'

'Your father was a German, Jack. Prussian, in point of fact.'

Jack gulped for air. 'And what was he to you, Mr Book?'

Book removed his spectacles. He did not want the tears to gather on the glass.

'What was Felix to me?' he repeated softly. 'He was everything, Jack. He was what the war took away. He was the whole damn world.'

'How did he die?'

'I don't know,' said Book, gazing at the boy. 'Shall we find out . . . ?'

The words were marked upon the moment, bold and clear and bright, like the last line at the end of a chapter. Jack knew his reply, but he took a breath before he gave it, knowing that to answer would be to turn the page of his life; to leap from ellipsis to question mark over a wide blank field into a new story, and all its unknowable immensity.

He took the leap.

146 Adelaide Drive
Santa Monica

25th December 1962

Dear Mr Book,

It is Christmas in California. Which means I am looking over the Pacific, kissed by the still heat of the air but wishing for the bite of those 1940s London winters. 1946 had sharp teeth, but the following year — that was the worst, wasn't it? Those cases we followed through the snow . . .

As for these adventures — the pit, the studio, the Walsingham Hotel — oh, Mr Book, what liberties I took. The assumptions I made. The dreams I had about private thoughts, private desires. I blushed as I read them. And wept a bit too, of course. For that vanished world, which now seems as far away as hansom cabs and Jack the Ripper. And for us, too, of course, and the people we were. You and Mrs Book and Dog. And that boy Jack. My brother. My co-conspirator.

I have to ask: was I really so morbid? The question puts me in mind of our trip to go to see the dinosaurs at Crystal Palace. Do you recall it? We were working on that case of the don and the iguanodon — the prof from the Warburg who was found dead with a dinosaur tooth in his pocket. We took a detour to the house where poor Harriet Staunton and her baby were starved to death by that terrible family, and none of the guests in the boarding house noticed a thing. Well, for the record: that was your idea, not mine.

You might be surprised to find that I have returned these stories. You say that they are my property, but that's only true if you believe that all property is theft. They are about you; they should be with you. And, dear Mr Book, I have to tell you that there are more. Plenty more. Think of how often you left me in sole charge of that shop, with that typewriter just sitting there.

Before I left for America, I placed them in a deposit box at the bank. Yusuf's daughter has the key. I should like you to have them. They are fiction, of course, but I built them from the material of your life. And your story belongs to you.

Yours ever,

Nora

PS Jack sends his love.

ACKNOWLEDGEMENTS

Bookish is a book. This was not inevitable. It began as an idea in the mind of Mark Gatiss – a place that may one day be designated a site of special scientific interest. Then, attended by endless conversations about scarlet fever, the Spanish Civil War, strychnine and chocolate, it became a series of scripts. Those conversations barely stopped as shooting started in the summer of 2024. And now, here is *Bookish* in its latest and most material of forms. Its stories even have a new author. She's called Nora, and you will know her already.

Here's an incomplete account of how this happened; how it led to the text before your eyes and generated a long list of people to whom I am profoundly grateful. Mark created *Bookish*. (Our friendship, two decades and counting, means more to him that he will know.) Its history bears the imprint of Walter Iuzzolino, Jo McGrath, Tim Morris, Christopher Arcache and Carolina Giammetta. Casting changes everything: those shadows in our heads became Polly Walker, Elliot Levey, Connor Finch and Buket Kömür – who made the characters on these pages as much as anyone whose name is on the cover.

Cassie Browne and her colleagues at Quercus suggested that *Bookish* should undergo the transformation undergone by most of the film and TV series I loved as a child. She and Kat Burdon were the best of editors. Amber Burlinson applied brilliant logic to the details of the story and gave me the best notes an author could hope for. Beth Wright sent it out into the world. The process was absurdly enjoyable. My family lived this one with me. (One has a cameo in the text.) Much of the writing was done at the Warburg Institute, that sanctuary for the bookish on Woburn Square. Its staff are due my heartfelt thanks. It is my favourite place in London and I hope one day to kill someone there.